DANGEROUS SALVATION

BOOK 1: ARMOUR OF LIGHT SERIES

DONITA BUNDY

JOURNEY
PRESS

ISBN:
Print: 978-0-6487823-0-8
EPub: 978-0-6487823-1-5

Editor: Belinda Pollard
Proofreading: Alix Kwan
Cover Design: Donita Bundy

Cover images copyright ©
Character: Warpedgalerie via Adobe Stock
Eyes: Sfio Cracho via Adobe Stock
Background: Petra via Adobe Stock

In memory of my Dad.
In gratitude to my Mum.

What if you could glimpse through the veil into the Unseen?
What if you were pulled through the veil, never to return?
What if you were handed a sword and told to fight for your soul?

In him was life, and that life was the light of all mankind. The light shines in the darkness, and the darkness has not overcome it.

John 1:4–5 (NIV)

1

DANIEL

"We're surrounded!"

"I see them. Quick, in here."

"You can't be serious. It's a dead end."

"We need to draw them away from the crowd."

"But what about the rules?"

"If we engage them in the middle of the shop, people will get hurt. Now move it!"

There was something fiercely wrong with these two women—apart from their conversation, which was another level of weird altogether. They'd first caught my eye as they moved through the store. Each time I looked at them, my eyes grew blurry. I looked away and all was good. I looked back and ... fuzzy.

I followed them because it offered a change from focusing on my own troubles. This whispered snippet carried as I edged closer, but the rest of their conversation disappeared down the hall into the department store's change rooms. Like them, I wasn't too keen on "engaging the enemy". For me, that was store detectives. For them, who knew? Blending into the background, concealing my contraband, I trailed the women.

Winter was closing in and, even though it wouldn't frost in town, the cold would ripple its way through anything weaker than hardcore insulation. I needed extra padding to get through this season. My bush shelter had been fine for summer, lost its appeal in autumn, and had absolutely nothing to offer for winter. But as a Loner, I couldn't make a claim on any of the decent shelters. The gangs now controlled life on the street, and even though I was desperate, I wasn't desperate enough to pay their kind of rent. I'd made that mistake before and learned the hard way. But I'd have to think of something soon.

The whispered argument was a great distraction. "Bossy" was large—not fat, but she was definitely a unit. Her face bore minimal lines, but her steely eyes suggested age. I would hardly call her a looker, but she was no dog either.

"Whinger" on the other hand was small and slight. Her darting eyes repeatedly scoped the scene. The speed with which her face changed suggested she was capable of thinking fast and hiding nothing. She was far easier to read. Probably around my age, early twenties or late teens, and as well-proportioned as a stick. Well, as much as I could imagine from under her bulky clothes. And, as peculiar as a Picasso. She was blonde, so I guess she had one thing going for her.

They were an interesting contrast. And not only to each other. Apart from the flickering, they both stood out from regular people in that they didn't stand out. They were plain, modest, and clean-skinned—they'd not had any work done. Obviously, their bodies weren't on show or for sale, unlike every other lost soul in this damned place.

I entered the men's section intending to take a cubicle when the hairs on the back of my neck buzzed. The only way I'd survived so long by myself was respecting this sixth sense. I went on high alert. But then some seriously weird skrat hit the fan. The temperature dropped. The smell of ozone floated down through the air conditioning and the taste of rotten eggs prickled my tongue. When my skin puckered into gooseflesh, I changed course and high-tailed it all the way through the men's section to the far end of the women's. I hid in a vacant cubicle as far away from the entrance as possible.

In a confrontation, more often than not I stand my ground.

However, when instinct overrides intellect I tend to go with it. So far, it's served me well. You know, the whole discretion–valour deal.

I shut the curtain and took stock of this fluorescent shoebox. Harsh light was intensified by the obscene number of mirrors, and stark white, reflective walls. There was nowhere to hide. And, with no gaps under the partitions, only one escape. Although I could possibly use the narrow bench as a boost over the side partitions if I had to.

The frigid air became a sickening electric cocktail of new clothes and body odour swimming in a pool of sulphur. I completed a three-sixty then faced the curtain. My reconnaissance complete without having to take a step. To free up my hands and keep the floor clear of obstacles, I hung my selections on every available hook to reduce the glare. Then I waited. For what? I had no idea. I was quietly freaking out.

"Which way will they come? Through the roof, or the floor?"

What. The. Hell?

Whinger and Bossy were in the cubicles near mine.

"Don't worry about those ones. The Warriors are on duty."

"What about Marcus? Will he be okay?"

"He's at the entrance. He'll slow the flow coming through to us. Any that get past him, I'll take care of."

Their voices moved into the hallway and stopped just beyond my curtain. I didn't move. I wasn't proud of being in the women's section. Or that I was skrat-scared. I hated that I was so damned vulnerable. But what choice did I have? None. Therefore, I was staying put till I could figure a way out of this mess.

"Stand there, and stay behind me. Whatever happens, don't let them in there."

My curtain twitched.

And again.

What. The. Hell?

I knew it hadn't been a good idea to take cover in a dead end. But it was too late now. I was trapped, just like them. So, I made ready for my last stand, giving myself as much room as possible. I've always been able to hold my own, even when the odds are stacked against me. Two on one, even three on one, I was confident I'd be okay. That's how I've managed to avoid being assimilated into the gangs for so long. Four at a time might be my limit though. But this didn't feel like any street fight I'd ever been in before.

I drew my knife and breathed deeply, forcing my muscles to relax. Dropping my weight and grounding myself, I did my best to prepare to defend another useless shelter.

My ears rang in the screaming silence of anticipation.

Whinger squeaked.

And it began.

The floor hummed and the walls vibrated. But apart from the occasional gasp and yelp from Whinger, the hallway was silent. I strained my ears for any clues as to when they would come for me. But all I heard was the faint ring of metal on metal. My curtain fluttered a couple of times and the air crackled, but nothing happened. I wondered for the third time what the hell was going on.

Without seeing or hearing a thing, I sensed a lull. My survival instinct kicked in and I realised I needed to make the most of this opportunity to achieve my primary objective. I stripped, donned my new clothes, and covered up ASAP. Regardless of how hard I tried, it was impossible not to be confronted by my multiple reflections in blisteringly artificial light from every conceivable angle. I was not a pretty sight—filthy, scrawny, and scarred.

It didn't matter how I straightened, tweaked, or tugged, I wasn't going to fool anyone. I was homeless, hopeless, and a thief. I don't know what was worse—being shut in a light box that was getting smaller, or being confronted by who and what I'd become. The sooner I could get out of there and back to the sanctity of the shadows on the streets, the better.

I decided to ignore the fact I had Buckley's of getting out of there undetected. I picked up the dummy shirt and turned my thoughts to what morsels I was going to sacrifice my precious coins on at Greasy Joe's. Hot, cheap, fried carbohydrates were their specialty, and the best I could do on a blisteringly cold winter's night, a skint budget, and an empty stomach.

I waited till I sensed the all clear.

"Is it over? Can we go?"

Still outside my cubicle, Whinger had plucked my thoughts from thin air. If I could just fly under the radar right out of here, I would consider myself well and truly kissed by Lady Luck. I just needed to wait until they left.

"Not yet. Don't forget, we came here for reason."

"Are you serious? We could have been killed. Can't we approach the Target later? Another time, another place?"

"We're fine, and we don't have a 'later'. You know Kait said we'd be heading out soon. Calm down. This is what we do. This is what you wanted."

The words, spoken like a slap, were followed by submissive silence. Bossy had once again put Whinger in her place. I was glad they'd made it through ... whatever the hell that had been. But now, I just wanted them to leave so I could get out of here. This coffin was closing in on me, making it harder to breathe. However, freaking out was a luxury I couldn't afford. So, my simmering panic would just have to shut the hell up.

Breathe in. Step one, make sure my blade was back in its sheath, out of sight. Breathe out. Step two, straighten the dummy shirt on its hanger. Breathe in. Step three, loosen up. I bounced on my toes, shook my arms out and rolled my shoulders. Not long now. Surely, they'd take off soon. Breathe out.

I almost choked mid-breath when the curtain of my cubicle flew open and I was hit by a truck. I copped the full force of Bossy's focus. I froze like a newb in a bust. Her eyes not only pierced me, they broke into my soul and read me like a picture book. I was completely exposed, weak and incapable of bearing the weight of her numbing gaze. I wanted to look away. Hell, I wanted to run away. But all I could manage was a stumble backward. When I hit the back wall, I ran out of ideas. I lost sight of everything but her eyes and the flickering lights that surrounded her.

Maybe I was having a seizure.

"Is that him? Is he the Target?" Whinger was upset, again.

Bossy, silent and unrelenting, didn't respond.

Whinger took that as a cue to continue in her ruthless appraisal. "He doesn't look like much. Are you sure?"

Bossy remained silent.

"Val, you have got to be kidding. Look at him. He's a gutter rat. He stinks and he's obviously a thief. He's probably hiding a knife or some other weapon in that ridiculous coat."

Her words were true, but cutting enough for me to break out of Bossy's glare. I looked her over, up close and personal. With a simple look, I let her know she had nothing, was nothing. She got the message. Her arms flew to cover her woefully small chest. Pathetic. Like she had anything worthy of protection.

Girls were so easy to destroy. I smirked. She hated it. Fragly little gnat. She had no right to the attitude, she was unworthy. I could snap her like the twig she resembled—skitchy princess.

"Ew, really? I need a bath. Please Val, not him, anyone but him." Whinger turned up the whine.

Without averting her gaze or turning down the intensity, Bossy spoke and I had no choice but to listen. "You have dreams. They frighten you. You don't want to sleep, but you can't stay conscious twenty-four hours a day. You wake in a cold sweat, shaking in a knot of pain. If your stomach had food in it, you would vomit from the shock and the distress of what you see and feel when you sleep. But you have little food, less money, and no shelter. You are too scared to talk about it. Who would you tell? You are alone and on the run with no one and nothing in your life. The scariest thing of all is that you don't understand the dreams you have, why you have them, or anything about them."

As the air rushed from my lungs I would have dropped to my knees, but I was paralysed, held prisoner by her knowledge. Like a bulldozer, she ploughed on.

"You are not mad, you are chosen. Sadly, there is no time for you to think about this. I am here to make you an offer. You can come with us now and you will be taught what it all means. Or, we will leave you here in your stolen clothes, armed with your blunt blade against the death of winter, and the harshness of the gang that wins you. Your choice. But make it now. Soon we will leave this place and never come back. Our time in this city is at an end. I know this is a lot to take in, but we are hunted and need to leave. What's your choice?"

I couldn't speak. I could only think: *What the hell!*

"What's your name, son?" her words wrapped around me, soothing the edges off my shock.

"Dan."

For the first time since she hit me with her eyes, she smiled. With obscure clarity, I knew she understood what I was feeling. Automatically, I flinched as she laid her hand on my shoulder. In contrast to her intimidating look, her touch was warm and comforting.

"Dan, my name is Val, and this is Tessa. We're not a gang and nothing like those you ran with in Gomorrah," she said. "If nothing else, consider this an invitation to a free meal and a warm, safe bed for the night. You can come with us, hear us out, and then take off if you want. But we really must go. You choose."

Her gentle touch warmed me through. Hits, kicks and abuse I could take. But this ... against this, I was defenceless. I couldn't remember the last time someone had consoled me, let alone touched me without wanting to kill me, or punch the skrat out of me. Tears formed in my eyes. I was powerless to fight them. But there was no way I was going to let them fall. Not in front of Whinger.

My brain was fried. How the hell did Bossy know? How could she know? I hadn't told anyone. But she was right. So, with no fight left I numbly nodded in agreement and let her guide me. All I was aware of was the firm yet comfortable pressure on my elbow guiding me through the crowd and out of the store. And Whinger's final remark, "Please Lord, not him."

2

———

CONTESSA

Far. Flaming. Out.

It was my first time on a mission, and I'd thought I was ready. I was wrong. I was not expecting that. Which part? The whole flopping lot. How can you be ready for something you have had no idea about? Thank the Light I was with Val. She was the best because she was scary as, a survivor, and kick-butt cool.

Shops were supposed to be pretty safe, especially on weekends. I was trying to copy my mentor by looking tough and playing it cool. But yikes, the shops. I hadn't been to anything other than charity shops for ... ever. It was perfectly normal to get a bit excited, right?

Look tough, play it cool. I played the chant on auto-repeat in my head.

I could do this.

The place wasn't too crowded but there were still enough people to provide cover. Normally, I stayed home with Abbot and helped watch the twins. But they'd all thought I was ready. So today it was Val, Marcus and me.

Look tough, act cool.

Right.

I'd been with these guys for about a year, healing, finding my feet, and training. I was still waiting to see what all my Badges would be. One was Serving.

Yay, right? Serving.

It wasn't as bad as it sounded though. If I didn't think about what it was called and just got in and did what came naturally, it was all kinds of cool. And pretty important. Generally, I lost myself in the tasks and helped the others prepare themselves for battle.

And today it was my turn.

We were all trained to do everything in case something happened to one of us. But each of us had different Badges that were a sign of belonging. Sometimes Badges didn't reveal themselves until you were in the moment—in the heat of battle.

Maybe I would be a real warrior, a Serving warrior ... or maybe not.

Part of our training was to know what to do on mission: only go if your armour is at full strength; don't go out uninformed; before entering a building make sure all the exits have been scouted; never enter a dead end; go out in twos or threes; don't be predictable or create a pattern; stay under the radar; keep an eye on all entrances to minimise the risk of surprise; stay with your guard; if it comes to a chase, each take a different route to designated Soteria Houses and wait till the next day to be picked up.

Simple, right?

Right.

Kait had said the Target would be in the shop. It was pretty weird how it all worked. Kait's badge was Knowing. But we never knew who the Target would be until we saw them. I say "we" but it was Val who could "see". Her Badge allowed her to identify Targets, or "Potentials", as they called them. She didn't actually pick them. They were already chosen. But once they'd been detected, she approached and made the offer.

That was the tricky bit.

The enemy was everywhere. All. The. Time. They didn't really care what we got up to until we approached a Target. That's why we normally picked populated places. We didn't want to be attacked, and the enemy didn't want attention. If the Target said no and walked away, it was game over. A loss for us, but an easy walk home. But if they said yes, or considered the invitation, it turned ugly. The enemy didn't want people to know about them, but losing a thrall was a price they weren't prepared to pay.

Our every move was monitored. There was nowhere we could hide from them, but we weren't defenceless. The thing was, as the deadline for this city came closer, they were becoming all kinds of agitated. So, at the moment, any sign of activity and they'd be all over us like a weepy rash.

And that's what happened this afternoon. We'd come fishing for our Target and just happened—tragedy, I know—to end up in the clothing section after scoping the store. Attempting "tough" and "cool" walking through the new season's stock was testing my focus. Red was definitely looking hot this winter. I have to be careful with red though. Yellow undertones are okay, but the blue-based ones eat me alive. I may not be a warrior yet, but this girl knows her colours.

The fabrics were lush and soft, they trickled through my fingers like feathery water. The smell took me back to when my mum would take me shopping for new season must-haves. These days I could never buy anything new, but I wouldn't have minded a bit of spare time to take it all in, and maybe dream, okay drool, a little. Running my hands through the racks, my eyes salivated. But then I caught sight of Val giving me the side-eye glare.

Right.

Hunting not shopping.

Look tough, act cool.

Back on track.

She was completely amazing, but colours were not her strength, or shopping for that matter. I mean really, the woman had no idea whatsoever about palette or style. But that was okay, we all had our weaknesses. Mine, it appeared, was staying focused in a battle scenario.

At Val's silent rebuke, I took stock.

My heart stopped.

I mean it literally stopped, then raced to catch up. White noise dissolved as time hiccupped. I hadn't noticed the enemy gathering. I knew we were heading into battle. But I had no idea we'd be so outnumbered.

Our guard had left to join the others covering the roof, and Val was leading us into a trap. I mean, I trusted her completely.

Why wouldn't I?

Val was an experienced warrior who lived for the fight. But seriously, what was she thinking? I shouldn't have argued or challenged her, but this was madness. My nerves had been jumping like the washing machine on spin. But Val had remained cool and indifferent to everything other than her purpose: locate the Potential and fend off the enemy.

And now, after my brush with battle in the change rooms, I was both exhilarated and gutted. I'd fought. Yeah, I know, it was minimal. But I'd faced the enemy in a real-life battle, killed a few, and survived. I was so high, I could have flown the whole way home.

But, of all the people in the shop, did it have to be him? He was completely disgusting, from the ingrained dirt breeding on his skin and his revolting clothes, to his unbearable smell. He really stank. And I mean eye-watering, gag-inducing stench. His hacked, greasy-bacon hair didn't do enough to cover his intimidating glare. He made no secret what he thought of me. He was just like all the others. But seriously, what had I done? Belligerence and body odour oozed off him.

Wordlessly, I had been stripped and reduced to trash ... again. The thought of making him the offer had made me physically ill. I hated it. I wanted to leave him to his hopeless future and walk away ... or possibly run.

When Val had propositioned him, he looked like he'd died but forgotten to fall over. The only evidence that he was still alive were the tears forming in his eyes and slightest nod of his head.

No. Please no!

We met up with Marcus at the entry to the men's change rooms. He'd had his share of the fighting but was unscathed. With our guard back in place, the four of us threaded our way out through the aisles and casually left the store. Well, as casually as you can with a stinking corpse, in stolen merchandise, surrounded by Warriors of Light.

Marcus took the lead, Val and Gutter Rat went next, and I fell in behind. The city was filling and the crush on the corso was building as crowds gathered for the weekend's sundown parties. And of course, where the doomed gathered, so too did the Others. Demons crawled over every surface, like ants cloaking spilt honey.

I knew that under our shield, with our armour at full strength, we were safe. But I was still edgy walking through the hordes. Dropping the visor into place on my helmet not only saved me from viewing most of the demonic activity, it helped block out the taunts and whispers, accusations and lies they fired as we passed.

Since moving in with these guys, I hardly ever come into the city anymore. Being reminded of what people do to themselves in the name of fashion, and what they do to each other in the pursuit of "pleasure", makes me sick.

Sodom was an overflowing cesspit of humanity engorging the Dark. I know, I know, just because I didn't see it every day, didn't mean it wasn't happening. But not being confronted by it constantly had been a relief.

Once we were clear of the city centre, we'd have to pass the main temple on our way out. As a kid, I loved Saturdays. Dressing up, joining the crowds and being a part of the temple scene had been a buzz. The stark white facade and the crowning spires in the goddess's colours of gold, purple, and blue had once been a trigger for a head full of happy memories.

But now, the pollution and exhaust from inside and out had coated everything in multiple shades of grey. Just like my childhood fascination had dulled with the knowledge of the soul-pollution the temples traded in.

Open seven days a week, now the temples had not only blended into the grey that surrounded them, they had lost the capacity to contain the growing number of worshipers. It used to be only the rich, or moderately rich like my family, who could afford to go. Now the desperate were welcomed, along with anyone who was prepared to pay the price. Regardless, everyone ended up in the same state. Wretchedness was a great equaliser. That, I knew from experience.

As we approached, my visor could not hide the full extent of the demonic activity. Like crows plundering the battlefield, they climbed over and fed off the inert bodies that spilled out into the street. Temple prostitutes wove their way through the melee, seducing and tempting the conscious to join the nightmare.

How the prostitutes looked so clean, I had no idea. Seriously, they were like beacons of pure in oceans of yuck. Each was covered in purple, gold and blue scales, like leaves, growing over the left-hand side of their bodies, to varying extents. From initiates with only hands and feet transformed, through to full handmaidens, whose goddess-scales completely replaced the skin on the left-hand side of their bodies. I couldn't help but stare. Women from different cultures, artificially modified to be perfect. Perfect bait. They were beautiful ... mesmerising. Even I felt the pull.

The closer we got to the entrance, though, the more like a maze it became. I quickened my step and kept in Val's shadow. I knew we were under guard, but memories of leering eyes and grabby hands lurking in every nook were hard to shake.

The abundance of incense wasn't enough to cover the stench of vomit and sweat. The mix of all three made me gag. As we negotiated the chaos, I held my breath till I saw spots, then breathed through my mouth before I passed out. I was going to shower in bicarb and vinegar, then rinse my eyes with bleach as soon as we got home.

I tried to take my mind off the horrors by going over what had just happened. Especially replaying what Val had said to Gutter Rat. This was kind of dangerous, because as I tried to see things from his perspective, a very small part of me felt sorry for him. From what Val had said, it sounded like he'd had it pretty tough and, well ... it would have been kind of frightening, even for us with all our training and experience. Poor guy.

But I tell you what, if he looked at me like that again, I wouldn't be feeling anything but the handle of my sword.

A girl's got some pride, right?

Well, actually, it was more than that. I'd once been where he was. Worse actually. But I'd received the gift of a fresh start with a new identity. And there was no way I was going to let some feral, stinking, gutter rat make me think of myself like that again.

No. Flopping. Way.

Walking behind, I studied him. I figured since he was processing some pretty full-on stuff, I wouldn't get caught. Even in a trance, he carried his weight low. He was poised and light on his feet. He looked ready to pounce ... or make a run for it.

I didn't really care if he got away.

Well that's not entirely true. I kinda hoped he would.

But since Val had a hold of him, I doubted he was going anywhere.

More's the pity.

So, for now, we were a pinprick of Light moving through a sewer of Dark. One thing I had learned over this past year was, no matter how small or apparently insignificant the Light was, it was always stronger than the Dark. I'd been rescued from the Dark and brought into the Light.

I was safe.

As long as I kept myself within the radiance, the Dark couldn't touch me anymore.

Thank you, thank you, thank you for saving me.

I must have sighed. Val turned. Her face was lit, and her eyes sparkled. She was buzzing with energy. It was probably her after-battle high. She loved it, the whole battle thing. Because she was free in the fight. As far as she was concerned, the bigger, the badder, the uglier, the better. Like I said, Val was scary as, a survivor, and kick-butt cool. But best of all, she was on my side. Or, should I say, we were on the same side.

We'd made it through the worst of the chaos and that's when it hit me. I'd been so busy focusing on myself, I'd totally forgotten about the twins. How were they going to cope with this intruder?

We weren't home yet, so I guessed there was still time for him to make a run for it.

3

MARCUS

Well that went down like a dog's breakfast. Bit of excitement, then it was all over before it had a chance to begin. Val had been happy as a pig in cream, as usual. If anything, she'd be disappointed it hadn't lasted longer. Not that there was anything wrong with that. I love a good fight just as much as the next person. But I reckon I'd have levelled up from enthusiast to fanatic like Val, if it gave me the release it gave her.

Now Tessa ... she was at the other end of the spectrum. Like me Kait, she was a tender-hearted soul who needed to get her "thug" on when it came to the fight. Well, when fighting Others that was. But she managed to hold her game together well enough this time. Not surprising though. Val'd kept her on a short lead. Not ideal to be blooding her in the last days of a city. But better to get her out while we still had a full number.

She was taking a while to come down though. Still walking on shells. Again, not unexpected. Could've been due to exposure to battle, her first visit to the city after being rescued, our particularly prickly fish, or a mix of all three.

But, now that the fluff and bubble were done with, I was keen to get home. We all were. That'd be the true test. Not sure how our two young pigeons would cope with this wild cat. Truth be, I suspected we were all in for a bit of a feather fluster this time round. Not sure how our small home was going to contain his raw energy. Just as well we had rubber walls. They stretched when we needed extra room and we could bounce off them when we went mad.

But this time, it'd be far different than when Tessa arrived. Or the twins for that matter. Maybe he'd take off. But me money was on him staying. If I was going by looks though, I'd say he'd already done a runner ... if he hadn't been hit between the eyes with a stunned mullet. Poor kid. Truth be, it was like that for all of us.

Once his rough edges were chipped away, and we'd all adjusted, it'd be good to have another body around. Good for the kids and Tessa too. You'd never hear her admit it though. I could understand why, seeing as where, and how, we'd found her. But she'd come round. When you were outnumbered on the scale we were, every extra body was a gift worth celebrating. And the prize of an extra blade in battle was worth getting uncomfortable over. It would take some adjustment. But as Abbot said, it added to the flavour of life. That's if I was right and he stayed.

Either way, he wouldn't have long to decide. Time was running out for Sodom and the Light was pulling His army out. We'd been searching for years, and as far as we could tell, we were it. On the one level, it was pathetic. On another level ... actually it was pretty scary on that level too. After all this time, we stood at seven. If the money wasn't already in the bank, I'd say we'd have as much chance as wax in hell.

But we weren't making the moves or calling the shots. Thank the Light. We just followed the orders. I reckoned any that came to us now would stay. I knew there was some kind of rhyme and reason to it. But blowed if I could figure it out. But truth be, when we all pitched in and offered up what our Badges revealed, we generally got a feel for what was going down. For instance, in a matter of weeks, Sodom was going to fall.

And you could feel it. I'd not been to the city for a while. Had no real reason to go, thank the Light. Wretched place. But despite not having Kait's badge of Knowing, Val's badge of Seeing, or Abbot's badge of Feeling, even I could sense the atmosphere was as hot as a docker's armpit.

Even though we had our guard and we trained for this daily, we were in for a rough run. The enemy were ramping it up. Numbers were growing. They were becoming more determined to claim as many thralls as possible before their time was up. In short, they were maximising damage before the plug was pulled. But thankfully they were on a short lead too.

We'd have to be extra vigilant when we were out, and at home. Constant attention to detail when running armour checks. Staying with our guard. No young'uns anywhere by themselves and definitely everyone in line of sight at all times. End times were never pretty. I'd be glad when this season was over. I tried not to think about how it might play out and who we might lose. It'd be good to get home.

It was a beautiful evening, chilly but fresh. I'd pushed Tessa out front. She needed confidence leading and finding her way. Just in case she ever had to make it home alone. Val and Dan followed, and I brought up the rear.

It broke me as I watched Val deteriorate. Apart from Kait, she was me closest friend. The closer we got to home or, more truthfully, the further we moved away from battle, her wheels well and truly started falling off. Not long now, then she could rest.

In the meantime, it gave me a chance to check our Potential. He looked part junk-yard dog, part caged tiger, and all edge. Probably seen and done far too much for one so young. And yet, I still had a good feeling about him. He'd come good. But I'd be keeping an eye on him until we were sure.

Yes, we were sent to rescue ones that'd allow themselves to be drawn from the Dark. But that didn't mean we were a walk in the park. We weren't just responsible for helping new ones out, we were responsible for caring for the ones we already had. That meant boundaries. And that meant standing strong. Always. Everywhere.

We'd tried to shelter the kids and Tessa as much as was wise. But as intentional enemies of the Dark, it had become increasingly difficult for those of us in the Light. In last days, everywhere we went we drew attack. From both the Unseen and the Seen. I doubt the people knew they were puppets of the Dark nailing down their own coffins. I guess that's the trouble with being blind to the Unseen; "the Others". Although, naivety was one thing, ignorance was a choice.

The Light had been warning the people of Sodom for generations. We'd even played a part in that. But, intentionally or not, the city had made its choice. It had run full-on into the arms of excessive perversion and was rolling around in bed with depravity. This place had become a sewer.

There was no other place as degenerate, except maybe Gomorrah. The Dark Lord had gained complete power. His demons were as high as helium sucking the marrow out of Sodom's heart. The temples proved that. You didn't have to be in the Light to see that what went on there was as wrong as a spit roast at a vegan's dinner party. What went on in this city just wasn't right by any standard. And the Light had decreed that their time was up.

If they weren't prepared to stop the carnage, He would —permanently.

4

DANIEL

We'd walked for years. Some guy had joined us early and taken the lead. I fell into a rhythm behind him, my eyes focusing straight ahead on the spot between his broad shoulders. His short, dark hair was generously salted with silver, but he moved with rhythm and balance. It was a dead giveaway. The guy was a fighter. His cauliflower ears and bent nose suggested he was experienced. His carriage and confidence testified to his talent. I would have to watch this one as well.

Mark ... Marcus ... turned to make a brief comment to Val walking beside me. His face was smooth and tawny. Definitely Caucasian, but a sun lover. It emphasised the laugh lines channelling from the palest ice-green eyes I'd ever seen. It was hard not to stare. They slapped me back to reality like a gulp of home brew on an empty stomach. He looked over and smiled, his eyes sparking with mischief.

Emerging from my brain-fog, the first thing I noticed in the absence of white noise was the eerie silence that filled the air. An echo of stillness. I hesitated. They didn't. We kept moving.

We'd walked to the outskirts of town to a rundown, abandoned area I was not familiar with. A sea of bitumen gave way to nature, both on the path and the road. I had one eye scoping the scene, and the other focused on the ground so as not to trip over clumps of grass and other greenery winning the battle against civilisation. The toxic blend of exhaust brewed in the city had passed, and the air almost tasted sweet with its absence.

The road was narrow, providing just enough space for two cars to pass. And the footpath was narrow too. With not enough room for two to walk abreast, we shuffled. Marcus fell behind, with Val at my front and Whinger in the lead. Great. I hope she knew where she was going.

Continuous barriers of concrete blocks hemmed us in on the street. Impenetrable facades painted white, naked grey or tagged with flaking graffiti. The only break in the monotony was the occasional roller door and odd half-door set into the walls. I couldn't imagine what secrets lay within so many fortresses. Each loudly proclaimed the same message: "Private. Skitch off. You are extremely unwelcome."

I had been trying to keep track of turns, but it was no good. I was completely and utterly lost. This place was a rabbit warren. My brain was cooked and I was exhausted, physically, emotionally and mentally. Mistrust and doubt began brewing and my imagination was buzzing. If they turned out to be psychotic freaks who wanted to kill me, then lamb-like I was approaching my slaughter. But I'd be damned if I didn't take out as many as I could when I went. Whinger first.

The farther we made our way into the maze, the more the hackles rose on the back of my neck. My apprehension increased with the sensation of being watched. If I were by myself, I'd be looking for cover. But, surrounded by this crew in this foreign territory, I was at their mercy. On the upside, anyone who wanted me would have to go through them. Small consolation, but at least they'd serve some purpose.

With them in charge of defence, I tried to make sense of what had just happened and what I'd agreed to. Feeling like a pushover. I couldn't get past what Val had said and how she'd said it. Something had given way when she'd broken through the barricade into my

private fears and nightmares. If I couldn't hide there, where was I
safe? I was now at their mercy. I just hoped if they wanted to do me
in, it would be quick and relatively painless. At least then I would be
able to rest and not have to worry about any of this skrat ever again.

Val turned to look at me over her shoulder. "We're almost there.
Then you can have something to eat, a wash and a safe place to
sleep."

What the hell? How did she know what I was thinking? This
woman was freaking me out and I was feeling very naked and unsafe
in her presence.

We turned down yet another street, identical to all the others in
this district, and stopped outside a grey half-door set with a high
stoop, low head and narrow frame. What its purpose was, I had no
idea—except perhaps, like everything else in this neighbourhood, to
keep people out. It was exactly like every other needle-eye door, set
next to a clone roller door, in a nondescript grey brick wall.

Great. I was having images of a man, a maze, and a Minotaur. I
was quite possibly very, very fracked.

Marcus did some weird manoeuvre with his hands, and then
opened the door and squeezed through, and then Whinger followed,
giving me a great view of her butt. So, she did have some assets after
all. Val smiled at me. Skrat, I hoped she hadn't read that thought. But
she merely gestured for me to make my way through and then
awkwardly brought up the rear.

As soon as the door closed there was a collective, silent sigh. They
were not a talkative lot, but they were more relaxed now we were
here. In a long narrow courtyard that ran along the front of the
house, surrounded by four tall, imposing grey walls and open to the
sky, I was surprised by a sudden feeling of comfort and safety. The
sun had almost gone, but it had left its signature in the surrounding
bricks and concrete, making it curiously welcoming despite the dullness of the space.

Now that we were all in, Marcus locked the gate, shutting the
world out behind us. Val slowly made her way to the front door of the
house, knocked once, then waited. This caused a flutter in the curtain

shielding a long, narrow window set high across the front wall of the building. Seconds later, I was invited into a room that was living with light, colour, and warmth. The pressure on my arm increased, forcing me to step forward. I began to panic, but then realised, in my shock I was blocking the entrance. The others wanted to come home.

There was an immediate chatter and a whirlwind of movement. Yet, in the eye of the storm, Val led me to a comfortable seat and told me to relax. "Dinner won't be long. I'll see if Raph can fix you a snack to take the edge off your hunger."

As I sat and took in the surroundings, the rest of the group gathered to catch up and share their news. The woman who'd let us in was wrapped in one of Marcus's arms and they were deep in conversation by the entrance. Whinger raced across the room to embrace a young Hispanic boy. And Val, who had become slower and stiffer in her movements, made her way across to them briefly, then joined Marcus and Gate Keeper for a quiet discussion near the door. This wasn't a gang. This was a family. I wasn't too sure how to take that and what to do with it. I was in uncharted territory.

The first thing that overwhelmed me was the light. Huge windowpanes in the ceiling released a flood of light into the building. The receding sun seemed reluctant to leave as it slowly ebbed away for the evening. The golden rays illuminated the interior walls, which were coated in a bouquet of rich colours and shapes. A garden had been drawn all over the concrete walls. It crept its way around the open room, stretching its tendrils to the back wall, which was panelled completely in glass doors. At this juncture, the avatar met real life—a beautiful, vibrant garden teeming with colour and texture.

Thankfully the doors were shut, as the outside temperature was dropping. On a sheltered patio, vacant chairs and a small two-seater invited relaxation, alongside a lush lawn dancing with the edge of a curving, vibrant garden. At the end of the high-walled yard, a chicken coop sat in the shadow of a glasshouse. Twilight revealed movement in the glasshouse, betraying two people within.

Over the corner of the imposing back wall, a gargantuan beast of a tree reached out its long, dark green fingers, desperate to take hold and claim a piece of this haven. A ladder leaning up against the wall gave access to its lower branches. I could sit here forever and never tire of this scene.

The "house" was just one big room, but the space had been divided up for function by furniture. The kitchen ran along the side wall across from where I now sat. An island bench separated the kitchen, where the Hispanic boy occupied the space masterfully as he talked with Whinger. She helped him lay out dishes and utensils. This would have to be the source of the painfully delicious scent of freshly baked bread, exploding with hints of garlic and other fresh herbs. My stomach reminded me, and everyone else in the room, I hadn't eaten for a very long time.

At the end of the kitchen was a door which I suspected led to the garage. To the right of the front door was a bank of desks with an old PC taking up residence on one, and a laptop opened upon another. Next to them was a set of battered shelves overflowing with books. A few had escaped and lay on the desk, unattended but accompanied by pencils and scrap paper. Someone had recently been working there.

On the other side of the entrance was the designated sleeping space. Several stretchers were stacked against the wall and there was an oversized beanbag in the corner.

When I'd first entered, I'd briefly noticed a hallway off the end of the sleeping space. It probably led to the bathroom.

I was planted in a garden of eclectic armchairs taking pride of place in the space before the glass doors. There was so much to take in. It was a feast of colour in a simple, uncluttered cavern. This sitting area was configured into a rough semicircle, making the most of the Eden outside. Behind me was a wall that created a hallway I briefly noticed when I came in.

This had better work out for me because, from my rapid reconnaissance, I knew there was no easy escape route. If I had to make a run for it, I had two chances—Buckley's and none.

The young chef approached me and introduced himself as

Raphael. "But you can call me Raph, everyone does. Val said you would be hungry." He obviously didn't know what to make of me. His nose flared and scrunched. His eyes darted everywhere other than my face. But it was the drag of his feet that revealed his dislike of the situation as he approached.

"Dinner will not be t-too long, but if you would like you can snack on one o-of my bread rolls, this one is plain, I am saving the garlic ones f-for dinner." His tumble of words betrayed his nerves, which he tried to disguise with bravado.

"Thanks, Raph, I'm Daniel, or Dan if you prefer. I've been dying since I walked in here. The smell of this bread is awesome. You're an amazing chef!" I tried to chisel away his guard with flattery and was rewarded when he flicked his eyes to mine. His face darkened to pomegranate. Mumbling his thanks, he skittered back to the kitchen. I took a huge bite out of the hot, airy roll and looked up to see Whinger staring at me. Weird chick.

"You've met most of us," she said, "but this is Kaitlyn who was here with the others to welcome us home. Abbot and Sariah are outside. And that's us, so ... welcome."

"And you are welcome, Daniel." Kaitlyn spoke from her station at the door. "Please relax, we know it's a lot to take in and, quite likely, very alien to you. But rest well. We will sit and talk over dinner. If you need the bathroom or would like to wash, Tessa will show you where everything is."

Kaitlyn was a very good-looking woman with a voice like honey and a body to match. Lush brown hair bounced around her shoulders and intellect smouldered in her dark eyes. Probably mid-to-late thirties, shortish in stature but with an edge that added to her package. She obviously took care of herself and gave the impression she could take care of herself. I wouldn't go out of my way to skitch her off. Kudos to Marcus.

Tessa approached with another bread roll, having noticed that I had inhaled the first one. "Come on, I'll give you a tour." Her huge dark eyes softened and her bird-like face relaxed. She even managed to radiate tepid warmth. I didn't know what happened to the twik in the shop, or the uptight princess on the way home, but she was different here. I didn't know what to make of her, which was scary. Reading people and situations is how I survive. Security always came first so, just to be on the safe side, I'd be keeping my distance.

I looked over to Raph and thanked him again for his delicious baking. His dark skin blushed to a deeper shade of plum as he busied himself with some task. I followed Whinger and almost walked straight into her as she stopped abruptly. I tried to keep my hands off her as I stumbled backward. She turned to face me and pointed fluidly around the room in a circular motion. "Kitchen. Study. Bedroom. Sitting room. And dining room."

We were in the heart of the building standing next to a huge, solid wooden table. The pale slabs of timber were well-worn and framed by equally aged bench-seats. Placed at each end were two armchairs dressed with ornate carving, similar to the work my grandfather used to create. A chipped bowl overflowing with tomatoes and avocados was an interesting centrepiece. This, and everything else about the place, was stamped with uncluttered, well ordered functionality. But far from being sterile, it was homey. A whisper circled and embraced me.

"Welcome home."

I would have to be really careful not to let my guard down. I didn't know these people and I didn't yet know what they wanted.

The tight line of Tessa's mouth softened as she turned and led on, showing me the other rooms until arriving at the bathroom. It was obviously an old building decorated eons ago. Whilst it was very clean, the tiles were cracked, and grout was missing. An old shower head extended over a deep, long bath taking up the length of one wall. It was hard to take in any other detail after I'd seen the shower. And the bath.

"Here is a towel and a change of clothes. In the bath you'll find soap, shampoo, and conditioner ... use as much as you want. Please. I mean it." With that I copped a full-on glare. "You can leave your dirty clothes in there"—pointing to a huge basket against the far wall. "I'm afraid we haven't got heaps of hot water, so ..."—she dropped her eyes —"please don't feel you have to rush ... but ..."

"Of course! I won't take too long, but listen, I really appreciate it. I can't remember the last time I had a proper wash." I was struggling to come to terms with their overt generosity, constantly looking for the catch.

"Yeah, I know, you reek." And with that, and a wrinkled face, she twirled and shut me in, leaving me to the bliss of a hot shower and the joyful anticipation of being clean. Even if they did turn around and kill me, I would be thankful for the bread and shower. Yet, I still wondered what they actually wanted from me. Because it was common knowledge, despite the slogans: nothing was for free. So, just to be sure, I locked the door.

5

KAITLYN

Not only could I not believe the latest news reports, I couldn't believe the lack of response from City Council. Unemployment, homelessness, crime and corruption had steadily been breaking new records. And not only for Sodom, but for the whole Eastern Seaboard. This boy, Dan, could well be presented as Exhibit A representing the ills of this city and how it had failed its people.

It was an embarrassment. If the situation wasn't so desperate, it'd be a joke. Anyone with the sense to see the writing on the wall, or who had a shred of decency, had long gone. I didn't blame them. If we didn't have a purpose here, we'd've been leading the exodus.

"You show 'em, love." Marcus's eyes sparkled from the sitting room. He was waiting with Val for the mission's debrief.

I looked down to the four wheat packs I'd been beating into submission. They had been intended to relieve Val's pain, not my aggression. "Tessa, sweetheart, could you please go and ask Abbot and Sariah to get ready to come in?"

Our beautiful girl twirled and danced out to the backyard. Once she was out of earshot, I took the packs to Val. "Did you read that fatalities at the temples have risen again this week? And no one seems to care. Or to be doing anything about it."

"To be honest, Kait, what do you expect?" Val welcomed the soothing heat with greater enthusiasm than my fussing. I knew she hated my "clucking", but until she was able to do something about it, she'd just have to deal with it.

"The decline has been in process for years," she said. "Corruption is a cancer that doesn't play favourites or show any signs of fatigue. It's a disease that has found a willing host and is breeding a colony of injustice, greed, and indifference." Val stilled my busy hands as I rearranged her blankets around her aching joints. "We knew it was coming. We were warned."

"I know, I just can't believe people would stand by and let it happen."

"Look around, love," Marcus said. "This suburb is a ghost town. Those who had the heart to fight have conceded defeat and departed. Other areas are the same." He nodded toward the door as the three came inside.

Riah and Tessa went to the kitchen to make a pot of tea as Raph busied himself finishing dinner.

"The divide is widening," Val said. "Those hungry for more of the Dark are migrating to the heart of the city. And those who still had a shred of dignity have left. As will we. It will all be over soon, Kait." She closed the conversation before the others could join us. It wasn't like the kids didn't know. They knew better than any, but they didn't need to hear us going on and on about it.

We sat in the living room and looked out to the garden. Tessa and Riah set the table as Raph finished dinner preparations. From the corner of my eye I watched the three of them move in harmony, complementing each other's actions wordlessly. They'd all come a long way and adjusted so well. Each one was a living miracle.

Holding the rim of my mug and blowing steam off the top, I allowed the aroma of chamomile to finish the work of calming my frustration. Darkness thought he'd won. Perhaps in a way he had. But not for long.

Sodom's days were numbered. The city had been warned and grace had been extended for the allotted time. The people had been given ample opportunity to come to the Light, but instead they had chosen to climb into bed with the Dark. And now, tested and found wanting, their day of judgement was coming.

The Dark Lord was avidly stirring the pot, striving to wreak as much damage, chaos, and pain as he could before the end. And, if he caused any of the remnant to lose focus or recant, or if he could steal any of our Targets, he'd have a bonus to his victory.

As always though, the Light was in control. And we'd been put on notice for our withdrawal. It was going to be hard to leave. With the addition of the twins and Tessa to our family, this had become a real home. More so than we'd had in years. It had been easier to make an effort to turn this shelter into more than a base, for the kids' sake. But I'd received word we'd be leaving; whether Dan would come with us remained to be seen.

My badge of Hearing provides words to help us discern our purpose in each situation. They aren't always actual words, sometimes they are more of an "understanding", a fuzzy but undeniable intuition. I had a very strong feeling about Dan. But in the end, it would be his choice. Those to whom we were drawn, with whom we shared the Light, were sometimes receptive to the idea. But when the pull of their known world became too strong, and the cost of leaving it too high, they sometimes returned.

There was always a choice. In fact, we were presented with the choice every day, in everything we did. For a few, the pull into the Light was stronger, and their ability to deny it was almost impossible. We didn't understand the way of it, we just charted the course as best we could.

Because of the current climate, heightened danger for us on the street, and the Dark being more overt, Words had been coming through thick and fast. Sometimes I didn't hear things till just before they happened. Other times, I heard in plenty of time to prepare. For example, I knew Daniel would be in the department store. But the nature of the attack hadn't been clear. Regardless, it had been important that we send Tessa. She'd had a small, insignificant run-in, was unharmed, and had learned to trust a bit more. Part of our debrief was to determine if any of her other Badges had been revealed. Although, it was still early days.

Tessa was going to struggle with Daniel. If he decided to stay, as Marcus seemed to believe he would, we were going to have to handle this very carefully. When we'd first arrived, there were just the four of us. The addition of the twins had taken a bit of adjustment, but that was mainly due to their extreme trauma. For the first year they had been our main focus.

When Tessa arrived the following year, it had benefited them to be the ones helping someone else. The three had become very close. And now, a year later, we had Daniel. Obviously, the Light knew what He was doing. I just hoped we could help the lad whilst still giving space and time to the other three. I guessed this was as close to parenting as I was ever going to get. And I loved every scary second of it.

This was not the first time we'd experienced the death of a city. However, it was the first time with kids, and that put us all on edge. Tonight, we would celebrate and welcome. Tomorrow, we would plan and prepare our defensive. But right now, we needed to debrief, regroup, and petition the Light that we would all make it out.

The others came and joined us, and we all took a moment to watch the dramatic change of guard as the sun trailed over the horizon, giving space for the night. Abbot had been quiet. More so than normal. I knew he was worried about the twins—we all were—but I thought there may have been more to it than that. I'd have to try to speak with him alone. Easier said than done, with our growing numbers.

6

ABBOT

Raphael had done a marvellous job with the meal. As he did with all the things we'd taught him. The lad was a veritable sponge when it came to absorbing information.

Of course, Marcus was a gifted teacher and a patient guide. I like to think I'd played a small part as well, offering my two cents' worth when appropriate, and helping where I could.

It had been such a pleasure being part of this family and watching them grow from seedlings to healthy, vibrant vines.

My, how things had changed over such a short time. When I'd joined Valarie and Joy, we'd become three ...

Was it really ten years ago? My goodness, you should have seen us then. Actually, I'm very glad you couldn't. Let's just say, transitioning from living most of my life in a cell by myself to living with two women took quite a bit of getting used to.

Then it was with great celebration we welcomed Kaitlyn and Marcus. Now that would have been, let me think ... yes, it must have been six years ago, because Joy was taken from us shortly after ...

But now look at us, we were eight. Or would be very soon. This one was in for a bit of a wild ride, but I was confident he would be hanging around ... in a manner of speaking.

They were all so keen to learn and so willing to give. I never thought I would ever have such a wonderful family of my own. It would be hard to leave them. But it was all too easy to fall into the rut of worry. One must continue to make the effort to stay on the track of hope.

I would carry on encouraging them to celebrate our victories for as long as I was with them. It wasn't hard to find the victories, but one must strive to keep them in sight. But for now, it was time for building up, gathering stones, and a time to speak.

"Come now, everyone, let us sit and enjoy Raphael's banquet."

Our young guest poked his head around the end of the hallway as we migrated from the sitting room to the dining table. "Perfect timing, Daniel. Please come and join us for our celebration and welcome-feast."

Distrust radiated off him like steam from an overheated motor. This was understandable of course, but it was encouraging to note that he wasn't too uncomfortable. Hungry and inquisitive? My word, yes. A dangerous threat? Definitely not.

They say clothes maketh the man, but I'd like to add that washed and clean clothes go a long way to helping a man to hold his head up. With his tail tucked between his legs, our guest edged his way over, waiting to be shown where to sit.

My poor Tessa was drowning in a wash of fear, resentment and anxiety, her yellow flickering to orange and red. Raphael was fighting his enemy—the red tide, as we often referred to it. Or, at other times, the Dragon. Sariah was a concoction of timid and curious. Yet, keenly aware of her twin's and Tessa's discomfort, she was focusing on her Badge and pushing out waves of peace. Bless the dear girl. Such a miracle. Such a wonder.

"Daniel, this is Abbot and Sariah. They are responsible for the oasis outside. And Sariah alone has created the one inside." Kaitlyn beamed at both of us before she continued. "They are the final two members of our family." She then indicated a place where Daniel could sit and join our table fellowship.

Sariah, as usual, took refuge behind my "skirts". I sensed it was more from a desire not to be the centre of attention as opposed to being overly scared. At times she was a little mouse. At others she rivalled Raphael's Dragon. However, she was understandably nervous around new people, especially men. But her desire to lessen the distress in others was beneficial in assisting her own demeanour.

From behind me, a blue blanket of peace was sent forth with comforting weight. We all breathed easier with Sariah's gift as it settled snugly over us at the table, even over the girl herself. Therefore, it didn't take Sariah long to warm up.

Nor did it Daniel, for that matter.

Under her influence, Daniel's charm escaped and worked wonders. The lad deftly brought our girl back into view by quietly coming around the table and squatting down beside me, meeting her eye to eye. He spoke softly, like one might reassure a timid animal, not patronising, just soothing and gentle. He encouraged her, "I think your work is amazing, I have never seen a more beautiful garden anywhere, ever. And I live in a park. You must have green thumbs."

Sariah peeked out from behind me, her face beaming and alight with colour.

This one had insight. Although, Sariah did tend to bring out the best in people.

Am I biased? Absolutely.

I was immensely grateful that I had lived to see them all arrive. There were times I wondered if I'd make it, especially since I knew it would all be over so soon. I felt ready. But then, is one ever truly ready to leave one's beloveds? Is the work ever fully done? I didn't know. But I was exhausted and knew I couldn't keep up anymore. I was more of a burden than beneficial. I guess when one has outlived one's usefulness, it is time to move on.

I did worry about my little ones, though. I knew Tessa would be fine. However, for Raphael and Sariah, my little sparrows, I tried not to fret ... with limited success. But then, that was pride. How was my love for them greater than that of the rest of the family? How could I care for them better than those they had been planted amongst?

I have always struggled with pride. Don't we all? I needed to let them go and be ready to leave when my time came. I would miss them ... and Valarie, my daughter in the Light. We had been together so long. Kaitlyn and Marcus had been gifted to me as two more children of my heart. Watching them come into the Light, grow, learn and become formidable, had brought such joy and warmth into my old age.

And now, this young man had just started his journey and had much to learn—I hoped I would have time to teach him. Teaching to me is like breathing. Not only a vital part of life, but a source of pure joy. To take concepts, turn them into images, and then use words to paint those pictures. It was a Badge I'd always been grateful for and revelled in.

"Daniel, I can't tell you what joy it gives me to welcome you into our table fellowship. I understand that you had a trying day, and Valarie gave you a bit of a shock. That can't have been easy for you."

7

———

DANIEL

"Yes ... ah ... Sir. It was a bit unexpected and I've never met anyone who can read minds before."

"Our dear Val has a special ability. But whilst she can 'see' more than most, believe me, she can't read your mind." His soft voice matched his aged, bent body. But his crafty chuckle and sharp eyes gave the impression of youth.

I tilted my head and snuck a peek at her, sitting up at the opposite end of the table. Her eyes were down and once again a hint of a grin appeared on her face. It was like her life was one big joke. Some of us didn't have that much to smile about. Sheltered up here, with all these people running around after her, she seemed nice enough, but what's her story?

She looked like she could single-handedly take down an army ... and thoroughly enjoy it. I would not be going out of my way to skitch her off, that's for sure. Maybe that was why they all ran around waiting on her hand and foot. She was one scary woman ... but she was also kind of warm and welcoming. Confusing.

Maybe this was where Whinger got it from ... she had a long way to go.

I hadn't had time yet to get a read on Old Guy, but he seemed nice enough. He definitely had pull, but I doubt he was top dog. That had to be either Marcus or Val. Trouble was, I couldn't see either of them playing second fiddle.

Normally I could size up a group pretty quick—another survival skill. Pick the leader and either bargain or take him out. Fastest way to end a skirmish. Whatever the pecking order in this nest was though, for now, everyone listened as Old Guy continued to run this part of the show with his gentle voice.

"Where to begin? I hope you don't think she was betraying a confidence, but Valarie told me about your dreams," Old Guy began. "I believe she also told you that we could help you understand them. The fact is, Daniel, what you can now see pales to insignificance compared to what you can't yet see. You have been offered the opportunity to enter into the world of the Unseen. To look into the Other. I believe you may have already had a glimpse. However, if you accept the invitation, you will not only enter that world, from it you can never return. You will be at war for the rest of your life."

For frack's sake, talk about dramatic. I'd read those books, snuck into those films. It was the latest thing—everyone wanted to be a freaking vampire, werewolf, demon or zombie, all the rich were getting work done to resemble whacked-in-the-head creatures. I might come from the streets, but give me break. I wasn't that gullible.

Although, to survive any longer, I had to align with someone in this town and these guys were nowhere near as whacked as the Commander and his pet, Soldier. But I was not going to hang around if they were going to feed me this skrat. I'd stay the night, but come tomorrow, I was outta here.

"Daniel, it's not what you think." The "not-mind-reader" was back at it. "Please, let him finish. Then you can decide. You are welcome to stay tonight regardless of what you think. And tomorrow you are free to leave, or at any point for that matter. But please hear him out."

I turned back to the old man, and he continued.

"Please, Daniel, I ask you to be patient ..."—he tilted his head, narrowed his ancient eyes and gave a sly smile—"in exchange for your food and lodging for the night."

I didn't really care too much about stealing stuff from the big corporations, but I never stole from the little guys. These people had taken me in and fed me, an unknown gutter rat. They even let me keep my weapons as an offering of trust.

I really didn't want to skitch them off, and I had been starved of decent human company for so long. It was a novelty to sit and talk with them—even if they did turn out to be complete nutters.

I guess he'd got a read on me before I'd read him back.

"I think it would be helpful to give you just a brief outline of our reality." The old man took a moment, leaned back and steepled his fingers under his chin, his elbows resting on the arms of his ornate chair. Rheumy eyes lifted to stare out the skylight into the infinite night beyond, and he began.

"There is, and always has been, the Light. But, discontented with inferiority and driven by pride, the Dark rose in opposition. And, like lambs, we followed when he beckoned. Now, we are all swimming in his sea of Darkness, and that is where we stay unless the Light awakens and calls us back.

"Once that happens, we are at a crossroads. We can stay in the Dark or we can turn to the Light. For alas, we cannot belong to both. It is impossible for the Dark and the Light to mix. You either choose to accept the invitation to come into the Light, or you choose to remain in the Dark. Simple."

At this point I gazed out the huge glass doors, for no other reason than to get away from the weirdness of this conversation and the faint flickering of the seven who joined me at the table. The rubber had definitely hit the road and they were going for the sell.

Outside, evening had blanketed the sky and turned the large glass doors into a dim mirror. But despite the reflection I could see tiny droplets of light were dotted throughout the garden like night flowers blooming in the dark. It reminded me of one of my dreams. And all of a sudden, I remembered Val's words in the shop, and I was all ears again.

The old man's gentle voice continued rhythmically. "If you accept the Light, you begin a journey of transformation; a journey into the Light. Light changes everything. But it is hard to choose something that you have no experience of. I expect you have had some experience of the Dark: chaos, loneliness, fear, bitterness, hatred. We all have. But Light is, by definition, everything 'other' than Dark. And whilst you are free to choose, you must be aware that there is a cost."

His gentle voice continued almost hypnotically. It was a weird contrast: a withered husk of a man attempting to enlighten me about cosmic warfare. But I knew about cost and the result of staying where I was. I knew all too well what my choices were on the street. I knew that I didn't have long before I'd be permanently integrated into one of the gangs ... or killed by them—the more desirable option of the two. I had seen, I had heard, I knew the fate that waited for me on the street.

The old man, if he had been a warrior, looked way past his prime, yet he had done nothing to earn my disrespect. I continued to listen.

"The way of Darkness is the easier way because it merely requires self-gratification. Humanity, in its basest form, functions for the sole purpose of self-satisfaction. You've seen the temples, where humanity crawls in to sacrifice itself upon the altar of self-worship. The Dark encourages this, rejoices and revels in it. For when this happens, humankind rips itself apart and the Dark dines on the carnage.

"The way of the Light requires discipline and hard work, because it is both opposite to and opposed to the Darkness. In the Dark, we're each the centre of our own universe, whereas in the Light we step aside. It is not easy because it is not our nature, but humanity in its highest form is motivated by love and functions for the sole purpose of Other."

Sounds like a blast. Where do I sign up?

"Darkness hates the Light, for the Light is superior in every way. Wherever there is Light, Darkness cannot be complete. The faintest Light is more powerful than the most intense Dark. Therefore, the Dark does not readily relinquish its prey to the Light. The deeper his claws are skewered into the flesh and mind, the tougher and more painful the battle for release. For those who choose the Light, there will be a fight. Yes, there's always a fight—inside and out. Mind and body."

Great! So, I'm looking at service, pain and more fighting. They really know how to sell a product.

"This has been a lot to take in, young man. But please be aware, if you do choose the Light, we welcome you as family for as long as you continue in the Way. You will be one with us, part of us, and home among us—sheltered and protected for as long as you desire."

A family. A home. A place to belong. These were fighting words that sounded pretty damn good right now. That other skrat about "Light" and "Dark" I could leave, but companionship, security, shelter, and food were harder to pass up.

Although, there was one issue. Well, one I needed clarifying now. "If this universal war has been going on for all time, and you say you're on the winning team, why are you so few? Are there other groups of you in Sodom?" It would help if they had back up. They talked about protection and shelter, but looking around I couldn't see how that was possible with so few. Most of whom were unviable. I needed to know the odds before I even considered jumping ship.

"We are always on the lookout and eager to find any who are aligned with us. The Light leads us to those He chooses, and we have ways of discovering other Communities. But, alas, here in Sodom, we know of no others," the old guy answered. "But there are great numbers in other cities around the world. Soon we will leave this place and join another Community in the next place the Light leads us to. Our specific job is to find potential recruits and offer them the choice to join the Light. It has been our immense joy to have discovered and welcomed Raphael, Sariah and Tessa from our time here in Sodom. There will be more in other places."

So, they were weak here, but they had numbers in other cities. The biggest plus was they were leaving soon. I could use them as my ticket out of this place, and shelter here in the meantime. I was sure this wasn't the whole deal, though. It sounded too easy. I wouldn't make a decision either way till I knew the catch.

"Enough for now. Time to withdraw for tea." He looked around the table and drew the business to a close. He then turned to the boy. "Raphael, another grand masterpiece, thank you. Tessa, dear, would you put the kettle on?" With orders issued, he turned to me. "Daniel, do you drink tea? Coffee? Or perhaps a hot chocolate? Our Raphael makes a splendid cup." Without waiting for my response, he stood and made his way to the sitting room. Once again, like a conductor manipulating a grand piece of music, the old man had manoeuvred the situation and the mood.

Everyone began to move, except for Val. She leaned back in her chair, studying me with an open face. She gave that same encouraging smile then stiffly rose and slowly made her way to the sitting room. As day progressed into night, so too her body transformed from warrior to a cripple needing assistance. I didn't know what the go was, but swallowed my curiosity, not ready to open that can of worms. Rather, without thinking, I slipped right back into the habits of my childhood. I got up and helped clear the table, taking a pile of plates and following in Whinger, Sariah and Raph's wake, but was stopped when I reached the kitchen.

"The first one's on us. If you choose to stay, then you can help. Tonight, go and have a seat. Raph, Riah, and I have got this. What will you have?" Whinger took the plates from me and passed them over to Sariah.

She was still playing nice and I wasn't complaining. Here, on her own territory, she was different. A different I could try to get used to. Or at least put up with until I'd milked this situation. The girl was definitely weird, and I didn't trust her. Even though she had her friendly face on, I was sure Shop Twik or Uptight Princess would be waiting to jump me when I least expected it.

"Ah ... a coffee would be great, straight up. Thanks heaps." I turned around to see the others taking their places in the sitting room. I met Val's eyes, and with a small jerk of her head, she indicated I should join them. I approached, hesitant, not knowing where to sit. Then I noticed there were eight chairs. Why were there eight, if they were only seven? They didn't strike me as folk who entertained regularly ... or at all.

A guttural rumble erupted from Marcus, which, I was soon to learn, was his laugh. "Come on, boy, take a seat, we won't bite you ... yet. We'll wait to see what you decide."

"Marcus!" His wife was shocked, or at least pretended to be. "Come on over, Dan, we prepared a place for you." Kaitlyn nodded towards the old armchair next to Val. It had high, wall-like sides I could shelter behind. It wore a cracked cloak of soft leather. I could see a permanent well had been made by the previous owner's butt. I already knew it was comfortable. It was the same chair Val had placed me in when I arrived. I hadn't known then it was actually to be my chair, a place they had prepared for me. After all I had been through, that was a big deal.

"Like Abbot said, you need to count the cost before you make your choice." Marcus's eyes indicated Tessa, who had moved from the kitchen to wipe the table. "The battle's nothing compared to having to work alongside that scullery maid!" Again, Kaitlyn let out her feigned protest just as a wet dishcloth came flying across from the table and hit Marcus in the side of the head with a satisfying splosh.

"Yes!" Whinger roared in victory.

"Very good shot, dear one. Your aim is improving," Abbot congratulated from the sidelines.

With a torrential roar Marcus stood and turned in one fluid movement, flying to the kitchen. Whinger ran for cover. For a split second, I was concerned for her. I looked to the others to get a read on the situation. Should we intervene?

8

RAPHAEL

"Run, Tessie. Run. I will stop him."

"You." Marcus changed direction. "You turncoat."

I knew it was play, but anxious tingles took hold. My blood ran fast and my heart raced ahead. I could not hold still, but I did my best to block Marcus the mountain as he approached. Low breath. My feet were roots reaching down to take hold of the Earth's core. I was a rock. I was the Light. Feet wide. Defence stance. I was a wall.

He stormed the kitchen. He came at me. I roared like a lion. He did not even slow as he swooped me up under his left arm and kept raging on to catch Tessa. I could not hold back the squeals or laughter. It poured out of me like a waterfall sourced from the ocean. Joy bubbled and frothed from my heart.

I could hear Tessie's laughter, chairs bumping, and Marcus's soul growling with love. Tessa was a cat. A beautiful, clever, sunny cat. She would run and dodge and weave. But Marcus would catch her. He always caught us. She could dance across thin air if she wanted. But Marcus was a magnet. A big, strong magnet that would not, could not break. Would not stop pulling us into his arms.

It only took one circuit of the dining room and he had her. She reached out from under his right arm and grabbed my hands, laughing tears painting her face. We knew what was coming. We hung on tight. We clung to each other and to him to prepare for the fall.

Rolling and tumbling onto the big soft field of carpet that sat in the middle of the chairs. Tessie and I held tight. Each trying to protect the other from the onslaught of tentacles that tricked their way to the tender spots and tortured us with tickles.

After years of torment, he stopped. We remained pinned under his saucepan-lid hands as he turned to Riah. She had run to the safety of her chair under the protection of Abbot the moment war had been declared.

"What say you, my fair princess?" It was a ritual. "Release or retribution?"

I looked out from under Marcus's arm and over Tessie's shoulder to watch the performance unfold. Riah squinted her eyes, pretended to ponder, then slowly reached out her hand, fist clenched, thumb parallel to the ground. This bit was not foretold. Riah would do what Riah would do, when Riah wanted to do it.

We waited. I held my breath.

Our eyes locked, the corner of her mouth skipped. I did not have to look to her hand to know what she had decided. Her eyes declared my fate as she turned her thumb to the ground.

"No," Tessie and I cried in unison. Our despair fuelled Marcus's energy for another round. Breathless eons later a tinkling clap rang out. Marcus turned to Riah again. With a slight shake of her head, and a wink to me, Riah indicated it was enough. We had been punished adequately. Her point made.

"Your wish is my command." Marcus climbed up from the floor, releasing us, and stepped over to where she and Abbot sat, secure in their thrones. He took a knee as Riah held out her hand. He leant over and he kissed it, back to the ritual. But it did not stop her cheeks warming and her eyes deepening.

Lightning fast, he stood and turned back to us. Bending at the waist, he held his hand out to Tessie. "M'lady."

Tessa snorted. I giggled.

He crushed her to his chest, wrapped her in his steel bands and laid feather lips to her forehead. Watching his love, my heart sang. Giddy, I waited. Not disappointing, Marcus scooped and cartwheeled me before setting me on my feet with a feather forehead blessing for me. I melted into his embrace.

"Back to the kitchen, the both of you, scullery maids!" Intermission was over. Marcus planted himself back on his throne. I waited. I watched. My eyes feasted on Riah, curled up within the protective arms of her chair, resting her head on the edge with Abbot's hand stroking her hair. Both of them stared into their Eden beyond the glass, salted with night lights. I watched how he loved her. I watched how she trusted him.

Thank you.

Kaitlyn came to me, knelt, took my face in her warm, warrior hands and repeated the blessing Marcus had laid on my forehead. "All is well, Raphael. She is safe. You are safe. Rest easy."

Kaitlyn let me listen to her heartbeat. It was my anchor. Just to make sure I did not miss it, I pressed in close and she held me in place. Once my timing had been recalibrated with hers, she stood and steered me to Tessie, who was waiting off the island of carpet.

The light in the room dimmed to a gentle glow as Kaitlyn lit two lamps, one between her throne and Abbot's, and the other between Tessie's and mine. The only other light in the building drew us into the kitchen.

With the break over, we returned to our responsibilities. Tessie hung her arm around my shoulders. I wrapped my arm around her tiny waist. In the kitchen she leaned over and gently kissed the top of my head. "Love you, little man," she murmured.

I turned and tried to break her willowy waist in two with my love. She never did break. But she did laugh. Then without words—we did not need words—we worked as one to complete our mission of caring for our family. The two of us were a team within the team. Tessie and I played a vital part in the Light. If we did not do what we did, caring for our family, they could not go out and kill the Darkness.

They needed to be looked after and that was our job. They could not function without us. One day I would join the battle, killing the Darkness, but until I was old enough this was my duty.

Tessa pulled us along the current of our roles with her quiet song. The quality was not pure crystal, like Sariah's. Instead it rolled and folded into and around the earthy nature of gold.

9
___

DANIEL

A peaceful hush descended on the room. The only sounds were of the comfortable companionship of the two in the kitchen as they finished their duties. I sat back in my chair and watched quietly.

A gentle weight descended upon me. At first, I thought it was tiredness and contentedness from having a wash, wearing clean clothes, food in my gut and a roof over my head. I hadn't felt such peace and security since those fleeting days with Abraham and Indy so many lifetimes ago.

A gentle hum sang in my ears. A hole had been cut in the top of my head, through which warm, golden oil flowed into my body, filling every part of me from the tips of my toes to the roots of my hair. Each crevice, every gap filled. Every bone coated. But it didn't stop. It continued to build and intensify. My heart swelled uncomfortably. Weight became pain. My eyes leaked. The pulsing hum intensified to a scream.

What the hell?

I panicked. This was way beyond my control. With more weight came a bursting heart, incredible pain and exploding ears, flooding eyes, and more panic. A fist clenched my throat. A sword pierced my chest. A vice bound my head—I couldn't breathe. The pain. The Light ... the pain. I was aware of gentle pressure on my right shoulder. "Don't fight Him, Daniel. Let Him in." Val came close.

I was losing myself to the onslaught. But damned if I was going to surrender. I'd never let anyone in ever again. It was unbearable. Searing pain. Overwhelming weight. Val was quietly humming a tune under her breath that was, in a way, distracting.

Regardless, the weight of the world closing in on me, the pressure of the cosmos forcing its way into my body, simultaneously crushing and tearing me apart, was unbearable.

There was an explosion of Light inside me. My heart burst, pain screamed through my whole body. A grenade within my flesh detonated, ripping every sense apart. Nothing was holding me together. Every neural pathway was electrocuted with high-voltage Light. I couldn't hold back the wracking sob that shook my body. I was completely and utterly broken.

"Daniel, you are my child; I know you, I formed you, I love you. I died and I live for you. I have come to invite you into a new life. A new start, washed clean, with a purpose, as a member of my family. But first, you must acknowledge me and confess your need for me."

His voice was as deep and as old as the mountains. It came to me from within my head, from behind the torn ribbons of my shattered heart, from the depths of the universe. The screaming in my ears had broken through to quiet angelic singing.

The chair cradled my depleted body. My mind was numb and broken. I had no control over my quiet sobbing, my defences were completely shot. I wept with relief that the torment was over, and I grieved for the truth I now owned. I was rebellious, wounded, filthy and insignificant.

Multiple images and memories raced through my mind like snippets of a horror movie flashing, marring and distorting a pure and perfect background. Something that could have, should have, been beautiful, I'd destroyed. My life had had potential, a wonderful canvas I'd turned to ashes. In the clarity and awesomeness of pure light, I was filthy. And I was ashamed. I was stained forever. The realisation finished the task of breaking me. I was reduced to nothing as my life's memories and suffering came flooding back.

Go away from me. It's too much. Too bright. I have nothing. I am nothing. I am alone. I have caused incredible pain. I have suffered unspeakable things. And I hurt. So. Damned. Much.

I could not speak the words out loud, but I knew He'd heard me.

"I know you, every part of you and your life, and still, I love you. I was broken so that you could be made whole, I suffered so that you may be free, and I died so that you may have life. I am here to invite you to accept my gift of a clean slate. All you need do is say yes, and it will be done."

No! Get out of my body, get out of my head.

I couldn't stand it anymore. It was too much. I bolted. I made it out the front door to the courtyard and fumbled with the skratty little door onto the street. I couldn't get the blasted lock opened, so I started punching it in frustration. The noise covered the sound of approaching footsteps, so I jumped when Marcus's arm reached over and he placed his hand on the latch.

"You are free to go, but remember, the way back will always be available to you."

With that, he opened the stupid door and I was free. I hit the pavement running.

10

DANIEL

I had to think. I couldn't breathe with all of them crowding me, standing over me and around me—with that thing in my head, destroying my body. They had tricked me. Lured me into their trap so that thing could get at me. I had to get outside where I could think.

I forced myself into a rhythm that would burn off the adrenaline and allow me to process what the hell had just happened. After losing my mum at three, and my grandfather eight years later, I had spent the next half of my life keeping people out. No one was allowed in. I had been close to Indy, but that was it. No one else. By the goddess, how had that thing got into my body and spoken in my head? How had it known all that stuff about me?

I didn't have any answers, but I had covered a lot of ground and worked up a sweat, which was a problem. The temperature was dropping and, in this condition, without my coat, I would freeze before morning.

It was too late to make it back to my tree, the makeshift shelter where I spent most nights. And walking through the city this time of night would be suicide. My best hope was to try to get back to their house. I didn't know what reception I'd get or if they'd let me in, but

Survival 101 sometimes meant swallowing your pride and telling people what they wanted to hear.

I turned on the spot and confronted my next hurdle. How was I going to get back … in the dark … on foreign ground?

The temperature plummeted unnaturally. My hackles stood, and goose flesh rose on my arms. Someone was watching me. I spun around. The street was empty. Or at least, as far as I could see.

I edged backward till I felt a wall behind me, and then strained every sense into the darkness. Damn it, I couldn't pick up anything. But I knew someone was there. I figured if they were "friend", they would have approached. So, I prepared for foe.

Since I was alone and had no idea who or how many there were, I started edging back the way I had come.

Okay, so if you're there and you're real, now would be a good time to check in. If you're not there, that's kind of okay too, 'cause it means I'm not completely mad. But on the off chance I didn't imagine all that skrat back at the house … a little help, please?

I felt an urge to move back the way I had come. So, since it was something I planned to do anyway, I followed. I was uncomfortable turning my back on the presence in the dark. I felt exposed and expected a knife between my shoulders any second. But damn it, I was not going to run away. I didn't exactly dawdle in my retreat either. I followed the "urge" until I got to a crossroads.

Okay, Light, or whatever it is that I'm supposed to call you, which way now?

It was only a faint hint of an indication to turn right, so I went with it, glad to be around the corner. I jogged a bit to put some distance between me and whatever was back there. I slowed at the next turn and felt the urge guiding me again; without hesitating, I turned left. As I progressed back through the streets, I began to recognise the sensation and didn't question it as I followed. I didn't know if I was going to make it back. But at least I was moving, I had a plan, a pretty weak plan, and my mind had something else to think about rather than whatever was out there following me.

Eventually, I turned down a street and saw light coming out of the wall. I ran towards it and found Marcus waiting in the doorway.

"Welcome home, son. Glad you made it back." He turned, and as I started to follow him inside, moonlight revealed someone walking past the end of the street. I'm sure they were looking at me. I strained to see more, but they'd gone.

A shiver took hold of me as I stepped into the light. Then relief almost undid me again, so I prepared my "sorry" speech. Not that I was, really. But I knew how to play the game. I needed a place to stay for the night. However, I was surprised to see that most of them were in bed. The room was dark except for the sitting room, where Val sat reading by the light of a solitary lamp.

Marcus claimed my attention again. "You'll probably want another shower after that run. It will make you feel better and help you sleep. When you're done, we've set up a stretcher for you in the study." He pointed to the opposite corner where a stretcher, blankets and a pillow waited. He handed me a pile of fresh clothes and a dry towel. Without another word, he went to his chair near Val and picked up a book. Okay, so, no speech required. Maybe I would try again after my shower.

Or maybe not. When I had finished, everyone was in bed and only a desk lamp illuminated my sleeping area. They'd reeled out more trust. The door wasn't locked, and I could've made off with their stuff. Not that they had much.

I lay on the stretcher, the most comfortable bed I'd slept in in the eleven years since Grandpa died. Warmer than I had been in any winter I could remember, with the luxury of a full belly—and I couldn't sleep. Thoughts and memories from my past, my dreams, and the weirdest day I had ever survived, attacked my mind like a strobe light. What did it all mean? Begrudgingly, I had to acknowledge it wasn't a trick. What Val said was real, what the voice in my head said was truth. And if part of it was true, was it all true?

I was being offered a new start, hope for a better future, and a purpose. What would that look like? What would it cost?

One of the lessons that'd been beaten into me throughout my life was: nothing was free. It had to cost. Eventually I fell asleep contemplating how much I was prepared to pay for this supposed gift.

At some point through the night, I was awoken by someone whispering my name. In my haze, I couldn't figure out where it was coming from.

"Daniel."

Definitely outside, in the street.

Who knew my name? And how could anyone possibly know I was here?

"Daniel, come outside, I just want to talk."

What the hell? Yeah right, like I was about to go out there in the dark to face an unknown, who knew far too much about me.

"Daniel, I have been trying to talk to you for a while. Indy told me all about you. I just want to talk."

Indy? It had been five years since we'd been separated. I'd spent every day since then fluctuating between hope of finding him, and grief over losing him. It was a risk I was willing to take to find out what I could.

Wrapping the blankets around me, I rolled out of my cot, tiptoed to the front door and silently eased it open. In the courtyard, the moon was still bright, and the air froze my breath as soon as it left my mouth. With a calmer mind, I easily opened the lock on the half-door out into the street and, very carefully, edged it open a finger to check who was there.

A well-dressed man stood in the middle of the street with his arms held out, indicating that he was unarmed. I edged the door open a bit more and quickly stuck my head out to see if he had company. He was alone.

"Good morning, Daniel. You are a hard man to track down." He was over six foot and classy. His voice was deep, calm and soothing, which was at odds with the hair all over my body standing at attention. He seemed congenial, but I knew from experience that looks, more often than not, were deceiving. I remained on high alert.

"What do you know of Indy?" I wasn't hanging around for pleasantries. I wanted answers.

"All in good time. First, I wanted a chance to meet you, to see what all the fuss was about."

"What do you mean? What are you talking about? What do you know about Indigo? Is he alive? Where is he?"

"Come now, let's not be hasty. I will tell you what you want to know. But first, I want to warn you about the danger you are in." His face changed to a mask of concern.

"What danger? Who are you?" I was tired, freezing, and this guy was starting to skitch me off.

"Daniel, Daniel, I have just come to warn you that these people are a danger to you. They seem harmless enough, but that's part of their disguise. I would not stay if I were you. If you weaken, and commit to their cause, you'll never get away." He held his hand out. "Come with me and I will show you a safe place to rest, where they can't get you."

The guy seemed genuine. And these people were pretty weird. I still hadn't figured out what they wanted from me. Why was it that, all of a sudden, after five years in isolation, everyone wanted to be my best friend?

"Come with me now, Daniel, before they wake up and lure you further into their trap. You are not safe here. I'll take you to Indy." He stepped forward, his hand still out, inviting me to go with him. Without thinking, I rocked forward. I'd raised my leg when the sensation in my chest that had guided me home pulsed, encouraging me to stay.

Then it occurred to me: how did this guy whisper to me from the street through two concrete block walls without waking anyone else? He was dressed only in a suit, despite the cold. His breath wasn't forming any mist. Why would this rich dude want to have anything to do with a kid like me? Something was off. I shifted my weight back.

"Not this time then? It was nice to meet you, Daniel. I look forward to chatting with you again sometime." The guy chuckled and the hand of invitation was dropped. And then he vanished. I kid you not. The guy simply disappeared into freezing, thin air. I pulled the gate wide open and stepped outside. The street was empty. What the hell was going on around here?

Confused, shaken and exhausted, I went back inside, carefully locked both doors and rolled back into bed. Tossing and turning, trying to rediscover that comfort I had previously relished, I pleaded for sleep to take me. Like that was going to happen. Lady luck had seriously ditched me this time.

11

RAPHAEL

"Raphael!" Kaitlyn had come over to the kitchen and, face to face, whisper-shouted at me.

"What?" I was not going to whisper. I had work to do. If Stink Face woke up, I could get on with it.

"I've asked you to be as quiet as possible so as not to disturb Daniel. He has had a very difficult night and needs to sleep." Kait was using her polite, stern voice, but very quietly. She was not our birth mother, but she was our mum, and she was a very good warrior. "Daniel is a guest in our home, and you will extend hospitality to him for as long as he chooses to stay. I commend you for throwing away Daniel's cold breakfast in order to make him a fresh, hot one when he awakes. That's exactly the kind of generous attitude I have come to expect from you." She knew perfectly well I had not been planning on making Stink Face a fresh breakfast, but now I would have to.

Things were changing. I did not want them to, because they could not, must not change. But I was drowning, defenceless in the war to stop it.

The heat flashed. Moisture prickled on my forehead and under my arms. Flames rose up my neck and consumed my face. Nausea gnawed at my stomach. The Dragon had arrived. Its red haze fogged my mind. Heart racing, I could feel its claws sinking deep into my chest, squeezing my heart. Lights stabbed behind my eyes. The air was thinning, and it was becoming harder to breathe. I was drowning. Sirens screamed in my ears and tears leaked out of my eyes. I was sinking into the haze as the cage around me shrank, squashing me. It would break all my bones. I could not escape. I could not breathe.

"I do not know how I am supposed to do what I need to do and do it quietly." The pain squeezed the words into an echo. My throbbing heart burst through my chest. "What I do is important, more important than letting some stinky stranger sleep. I have a job to do. It is my job. I need to do my job." The room was spinning. The Dragon roared. I clawed at my head to get it out. My fingers locked around the chaos fighting for supremacy in my mind.

Firm bands encircled me. Soft words blew against the heat of my ears. A strong, slow beat called to me. Tapped a memory. Searched the shadows. Reached to me. Anchored my flight. Comfort ebbed through the noise, "It's okay, you're okay. You're safe, Raphael. You are loved and you are okay. Just breathe with me, honey. You're okay."

Essence of lavender and rose swam around me. Kait. I stopped fighting the bonds around me. She came to help me fight the Dragon. I tried very hard to focus on breathing with her ... deep ... long breaths. I shut everything out and focused on the Light, just like they taught me. Breathe the chaos out ... breathe in the Light ... let the chaos out ... welcome the Light in. Kait gave me a raft and I used it to ride the wave out of the storm.

Hours later, the mist started fading and as she continued to hold me, I could feel my throbbing body calm down. I was held, not in iron bands or sharp claws, but in secure arms. We breathed in and out together. My heartbeat recalibrated with hers. My ear the conduit for the solidity she offered. Forever later, I was able to step back, and tried to think clearly.

"I am sorry, Kait"—I hated that I sounded weak and shaky—"but I do not want him to stay. I was sorry to see him back this morning. I had hoped that when he ran away last night, we would never see him again. I do not like him. He is smelly and stupid, and … and he scares me." I hated my weakness even more than I hated him.

He was not as big, or quite as tall, or anywhere near the mountain Marcus was. But Daniel was a lot bigger than me, and the wilderness of his Danielness invaded my safe place. Our house was small, and he was a stranger and he did not belong. It was different when Tessa came. She was sunny, soft and small. She was not scary at all. I loved Tessa and she loved me.

12

KAITLYN

"How did you sleep?" Obviously, he had slept well this morning, but we were aware of him stepping outside during the early hours.

"Not too bad, thanks. Sorry for sleeping in. And about last night—"

"You don't have to apologise for anything. There is a lot for you to process and think about. We understand. Now, after your breakfast, I would like to offer you a haircut."

"What?"

Daniel's face was an open book. Poor dear, we weren't mind-readers, we didn't have to be. He broadcast everything that passed through his head.

"Well, no offence, but you look like you could use one. It's one thing to be clean and have fresh clothes. Why not finish the deal with a trim? Make you look a bit more human."

"Thanks ... I think?" He had a nice smile. The first I'd seen.

He finished his breakfast, took his plate to the sink and started to rinse it off and clean up.

"Actually, Daniel, I believe Raph would like to do that for you this morning. Wouldn't you, Raphael?"

"It's no trouble, I don't expect him to cook and clean up after me. I can do it. I really appreciate the meal." Turning to Raph, he said, "Cheers for that, it was brilliant. Seriously, that was the best breakfast I've had in ages."

I watched Raph, interested to see how he would respond. He dragged his eyes up to meet Daniel's. "Really? Well ... I guess you are welcome, Stin— ... Daniel." He dropped his shoulders. "I will clean that up for you. I am glad you enjoyed your breakfast."

"You are seriously cool, Raphael. I've never met anyone who could cook as good as you at your age. That was amazing." Raph turned to the sink as Dan followed me outside.

Please let him see Dan is not a threat. Encourage him and teach him your ways through this.

Out on the patio, I pulled out a chair, faced it towards the garden and offered it to Dan. "We're going out later today to get some supplies and to check the Soteria Houses. You're welcome to join us. We could give you a lift back to your home if you want to return there, or you could pick up any things you might need if you decide to stay longer." I indicated he take a seat and I ran my fingers through his hair to see what I had to work with.

"Thanks, Kait, I'll let you know." In the warm winter sun he breathed deeply, shut his eyes, and let me loose on his mane. He didn't even ask for anything in particular or what I was planning to do. I suspect he didn't care. He had an open face, a beautiful smile, and his natural hair colouring was really interesting. I would cut it to make the most of all he had, clear away the camouflage to reveal the human being beneath.

Whilst he was here, it might be good to share our story with him too. Hopefully it'd help him understand that it was hard for all of us. And how we all felt completely overwhelmed and useless at times.

Please, let these words be received as they are intended. Let them take root, giving encouragement and hope rather than being a burden or an overload of information.

"Dan, we do know how you feel. I mean, about what happened last night. Even though it's different for all of us, some things are the same for everyone. Your introduction to the Light was probably more intense than most, but it will never be like that again. You've been offered an invitation. And that's exactly what it is. The choice is yours. You don't have to accept.

"But, if you decide you would like to, all you have to do is say yes. He is waiting, but He won't rush or force you." I continued snipping away, gently pulling at his hair. My heart swelled when he exhaled and relaxed deeper into the chair. He trusted me. That was an honour I didn't hold lightly. "Before you make your decision, though, you need to be aware that there will be a cost."

His body stiffened slightly. "What kind of cost?"

He had to know. It wasn't fair for him to be led into making a decision without the facts. "As Abbot explained, the Darkness has a hold on the world around us. And since the Darkness hates the Light, those in the Dark are opposed to those of us in the Light. If you were to join us, you would also be in their sights, so to speak." Best to be blunt and clear. "We are not popular, and our ways are seen as foolishness. We are derided and discriminated against because of whom we belong to. Along with the indescribable joy, there are many types of suffering in our world."

"To be perfectly honest, Kaitlyn, I can't really see the difference between your reality and mine at this point. Apart from the joy part."

"Good point." I chuckled and continued working away at his hair. "The difference then would be that we are in the Light, and He is gracious and loving. He is protective and generous. But He is also jealous. If you decide you want to join His family, He will always have to come first. To be your priority." I felt him tense again, so I hurried on. "But you never have to be worried that He would ask you to do something that is beyond your capability, that wasn't beneficial, or that He hadn't done first. It might hurt at the time, but you'll be better for it."

"'What doesn't kill you, makes you stronger', you mean?" He brushed stray hairs off his face.

"Exactly. Always remember that, by definition, the Light is Love. But, as is the way, if it's worth having, it's worth fighting for. It's different for everyone. But the journey is not easy, and I would like to tell you the worst is over, but I would be lying. If you join this family, your future will be full of more pain, joy, laughter and tears—but there will also be purpose, community, and love. It is many things, Daniel, but this I promise you. If you say yes, your future will be full, and we will be with you."

His posture relaxed once again, so I asked permission to share Marcus's and my story. He didn't openly object, so I went ahead.

"Marcus and I have been together since we were teenagers. I wouldn't let him marry me till he had a job, and I wouldn't say yes to kids till we had a house. Well, we got married as soon as he signed up as an apprentice mechanic. I was twenty-one and he was twenty-two. I can't believe almost two decades have passed since then. Anyway, I got work as an orderly at a hospital and later went on to train as a nurse. All the while, we were saving for a house." I couldn't help but pause my hands at the memory.

"But before we got the chance to do anything about it, some pretty serious things started happening, and we found ourselves in a situation similar to where you are now. We couldn't stay where we were. We didn't want to leave. We had commitments, friends, and a life, but it was too dangerous to stay.

"We were aware something was happening to us. We couldn't 'see' as we do now, but we could sense there was more to the world around us than what we could physically see. At that time, not knowing what was going on, it was really frightening—being in the Dark, knowing we wanted to get out. We always felt watched—it was creepy. If it had been just one of us we would have suspected paranoia, but we felt it together. We didn't have many belongings worth keeping, so we packed up the essentials, withdrew our savings and planned to get out and try our luck in a new place.

"That day was the start of it all. On a bus out of town all hell broke loose. It was frightening. Things got very ugly and a lot of people died ..."

"Died? What do you mean 'died'?"

"All I'll say is that we were right to be scared, and our feelings of something dark and dangerous hunting us were validated. I have never been so frightened in my whole life. If Val and Joy hadn't come to save us ... well ... we made it out. But no one else on that crowded bus survived.

"It was the start of our new life, and a pretty terrifying introduction to the Dark. And whilst we didn't have your intense meeting with the Lord of Light, we did receive the invitation, a welcome, Badges ... and the knowledge we couldn't have kids." This wound had been eased in Sodom. "I remember that time with such a mixed bag of feelings: intense relief, incredible joy, indescribable peace and gut-wrenching grief. Val, Joy, and Abbot offered us a safe refuge and the beginning of understanding. We've not looked back since."

Dan sat quietly taking in what I had to say as I continued snipping away at his hair.

"Over time, the Light has grown our family. Over two years ago, we were given the twins, then Tessa about a year later. I know you have a lot to think about, but if you do decide to stay, you will also be a welcome member of this family. It's not an easy transition, but we'll help you as much as we can. But there is no pressure to decide either way."

He sat silently as I continued to cut away his dense mop of hair. When I finished, I stood back to survey my work. I was pretty impressed with how well it had turned out. Neither of us spoke. I could see he was contemplating what I had just said. In silence, I left him with his thoughts as I cleaned up all the excess hair.

13

***

CONTESSA

After hanging the washing, it was time to help Raph with morning tea. Afterwards, we'd do a supply run. Perhaps Dan would come with us. I was kind of hoping not. The showers and clean clothes had helped him become less feral on the outside. But he still glared at me and looked ready to snap me in two. I tried being nice, but it didn't seem to help.

Riah didn't have a problem. He was a different person around her. And Raph. You could see the wheels in Daniel's head turning with the effort of being nice to them. Actually, now I thought about it, he seemed personable with Kait and Abbot as well. He was still standoffish with Val and Marcus. He didn't glare at them. But then, no one glared at Val and Marcus ... except Kait ... and stupid people.

Maybe there was a semi-decent, half intelligent human being underneath that horrible exterior.

Not that I would know.

Maybe he was exhausted from trying so hard to be nice to everyone else he'd run out of "nice" when it came to me.

Typical.

Please make him go away. Can't you pick someone else? Anyone else?

If he decided to stay, it was going to be weird. Weird and awkward. Weird, awkward, and all kinds of horrible.

I guess they'd all had to adjust when I got here. But I was not as weird and horrible as him.

Kait had tried convincing me that it'd be kind of nice to have someone my own age to hang with. But I told her I'd got the impression Dan didn't really do "hang". So, I asked her for a dog instead. Or a goldfish.

I told her Riah and Raph were like my kid brother and sister and I loved them to bits. They were half my age, but there was heaps of fun stuff you could do, hanging with ten-year-olds.

And of course, there was Abbot. He was the coolest old person I'd ever met. Funny as all get out. I loved hanging with him. Except when he needed his naps ... and sleeps ... and quiet times.

I told Kait that I loved hanging with Val. Except when we were battling. She kind of scared me then. And when she was reading. Val didn't like company when she was reading ... or behind her wall. But all the other times, Val was awesome.

Obviously, Kait and Marcus were amazing too. Except when they went all mother-hen. It was nice, but, well, you know, when they were in parenting mode, we didn't really hang. After I had explained all of this to her, Kait had smiled and hugged me.

But for now, it was time for Riah and me to help with morning tea. And just my flopping luck. We'd come around from the laundry to the patio and run straight into Dan. Kait had cut his hair and ...

Oh. My. Word.

Wow ...

I mean, eeeks.

Trying to look anywhere but at him, and at him at the same time, I walked right into the glass doors. Not my best look. And now, not only had I humiliated myself by tripping up, I was going to be as red as a pepper and have a flopping great bruise on my forehead to remind everyone for weeks to come.

"You okay, Tessa? Watch where you're going, love. You could hurt yourself." Kait smiled gently at my humiliation.

Please, please, please could you open the earth so I could hide for a few years? And maybe you could stop my face flashing like a red-hot poker against pure white snow? Please!

"What's that all about?" Marcus attacked as soon as I managed to coordinate my uncooperative limbs through the door into the sitting room.

He'd been sitting in his chair reading. In other words, he'd had a front row seat. The man was far too sharp for my liking. Sometimes it really sucked, living in a fishbowl. I'd tell Kait I didn't want a goldfish anymore. A cat would be better.

Hopefully, Riah had been oblivious and we could just move right on and forget it ever happened. Buoyed by this hope, I met Marcus's glare head-on and went for denial. "What do you mean? I just tripped over is all."

"Hmm, whatever you say." Marcus sat back, staring at me. Which, of course, really helped cool my face ... not.

Val whispered something to him, and he slowly turned away and returned to his book.

"Come on, Riah." We made our way to the kitchen and Raph. "How can we help, little man?"

Looking up from a recipe book, Raph craned his head to look behind me. "Who is we?"

"What?" I turned, expecting to see Riah just behind me. "What on earth ..." I couldn't believe it. She was oblivious alright, of everything but Daniel. She still stood on the patio, frozen, staring goggle-eyed at him.

Please don't let that be what I looked like.

"What is wrong, Tessie? She is just talking to Stink Face. Are you okay? Did you get sunburnt this morning?"

Great.

"Stink Face is not a nice name. You'd better be careful no one else hears you say that."

"Sorry, Tessa." He dropped his eyes, but not his voice. "I do not like him. He scares me, and he does stink."

I wrapped him in my arms, my heart softening. Sweetheart. I had to keep reminding myself that I wasn't the only one put out by Daniel's presence. Raph was younger, smaller, and had suffered all kinds of horrible. Not that I knew the full extent, but he and Riah were carrying serious baggage.

Rather than focus on how uncomfortable and upset I was, I could try to help the twins—Raph especially—to adjust. Hopefully it was only for a couple of days, then we could go back to normal once again.

"Actually, he doesn't smell anymore. And all I'm saying is, the adults won't like to hear you calling him that." Releasing him, I turned him back to the bench and tucked him under my arm. "Now, what should we do for morning tea? Pikelets or scones?"

"I would like us to make pikelets. We have not had them in ages." Once again, distraction did the trick. He was such a good kid.

Now, if I could just get Riah out of the lion's den.

14

KAITLYN

Oh dear, this was going to be interesting. "Dan, why don't you go and have a shower to wash all the hair off, then get changed? By then, morning tea will be ready, and we'll make a plan for the day."

"Thanks. And, ah, thanks for the trim." Looking down at the extensive carpet of hair around him, Dan ran his hand over his newly shorn head. "I'm feeling kind of bald, though." He didn't look too worried, just matter-of-fact about the whole thing. He offered a quirky smile. "I am glad, however, you left me something to hide behind." He raised his eyebrows into his tidied fringe.

He went inside, making room for Abbot to take his place for a haircut, and the kitchen erupted with the crashing of bowls and utensils.

"We're all good, nothing to worry about, I'm just going to hang out the next load." Tessa tripped out of the kitchen and dashed down the hallway.

Abbot and I exchanged a look and Dan made his way toward the bathroom, running his hand back and forth across his shortened hair.

"So, Abbot, what's up?" I knew he would only tell me what he wanted to and no more. But I wanted him to know that I was aware something wasn't quite right.

"Kait, my dear, you of all of us would be best to answer that one."

"I know that poor Dan is in for a wild ride, Tessa is in uncharted territory, Raphael will be okay, and you're evading my question."

"Clever as always, dear heart," he responded, but said no more.

Silence followed comfortably as Abbot's soft, trimmed hair floated to the ground like peaceful autumn leaves ready to rest permanently in the earth's embrace.

And then I knew.

Involuntary, unrestrained tears made their path down my cheeks. I was thankful that our backs were to the doors. With great care, and a broken heart, I slowly, tenderly, and with great care gave him his last haircut. I gently kissed the top of his head. Not for the first time, I railed silently against the reality of living in a shoe box with six, maybe soon to be seven, others.

Abbot didn't want the others to know it was his time, so I wasn't at liberty to share it. But I needed time to compose myself before I was capable of hiding it from the others. I would never be able to keep secrets from Marcus and Val. But neither would they push me to tell if it wasn't time.

I left Abbot sitting in the warm sunlight whilst I took a turn around the garden, stopping regularly to immerse myself in the beauty of this haven. As the sun hit the herbs, the scent of basil and coriander blended with the stem of lavender I had plucked. The chickens cooed and scratched in the compost as the butcher birds waited for any spare morsels they'd missed. Our place may have been small, but it was a blessing, beautiful and bountiful. It was self-indulgent but natural to grieve what we would lose when we left. The weight of loss would incapacitate me if I let it.

Enough. This is not the time. Please help me stay focused on the job at hand.

Back inside and back to work, feeling Marcus and Val's eyes on me, I smiled at them and made my way to the kitchen to see what the kids were up to. Tessa had managed to compose herself and was back helping Raph with the pikelets.

However, all went pear-shaped when Daniel appeared around the end of the hallway, his hair darkened and spiked from his recent shower. Scars punctuated the defined lines of his bare chest and abdomen. The muscles on his arm danced as he continued to stroke the back of his head. His other hand grasped a towel loosely wrapped around his hips. "Would it be possible to grab a few extra clothes? The others are full of cut hair."

Oh dear.

Laying a gentle hand on Tessa's shoulder, I said, "Marcus, perhaps you can show Dan where we keep our clothes? Tessa, could you please go out and see if we have any more eggs this morning?" He had no idea what effect he was having on the poor girl.

Or Riah for that matter. As Marcus led Dan to the wardrobe, I noticed her eyes were no longer focused on her latest drawing on the study wall. They tracked his every move, mouth agape.

"Riah, could you come and help us out in the kitchen please? These are almost ready to serve, and we need you to set the table."

Val and I exchanged a look and it was all I could do to stop myself from laughing out loud.

Please give us the space and time we need to settle things within our family before the big battle begins. We are going to need as much of both as possible.

15

———

MARCUS

That boy didn't have the sense the Light gave geese. What was he thinking? Was he thinking at all? Or maybe he *was* thinking. I didn't like this at all.

Sure, he was a nice kid. But he had another thing coming if he thought he could come in here and have his way with our Tess. She'd been hurt enough. I was not going to stand by and let this new young thing come in here and rock her cradle. He may have been called into the Light, but if he was going to cause trouble, he could go jump into someone else's sunbeam.

Around the table, morning tea was laid out for everyone, as were the plans for the rest of the day. The schedule did not come with as many choices as the pikelets.

"Today we'll do a run of the Soteria Houses. We'll stock up on any last-minute supplies we need and get some extra clothes and things for Dan." I looked to the boy. "Have you decided what you're doing yet?" He'd just stuck a pikelet into his mouth. With "deer in headlight" eyes he shook his head. "Is there anything you want us to pick up from your shelter? We could call by this morning if you want?" I wasn't his biggest fan, but I knew the rules. He needed to be given the choice.

He finished swallowing. "There's a good chance it will be ransacked by now, but I wouldn't mind cruising by in case my guitar is still there. It isn't much, but it's the most valuable thing I have, which is pretty sad, as it's a piece of junk." He tried to lighten the mood. "If it's okay, I would like to stay another night or two? I'm happy to help out with any chores or things that need doing ... ?"

I knew an invitation to sleep inside, on a bed, was too good to turn down. I couldn't blame him. I'd done me own time on the streets. Being offered shelter and safety had been a turning point for me. Even now, long in the past, it was shallow in me memory.

"Right," I cut him off, "we'll go there first and see if you can salvage it, and anything else you want to grab." I tried for a softer approach. "And you're welcome to stay for as long as you like."

Back to business, I took in the rest of the crew. "Abbot, you and Raph make a list of kitchen supplies. Tessa, work with Kait and figure out what household stuff we need. Riah, I'd like you to make sure we have the cage, water container, and enough food for the chickens ready to go at short notice. Tell me if we need a bag of pellets for them if we don't have enough of our normal food. Kait, can you let me know of any bills we need to pay to finish things up. We'll drop by the postal and square things away on our run. Have I forgotten anything?"

"Can, ah ... can I do anything to help?" Dan was hesitant.

"You can lend Riah a hand with the chickens. She'll teach you what's involved in caring for them. Anything else?"

Faces ranging from poker through to thunder made it clear that had come out harsher than I'd intended. "Okay guys, let's aim to head out in forty-five to an hour." I forced a smile. It didn't help.

Me bad mood spread like a virus. The ease and joy of the morning had evaporated like the pikelets. Everyone was doing their tasks, head down, butt up, and speaking in whispers.

I dropped meself next to Val, ready for her inquisition.

"So, what's up, old man?"

And it began.

"There's so much to do and we're not ready," I said.

"How has thirty minutes passing made all that difference? You were in fine form this morning after hanging out with Kait in the garage." Raised eyebrows. "What's changed?"

"You know as well as I do that the Dark Lord is not going to give us a free pass outta here. He owns every part of this city except us. And he's going to throw everything our way. Shooting fish in a barrel is what it'll be. We're not safe anywhere. Even in here." I couldn't help the hackles. "The countdown to us leaving this damned city is going to be a skrat fight. They're all so green and young ... and old ... how are we going to do this?" I pictured each member. "What if Raph has an attack in the middle of a fight? What if Tessa loses it when it matters? What if Abbot isn't up to it anymore? What if ..."

"Enough. None of this is new and none of this is our concern. We have one thing to do and that is to do what we are told." She wielded the steel of her eyes and fractured me argument. "Marcus, what's the matter?"

I didn't want to answer her. To be honest, I didn't exactly know what to say. She waited. Pinned me with that bleeding unrelenting glare of hers. Dared me to lie to her again.

She waited.

I felt stupid saying it out loud.

She waited.

Oh, for bleeding heck. "I don't like the way he looks at her, alright?"

"Ah, now we're getting closer to the truth." She released me and sat back. "You've seen as much as I have, and I can tell you, he doesn't look at her. Not in a way that warrants your reaction."

She was right. Damn it. You just couldn't hide anything in this bleeding family.

"I don't like the way she's at sixes and sevens with him here. The girl's a cat, but today, she can't even walk. Never blushed in over a year, today she's a fire hydrant, with butter fingers. I don't like it. I don't want her to get hurt. I don't want her back in the place we found her. She's too fragile. I won't let her get hurt again."

"You finished?" she countered without heat.

"Yeah, I guess so."

Tessa had been such a mess when we rescued her, broken inside and out. But she'd come so far. We already had one little girl who wouldn't heal. I couldn't bear the thought of another.

"Believe it or not, Marcus, I understand your pain. These kids fill the hole in both of your hearts. You know I feel the same. The four of us would do anything to protect them. But some things are out of our control. So far, Dan has not disrespected Tessa in any way.

"Consider what the boy is going through. Think back to when you came into the Light and how frightening and confusing that was. He's not used to living in a group." Her lips twitched. "And we are not your average family.

"He's trying to process so much. He hasn't had time, nor does he have the head space at the moment, to consider her as anything more than another person in this house." She placed a hand on me arm. "Tessa will always need you to look out for her and to watch over her. You are, and will continue to be, special to her unless you sabotage that. But she has to make her own way in the world as a young woman."

"But she is not a woman yet. She is too young."

"She is twenty-three and has been through things no one should ever have to face. She is well and truly a woman. It's hard not to be swayed by her looks, but we can't let that stifle her growth. Even if her childhood had not been stripped from her, she is definitely old enough to be making up her own mind on who she wants to connect with. How old was Kait when you two got married?"

"That's different."

"Yes, it is. You were only eighteen when you started living together and twenty-two when you asked her to marry you."

"We didn't know the Light then. We would have done things differently if we had."

"And these two do know the Light or will soon enough. They are older and they haven't even shown mutual interest yet. Don't you think you're jumping the gun?" In a softer tone, she continued, "Be there to support her. Don't smother her or you'll push her away. She respects you and loves you, but you will ruin that if you don't allow her to make her own choices and mistakes." She stopped, and I followed her gaze to the garden. "And perhaps you could look to Dan. He has been adrift for a long time. You, better than anyone, can understand what it's been like for him—taken in and kicked out more times than we know. He may very well soon be part of our family too. He'll need you just as much as the rest of us do."

We sat back in our chairs, thankful that everyone was out of earshot. We both continued to study the garden. Dan chased Riah, flapping around like a headless chook. Her face flushed with laughter. A flap of fabric flashed near the clothesline. Tessa was watching as well.

Help me deal with this and do the right thing by all of them. I want to watch over them and protect them. Help me figure out how the hell I'm supposed to do that and what the hell that looks like.

Now that I had started, I may as well get it all out. "I'm not sure about today." Now that I had started, I may as well get it all out.

"What do you mean?" Val asked.

"I think Tessa needs to come, to make sure she has a positive experience after yesterday. Dan needs to come, obviously. Regardless of whether he stays or not, he'll need clothes and I promised we'd go by his tree. Raph normally comes to do the shopping, and if we leave him, he'll resent Dan even more and it'll ramp his anxiety up. I think it'd be best for him to come along, but I'm worried about him. If we're attacked when he's so fragile, it could be his undoing. Sariah can stay, but someone will have to be here with her, and I don't think Abbot has what it takes to protect her if there's an attack here whilst we're out."

"It's your mission, but I agree about Raph. I think it'd be best to take Kait, because, apart from Sariah, she's the best at calming him down. Apart from cruising past the tree, you'll be in the suburbs, so it should be pretty quiet. Just don't hang around. I can stay, but it's your call."

"Sounds good, we'll go with that." She'd always had a way of giving advice and allowing me to save face. Full respect to her for that, and I appreciated her help. Feeling lighter, I looked around to see everyone had come in, loitering by the kitchen waiting for instructions. I called a quick meeting and ran through the plan for the morning. So far so good.

Thank you.

I knew Val was right and I had to try to let go. I joined in the tussle at the main wardrobe, rugging up for going out. In last-minute checks, I saw Tessa glance sideways at Dan and me brain snapped. "Tessa, you're up the front with me and Kait this time. Dan, you're in the back with Raph."

"What? Why? I always go in the back with Raph!" She didn't quite stamp her foot, but her fists were clenched, and her jaw was set.

"This time you're in the front!"

All eyes turned to me. Deja vu. An assortment of unhappy. And then the protests started. Great. So much for letting it go.

Kait just raised her eyebrows. Val gave a small shake of her head. Abbot widened his eyes and Dan, as usual, kept his head down. But none of them said anything. Tess and Raph, however, wailed in unison, "Marcus!"

"The back of the truck is already partially loaded and there is less room, so you're coming in the front, Tessa." End of conversation.

"It's too cramped with you two. Raph should go," Tessa countered.

Raph threw his oar in. "I do not want to go in the front, I always go in the back." I was surprised that he volunteered to be that close to Daniel. But if it's what he wanted, he could have it. Anything to keep him happy for now.

"See, he doesn't want to go in the front, so you are. Final." I didn't clench me fists, but I could set me jaw good as any.

"Val!" Tessa looked for support from her champion. That used to be me.

"Sweetheart, Marcus is leading the mission, so it's his call."

"Maybe there are reasons why he wants you in the front, Tessa. I'm sure he doesn't want to upset you. Maybe you should just do what he says." The collective heart stopped. We all turned to stare at Daniel. "Sorry, just seems you'd have your reasons."

His wall came up, and he fired off at Tessa, "Well, you're lucky he doesn't beat the skrat out of you for dissension. That's the way it happens in the real world."

Their eyes locked horns before she marched out to the garage. Slamming of the cab door confirmed that she was skitched but had complied.

Raph edged closer to Kait, who shot Daniel a smile before she and Raph followed Tessa's path, less dramatically, to the garage.

This could actually work. "Come on, Dan, let me show you the way." Clapping him on the shoulder, I led the fine young man out to the truck as he handed me the directions to his shelter. Today might just turn out sunshine and roses after all.

Before I pulled out into the street, Val came to watch the door and secure it behind us. Thankfully, with Dan on board, we were gifted with a reinforced guard. The truck would be safe, but we weren't too sure who or what would come by in our absence. But with the seals back in place, Val and the Warriors would keep our house safe.

It was another reason why I wanted Tessa up front. If we came across an ambitious attack, the three of us would be unhampered to take care of it. And now, with Tessa's armour and mine dimmed, I knew to expect it. The streets being lined with applauding, drooling minions was also a bit of a giveaway. Great time to let me armour fade. Sometimes, I could be as smart as bait.

Sorry.

The glow from above let me know the guard were in place. How game would the enemy be? Kait drew her sword. I drove. We turned the corner straight into a horde. I didn't slow. It would've made no difference. The Unseen are not affected by the physical.

Three threw themselves onto the windscreen, others leaped at the sides. These guys were ugly at the best of times, but up close and personal they redefined feral. And the reek. Sulphur seeped through the vents.

More than anything, they were a nuisance. A reminder that we could never let our guard down. Kait was onto it. I didn't have to say a thing. With a flick, a parry and a punch, they'd disengaged. One was hauled up over the top and I watched it fly, without wings, into the tarmac.

Like I said, they weren't serious about taking us down. They were here to remind us that we could not slip up ... at all ... ever. They saw everything. Every bleeding mistake. They took advantage of everything. Every bleeding weakness.

They'd made their point. They backed off.

Tessa was so caught up in her anger, she didn't even flinch. Trying to talk to her was like trying to melt an iceberg with a burned match. The arctic conditions both inside and outside the cab stunted all conversation. But she'd come round. She always did.

16

CONTESSA

I hated him. So. Much.

And I was right. He was just like all the others.

I mean, seriously, who did he think he was throwing his two cents in? He had no right.

Trust him to suck up to Marcus.

I had made a real effort. Gone against my instinct and been nice to him, welcoming even. Flopping gutter rat. He wasn't really so scary, more a pain in the butt than anything else. I couldn't believe I had come round to actually thinking he might be different. Turns out looks weren't deceiving ... his old look that was. Not the new look Kait had given him. That one had sucked me in.

I couldn't trust him.

I wouldn't.

Well, just because he moved in for a bit didn't mean I had to speak to him. Idiot.

Why did you invite the enemy in? Please, just make him go away.

I hadn't noticed where Marcus was driving, I had been using all my energy to find ways to ignore him and reasons to hate Daniel. I even ignored Kait's attempt to reach out. I hated them all.

Stupid, ignorant family.

We pulled up within the grounds of a park sandwiched between the city and the river. As ugly as Sodom was, this part was really pretty. That was, if you dropped your visor into place and blocked the sight of some of the demons dripping off the trees. Seeing them brought me back to reality with a slap, and a chill that sobered me real quick.

I waited till I saw that we had a full set of Warriors in place before I left the cab. It did the trick. The enemy stayed put. With the extra guard in place, I suspect because we were hosting a Potential, the Others didn't approach.

They just stared.

And leered.

And. Totally. Creeped me out.

Yet, inside the honey glow of my own Warrior guard, I felt safe enough to dawdle behind everyone as they followed Dan across an expanse of grass to a far-off group of trees.

I turned to look out over the river and did my best to block out the noise of traffic. Pretending the city and demons didn't exist, with my visor in place, I focused on the tiny birds jumping from branch to high branch in the massive trees. And the thin carpet of dead leaves crunching under my boots. When I was sure none of my family were looking, I kicked the leaves and watched them do cartwheels in the chilly breeze.

Why did life have to be so flopping complicated?

The sunlight was soft and weak. Like, as hard as it tried, its fingertips just couldn't reach this damned place. Whatever warmth it sent our way dissolved before it could take a firm hold.

Or maybe it just didn't care.

I hate winter.

But I love parks. And it saddened me that this oasis was neglected. Huge clumps of trees huddled together randomly in isolated groups, clinging to each other to fight off the toxic civilisation and overwhelming Darkness. I could relate. Some trees had merged into each other, transforming themselves into giants of ridiculous proportions.

Up ahead, everyone was standing in front of one particular beast which had partly devoured a park bench on its left, whilst a metal fence had fallen victim on the right. Roots hung from the branches, stretching down to grab hold of the ground and everything else within reach. Layers of impenetrable protection had created a fortress. As I got closer, I wondered what they were all looking at. But then Dan disappeared.

Yep.

Disappeared.

I raced over.

"Someone's been here!" his muffled voice sounded from inside. His head reappeared from a concealed entrance. "I try not to come here in daylight for the sake of secrecy, but someone's been in here." Lines creased his forehead. "Nothing's been taken or broken, but everything's been moved." His body then rejoined his head as he re-emerged. "No one cares about my tree. It's pretty useless as far as shelters go. They just like to hassle me because I'm alone." He turned back to the tree. "Why would someone go in and not destroy it or nick my stuff?"

Turning a slow circle, he surveyed the park, but was apparently distracted by Raph's jiggling around him, trying to see inside. "If you want, you can go—"

Raph disappeared before Dan could finish the invitation.

He looked to the rest of us. "There's not a lot of room, but a couple of you could fit if you wanted to."

I didn't want to show any interest, mainly because I hated him. But then I realised how annoyed Marcus would be if I went in.

So, I did.

There was a narrow gap hidden in the folds where the trunk and roots blended. It wasn't a tight fit ... for Raph and me. The others might need to squeeze, though.

Just before I slipped into the darkness, I shot a glance back to see Dan standing with his arms crossed, and one side of his mouth hitched.

Idiot.

I still hated him but went in anyway.

My anger evaporated as soon as my eyes adjusted to the dim light. Oh. My. Word.

It was cramped. A cold, damp mustiness mingled with body odour. There was a small clearing, just big enough for him to curl up in. Half a battered guitar peeked out of a natural alcove. An old sleeping bag almost covered a piece of folded blue plastic, nestled on top of a bed of dead leaves. He must have brought extra mulch in. They weren't all from this tree. I was sure they wouldn't do enough to soften the thick, web-like roots that covered the floor.

The trunk walls were solid. No one could see in, not even the half-hearted sun. Its filtered light did nothing to cheer the place. Or warm it.

It was freezing.

Like, seriously-damp, stinking, freezing.

Raph and I looked at each other. His face mirrored my question: "What do you do if it rains?"

Dan had eased his way in. His body uncomfortably close and warm. "I have an old tarp that I sit under. Most nights I sleep on it to keep the damp out, and when it's really cold I wrap it around my sleeping bag. When it rains, I just pull my guitar and sleeping bag up and sit under it." He said it matter-of-fact. As though living like this was perfectly normal.

This was not normal.

This was crazy.

"Is this all you have?"

"Well, it's the basics. There's a toilet block not too far away where I have a simple wash each day. I don't have a lot of clothes, so in winter I tend to wear everything I have." He shrugged and the space shrank even more. "In summer, I occasionally have a dip in the river and try to wash my clothes there as well. But I don't do it too often. Have you seen the river?" He chuckled. Like that was funny.

It wasn't funny. It was scary.

Raph's hand slipped into mine. I would never swim in that river. I mean, seriously, who would? The junk, the disease—the sharks.

Yep. You heard me. The sharks!

Dan continued, "I busk most days and earn enough for simple food and a cup of bad coffee from Greasy Joe's. But, sadly, I don't generally get enough for good quality clothes. But I know where I can go to get a bargain." He looked sideways from under his very long lashes, daring me to challenge him.

I was speechless.

Raph and I turned in silence and tried to leave. But it was too cramped. In the end, we followed Dan out and moved away to let Kait have a look. Raph and I gravitated to a weak patch of sun. I took him in my arms, as much for my comfort as for his. Silently, we warmed each other.

The murmur of Kait and Dan's conversation was distant. Extra warmth surrounded us as Marcus embraced us both.

No words.

Just warmth and strength.

Dan's voice broke our huddle. He approached, bringing his guitar and nothing else. "I don't know if it'll all still be there if I choose to come back. Maybe I'll find somewhere else and move on."

Without looking back, he walked away from what had been his home for ... I didn't know how long.

There was a lot I didn't know. I didn't want to know, because knowing was dangerous. The more I knew, the more my defences cracked. The more I knew, the more I cared. And I didn't want to care, because caring involved risk, and vulnerability, and pain.

I welcomed Kait's arm around my shoulder as we walked back to the truck. I forgot that I hated everyone and that I was angry with them all.

Even though I didn't want to learn more about Dan's story, and even though I still hadn't forgiven him for siding against me, I had to admit he was brave. Brave enough to go it alone rather than giving in to the gangs.

And he'd succeeded.

He'd not sold out.

Not like I had.

I'd been too scared. I'd sold myself for the promise of security. It'd been a lie.

He'd survived by himself with no help, and gone without so much, even though part of that involved stealing. No way could I have done that. I didn't have the guts. I'd have been petrified of being caught. I didn't know what he really thought about surviving that way. Or if he thought anything of it at all.

I, however, was ashamed of so much. The least of which was so much worse than theft.

I am so useless and weak. What could you possibly see in me? Why did you choose me? I have nothing.

Back at the truck, without protest I climbed into the cab. Taken hostage by my memories, I retraced roads I didn't want to travel. Ever. Drowning in all the skrat I'd been rescued from. All the things I'd done. All the things I'd been too weak to stop or walk away from. Things I was too scared to stand up against.

I was aware of the truck stopping at several places, of Kait and Marcus talking over me. But I was too distracted to care or notice what they'd been talking about. I was pulled up short however, when Marcus kissed the top of my head and Kait removed her warmth from my shoulders.

I could never hate them.

They made me angry, but I loved them. They were my family. They gave me the safety and security that I craved. That I needed.

Thank you so very, very much.

"Tessa!" Kait gave my shoulder a gentle shake.

"Sorry Kait, what were you saying?"

"Marcus, Raph and I are going to do the shopping. We have given Dan some money to buy clothes from the charity shops in this street. Could you go with him and show him where they are? I've been given a word that the enemy is not around. But nonetheless, keep your eyes open and don't dawdle. We'll meet you back here when you're done. If we finish first, we'll come and find you." She was offering me an olive branch.

"Are you sure it's going to be okay?" After yesterday, I was a bit nervous. With this request, they were showing a great deal of trust and giving me a pretty big responsibility. I was in charge of protecting Daniel in a skirmish. I knew my Guard would be with me and would be first line of defence in an attack from the Others. But I was Daniel's last line of defence. They knew very well how I felt about him.

Like I said. A lot of trust.

I had no reason to doubt Kait, though. Since coming to the Light, life had been a battle, not that life before had been a walk in the park. But from the moment I said yes, I had never been lied to by the Light, or by my family.

Kait stopped, took my face in her firm, warm hands and looked me in the eye. "It'll be alright, beautiful girl, we love you. You are a child of the Light; your past is past and your present and future are bright. Don't dwell in the Darkness, you don't live there anymore. I have been assured the Unseen enemy is not lurking here." Kait soothed my wounds with insight and then kissed my forehead as I hugged her. Tight.

Looking around, I saw Dan waiting a polite distance away. I gave him a weak smile and we headed off down the street to shop.

Yes. You heard me. Shop.

Shop. For. Clothes. Yikes! Happy dance.

It didn't matter that we weren't shopping for me. This is my forte. This is where I am king ... or queen. It helped relight a spark of joy.

I knew Kait was right. I had been rescued from the Dark. My past had been eradicated. But this kind of stuff was easier to say in your head than it was to believe in your heart.

17

DANIEL

I wasn't sure what to do. But I was sure Suit Dude had been at the park. The guy was freaking me out. Having someone go through my stuff was also really weird. I would have understood if they had trashed the place or stolen stuff, but to just neatly rearrange everything? It was like they wanted to let me know they had been there. Like they could get to me whenever they wanted. It was a skrat hideout, but it was all I had. It'd been my sanctuary, and now I felt kind of violated.

One thing for sure, I'd never be safe there again. But I guess I hadn't really been safe there in the first place.

Things at the "Light" house were tense, but with the alternative not looking good, I weighed up their offer.

The pros: an offer to stay, shelter, food, clothing, warmth, and protection of a group.

The cons: Little Skrat, Shop Twik, figuring out what the hell I did about this "Light" stuff, and having to consider other people again.

Little Skrat a.k.a. Raph and Shop Twik a.k.a. Whinger were small fry compared to the plinting krets I'd left behind in Gomorrah. I could pull my head in and mind my manners if it meant getting off the street. And I'm sure the Light problem was all in my head ... well, pretty sure. Although, I couldn't shake the memory of being hunted through the street, and how Suit Dude did his freaky disappearing act. Kait's story about how she and Marcus came to the Light just added to the confusion. I'd decided it was best if I just filed everything away in the "think about this later" folder.

Because now I had to figure out how I was going to play nice with Shop Twik, or perhaps it was Uptight Princess. To hell with it, there wasn't that much difference between the two, "Twik Princess" covered all the bases. I never did understand girls. If I didn't need them to scratch my itch, I wouldn't have anything to do with them at all.

I had no idea why she got so skitched off with me this morning. Then when she saw my place, she went all kinds of weird. Maybe she wasn't right in the head. Not sure, but no doubt I'd figure it all out at some point ... or maybe not. No big deal really. I'd just play nice and not have anything to do with her for the short time I planned to stay. I'd just give her heaps of space ... in that small ... fishbowl ... box of a house.

I'd give her one thing though. She was a confusing creature. At first, I thought she was just butt-ugly, but later I realised she wasn't actually that bad. Her face was just ... peculiar. When she was scared or angry, she was like a little predatory bird.

But when happy, everything softened, and she took on more of an ethereal quality. I'd caught myself staring at her a few times. Not that I was interested or anything. It was more in an effort to make sense of her. She was like a 3D picture. There was definitely more there than met the eye. And what met the eye was ... intriguing. I'd try not to push her buttons, except maybe when I was bored ... or in need of a laugh.

TP led me down the street to start shopping. Or in other words, the gateway to hell on earth. She said we'd work our way back to the truck so that if the others finished first it would be easier for them to find us.

"Wait." I stopped dead. "There's more than one shop?"

Tessa kept walking. "Always."

"Why can't we just make one stop and get what we need there?"

"One?" I had her attention now. She stopped and came back to where I stood frozen, trying not to hyperventilate. "One shop? Where's the fun in that?"

"Fun? Are you serious? Shopping for clothes, or anything for that matter, is a necessary evil to be avoided except for extreme emergencies. Much like needles ... and dentists, and ... other forms of torture."

For some reason my clarification brought a spark back to her dark eyes and the start of a genuine smile. She was definitely not right in the head. "Don't be silly. Come on." She walked away again, this time calling over her shoulder, "I'll protect you." She giggled.

It was time to make a peace offering. For what, I didn't know, but it felt right. So, I followed.

Hey, if you're still out there, not that I'm saying you are, but a bit of help with this would be really appreciated. That's if, in fact, you're real. Um ... thanks ... over and out? Or whatever. Cheers.

I could not believe she actually wanted me to try things on. And not only that, she insisted on me showing her everything. Everything. But in all honesty, the most confusing thing of all was that she seemed genuinely happy about the whole process. It was killing me. And I wanted it to stop. So, I told her. But you know, politely. I didn't want to break the fragile truce we had going.

"Tessa, don't we have enough already? Please. This is seriously doing my head in. I really don't need any more."

She considered me with her deep, dark, predatory eyes, then softened and let me off the hook ... almost. "Just one more. These jeans are an awesome cut, not like those baggy things you were wearing. They might actually fit you."

"My pants fit. They aren't too tight, and they don't fall down. What more do you want?" I took the pants she handed me, honestly baffled.

"No, Daniel. Your pants do not fit. They simply exist around your hips. And they need to fit you properly."

Not that I could figure out why it was so important. But I let her go on. You know, in the spirit of keeping the peace.

"I have finally discovered what's best for you, and I believe these are they. Please, for me." Her eyes grew to the size of frying pans.

"The last ones. I promise." Then she hit me with that smile again. The nice one.

With that compromise, I headed back into the change room for what I hoped was the last time. Outside, I could hear some louts had entered the store and were talking themselves up. I didn't pay attention as it didn't involve me—or "us", I should say. A word I hadn't used in a very long time.

I was ready to be the exhibit again, but when I opened the curtain, Tessa wasn't around. Which was odd. Normally she was outside tapping her foot, waiting for me. It was all I could do to keep her out and not in the cubicle actually dressing me.

"Hey, dog, where have you been? We've missed you."

"Yeah, who said you could up and leave us, twik? Get a better offer, did you? Someone who did you better?"

"Not bloody likely, bro, I was the best she eva' had."

"In your dreams, plinter, I was the one she moaned for most."

"That wasn't her moaning for pleasure, dumb butt, that was her trying to get you off so I could have a turn."

"Skrat for brains, what would you know? You're just lucky to get my seconds."

As I walked through the small shop, I noticed the staff had made themselves scarce. I rounded a clothes rack and walked into two primates. My brain snapped and everything froze when I realised these two thugs were grabbing at and fighting over Tessa.

She stood dwarfed between them, wide-eyed and white, a frail daisy crushed between two witless boulders.

I was used to working my way through street negotiations. But I had only ever had to fight for myself and Indy. And he could definitely hold his own. As a rule, I'd try talking first. And if that didn't work, Plan B was to smash the skrat out of the opposition, taking down as many as possible before I ran for my life. There were only two of them so it shouldn't be a problem. But I didn't want Tessa caught in the crossfire. I got the impression yesterday that she hadn't done much actual fighting.

And by the things they had been saying, to her ... about her ... I realised she was in real trouble. And I snapped. She may have been a Twik Princess, but she was my Twik Princess.

When I saw her trapped and terrified, a powerful feeling rose up in me. All of a sudden, I wanted to kill the krets that were hurting her. I hadn't felt that strongly about anything or anyone for a long time.

It felt good. I was alive again, fighting for something other than myself. I opened myself to the rage and drank deeply.

"Hey Tessa, there you are. I was wondering where you'd got to. Could you give me a hand with something?"

"Get in line, skrat-for-brains, she's going to give me a *hand* with something first. Just like old times, eh, twik?" He leered, turned his back on me and grabbed her chin. Leaning down, he forced his ugly mug onto her face, mauling her in what I expect he mistook for a kiss. She was white, shaking with fear. I was red, shaking with rage.

"Back. Off. Now." Low, slow and quiet. It had the desired effect. Frugly Thug One, who'd currently snared her, turned back to face me.

"Who's gonna make me, plinter? She's mine. I claimed her and used her most, so she is my property. She might'a got away for a bit, but I'm taking what's mine and no one's gonna stop me."

I was taller than both of them, but they were about three times as wide, four times as heavy and five times as strong. He didn't perceive me as a threat, just a tall annoying fly to be swatted. Just the way I liked it.

"Tessa, this is your choice. Would you like to come home, or would you like to stay? If you want to come home, I will make sure you get there. You are no one's property."

She looked me in the eye, a ghost, trembling and mute. She mouthed one word, "please".

"What the hell is all this skrat? Like you're going to stop me taking what I want," Frugly Thug One said.

"She doesn't want to be with you. This is your last chance. Let. Her. Go."

He snorted so loudly, snot sprayed, and Frugly Thug Two doubled up with laughter.

"Sure thing, Lancelot, I'll just step aside and let you have your—"

Before he finished his sentence, I stepped in and buried my fist in his face. I welcomed the fire that consumed me as he stumbled.

I didn't have to think. Instinct stepped into the driver's seat and I shifted into autopilot. His falter drew me closer and I kneed him as hard as I could in the balls. As he went down, I was presented with the back of his head, so I helped him on his way with my elbow.

Man, I love a fight. Nothing makes you feel more alive than smashing an opponent.

Frugly Thug Two stood there, as big as he was brainless. He swung a right that connected with thin air, and I dropped to one knee and speared my fist into his diaphragm.

"Okay, that's enough play for now. I suggest we get a move on before you girls break a fingernail," thunder rumbled behind me.

I looked around to size up the situation, ready to kick on if need be. But I was confronted by Marcus, full height, full breadth, and fully-intimidating game face on. To my shock, Kait was there too, battle-ready. Mother hen had morphed into skrat-scary mother bear.

Frugly Thug One was moaning and rolling on the ground whilst Frugly Thug Two gasped like a fish out of water. Tessa, frozen on the spot, stared at me. Marcus and Kait raced to her, wings flapping, feathers fussing, checking to see if she was okay. I then lost sight of her as she disappeared into Kait's arms, dissolving into tears.

I looked around and spotted Raph staring into space. He didn't look too good. So, as I went to leave money on the counter, I asked him to get my stuff from the change room. He didn't respond, so I gathered it myself and raced back to see what the go was. He seemed pretty traumatised by the whole thing. Probably best to get everyone home.

As we made our way back to the truck, Kait and Marcus refused to release Tessa from their embrace. When Kait scanned Raph, I was touched by the concern on her face. Since she was tied up with Tessa, I mirrored their example and placed an arm around his shoulders. The kid was shaking, stiff as a board, and cold as my old shelter. I couldn't figure out what his problem was. It really wasn't that big a deal. But then again, I didn't know what he was used to. Maybe he'd had a sheltered life.

When we arrived at the truck, everyone disentangled arms, but only so Kait could engulf the unresponsive Raph as she kissed him on the head. "You're okay, everything is going to be okay. We're going home now, Raph. You are safe."

We guided him into the back, and Kait shut us in. I knew warmth was needed to treat shock, so I tucked the kid under my arm. He didn't reject me, so I left it there for the trip home. His stony silence gave me space to think about all the things I had just heard and seen. It raised questions I didn't have the right to ask. But I wasn't an idiot. I already had answers to most of them.

The mood was subdued when we returned. I heard Tessa leave the truck, and when we were released from the back, Raph followed her robotically. There were happy cries of greeting from inside that were left hanging, unmet.

I helped Marcus and Kait gather the shopping. We lugged everything into the kitchen where Abbot and Val got up to help us. I could see Raph and Riah huddled at the back of the garden. Tessa was nowhere in sight.

"I am feeling a bag of emotions right now—a whole lot of shame pouring out of the laundry and a fair bit of anger, fear, and confusion coming from the back garden. I guess you had an eventful trip?" Abbot questioned politely.

Marcus gave a rough outline of what had happened. I stayed in the kitchen pretending to make coffee, while listening intently to his version of events.

"Raph's taken it pretty hard. Maybe witnessing what happened has brought on a flashback." Marcus threw in his two cents.

"It's PTSD for both of them. We need to handle this carefully," Kait pointed out. "For now, allowing Riah space and time to calm her brother down is best. But I suggest we don't leave him too long."

"I thought we'd gotten over that. Moved on?" Marcus moved to the sitting room and slumped into his chair, staring into the garden.

"You never really get over it," Kait said. "That's why Riah doesn't talk. They are getting better, being further away from it. The breathing exercises we do, our morning sets, all the talking we did with them early on. The routine we set up, the skills and responsibilities we give them, it all helps. But they may never be healed from it. It's the root of Raph's anxiety."

I couldn't stall any longer, so I carried the drinks over on a tray, handed them out and then took my place in the circle. Sliding down in my chair, I mulled over what I had just heard.

"Sorry to interrupt, but what is PSD ... ?" I had no idea what they were talking about but felt sick thinking about what could cause Raph to have this reaction. So much for a sheltered life.

"PTSD. Post-traumatic stress disorder," Kait said. "They have all been through very traumatic experiences. The twins' ordeal was hideously unnatural. And as a result, like all people, it's had long and lasting effects on their minds. When something happens that triggers a memory of that experience, they are transported back to that time and they relive it all. It's very frightening for them."

"Dan, I owe you an apology." Marcus could have knocked me over with a feather.

"What? What on earth for?"

"I had you completely wrong. Well, not really. From the start, I had picked you right, but then in a rush of blood, I stuffed up. I'm sorry. Thank you for what you did today and for looking after Tessa. I have to learn that I am not always going to be able to protect her, or the others for that matter. I can't even guarantee Kait's safety." He looked at her sitting next to him and took her hand. "I'm having trouble letting go of those I love and trusting them to the Light."

I was too shocked to say much, but thought if we were being honest with each other, I may as well say my bit as well.

"Thanks, Marcus, not for the apology. You don't owe me anything. I am just so incredibly grateful to be here. You have no idea what it means to me to be safe, to be warm, to not be hungry —" I had to stop to get my emotions back under control. "To be clean—" I coughed to cover the break in my voice. "Yeah, well, thanks for letting me stop here for a while. And for letting me handle things in the shop. Smashing heads always helps to relieve stress."

I couldn't help but smile when I saw the glint of recognition in Marcus and Val's eyes.

Kait sighed and shook her head. "Not another one. How's the hand?"

It was sore, but nothing I couldn't handle. Eventually it would settle, and I told her so.

We sat in silence, everyone lost in thought. I couldn't stop thinking of Tessa and the shame she was drowning in. "Do you think it might help if I offered Tessa a coffee?"

"I think that is a very good idea, but before you do, I think we'll spend a few moments in the Light asking for wisdom on how best to help all our family right now." Abbot's gentle words were spoken from many years of experience. He went on to explain how to do this.

Apparently, we needed to sit quietly and focus solely on the Light, pushing all other thoughts out of our minds and only focusing on His greatness and ability to help. Once we had done this, we brought forward our "petition" for the others and asked for wisdom, healing, and assistance.

He also asked for patience, grace, and humility for us all and that we would find a way forward. I thought it was interesting how they spoke to the Light-god, and that they would ask these kinds of things.

What other stuff do they ask you for?

With a new sense of calm, I went to speak to Tessa. I knew that I would never refer to her as Whinger or Twik Princess again, especially after hearing how those guys abused her. It made me realise I was as repulsive as they were.

She was just like the rest of us, doing what we had to do to keep from being chewed up, spat out and obliterated by the skrat we called life.

I went to pour another coffee and Marcus went outside to the twins. They sat cross-legged opposite each other, foreheads touching, huddled at the back of the garden under the arms of Raph's tree. He had turned defensive and shut ranks, keeping everyone out. Of the two of us, I think Marcus had the harder job of working reconciliation.

As I rounded the corner to the laundry, I caught a snippet of the conversation coming from the sitting room. "He's catching all the foxes before the battle," Abbot's soft voice offered.

"Looks that way. This is healthy, but we need to manage it carefully. It will make them stronger if they let it. These wounds need to be opened before they can be cleansed," Val replied.

18

CONTESSA

H e was outside.

Funny thing was, he was the only one I wanted to talk to.

But he was the last person I wanted to see.

I was so ashamed.

Yet equally grateful.

Yeah, I know. Confusing.

I'd insulted him. He didn't like me, obviously. Yet, he'd stood up for me. He hadn't run. He even took them on; one on two. He'd had no idea that Kait and Marcus were in the shop. But he took them on anyway.

I'd tried not to look at them. When Marcus's face morphed to rage, I had to look away. His body had tensed, building to an eruption of epic proportions. Kait had gently laid her hand on his arm, and it had halted him. I'd caught a glimpse of the shock in his eyes. The dawning of realisation. The truth about what they were saying about me.

But I'd had to look away then. Kait had known from the beginning, but Marcus had not ... and now Raph knew too. Every foul, disgusting truth had been ripped open and laid bare before them.

I was so ashamed.

They had accepted and loved me before this, but how could they accept me now? Knowing ...

Hot tears came again as Dan clumsily made his way through the door, trying to manage the handle and carrying two mugs of coffee in one hand. His thoughtfulness made me feel even worse. I dropped my head into my hands and continued to weep. I heard the gentle tink of the cups being placed on the tiles. The washing machine flexed and bumped as he slid down next to me. His body heat reached me once he'd settled on the cold, hard floor.

We sat, still, silent and solemn.

After a while, he tentatively reached over and passed me a coffee.

"Why did you do it?" I couldn't help it. I had to know.

"What?"

"Today in the shop. Why did you help me? You don't even like me."

"I wouldn't say I don't 'like' you." He blew across the top of his cup. "But you are ... different." He rushed on, "Different's not bad, it's just ... you know ... different. Well, different from what I'm used to, that is." He looked out the window in the top half of the laundry door. "I guess we had a bit of a rocky start. I figured the feeling was mutual? I seem to skitch you off pretty easily." He bumped my elbow. A small wave of coffee slopped over the side of my mug. It burned my fingers. I didn't care.

Truth was, he was right, and I didn't even know why.

I stalled by putting my cup down and grabbing a relatively clean shirt from the dirty clothes pile to wipe my hands and mop my hideous face.

What a mess, please help me here.

"Why'd you do it?" He returned the challenge.

I couldn't hold my head up anymore. Nausea washed through me, the shame was too much. "I was trapped."

He was silent for a moment, then went on in a rush, "No, not the thing with those plinters. That, I get." He seemed to zone out for a moment. I couldn't believe he was ready to dismiss my situation and suffering, my whole past, as simply as swatting a fly. Like it didn't matter.

I had looked down on him because he'd lived on the street. I had considered him dumb. Scary … but dumb, because of how we found him. But he'd had the courage to do what I couldn't. Break away from the gangs and go it alone.

He had been filthy on the outside.

I was filthy on the inside.

He came clean with water and soap, but I was scarred with scum. But maybe he wasn't brave, maybe he was simple.

"Dan, you do know what I did? What I let them do to me, just so I didn't have to live on the street. Like you."

"I'm not an idiot, Tessa." But he looked at me like I was. "You and I have experienced the skratty side of life. I've seen and done far worse in the name of survival. I'm just glad I haven't been caught and had to do time in a real prison." He looked at his hands. "Yes, Tessa, I have a pretty good idea of what you have done and been through." He turned back to me. "Doesn't mean you liked it. It was the choice you made to stay alive."

His eyes lifted, his face tilted. "No, I meant, why'd you sign up for this 'Light' gig. Why'd you say yes?"

Those eyes. They pinned me like I was a dead bug, extending my wings and casing to expose the truth underneath.

"Oh, that." I cleared my throat. "It's simple … and complicated." The weight of his complete focus was uncomfortable, so I raced on. "When they came for me—Val, Kait and Abbot—I wasn't as far along as the others had been when they were rescued. I couldn't see demons back then."

"Demons?" His voice rose.

"Yeah, they were running our gang through their puppets. But I had no idea. I had been marked for the Light, so I figure that's why I was having such a hard time of it. It was all pretty much a blur. But at least, hardly any humans were killed. Not like when Kait and Marcus were rescued."

"Killed?"

"Well, yeah, weren't you listening last night? We're at war. And in war, people die." I looked at the piles of washing, the shelves, the cracked tiles, anywhere but at him, as I relived the nightmare. "Anyway, I was given a choice. To start over, fresh and new, with hope and joy and peace ... so much peace." I couldn't hide my smile.

Thank you.

"I was invited to leave my old life behind and start again where I was safe, valued and loved. I was told my life could have meaning and purpose. Or, I could stay where I was, used and abused. No-brainer, if you ask me." I looked down to where I'd made macramé out of the shirt I was holding. "These guys offered me a home and a family, safety, and security. It's not a free ride, but I have an important role here. Oh, and I train hard, really hard, for battle—hand-to-hand and with weapons."

"Weapons?"

His rumble of appreciation snagged my attention. Maybe he was simple. "Did you get knocked in the head? What's with the parrot imitation?"

"Sorry, Tessa, it all seems a bit far-fetched, that's all."

Seriously? After what I'd heard about him, he had the nerve to call this far-fetched? "What spooked you last night and made you run? You don't look like someone who's easily intimidated."

"I was feeling ... crowded ..."

"Why did you come back?"

"I ... needed shelter."

"You've lived on the streets for years, Daniel. You could find shelter anywhere. Why did you come back here?"

"I needed to get off the streets."

"How did you find the way?"

"I ... don't know." His eyes darted around the room.

"So, you ran off because we crowded you, then for 'some' reason you needed to come back and 'somehow' you managed to find your way in the dark, after only being here once. Sorry, Dan, seems a bit far-fetched to me." I had him. And since we seemed to have unofficially entered a truce, in the spirit of honesty I decided I'd probe deeper. "It's pretty scary, isn't it?"

"Yeah. It is. How can I know what to do?" His vulnerability eroded a bit more of my defensive wall.

I had the urge to reach out to touch him.

I resisted.

"What do you feel? Inside, here"—I tapped my heart. "In all honesty, what do you know? Here"—I tapped my temple. "Do you believe that there is something 'Other'? Other than the Seen. Can you stretch your belief to accept that there is an Unseen world around us?"

He was silent for ages. I figured he was fighting all kinds of denial. But then he answered. "Yeah, I can't really deny that there is something. My dreams, Val in the shop, here last night, being 'led' back, and Suit Dude out on the street. The evidence is stacking up."

"Well, in light of all that, look at us. Look at how we live as Children of Light. Then look at the world and see how the rest live. We aren't perfect, but we don't fit in with them. And I don't want to." I couldn't help the shudder as I recalled the temple, and my past life. "All you have to do is choose between the two. Your choice. Say yes to the Light or say yes to the Dark. Simple ... but complicated." I couldn't help but laugh at the pained expression on his face. This time I gave in to the temptation to reach out to him. But I disguised it as a return elbow bump. "Things will become clearer when you make your choice.

"Now, your turn. Why'd you save me today? You could have walked away. You could have hidden. If you'd waited two minutes, Kait and Marcus would have been there. But you didn't. Why?" Again, he took for-absolute-ever to answer.

Maybe he didn't have an answer.

Maybe he didn't know.

Talk about crushing a girl's ego.

Then, like lancing a boil, it all poured out. "Those plinter meatheads skitched me off. They deserved to get their heads smashed for being so skrat stupid. You don't deserve that. You aren't the product of your past, or what those guys did to you. They could hurt you, but they can't change you. You were just doing what you had to do to take care of your chil—" He stopped, looked at me, took a deep breath. "You were just doing what you needed to do to take care of yourself." Another deep breath. "You've just admitted to being different, and you are. That's the point. You're not scum like them."

My ego rebounded. But I was speechless. And even more ashamed. "Well, I'm feeling pretty skratty at the moment."

"Listen, you were in a tough place and had to make a tough choice. You did what you had to do to survive. That's not weak, that's the harsh reality of life. You are not filthy." Then, more quietly, "You're ... intriguing."

I snorted involuntarily. Our bubble of honesty has just burst.

"Well, so far, from what I've seen, this is not one of your best looks." He smirked. The tension was relieved, and the immensity of his previous statement had been suitably sidestepped. But nothing could take away from the grace he presented to me. It was a gift that was both unexpected and unwarranted. A cloak I gratefully accepted as it enveloped me, warmed me and, most importantly, washed me clean.

We stayed like that for an eon, side by side on the laundry floor, leaning against the washing machine as our coffees, forgotten, went cold.

19

RAPHAEL

The breath I inhaled was full of musty history. Watching Tessa pinned, pushed and passed between those men like a piece of dough had taken me back to when Riah was hurt by the Bad Men.

I exhaled through gritted teeth, suffocated by the hell of that time. That place. That experience. I had to get home to her. I had to save her and take her away. I had to protect her. We had to escape. The Dragon threatened to conquer me. But even the Dragon has no sway against my fight to save Sariah. I was rage. I was fear.

I let the Dragon come and I rode the beast, whipping it onward, all the way home.

Scents of stale sweat, cigarette smoke, sweet spirits swam. Icy fingers parted my vertebra and walked their way up to my skull. I tried to spit out the bitterness, but my mouth was dry.

I had to get Riah. We needed to escape.

The door of the truck cracked open. I was ready, flattened on the floor. I rolled out the crack as soon as it was wide enough. I hit the ground, stumbled, then shoulder tackled the door into the house. Where was she? Over by the window in their thrones, sitting, smiling, talking.

No. No time. We had to run.

Grabbing her by the wrist, I ripped her from Abbot ... no one could touch her. We were the same size, but I had taken her by surprise. She could not find her feet. It did not matter. I dragged her through the back doors out onto the lawn.

No one could have her. I had to get her to safety. I hauled her to the farthest safe place. The garden, my tree. If I could have pulled her up through the branches, I would have. But for now, the base would have to be good enough till I could explain. Then she would join me.

But for now, she was confused, resisting. She did not understand.

Conceding that I knew best, she gave in and escaped with me. I hugged her and ... hugged her and ... then, I could not stop the tears. I cried and cried, and I did not know why. I had to make sure she was okay. I had to see her. Without releasing my grip, I pushed her to arm's length. Then held her close. I ran my hand through her hair. It was clean and smooth. My shaking fingers knotted and tangled.

I could not breathe. The Dragon was shaking me from the inside out. The fire and the fog were taking over. I was confused and angry and scared and I could not stop crying. We sat on the grass knee-to-knee, eyes closed, hands entwined, forehead-to-forehead. I cried and tried to force healing into her. She sat quietly and lent me her peace. I drank deeply.

The half of my soul that lived in her was a deep, cool reservoir. It did not matter how deep the Dragon's fire burned, Sariah's waters were always stronger. Inhaling her endless spring tide, I was able to tell her what happened in the shop. I revealed Tessa's truth. I condemned her for not running.

Why had she not escaped? She was not trapped. Why had she stayed with the Bad People?

Like a jigsaw puzzle being reconstructed with no picture, I told the story in fits and starts. I was still gasping for breaths between clouds of confusion. But Riah had helped calm the wild storm. My heart did not hurt anymore. The red haze was lifting.

Equally difficult was revealing the truth about Daniel. I had not liked Daniel. I had not trusted Daniel, but he saved her. I had called him bad names, but he held me together all the way home. I rode the Dragon and he braved the storm.

When I had finished, we sat without moving. Riah was taking it all in. I know she was sad. She was doing her not-crying thing, when the tears run but her face does not change.

She was hurting. She looked at me with her strong face on. Sad inside but fierce on the outside. Thank the Light she agreed with me. Tessa was weak, Dan was strong.

I did not know what to do. We could not leave, but we had to get away. Where could we go, we could … we could not …

Marcus was coming. He would know what to do. He always knew what to do.

"Hey, young man. That was a bit of a shock this morning, wasn't it?" He started to fold onto the grass next to us, but before he could sit, I stood to meet him.

"We have to get away," I confirmed.

"You know that we'll be leaving soon. We will leave this place and never come back. The Bad People who hurt you won't be able to hurt you or anyone else ever again."

"You are strong, our mountain, we can stay with you. Dan is strong, I can see that now. But what are we going to do about Tessa? She is too weak."

Marcus's tanned face turned to milk, and his icy eyes went wide as his jaw dropped. He knew the truth. Only the strong could stay. He would have to get rid of her. He would understand. He was a warrior. As I was waiting for him to answer, to come up with a plan, Riah stood and grabbed my hand.

She did not have to worry. We would protect her. This would be hard for them, but they knew that only the strong survive. The weak would destroy us and let the enemy in.

I tried to ignore her while I waited for Marcus to decide. But her actions were getting too loud to ignore. For once, I wished she would just let me lead. Did she not know that I was looking after her?

Her angry eyes drilled through me.

Calmer now, I re-explained that I was looking after her. She shook her head and scowled at me. Shoved her palm out at me, many times: *Stop! Stop, stop, stop.*

"Stop what? What is wrong? Marcus and I will sort this out. You must be patient, Ri."

I staggered under the force of her open hand connecting with my shoulder.

"What? Why are you angry at me? I am protecting you! Don't you see?" She must have misunderstood me. "I have to protect you from the Bad People."

She pointed her finger to the ground and made a circle: *everyone here*—making a fist, she placed it on her heart, then covered it with her other hand: *is family, is community, is one.*

She then took her finger and shook it at me: *no*—then, taking that finger, she pointed behind her: *enemy*—circling her finger again: *here.* She wagged her finger at me again: *none!* Once more she made the circle motion with her finger pointing to the ground: *everyone here*—bending her elbows, making a straight line as her fingertips met in front of her chest, then breaking the line, making an angle: *broken, weak.* Circle again: *everyone here*—gripping wrist-to-wrist: *strong.*

"But Ri, I just told you what she did, what she is like! You of all people should agree with me."

It was more than a stagger this time when she hit me. I had to step sideways to stop myself from falling. Forming a T with her hands: *Tessa*—and then one fist covered with her other hand over her heart: *family. We are one.*

"No!" I yelled at her.

I turned so my hunched back took the rain of her blows.

I could not believe it. She was betraying me. I was protecting her. I was keeping her safe. She did not understand.

My soul tore.

We had been together forever. I looked after her, I told her what to do. I kept her safe. She had sided against me.

It was too much. The fire exploded as the snarling Dragon lurking in the shadows launched and consumed me. Its roaring breath entered my head. A whirlwind, a tornado picked me up, it violently ripped me away from everyone, carrying me away.

An angry flock of birds attacked my head, pecking my brain, tripping colours and electrifying nerves. Their screeching and squawking blocked out all other sounds.

I was back in the locked room. Darkness was inside me, all around me. Suffocating me. I could not breathe, I could not think, I could not speak. My heart was pulsing, pounding. Too strong. It was going to explode. It hurt. It told me to run. To get away. I turned, but there was nowhere to hide. So, I ran ... straight into Val.

I was trapped. Strong arms surrounded me. I fought against her. I punched and kicked. She had me pinned. I bit, and used my head to smash her. I had to get away. I had to hide. But there was no escaping Val.

I was completely bound in steel. A mantra wove its way through the wild wings and raging winds. Whispered words subdued the enemy and bound my wounds, pulling me back together, piece by piece. "It's okay, you're okay, Raphael, you are safe. Sariah is safe. Be at peace, it's okay, you're okay ..."

Her chest, bound to mine, grew and shrank. Out. Slow. In. Slow. I couldn't get out. But in this cave she had made for me, no one else could get in.

In this cage I was safe. I joined her ... in ... slow ... out ... slow. The wind died down, the roaring dulled, my heart steadied, and the killer wave broke out from within me and rolled over the top of me. And escaped.

Big ... slow ... breaths. The storm passed on and drew with it all my anger and hurt and frustration and pain. A poultice, like Kait used to draw infection from a wound.

Big ... slow ... breaths. I collapsed in her arms. Val swam in my tears.

The storm had passed, but its savage tail pulled with it everything from inside me. I could not stop the tears. The sobbing.

Val, an anchor, pinned me to the thin line of sanity, whispering,

"You're okay, sweetheart. You're free, it's over. Sariah is safe. You are safe. The Light has you. You're okay."

Lavender and rose cleared the final wisps of fog. Warm warrior hands stroked my hair, a soft cheek pressed against my crown. I remained inside the fortress of frighteningly fierce arms and allowed the love and safety to seep in and restore me. I was surrounded by love, by my family.

After a while, I released Val and turned to drop, exhausted, into my safe place ... the comfort of Kait's arms. She was kneeling behind me on the grass. I looked over her shoulder and saw that Riah was also being comforted by Abbot and Marcus.

I was still confused and scared by the storm, but I was not angry anymore. I did not know where those thoughts had come from. I loved Tessie ... I was sad for her. I was confused by her ... but I loved her.

Riah looked up at me and broke away from them and came over. I stood up to meet her. She took my face in her hands and stared deep into my eyes. She was so strong, so determined.

In silence we acknowledged the truth. I bowed my head to her. She kissed my forehead and hugged me. Again, finger pointing to the ground, circling—"Everyone here"—fist covered by her other hand placed on her chest—"family, we are one."

"You are right, Ri. I am sorry. I could not fight the Dragon. He is too strong, and his lies turn me inside out. They call me down dark paths ... and I follow."

20

CONTESSA

We'd been lost forever. And now it was time to get back. I hated to think what the others would be thinking. I tried to move, but first I had to get circulation through my frozen joints. My butt was a block of ice. Dan took our cups and, standing easily, offered me a hand to get up. I accepted. We made our way out to the living room and saw that everyone was outside.

Something was wrong.

I bolted outside and grabbed a patio chair on my way past. I asked Daniel to grab another, and motioned for him give his to Val as I set mine up for Abbot. Both looked up, grateful. Marcus and I assisted Abbot into his.

I raced back inside to get them each a blanket. The air was frosty, but it was the way everyone looked at me that chilled me the most. And what really hurt was the look Raph shot me before turning away. I couldn't read it. I could always read Raph. But now, he made every effort to shut me out. I stepped toward him but Kait laid her hand on my arm. "Not just yet, sweetheart."

"Why? What's up? Raph, what's wrong?" I looked around the group. "What's happened?" He still wouldn't look at me. My new cloak of comfort torn to shreds, once again I was exposed and alone. I dropped to the ground between Kait and Dan. "Could someone please tell me what's going on?" I could hardly speak.

"Today's episode in the shop was as devastating for Raph as it was for you, sweetheart." Kait took my hand. "It reminded him of how things were when we rescued him and Riah. The trauma they went through hasn't left them. You know what it's like." She gave me a small, joyless smile. "When something happens that triggers those memories, you're transported back to the time and place, and relive the experience vividly." She took my other hand and folded both in hers. "Like you, Raph has no control over it, and it's extremely distressing for him. We believe it would be the same for Riah"—she shared her smile with Raph's twin—"but she is not exposed to as many things as Raph. There are a few things we can do to help them, but it is something they may never be rid of."

Releasing one of my hands, Kait shifted and spoke directly to Raph, "It would be helpful for you, and the others, if you would be brave enough to share your story. It is hard for us to hear, but I understand that it is far harder for you to share."

He looked at her, wide eyes glistening. His head trembling from side to side. Like a goldfish, his mouth silently opened and closed. Riah went to him, leaned her forehead against his, shut her eyes for a moment then stepped back. She held him with her gaze and nodded her head. Then standing at his side, leant her shoulder into his. Her fingers entwined with her brother's.

Raising her chin with steel in her eyes, Sariah defied the world.

The air was cold, the ground was damp, and we waited, frozen, for Raph to tell his tale.

"You know," just above a whisper, he began, "I can make some wounds heal. Abbot says it is my Badge. That is why we were sold. I do not remember our parents. I do not remember our home. But I remember when we were young, the man we lived with would take us out to the streets during the freshness of the morning, and the cool of the evening. Riah would sing for people and I would lay my hands on them and make them feel better. Riah has a beautiful voice, everyone would come to listen. The man would collect lots of money from the people who liked what we did.

"One day, a man from here visited our country and our owner sold us to him. We came to this country by boat. A big boat. It was a long trip. I know we were lucky to be together. I do not know how I know that. But I know we are a 'package deal'. I was sold because of my 'magic' powers, and Riah was bought because her voice is pure and perfect."

Pale and frozen, metronomic and monotone, he continued, "When we arrived in Sodom, he took care of us. In the evenings he would have parties. We would both be brought out for entertainment. But mainly for Riah to sing. He would get me to lay hands on people and do my magic.

"He was not mean. He was not kind. He just was. We were fed and clothed and safe. We did not like the way he dressed Riah for his guests. The lady staff painted her face and he made her wear small, sparkly dresses. Riah said the beads were pretty. But her night clothes were not good. We did not like them. We did this for a while. But mostly, when he was alone, he would get Riah to sing for him and get me to lay hands on him. He said it helped. I think after a while he must have got tired of us." His voice developed feeling and volume.

"One night we were pulled out for one of his dinner parties. But this time it was different. The Bad People were there. We did not like them from the start. They liked Riah's singing, but they would not let me touch them. I was happy. They were scary. Scarier than anyone we had ever met. We were glad when the show was over, and we could go to bed. We did not have to see them again. But the next morning the staff packed our bags. No one would speak to us or tell us what was happening. We thought we were being separated. But all our belongings were being packed. We were relieved. We'd still be together."

He was silent for a while. Sariah's face was still stoic, whilst tears streamed down her cheeks.

No one moved.

No one breathed.

We waited, sick, for Raph to continue.

"We were taken to the Bad People's house. They stole everything from her ..." Raph, was a hollowed, empty shell. His words a lonely wind through a deserted house.

"I tried to stop them, to protect her. I fought and kicked and bit. They laughed. She screamed and screamed and screamed. They laughed. After that, she never screamed ... ever again. Never yelled. Never sang. Never spoke. Never even whispered ..."

He drew a shuddering breath. "It turns out I can fix others. But I cannot fix myself. I cannot fix Val." He looked to her, eyes blank— "and I cannot fix Riah."

I was going to be sick. Slumped on the grass, I was prisoner to Raphael's story, watching Sariah stand iron-like by his side.

Him broken.

Her defiant.

"They were the Dark's men. Darkness was all around them ... in them ... they breathed it in ... and out ... and poured it out all over her. It changed them. I did not know about the Light then, but I was already starting to 'see'. I could see they were Dark. I could see we were Light. And I knew I would kill them. Kill them all, slowly and painfully." His voice now full of grit, lilt, and life.

"When they finished, they let me hold her. They would have to kill me to get to her again. They laughed. I sat and stroked her knotted, sweaty hair, cradled her and planned the most horrifying, painful ways I would kill them. Each a different way.

"But I did not get to live my dream. Val came and stole it from me. Marcus and Kait were there too, and Abbot. But Val killed them all." His eyes cleared and narrowed at her. Red and shaking he spat out, "I was so angry with you. That was my job. That was my right. That was my dream. And you took it from me." He yelled his accusation.

Val clenched her jaw, narrowed her eyes and slowly nodded her head, once.

With a ragged breath, Raph continued, "You said that you understood, but it was not my time. But if we went with you, you would teach me how to do it properly. With real weapons that would work.

You said it was important that I did not strike out in grief and anger. But when the time was right, you promised that I could fight alongside you. And I could kill them." Light sparked from his eyes and steel threaded his words. Val nodded again with mirrored steel and a hint of a very scary grin.

"You said, when I was ready, when I was a man, when I could prove I had a pure heart and was worthy of the weapon I would be given, I could kill as many as I liked." He broke away from Val's focus and looked at Dan and me. "I did not understand most of what she said, but I heard 'weapon' and 'kill'. I saw how Abbot held and wept over Riah"—his eyes filled—"and how she clung to him. So, I agreed." His head dropped.

Dumbstruck and numb, I knew I shouldn't overreact. I had to stay calm. I would process this later. There was a barrier between us, but for the life of me, I couldn't understand why. But I sensed that I had to be very careful.

Please, give me the words.

Taking a long, deep breath, I made a start. "I cannot even begin to imagine what that was like for you both. All I can say is that, I would have loved to have had a brother like you to care for me when I was in trouble, Raph." I swiped my face on my sleeve. "But, when I was trapped, I didn't have anyone to protect and care for me. And I didn't have the skills of Marcus, the experience of Kait, or the knowledge of Abbot. I didn't have the wisdom of Val or the courage of Dan. I didn't have the talent of Sariah, or your determination. I was weak and alone. I couldn't have survived on the streets by myself. But I know for sure, if I had had a brother like you, I would have been able to leave. I wanted to. I hated it and I was so scared. But I had no one, and nowhere to go. I had to decide between living in hell and dying on the street."

Once again, I was reduced to nothing.

Worthless.

Weak.

Filth.

I had nowhere to hide from these kids, from these people.

I didn't know where it came from, but I felt the need to apologise to him. "Please forgive me for being weak and incapable. Forgive me for staying. You had physical chains holding you captive in your torture. I had unseen chains that held me in my hell. But like you, like Dan, I should have tried. And I am sorry."

More flopping tears. I was so sick of this.

Dan's hand covered mine and gave it a squeeze. I clung on tight, but only had eyes for Raph.

I waited.

We all sat motionless. Breathless. Waiting to see if the bomb would go off and how devastating the damage would be.

He didn't move.

He didn't speak.

He just stared at me.

I wanted to scream. To hit something really hard. And smash it. Completely.

Whether Dan was a mind-reader, or just as desperate for Raph to respond as I was, I didn't know, but he gently returned the pressure on my hand, holding me firm. Giving me an anchor. The waiting was unbearable.

Riah rolled her eyes and shoved her brother in the back. He wasn't expecting it and almost fell to his knees. He glared at her. The volley of expressions and hand movements between them was a blur. This was how they were when it was just the two of them. We called it their secret language.

In the end, she set her face and forcibly shoved his shoulder and pointed to me. Her directive was enforced by set feet, crossed arms, tilted head, then, very slowly, she narrowed her eyes: *end of conversation.*

I saw Raph's eyes roll before they were hidden behind a dropped fringe. He made his way over to me.

Help me.

"Tessie, I was angry at you. I do not know why. Kait tried to explain it to me. I am confused. But I know Abbot says we cannot judge others. He says ... we all do the best we can ... with what we have … at the time." He recited the well-known saying. "He says we are all different. But we are all the same. It is what makes our family tapestry so rich. Like one of Ri's pictures." He flicked a glance at his sister.

As he twisted, I could see Abbot and the smile that lit his face. Some of the tension dissolved.

"You have a family now and you do not have to pick between living in hell and dying on the street. We will protect you." He looked from my face down to where my hand was held by Dan's. His eyes clouded.

"What about you, Little Man? Are we still good?"

Help me, please.

I couldn't bear it if he rejected me. But I had to know.

Silence.

Every muscle in my body clenched. Every nerve was on fire. My heart hurt.

Raph tilted his head. "I do not know what you are talking about. I said I was angry. I am not anymore. I just felt so guilty and ashamed when you came out. I thought if you saw my face you would see all the horrible thoughts that I had had. I am so sorry. We will always be good, Tessa. I love you." And with that, he launched himself into my arms and finally the tension was broken. As we tumbled backward, I managed to catch a glimpse of Abbot hugging Riah. And Kait dropping her head to rest on Val's.

Marcus's roar sent birds from the trees. "Right then!"

Far too supple for his age, he pounced like a cat. Everything was overwhelmed by his warmth and strength. There was no room for sadness, fear, shame or regrets in the fold of Marcus's arms. Both Raph and I were swooped around the garden. The horror of his war cry was muffled as he pinned me between his arm and chest.

We ended up on the ground. We always did. I cradled Raph's head to my chest, as both of us were cradled on Marcus's. He held us firmly, gently, possessively. We struggled to breathe from the laughter. We always did. But this time, he couldn't hide his tears of relief. But then, neither could I.

21

DANIEL

As I surveyed the scene of this family in recovery, I couldn't help but remember Tessa's words: "All you have to do is choose between the two. Say yes to the Light, or say yes to the Dark. Simple, but complicated."

Raph's story had made me want to vomit. I couldn't deny the vein of Darkness that ran through it and identified the Dark Lord's signature throughout my own life. By saying no to the Light, was I, by default, saying yes to this? Were there any other options? I knew that whatever choice I made, I couldn't go back to ignorance, denying the truth about the world that existed in the Other.

Everyone was inside. Tessa and the twins were preparing lunch and the older guard were relaxing in the sitting room. I took my time and brought in the chairs and rugs that were left behind. By the time I joined them, my knuckles were swollen and my hand was giving me some grief.

Despite the pain though, I was having trouble keeping my eyes open. So much had happened in such a short span of time. I joined the crew in the sitting room, slumped in my chair and, with my wrist gently laid over the arm of the chair, I shut my eyes and zoned out.

I heard Abbot clear his throat and very soon afterward there was a bustling around my chair as the air filled with activity. I pried my eyes open to see Kait, armed with a first aid kit, preparing implements and potions I had never seen before.

"Dan, why didn't you tell me your hand was this bad?" she accused me.

"Well, there was quite a lot going on. And to be perfectly honest, I've had worse. It's not that bad, really."

"Dear boy. It looks a bit more than 'not that bad'."

"Kait, I'm not one of your chicks." I smiled at her.

She raised her eyebrows and the corner of her lips twitched. "When you're under this roof, honey, you're one of my clutch, regardless."

"Well then, feel free to cluck away. Do you mind if I leave you to it though? I'm shattered."

Val and Marcus had leaned forward to get a better look and Tessa called out from the kitchen. "What's wrong, what happened to his hand?"

I then realised she had no idea. Marcus, Kait and Val looked to me, waiting for my interpretation of the events. "Well, I kind of hit a big, ugly brick with it ... as hard as I could, twice ... and it hurts. But it's okay really."

"What a dumb thing to do. Why on earth would you ..." She trailed off when she realised what I meant, and once again the red comet raced up her neck revealing her embarrassment. "Oh."

"Don't feel too sorry for him, sweetheart. He kind of got a kick out of it at the time." Marcus covered the awkwardness with truth.

"Is there anything I can do?" she offered meekly.

Kait jumped in. "You can crush some ice for me, thanks. Although it might be a bit late for that." Immediately Tessa left Raph and Riah to the lunch and set to the task whilst Kait finished examining my trophy. "The good news is that it's not broken. It will be swollen and sore for a while, but you'll live." She said it with a smile and a hint of pride.

"Thanks, Doc. I could have told you that myself, but I feel much better in your tender care." My hand was examined, iced, elevated and rested. I could get used to the pampering thing. I'd add that to my list of pros.

There was a gentle eddy all around me. I heard Marcus and Kait leave, possibly to join the crew preparing for lunch. I didn't know, and I really didn't care.

I sat in the peaceful eye of the gentle flurry as years of tiredness, and the inability to relax, threatened to overwhelm me at the first hint of safety and the beginning of trust. Yet—despite the exhaustion—thoughts, images and memories occupied my mind.

I had already acknowledged the existence of Other. And I could no longer deny the reality of Darkness. But just because there was Dark, it didn't prove there was Light, regardless of what Abbot said.

However, these guys were different, in every possible way. They stood apart from the world around them, but not in a bad way, in an ... unadulterated way. And I had been invited to be part of that with them.

I had no idea why. Why me? I was nothing special, and I had done my share of dark things. Things I was really ashamed of and I fully regret. Nothing as bad as what had happened to Tessa and the twins, but maybe I had been a "puppet" and not known it.

Closing the others out, I leaned forward in my chair, cradling my head in my good hand, resting my other arm on my knee.

If you're out there, I just want to say, I'm sorry for all I have done that has caused pain and trauma, especially if it's anywhere as bad as what these guys are carrying around. I really like the sound of that clean slate you spoke about. I don't know why you want me, but I feel kind of special that you've asked me to be part of what you're doing. I don't really know what's involved, but if I have to pick a side, I choose you ... if you'll still have me.

Deep within me, a seed of hope, of a new beginning, sparked to life and grew to consume the soul-weight I'd carried my whole life. I felt light and free. All the pain I'd carried, all the loneliness I'd felt, the longing I'd harboured, the sadness I'd held, and the bitterness I'd clung to were being gently washed away with silent, unbidden tears.

I felt Val's presence as she took her seat next to me. But I didn't open my eyes when I heard her humming a comforting tune as she rubbed my back. I felt another hand comfort me. I had no idea whose, and I didn't care.

I didn't lift my eyes. I couldn't. There was an irritation. An object, sharp and painful, was lodged in each of them.

"It's okay, let it go," Val said.

The tears eventually washed the sharpness away. But something was working its way out of my eyes. I tried not to panic when warm fingers feathered my cheeks.

At that point I had to lift my head and was frozen in astonishment to see Sariah kneeling in front of me, smiling. Holding out her hands in victory with what looked like small scales balanced on her fingertips. I looked from her hands to her eyes. I had never seen her eyes before. Such depth, such incredible beauty. Purity.

I continued to lift my eyes. They'd all gathered around to comfort and help me. But I could see. For the first time, I could see them as they actually were. "Ho-leee fra— far out."

They were each clothed in ethereal armour of a different hue, yet they were still visible under it. They gathered around me, each giving off a dull glow. Riah in red, Abbot in orange, Kait in green, Marcus in blue, Tessa in yellow, and Val in indigo.

A hysterical giggle bubbled up within me. They were a veritable rainbow. I had to double-take when I glanced over at Val. Her armour was spectacular, elaborate and fearsome. All over her were knife hilts. Her feet, ankles, knees, hips, hands, wrists, elbows, shoulders ... even her finger joints. At each joint she had a knife hilt stuck to her. It was majorly creepy. I wondered if it was her own design.

I was going mad. For. Sure. "Well at least you're not vampires," I choked out.

Tessa snorted. The tension broke.

"Ah, he has seen your adornment, dear heart," Abbot said to Val, who merely nodded her head with that wry smile. "Tessa, I think that a strong, sweet coffee might be very apt right now, dear."

There was a movement to my left and my eyes were drawn to her yellow glow. Tessa's armour was not nearly as ornate or thick as the other's, yet she too was clothed in Light like the rest.

"Tessa is still growing her armour. It will develop and strengthen with time and experience. She is doing splendidly well though, and we are all so very proud of her." Abbot's affection caused her to blush as she turned to the task of making a coffee. Raph went to her aid, similarly clad in pale violet.

So, why'd you give those two thinner armour than the rest?

I snapped my mouth shut as soon as I realised I had been gaping. Speechless, eyes flicking rapidly from one to the other. Abbot's armour was thick and ornate, as was Marcus's and Kait's, but none was nearly as intricate and intimidating as Val's.

All of a sudden, I was cold and started shaking. Probably shock. Kait came to me with a blanket, Tessa came to me with a steaming hot, sweet cup, and Raph came from behind and laid his hands on my shoulders.

I accepted all three as heat radiated through my body and the peace and comfort I had felt previously returned. But this time it didn't get out of control. Shutting my eyes, I bowed my head, letting the warmth of all three pervade, returning calm and peace.

Raph finished and walked back to the kitchen while I sat there, mesmerised at how he had eased my suffering and warmed my soul. I was still in a whirlwind of wonder by the time they both returned with hot drinks for the others.

When everyone was seated, Kait asked, "How do you feel now, Daniel? I believe you might have just made your decision?" Her soft, warm voice smiled, honey flowing over the sharp edges of my shock.

I looked to her and stared. It was going to take me a while to get used to this. How could I have been with them for this long and not known, not seen? I felt like I had been walking in the ... well ... walking in the Dark, blinded. And now I was seeing everything for the first time in the ... Light. It sounded so clichéd, even in the privacy of my head. But it was the only way to describe it.

"I ... I feel warm, I feel the Light. I don't know, I feel ... different. You're all so ... different."

"And now you have experienced the Light, young man," Marcus's voice gravelled approvingly. "Your introduction last night seemed pretty extreme, but there will be a reason for that, no doubt. But, however it happens, all of us have to shed the scales in order to see, have our ears cleared so we can hear, and have our heart broken so we can love." He rose and held out his hand. "It's a joy to be able to welcome you to the family, son."

Still gaping like a cartoon fish, I removed the ice pack and rose to have my sore hand engulfed, while his other hand firmly clapped me on the back.

Kait came around him to embrace me. Only as tall as my chin, she laid her head on my shoulder and I allowed her to engulf me with her mother heart. Her fresh lavender-rose fragrance seeped into my mind. Forever I would associate this feeling with her scent. "Again, and more truly I say, welcome. You are one with us," she said.

Tessa jiggled on the spot and when I had been released from Kait, she sprang into my arms. Shorter still, she tightly squeezed my waist. It was weird. Holding the little oddball felt right and good. She was a good fit. I looked down at her, briefly astonished, as she looked up squeaked out a "Yay!"

Yep, she was definitely one interesting chick.

"Yay, indeed, young man. It is a pleasure to have you with us." Abbot edged forward to gently shake my hand. "Your timing, once again, is perfect. May I suggest now might be the most appropriate time for a thanksgiving meal?" He indicated lunch all ready and waiting. "Shall we?"

I waited for the crowd to pass and went to follow, but found my hand once more firmly grasped. This time by Riah. I stopped and turned. She tugged twice, so I sat back down, perched on the edge of my chair. "Yes, princess?"

I hadn't meant to use that name, it just flowed from my lips. Her eyes again blew me away. They were beautiful and pure, but there was an intensity, similar to Val's, that had taken over their depths. I had to be careful not to drown in those waters. She stood in front of me, kitted out in her own strong, intricately-woven red armour, detailed with vines and flowers. Her jaw was set, her eyes on fire. I had a glimpse of the intimidatingly gorgeous woman this young girl would grow into.

Whether her ordeal had stolen her ability or desire to talk, I didn't know. But I did know she had suffered terribly. To have that intensity in one so young was frightening.

Then, in an instant, she switched to the most beatific smile and fiercely embraced me, knocking me back into my chair, clinging to my neck. I knew then I would give my life to protect this kid.

I eased her up and got back to my feet. I was trying to protect my sore hand—made all the worse from the welcoming—when Raph came and stood before me. He didn't say a word.

I knew he struggled with me being there. I had heard this morning's conversation with Kait. But now I sort of understood why the boy would be uneasy. I perched back on the edge of my chair so I could meet him eye to eye, and waited. He reached over and took my swollen hand in both of his. This time I couldn't hide my grimace and may have even groaned. Quietly, mind you.

He just closed his eyes and murmured something I couldn't quite understand. My whole body relaxed, and my jaw dropped as all the pain, even the pain I hadn't yet registered, diffused then disappeared. Now it was my turn to be speechless.

"You have not had a family in a while, have you?" He still held on to my hand. "We know what that is like. It is not nice. But we never had to live in a tree. That must have been horrible ... and lonely. We have a spare bunk here if you decide to stay." He gently laid my hand back on my leg, then, with his eyes glued to the ground, he went to join the others at the table.

I flexed my healed hand but stopped mid-step on my way to the others. Something had caught my attention in the backyard. I could have sworn I saw someone walking towards the clothesline hidden behind the patio wall. Fear trickled down my spine and I raced to the glass doors to check it out.

"What is it, Dan?" Val was the first to come to attention.

"I thought I saw someone in the backyard. I must be seeing things. How could anyone get in?" At the silence from the table, I turned to see glances being exchanged and felt the tension increase around the room. "Should I go and check?" I didn't really want to. The hairs on the back of my neck were standing and a chill caressed my spine. But I'd just signed on the dotted line, so I guess I had to offer?

"Nonsense, come and join us for lunch, Daniel. What will be, will be. We are about to give thanks to the Light for all he has given us and for bringing you into our family. What's out there can wait." Abbot said.

Would I ever get used to the weirdness of this crew? Someone could be about to break in. But apparently, they were going to have to wait till Abbot was ready to receive them. Which, by the looks of things, wasn't going to be until after lunch.

Finally making my way to the table, I couldn't help but feel a sense of calm. I took my time to survey my new "family" as they sat around the table. I mean, what could I possibly have to fear when I was surrounded by a small army of freakingly intimidating warriors, each of whom had their own huge, skirt-scary sword strapped to their back?

I allowed myself to get swept along with their celebration and thanksgiving focusing on the Light. Abbot spoke out loud to Him as they all respectfully bowed their heads in His presence. I wasn't quite sure what to do, so I just watched them and listened to the words.

It was pretty cool. It was like the Light was a real person there in the room and He was being included in the conversation. Soon all else was replaced by Raph's brilliant lunch, and excited conversation.

Up until now

I had been living in a two-dimensional picture but then, all of a sudden, the ground, the horizon, the sky hurtled away from me in every direction at the speed of light. A hook had been attached to the inside of my gut and I had been forcibly ripped inside out, and I was left standing as a tiny speck, with no grounding, in a limitless universe.

In a weird sense, I felt like I had just been born and everything—every experience, taste, sight, touch, smell and sound—was all new. All I had known was still there ... but gone. How could I climb back through the infinitesimal hole through which I had been inverted?

It was definitely frightening.

So much that I had never even imagined.

But, how could I?

How could anyone imagine something they have no previous knowledge of? What words, what pictures do you use to describe something totally beyond your comprehension? Something so utterly alien to your existence?

I had always been the centre of my world—my safety and my survival had been my only priority. But now I was nothing ... no, not nothing. I was something. But something very small in a very big picture, and I had no idea what that picture looked like or what part I was supposed to play.

Last night, the voice said He'd had a plan and a purpose for me. Now I knew that truth with a certainty, and it was part of what felt so incredibly right about it all. Not only the people, the comfort, and the peace, but now I had a hope for the future and a purpose. That was new and it was exciting. The promise of being useful and to play a significant role for others.

Turning to Raph who sat beside me, I said, "Thanks for what you did for my hand, and thanks for this amazing meal." I would never look at this kid in the same light again, regardless of how annoying he might be. "I don't know how you make so much out of so little, and how you make it taste so good. You're a pretty special guy, and I just wanted you to know I appreciate what you've done for me, and the invitation to stay." It wasn't much, but it was genuine, and it was a start.

He didn't look up or respond, but his cheeks reddened to tomatoes and he dropped his head to his chest.

Skrat, did I just make things worse?

Despite my uncertainty about Raph's feelings, the mood after lunch was relaxed and peaceful. I was full, clean, warm, and feeling pretty excited about the potential of my future when Suit Dude walked through—yes, that's right, through—the closed glass doors from the patio.

"Frackety skrat ..." I was at a loss for words, or at least socially appropriate ones.

"Oooh, Daniel, keep it up baby, you're making me all hot and bothered." He made his way over, pulled up a stool next to the kitchen counter, and leaned back like he owned the place.

"What the hell?" Something other than my brain had taken control of my mouth.

"Oh yeah, that's it." He started fanning himself. "You're speaking my love language, baby. But I know you can do better than that," he purred.

I quickly glanced around the table, trying to get a read on everyone else. Was I the only one seeing this guy?

Abbot wore a rueful smile. Marcus and Kait had clenched jaws. Tessa and Raph were white. Riah's eyes sparked with rage whilst Val's were calculating. So, they knew Suit Dude, but still, no one was saying anything, so I asked, "Who are you?"

"Well, I kind of like 'Suit Dude'. That's not one I've heard before, and believe me, I've heard them all. Some call me Lucifer." He dropped his head and waved his arms in an expansive bow. "Some call me Baal." He morphed into a beefed-up body builder with a loincloth and a bull's head. "I have many names, but here in Sodom, they call me Ashera, or the goddess."

"He" then turned into a "she" of significant proportions. The green and blue scales imitated by her acolytes—the temple prostitutes—were her only covering. "But enough about me, I'm here to talk to you." He turned back into Suit Dude.

"I warned you, Daniel. I told you if you stayed with them, they would trap you. You should have left whilst you had the chance. Now you and I are immortal enemies, and I will do everything I can to destroy you, unless ...?" His voice was deep and mellow and would have been comforting if it hadn't been for the fact that my blood had chilled, my heart slammed, and every sense screamed at me to Run. For. My. Life.

I snuck another quick peek around the table and still, no one had moved or said a word. "Unless what? What do you want?" I was freaking out of my fried brain.

"Unless you change your mind and join me instead."

22

ABBOT

It was, sadly, inevitable. No one can come into the Light without drawing attention and attack from the Dark. Poor Daniel was in his crosshairs. I knew he was coming, but the Light let us celebrate first, as I suspected He would. In his way, the Dark was putting on a show for the lad and trying to be as off-putting as possible.

"Ooh, Daniel, I warned you, if you kept talking dirty, I wouldn't be able to control myself."

Daniel must have been rattling off a chain of expletives in his mind.

"What the ..."

"Go on, say it," the Dark purred.

"No, you freaking weirdo."

"Careful, sweetie, you're playing with fire and you're about to get very, very burnt." The Dark cackled malevolently at his own joke. Valarie, sitting to his left, laid a hand on Daniel's arm, trying to warn him to stay quiet. The fear and confusion pulsing out of him were not enough to shut down his other senses completely. He complied.

"Good call, my dear Valarrrie. Daniel, I am being a bit unfair, I really should introduce myself properly so that you may give me my due honour." He bowed theatrically. "I am ... the Dark Lord, and it is a pleasure to be with you all again, *dear* ones." He looked over at me, obviously making fun of my endearments. For a being as old as time, he really could be quite childish.

"I really must make an effort to visit you more often," he continued. "You are all looking so well. So deliciousss."

He then allowed the physical tent he walked in to melt away, and the enormity of the evil within him was released to pollute the room. The intensity of the Darkness shrouded us all. Warmth departed and hope diminished. His disembodied voice continued like the stench of fetid food and oozed its way around the room.

I am a child of the Light and I knew I was safe in His care, but even still, icy fingers of fear tickled my spine and attempted to worm their way through to my heart. I resisted the sharp fear, driven firmer and deeper than anything mortal could instil.

His disembodied voice slithered smoothly from one corner of the ceiling to another. The bottomless well of the universe's shadows clung to him like a cloak. To see within the folds was an impossibility —and it was a mercy not to.

"Valarrrie ..." The word uncoiled; a snake departing a rotting corpse. "Ssso good to chat with you again." The irony dripping like acid, licking away at a shield of faith. "I come once again to tempt you with my offer, child."

Dreadful weight meshed painfully with frozen anticipation. Silence screamed.

"Come to me, be my queen of Sssodom. I have been cultivating this city for yearsss and, finally, it has come of age. After only one pitiable generation I possesss it all and the pathetic little beasssts who ssspawn here. But, say the word and I will withdraw, and it will be yoursss. You will all be free to walk in the light." The last word was spat like poison across the void.

Val knew what was coming. She inhaled deeply. Slowly. Her eyes closed. On her exhale she answered, "My Father is Light. It is written that you are the 'Father of Lies'. There is no truth in you, and when you lie you speak your native language." Quiet. Polite. Humble. "I choose the Light."

"Oh, how quaint, my dear Valarrrie. Come now, give me one of theesse and I will remove your burden. You will be free from pain for the ressst of your life." The temptation was presented like a poisoned apple.

"I wouldn't mind housing Daniel in my ssstable. To think, I almost had him in Gomorrrrah ..."

A lion's purr prowled around the table.

"But then again, I've alwaysss been partial to my sweet Contesss-sa." His throaty chuckle turned my stomach. "However, they are getting a bit long in the tooth, so how about I have them both? What do you sssay? It would be ssso easy. They are untrained and a liability. Give them over to me and you will not be responsible for them anymore."

Silence.

"No? Then return to me Ssariah and Raphael. I will place a banner of truccce over them. They will be under my protection, never to be touched by my minionsss again." He crooned, "Imagine the peace, Valarrie, knowing they were sssafe."

The silence between his propositions rang like a clanging bell. My lunch threatened to return. My sweet, beautiful children bargained for by the Beast.

Val's chest swelled then relaxed.

"I cannot give what is not mine." Quiet. Gentle. Humble. "Yet, I have been called as a child of the Light to fight the good fight and to guard those in my care. For it is written, 'The Light entered the world as one of us, to be with us and to save us.' He has already won the eternal victory over Darkness. I choose to stand for these in the Light."

"Oh, how terribly brave, sssilly girl. Do you feel like a victor, Valarrrie? I have made you a human pincushion. I have buried bladesss deep into your flesh; knivesss lodged into every joint in your body. Foolish woman."

Silence.

"You'd rather be buried beneath this conssstant, exhausssting pain? You'd choossse a life of balancing on a razor's blade; battling to keep going, fighting to stay in control and not lash out and destroy everyone and everything around you?"

Silence.

"You know it isss for nothing. No one knowsss, no one seesss, no one understands your sacrificcce. You are completely alone ... and pathetic."

The air was charged with sulphuric electricity.

"Where is your precious Light now? How can He love you and let me do thisss to you? You are nothing to Him. Curse the Light and I will take it all away."

Val breathed in. Breathed out. Breathed in.

And answered, "It is written, 'the Light is love', and He says, 'Come to me all who are weary and heavy burdened and I will give you rest, for my burden is Light.'" Quiet. Gentle. Humble. Valarie parried, "I choose the burden of Light."

"If it's a burden you want, a burden I can give you. I will take each and every knife buried in your body, roughen the blade and sink them all back in again, deeper, wider, heavier. Orrr"—the word hung in the tension, a worm on a hook—"I can remove them all; all the pain. This is your lassst chance. I can *lighten* your load or increase your burden ... your choiccce."

Valarie looked to me. She knew, because of the bond we shared and the Badge I carried, the increase of her personal suffering would cause me emotional pain. Nothing compared to hers, of course. But she was asking my permission. In the midst of her greatest trial, she put me first.

How could I allow anything to increase her suffering or cause her greater anguish? I gave her the smallest of nods, then shut my eyes and wept as the pain of her suffering and the cost of her sacrifice pierced me like a blade to my own heart.

Quiet. Polite. Humble. Valarie conquered. "I choose the Light."

"Foolish, stupid little girl. Ssso be it." Viscous insolence, vile indifference, vicious malevolence, the true character of the Dark Lord.

Within a fractured heartbeat, the air was teeming with frenetic creatures. Miniature monkeys, with long snaking tails thrashing wildly and whipping anything within their reach. Everything on the table was jettisoned around the room, spilled and shattered.

Talons, short and jagged, razor sharp, carving, cutting, creating havoc. Strong sinewy arms snapping, sawing, grasping everything in reach. Human heads with fangs dripping, saliva spraying, and foul breath wrapped around us.

And all of them converged on Valarie. Before she could draw her sword or had a chance to throw her arms over her face, she was swamped. Her body disappeared beneath a cloak of demonic beasts.

Her cry was muffled as she sank beneath the onslaught. There were too many of them. Each time she raised an arm to swat them away, she left herself vulnerable. They got underneath her arms, around her legs, under her chin, and with their tiny claws worked away at her armour's bindings.

Dan reached for her, unaware that we could not help her. We could not protect her. This was her burden to bear. We were all torn as we watched her go under.

Her cries were muted as she tucked her head and arms into a ball to protect her body. However, this created gaps. Needle-like fingers worked their way in and dislodged her helmet. They dug their way in under her gauntlets and grieves.

Time paused. The room froze. The beasts stilled. Then each one grasped a knife buried in her body. As one, they removed each blade from her flesh and bone.

Stillness.

Valarie unfurled with a gasp and filled her lungs with the peace that comes with release from deep, bone aching, nerve-fraying, pain and torment. Her eyes wide open. Shocked white orbs surrounded by opened, bleeding flesh. Blessed relief and freedom from chronic suffering.

Stillness.

She held that breath and all that she could of that sweet moment, as each of the blades increased in length and width. With quiet snickers, saliva dripping and hungry eyes, the creatures waited for the command. As one, they each plunged their knives back into her body.

All control was gone. Her restraint broken. Valarie screamed.

Her cry blended with screeches of laughter. Branches clawing glass on a windy night.

My heart shattered into a myriad of iron shards and I slumped under the weight of her additional suffering.

With their job completed, the demons were gone. A void opened and we were pitched into emptiness. We hung over a chasm of despair. Then the cloak was lifted, the warmth returned, and a glow radiated once more.

Valarie dropped her head as tears rolled through the blood leaking from the multiple gashes across her face. She rested her bloody arms across her torn legs, forearms up, palms open, fingers cupped. A quiet moan escaped her. The pain was back, and her burden of inescapable illness had increased.

Tessa ran to the bathroom to fill the bath. I sat and tried to adjust to the new weight of Valarie's suffering and not break underneath her torment. Raphael came to me and wrapped his arms around my frail shoulders, cradling my heavy head, lending strength and warmth and comfort as only he could.

This however was tainted with the added grief that he could not assist Valarie in any way. A lesson learned from experience. His gift was an immense blessing, but one that did not cover all those who suffered and all types of suffering. We struggled with the truth of limitations. Our Badges were gifts of grace beyond our imagining, yet they came with restrictions. Why Raphael could not heal or reduce the suffering of Valarie was a mystery to us all.

I watched Sariah pick her way to Valarie through the smashed remains of our meal splayed across the floor. She knelt in front of her and gently leaned in, resting her forehead against Valarie's. It was red from multiple gashes, but it seemed the only place free from knife hilts.

Sariah raised her hand, placing her palm on Valarie's shredded cheek, forcing all the peace she could into the woman's shattered body. I could sense the child's concern and love, and the question she longed to ask.

Slowly Valarie opened her eyes and responded with the hint of a smile. Everything was going to be alright.

Moments later, Tessa returned and, together with Kaitlyn, led Valarie to the bathroom.

23

———

DANIEL

What the hell was that?

I know one thing it was. It was the scariest skrat I'd ever seen or felt. Ever. I didn't belong here. The Dark asked for me. They could have turned me over. But they didn't. Val said she would protect me, all of us.

I didn't know what was going on, I felt so utterly lost and confused. I had walked out of a wilderness I knew into a jungle I couldn't fathom. I'd been scared before. I had been given to Soldier as a toy for public humiliation and torture, for crying out loud. But that, I knew how to fight. I knew how to run and hide when I had to. But how the hell was I supposed to fight the Dark Lord?

I could take care of myself, but I was not ready to go up against that thing. Freaking "immortal enemies". What the hell did that even mean? I didn't know how to defend myself against it. It'd been years since I'd felt so weak, so vulnerable …

Skrat a fracking cat!

Damn it, I would not go out without a fight.

I will stay as long as they let me, I will learn this new way and I will do what I can to help. I will not be powerless. I will not be intimidated. I will learn. I will fight and win. Or die trying.

Twice in two days, I'd had my mind invaded and my soul stretched to breaking. The peace and excitement I had been revelling in from the first had dissolved into a fractured nightmare at the second.

24

ABBOT

"And now you have experienced the Dark, young man."

You must pull yourself together, old one. Now was not the time to drop the ball, burdening others to carry a load determined for me to bear. Raphael was such a blessing, not necessarily helping to carry the weight of Valarie's pain so much as bolstering me as I donned my figurative harness and ploughed on. He was a true gift of the Light at the time I needed it most.

It saddened me to admit I'd reached my limit. The weight of others' burdens had become too heavy and taxing. I was far too tired and weak to continue swimming through the slurry of afflictions, pain and sorrow that surrounded me. I had lost the ability to deflect their anger, frustrations and fear. Now I drank the cup and it was a toxic tonic indeed.

Yet there was little room for self-pity. I was also buoyed by their happiness, joy, and laughter. Once again, the Light had proven gracious to gift me with the healing of Raphael, the joy of Tessa, and the peace of Sariah in my final days. What a journey it had been and what a wonderful way to pass the baton, so to speak.

But, now was not the time for war, it was a time for peace. For it was the best way to deal with the current chaos. Busy minds had facilitated busy hands and the carnage of our dining room had been cleaned up quick smart. Presently, we adjourned to the sitting room.

Daniel's peace had been shattered along with Raphael and Tessa's. Marcus and Kaitlyn were enraged and ready for battle, spurred on by their protective instincts for their children, and in defence of their mentor and valued friend. Sariah's red armour was a flickering inferno. She was a burning fire whose coals had been stoked to a greater intensity. Time to act before someone behaved rashly and more damage was done.

"Daniel, I wonder if you would mind terribly if I unburdened my story onto you. It may help you understand a bit more of what is going on and perhaps you may understand a bit more of our sister, Valarie. I know she won't mind me telling you as this is my story, but I doubt she would ever tell you herself."

Raphael came to sit in Sariah's chair and laid his head on the armrest between us. I rested my hand on his head, stroking his thick, raven hair, and even there I felt his healing waves being cast out to me. Sariah came to sit on my lap. She was getting a bit big for that now, but, since both of us were small, it was comfortable enough. We were two small sparrows sharing a perch.

Raphael noticed Kaitlyn making her way back to join us. "Did she pass out this time?"

"No, sweetheart. She is better at dealing with it now, and each time she is attacked, she gets stronger. We've put her in a hot bath to give her some relief. But be assured, when Val is ready to ask for help, we will do what we can. She'll definitely be out of action for a few days, but she'll be alright." Kaitlyn took her place in the circle, via the twins, laying a hand on each of their heads as she passed. "Did you know her name means 'strong' and 'brave'? I think that's more than just a name, don't you?" She winked at Raphael. "Abbot has known her longer than any of us, and I think you'll enjoy his story." Kaitlyn graciously handed the focus back to me, so I began:

Many years ago in my home of Hormah, Children of Light
used to gather in the open to worship. I led a small gathering,

but times changed and it became dangerous to meet in public,
so we met in a grotto by the river—a beautiful wide-mouthed
cave at the edge of the water, with a small cave at the back
where I made a simple sanctuary. I didn't have much but my
needs were few; I was content and at peace ... for a while.
As the Dark Lord took hold of our city, many who had said
they were Children of Light were in fact not. Or had decided
they weren't anymore, the lure of the Dark too strong. And
with that, the Great Persecution started.
I never knew whom in my flock I could truly trust. True Children of Light became hunted—prized trophies.
The day came when I had to face trial. If I could convince the
authorities of the truth about the Light I would earn my right
to continue. If they weren't satisfied, I would be condemned.
They set up a gallows in the cavern. And like flies to a carcass,
a crowd gathered.
What was I going to say? It was hard to concentrate with the
noose ready and waiting.
I didn't even notice a young woman push her way through the
growing crowd. 'What's going on?' she inquired, as if she
couldn't see.
'They are going to hang me. I have to make sure everything is
ready.' I was surprised that my voice belied my nerves.
'Peace be with you,' the girl said. I remember thinking, 'Silly
thing, can't you see I am about to die?' but strangely enough, I
was at peace. She said it again, 'Peace be with you.' But this
time her voice was different.

"I believe you might have heard that same voice earlier this
evening, Daniel?" He was focused on my story, hanging on every
word; they all were. So, I continued:

I was captured by the Light in her eyes. Valarie was merely a
conduit for the Light; a vessel. The Light spoke to me. He
showed me and told me many things, but finally He declared,

'You will not die here today.' Valarie reached out and steadied me, noticing that my legs were about to give way.

'Who are you?' I said.

'I am no one. He spoke to you, didn't He?' she replied softly. All I could do was dumbly nod my head. She continued, 'Well then, you are not going to die here today.'

I was still in shock from hearing His voice and trying to come to terms with her bizarre statement. 'How can we stop it?'

At that point, the Councillor looked up from his watch and declared, 'It is time!' Valarie's face changed. She was so fierce and intimidating. I caught only a glimpse as she spun to confront my executioner and openly defied them all: 'Stop.'

I continued by imitating the gruff voice of the Councillor. This brought forth a giggle from Sariah.

'Who do you think you are to interfere with this official proceeding?' He was outraged and stiff with resentment. He had planned a hanging and that is what the crowd had come to see, and no young upstart was going to ruin it for them. She was only a few years older than you are now, Tessa.

Valarie raised her voice so that everyone there, including the hangman, could be in no doubt. Her voice rang like thunder. 'This man will *not* die here today.'

Indignation slithered through the muttering crowd. Then silence echoed throughout the grotto. No one moved, no one spoke. So she repeated her bold declaration, 'This man will not die here today.'

'By whose authority do you stand in our way? What powers have you to interfere?' the hangman demanded.

Standing there behind Valarie's right shoulder, I seemed to see her for the first time. She was in her armour of course and shone with indigo Light. It was beautiful—fearsome and frightening, but stunningly wonderful at the same time. And I was only seeing her from the back. I couldn't help but be encouraged.

I, too, was filled with the power of the Light and saw that I was clothed in my own armour of orange. I remember looking down and thinking I was like fire. The Light flickered all over me, creating its own design; it gave me such courage. I stood taller and stronger behind her, ready to take them all on. I was not going to lie down and die. They could kill me, but not before I gave them a jolly good fight.

Valarie turned to the river and held up her hand, and His voice came forth from her mouth, 'Stop.'

It boomed throughout the grotto and ricocheted to the water. The river bucked and roared, but did not, could not, continue past the platform in front of my cave. The water upstream had nowhere to go, so it banked up into a monstrosity; a violent wall of raging water, desperately seeking an outlet. The sky turned black with thunderous clouds, boiling over with fury. The whole of nature was violently opposed to being restrained.

The entire crowd walked out onto the platform, curious to see this 'Act of God'. The executioner furiously pushed his way to the front, expecting to take charge of the situation. Valarie turned and put her arm on my shoulder and we walked into my retreat.

We heard an almighty crash and a deafening roar of released water. A small wave licked around the corner of where we stood and receded, inviting us to follow. We stepped out into the bright sunlight reflecting off the rock platform that had been washed clean, and stood in shocked awe.

The sky was the clearest blue and everything was freshly cleansed. A hint of frangipani infused the air. The crowd, the executioner, the gallows and noose, my lectern and everything else had been swept away.

That day, Valarie introduced me to her mother, Joy. Together they invited me to join them in their exodus—the Light had determined destruction for Hormah. That was how I met Valarie—and Joy, who became very special to me in the short time we had together.

Kaitlyn had slipped out unnoticed and now returned, assisting Valarie. As one, we all turned to stare at Valarie. Poor dear, she hated being the centre of attention, but sometimes that just couldn't be helped.

Kaitlyn did her best to offer a diversion. "You will all be happy to know we have been given a few weeks' peace and respite. Time for Val to adjust to her new burden, for us to prepare, and for Daniel to start the adjustment to this way of life ... if he decides to stay.

"During this time, we are covered. We'll be safe in public and won't be vulnerable to physical attack. After this, however, the final battle will take place."

She and Valarie had made their way to Valarie's chair, and after she had been made comfortable, Kaitlyn turned to the twins. "But just because we have a break from attack, doesn't mean you get a break from schoolwork."

Glancing at her watch, she continued. "You guys have fifteen minutes. Raph, get your head around what needs to be done for dinner and make a plan. Riah, let the chooks out, check their water and rake the pen. Then, both of you meet me in the study." Tessa came under her scrutiny. "Do you need to finish anything in the laundry?" Even though this was presented as a question, we all knew it was not. And with that, Kaitlyn began clearing the room.

25

DANIEL

I felt so out of place. I hadn't been sent off with a task, but I wasn't sure if I was supposed to go as well. So, with no better option, I stayed in my seat next to Val's. Marcus came and squatted in front of her and Abbot took his vacated chair.

"Is it really bad, old girl?" Marcus's voice broke.

But instead of answering, Val looked to Abbot, whose face was wet with tears. "Are you okay?" she asked him.

He nodded slightly, eased himself out of the chair, smiled through his tears and gently kissed her on the head before leaving to join Sariah in the garden.

Marcus shuffled his chair closer to Val's, so she could rest her head on his shoulder. The multiple cuts on her face shone with freshly shed tears. I felt like an intruder, but Marcus explained as he lightly stroked her hair.

"Abbot's badge is Feeling other people's ... I guess you'd say, 'feelings'. He feels other people's joy and happiness but also their pain and suffering. The closer he is to them, the stronger he absorbs it.

"Abbot and Val have been together now for about ten years and he feels all of her emotional pain—not the physical pain, but her anguish, and fear." He shook his head and chuckled at my reaction.

"Yes, she experiences fear." Then he continued, "When Val encounters the Dark Lord, the consequences aren't just hers to bear. It's made all the more difficult, because she knows how much Abbot will suffer from her decision."

It was the first time that I had seen Val give any evidence of something softer than steel inside her. She allowed Marcus to comfort her and showed no embarrassment. The flow of her tears slowed. I found it hard to get my head around her being so vulnerable. It softened her facade and made her more human.

But it also intensified my admiration for her. She had let me see all her brokenness, her vulnerability, her weakness, and I was honoured. In a way, it was the most welcoming, inclusive gesture I could imagine.

"If it's okay with you guys, I think I might stay for a while longer. I know I have heaps to learn, I feel as useful as a chocolate teapot but ... I really want to help. I really want my piece in all of this. I've never been so skrat-scared, freaked out, felt so bloody useless, or completely ignorant, but I have never felt so alive and ..." My gut turned at the thought of that freak and what he'd done to Val. But then my blood boiled when I thought of the twins, of Raphael and how he'd been—was still— tormented. Of Tessa and how she'd been used. But most of all, I was ready to split heads when I thought of Sariah and what he'd done to her.

"Well, I just really want in. I want to do whatever I can to fight that kret, whenever and wherever we find him. And I'll do what I can, whatever it takes, to learn to do that to the best of my ability."

Val looked at me through her glistening eyes, gritted her teeth and nodded her head. Deal. Then, before I knew what was happening, Kait was back and I was being hustled out the front gate with Tessa, apparently on a tour to familiarise myself with the area. So, I guess that answered that question. I, too, was to give Val some space.

Later that evening, lying on my cot, not in the "study" but amongst the others, I had time to think, and try to regather my thoughts that had exploded like a deck of cards around the room. My new sight had allowed me to see not only the armour they all wore, but the Warriors of Light who constantly accompanied them. They were stationed all around the house. When we'd left for our walk, some had peeled off and joined us. The rest stayed put.

Tall imposing figures, pure and unblemished, stoic and intimidating. Each unique in features but emitting the same bright golden light. Tessa reassured me that they were on our side and would follow us wherever we went, to help in the fight. "They are actually our first line of defence," she said.

If I'd known about these guys earlier, I may have been keener to join up. I looked up at the one standing next to me. "Hey." I felt a bit lame when all I got was a smile and a nod in response.

"Yeah, we don't"—Tessa screwed up her face searching for the right word—"socialise. They stay with us and protect us, but they have their own orders." She'd beamed a smile at the one closest to her. "We appreciate them." He smiled back. "But whilst we're on the same side, we have different orders or ... roles." She tilted her head. "Does that make sense?"

"Possibly?" I had trouble not tripping over my feet during the walk, turning myself inside out in an attempt to check these guys out. Two stayed close, one to me and one to Tessa, but there were several others who scouted the periphery. By the time we made it back, I'd made up my mind. When I grew up, I wanted to be just like these guys.

Tessa had been pretty cool that afternoon, giving me space to get over my initial fandom for the Warriors of Light, and start trying to come to terms with what had just happened. She was supposed to be showing me around, but since we'd been declared "safe" for a few weeks, we both knew it was a convenient guise for our eviction, to give Val some privacy and for me to begin to adjust.

I snuggled down under the warm blankets and rolled my head over the pillow inhaling deeply. Clean, crisp, and cool with a hint of fragrance. Lavender? Eucalyptus? I couldn't tell exactly, but it was a blend of pure luxury. It reminded me of summer days, clear skies after rain, of outdoors and gardens. The freshness of the cotton, the softness of the pillow, the hug of the cot under me was blissing me out. I would never take this splendour for granted.

This crew really were different from any other people I knew, except perhaps Abraham. They hadn't known me but had taken me in off the street and brought me into their home where they were vulnerable.

They'd fed and clothed me even though a couple of them really didn't want me there. Raph, a traumatised kid, put his own feelings aside and invited me to stay. Tessa, whom I rattled, on purpose, opened up and was honest with me. Kait considered me one of her kids and Marcus called me "son".

But perhaps the most revealing and trusting gesture of all was Val letting me see her broken and weak, needing the support of those around her. She was the antithesis of Commander.

They'd put my needs first, despite the serious pain in the butt of having a stranger in their midst. And they had extended their boundaries and their limited budget to include me. But more than anything else, they had looked beyond my wretched exterior and awarded me value far greater than I was worth.

26

DANIEL

Even in the hazy world that exists between sleep and consciousness, I knew I was bathed in light. I clung desperately to the mist until, inevitably, memories crowded my awareness. One, I had slept dream-free for the first time in ... forever. Two, my internal alarm was offline, and I had slept deeply. Three, I'd not been woken by cold, hunger or whispering freaks. And four, the most intoxicating aroma sang like a siren, tempting me from the comfort of my bed.

Muffled music forged its way through a door from behind me. The hum and thump of some form of machinery worked away down the hallway. But more importantly, my bladder demanded attention. I reluctantly brought closure to the security of slumber and slowly opened my eyes, wondering what on earth this day would bring.

I was met by a living wall of colour, starting from Riah's corner where she had drawn a tree, which in turn, had taken possession of the whole space. Twisting tendrils claimed purchase of the surrounding walls and converted grey concrete into spectacular life.

In the morning light I had ample opportunity to take in the wonder of her creation. The lines, colours and textures were enough to take my mind off my other needs, but not for long.

From the bathroom, I made my way back out to the living space and now heard faint laughter mixing with the music coming from the garage. Out of the large glass doors I saw Riah and Raph, working with Abbot in the garden.

"Good morning."

I looked around and saw Val wrapped in a blanket, sitting in her armchair. Her feet were propped up on a stool and she too was gazing at the scene outside. "Why don't you pour two coffees and come and join me?"

My head was still foggy, my eyes were blurred, and my body ached. I was completely disorientated as I dragged myself to the kitchen. Once again, I had slept like a baby but woken feeling like I had gone the full ten rounds.

Normally I stirred at first light, adrenaline pumping and on the move—mostly because I was too cold, hungry and exposed to sleep or stay put. On the streets, coffee was a supreme treat. I could normally pull in a few coins by busking, but since I couldn't afford the bribes, I had to keep moving my patch. It wasn't big money, but it kept me from starving and supplied the basic necessities.

Placing the cups on a small table near the seats, I collapsed into my chair, slid into a comfortable slouch, and feasted my eyes on the garden. Raph and Riah were laughing with Abbot as they struggled to pick up and carry something that kept falling out of their over-loaded arms.

Out of the corner of my eye, I caught a glimpse of yellow fabric. Leaning forward, I saw Tessa round the edge of the patio partition, hanging out clothes. She was somehow involved in the game and they were all laughing. The glass doors were shut so I couldn't hear them. It looked like fun, but I didn't have the energy or inclination to pursue that any further. I was perfectly content to sit, slouch, and spy. And give the caffeine time to work its wonders, whilst not getting too freaked out by the armour they all wore. And the ridiculously large swords they all carried.

As I was blissing out, memories of yesterday started to creep back through small holes of clarity. Soon the thin layer of denial was shattered by a tidal wave of reality. "Val, can I ask you a question?" I started.

"Only one?" she chuckled.

"What's with the knives?"

She didn't turn or protest, she continued to stare out the window. I started to think she wasn't going to answer, when she began, "In the world you have just come from, where we all begin, fighting is a three-dimensional experience. It involves your body, your will and your mind." She paused, took a slow, steady breath, then continued, "There is a trigger, a tension, and an end. Your opponent either hits the ground and stays down or gets up and crawls away. They may or may not come back to fight another day. Physical fighting is external—you can leave, and you can rest. It may haunt your memories and dwell in your consciousness, but that's your choice. It doesn't matter what kind of fight it is, or how long it lasts. It always follows that pattern."

She slowly turned to look at me. She knew I understood. However, I didn't bother suggesting the alternative ending of perhaps your opponent winning and you hitting the ground. That didn't seem to be something she understood.

"In your new world, fighting is four-dimensional. You still need to use your body, mind, and will, but it is also internal. And it never stops. You never get a rest, because it doesn't end, until you die." She smiled to herself, like it was a personal joke. But I didn't think that sounded funny.

"You simply can't walk away. It's like Abbot said, we are born in the Dark, it is our culture—ingrained into everything we do, think and say. When we enter the Light—or I should say, the Light enters us—the Dark has to be cut back to make room.

"But even though it has been pruned, the trunk and the roots of Dark are well and truly embedded in our being. The Dark Lord does not control the darkness in us, but it is the part of us he has a grip on.

"The Lord of Light has a grip on the Light that lives in us. Spiritual battle is about reducing the Dark and increasing the Light. This fight is over the territory of our being—our soul." She looked back out the window.

I wasn't really sure I was ready to hear all this, but I guessed forewarned was forearmed. So, I waited quietly till she was ready to continue.

"Abbot explained, the way of Darkness is to worship and satisfy self. The way of Light is to serve and consider others. More specifically, to love the Lord of Light and, out of that, love others. Basically, in everything we do, we decide whom we glorify: ourselves or Him."

She waited till I'd given her my full attention. "But listen, there is a big difference between self-care and self-worship, and we must understand this in order not to turn that which is good and right, into something that can be a hindrance. This will be part of your training. Self-discipline is self-defence."

I let that sit. It was going to take time to get my head around it all. But it still didn't answer my question. "I can kind of get that ... but what has that got to do with the knives?"

"Because nothing drives you further inward, nothing makes you more selfish, more self-absorbed and more self-centred, than unrelenting physical pain." She ended in a whisper. Her face was grey and her body slumped in the chair.

I think the mention of it brought her suffering back into focus. I allowed the soothing aroma of my coffee to calm me. I tested the temperature with the edge of my lip. It was still too hot. I snuck a sideways glimpse at Val. Her eyes were fixed to the scene outside, her coffee untouched, her body held in a way, I suspected, offered the least pain possible. Whilst I could sort of see her point, I was still confused. "If the Lord of Light is supposed to be Love, and you said he was stronger than the Dark, why does he let you suffer such horrible pain?"

She offered a small smile that didn't reach her eyes. "To live life is to experience pain, Daniel. We can't escape it. And to live in the Light is to offer sacrifice. We don't seek pain, but we don't run from it either. We don't enjoy it, but we don't let it stop us, or shut us down. We can't be afraid of pain, but when we can see past it, and choose to freely offer ourselves in sacrifice despite it, we are demonstrating love. It is to this Love we are called."

"But Val, why do you have to suffer so much? I don't think I could do it. It's too hard. I don't get why such a 'loving Other' could let you pointlessly suffer like this. Why?"

Colour came to her cheeks, and a glint returned to her eyes. "Because He knows me, loves me and wants me safe. I love to fight and I'm good at it. It is my purpose—I am a warrior and I am His." She paused and looked at her hands still covered with fresh wounds. "But I am proud and arrogant. And this is the Dark's handle on me. It's a major chink in my armour.

"Through my pride and arrogance, the Dark can get to me and cut me down. I am unprotected in battle and therefore useless because of this weakness in my armour. The Light knows my weakness and is helping me overcome this so that I may be strong, protected and safe. My stumbling block is pride, and nothing has such a conclusive victory over pride"—she turned to me, ramped up the laser beam in her eyes and pinned me to the back of my chair—"than humility."

That was such an ugly word. "I don't know, Val, it just seems too much."

"Don't for a moment think I like this. Or that it's easy. In my whole life, this is the hardest thing I have ever had to bear. If I didn't have such an amazing family around me, I don't know how I could do it. On one hand, I accept it and acknowledge it for the blessing that it is —it's growing and strengthening me. But on the other hand, I hate it with every fibre of my being. I long for the day when it will end."

Suddenly, the laughter and music that had been muted by my focus on Val, burst into the room. I jumped when Marcus and Kait tumbled through the doorway, eyes sparkling, cheeks glowing, faces flushed, embracing each other. Totally preoccupied, they waltzed their way across the room.

27

KAITLYN

Knowing we had a few weeks of protection and freedom was such an incredible blessing. A gift of stress-free, quality time. Well, as stress free as a traumatised family in transition could be. We had some planning to do, but we had space.

I had been given the gift of opportunity to make one-on-one time with Marcus, my bear of a man. No one could infuriate me, anger me, make me laugh or cry or want to destroy things or rip my hair out, inspire me or love me like Marcus. He was far from perfect ... very far, as was I. But he was perfect for me. The Light filled me, but Marcus completed me.

The truck was organised, and we'd made a start, going through the garage, sorting what needed to come with us and what could stay. This took a lot longer than it should have as we made time for some significant one-on-one distractions. But now it was time to get back to the others.

"Hey Val, are you ready for a change of scenery or are you okay there?" I asked.

"Thanks, Kait, I'm good. Just need a hand with my coffee." Val flicked her eyes to her cup.

"Come on, old girl, let me help you with that." Marcus pulled his chair close to Val's, reached over and held her cup to her lips. This was hard enough without an audience and Dan was making it awkward. Not that he meant to, but it was time to get him out so Val could have her coffee without him gawping.

"Daniel, I would like to ask something of you." I turned him to face the garden where the others still played.

"Um, sure ... what can I do?" He followed my gaze to the others out the back.

"Riah doesn't go out often, but we can't afford for her to be sheltered too much. It's such a beautiful day, I was wondering if perhaps I could ask you and Tessa to take the twins for a walk?" Thoughts flickered across his face like a prize wheel till it landed on "confused".

"Are you sure? I know you said we'd be safe, but surely if you're expecting an attack or going to have to fight, now would be the best time for the enemy. We are so vulnerable. I'm a dead weight and, no offence, but Tessa doesn't seem battle ready, and the twins ...?"

"You're right, and if the enemy had any say in the situation, I'm sure he would use this to his advantage. But the Light is the true Lord, and nothing happens unless He allows it. He has said we have this time. So, for now, we are safe from physical attack. Why do you think I let you and Tessa out yesterday?" I continued before he could protest, "You will be fine. But we'd really appreciate your help."

He needed confidence out there, just as much as the others did, and now was the perfect opportunity. It might also strengthen the fragile bond that had started to develop between him and Raph. I would never demand that someone offer their gift. That was the whole point, it had to be freely given. But when Raph healed Dan's hand and then invited him to stay, it showed humility and maturity. I was so proud of him, Tessa too. Both of them were working at reversing their initial judgement of Daniel.

After I'd packed them all off, it would be a good time to sit and consider a plan of attack for the next few weeks. We had been given a window of peace and we couldn't afford to waste one minute of it.

28

RAPHAEL

Just because he was family now did not mean it would be easy. Everything was going to change because of him. It already had. I should have been at home overseeing lunch. Then Tessa, Riah and I should have been having our morning training. Instead, we were out here babysitting Daniel. It had only been three days and even he had changed.

We should not have been out without an adult, it was too dangerous. Riah should not be out here at all. I bet this was Daniel's idea. This was all his fault.

I was so confused by him. Sometimes I forgot I was scared of him. And some of the changes he brought were not bad. But being out was not okay. I could feel the Dragon approaching, its breath pinching the back of my neck, red haze rising, its whisper building in my ears. It was drowning out Daniel and Tessie's conversation.

I had to stay in control. He might have been okay at handling threats from people, but I was the only one who could protect Riah and Tessie from a real threat. I knew the Warriors were with us, but I was the next line of defence. I had to stay focused and breathe. Tessa had a firm grip of one of my hands and Riah's cool hand pumped my other twice. It meant, *I love you* in our secret language. I knew I could do this. I would keep the Dragon subdued.

"So, Raph, you must think I'm a lazy slob. I've only been here two nights and I've slept in both times. What'd I miss?"

"Everything." If he thought he could talk his way out of work and training, he had another think coming.

"Ookaaay ... perhaps you could fill that out a bit for me? Then I could be better prepared for tomorrow."

"We get up pretty early you know. First light. Well, Kait gets up first and starts coffee, then Riah is next up. Tessa or I get up after them and make hot chocolate and coffee for everyone once it has had time to brew. Val and Abbot get up after us, and finally when everyone is up, Kait takes Marcus his coffee.

"He does not like mornings, so you have to be really quiet and wait for Kait to wake him. Once he has had his coffee, he is okay. After reflection we go outside for sets at sunrise, then back in for breakfast and the start of the morning routine." That would show him. In the time he had spent with us, we had done heaps before he even woke up. He was right. He was lazy.

"Wow, I can't believe I slept through all that. Twice. I must have been in a pretty deep sleep. I can't remember the last time I've been safe enough or comfortable enough to do that. I can't even remember the last time I slept past sunrise. It must have been when I was a little kid with my mum, or maybe when I was a bit older living with my grandpa."

"Why did you leave your mum?" I did not want to talk to him, but I could not stop myself asking. We had lost our parents when we were young, too.

"She was taken away from me when I was about three, and then Grandpa looked after me till he died."

"Why did he die?" I asked.

"He got sick when I was about nine. I cared for him for two years till he finally gave up. He was pretty sick and in a lot of pain. I was shattered, but in a small way I was happy for him not to have to suffer anymore."

"Who looked after you then?" We were almost eleven. It would be horrible if anything happened to someone in our family.

Dan chuckled, but it did not dance with humour. "No one. I was on my own. There was no one else. I stayed in Grandpa's house for as long as I could. But when the authorities found out, they took everything. They tried putting me in care, but I didn't like what happened there ... so I left."

We had come to a T intersection and everyone waited for me to pick the route. I chose right and we moved on. "What about your dad?"

"I never had a dad. The closest I had was Abraham, the father of my best friend. I met Indy when I was about thirteen. His tribe was huge, and their house was always packed with people coming and going. Come night-time, there was never a spare flat surface to sleep on. They didn't have much, but what they had they shared around. But Indy and I were too stupid to realise how good we had it. At fourteen we ran away to join the gangs—to make our fortune." He kicked a small pebble along the ground. It pinged off the wall of an abandoned building and rolled to a stop in a tuft of grass.

"What happened to Indy?" The question jumped from my mouth before I had finished thinking it.

"I don't know. Things turned bad in Gomorrah. Abraham had warned us, but we didn't listen. We tried to escape the gang. It was pretty scary, but in the end they caught me. In the process, though, I was able to give Indy the break he needed to get away." He was silent for a while. My pace had slowed as I peeked into his memory and it formed images around me.

"Eventually, I was also able to escape by the skin of my teeth. I don't know where he is, or even if he's alive. I can't go back to Gomorrah to look for him, or Abraham. Commander would have me killed as soon as I entered the city limits."

"But that is horrible." It was more than horrible, but I could not find the words to paint the picture.

The others were quiet. Were they thinking the same as me? That

Dan was a battered old suitcase with heaps of surprises crammed inside. Each time you opened the lid, more puzzles escaped.

"I think I can understand why you slept in." I looked up and saw he was in the halo of his Warrior's light. I saw a baby losing his mother and a knife twisted in my stomach. I thought of what it would be like to lose Abbot, and my heart broke. I imagined a young man losing his only friend and my eyes filled.

He had been totally alone. Cut adrift. No one to care for him, or to care for. It was a hard story to hear. Kait said Riah's and my story was hard to hear. I wonder if it was just as hard for Dan to tell. I was dying to ask what happened to him in Gomorrah. But I did not have to hear that to see that his path had been cobbled with obstacles from the start.

He was like us.

I remember when we arrived in this family. I remember how they treated us like treasure they had strived and starved for. We had been washed and wrapped in the love of the Light. They had cleansed and comforted, and poured themselves into putting us back together.

How could I open my hands to receive this wealth, not deserving it, but greedy for more, then stop another from receiving the same? It would be selfish.

But it was hard. I could see he was like us. I could accept that he had just as much right as we did—none at all. And I could try to deal with the changes he brought, the good and the bad. He had walked a rocky path to get to our door and the Light had invited him in. I must not shut him out. "Daniel, you are safe with us."

The blue of his eyes rolled like storm clouds. They were deep, dark and dangerous. He looked at me and did not blink. But I was not scared. Because he looked at me as an equal. With respect. He nodded once.

As I was leader on this mission, it was up to me to call the shots. To be responsible. "It is time for us to get back. I have to prepare lunch and we need to do our training." Talking to Daniel had stopped the haze, but we needed to go home now.

Tessa understood. "Okay, little man. We'll head back."

There was a plan, the plan kept us safe, we had to stick to the plan.

29

DANIEL

Lunch had been cleared away and the twins were doing homework with Kait. Tessa was involved in some kind of study prompted and punctuated by Abbot. Marcus was in his cave tinkering on the truck and I was sitting in my chair zoning out.

Looking through the doors into the garden, I reflected on how spending time with Raph was like doing the Skratoosie two-step: one step forward, five steps back. And how Tessa was a complete enigma: you thought things were going fine, but then, like some defective pop-up doll, she sprouted thorns from every surface. Between the two of them, I was walking on eggshells. I wondered if this was one of the "costs" Kait had talked about.

But my train of thought flew into the aether when I focused on what was actually in front of my eyes. Val was in the middle of the garden imitating a praying mantis in defensive mode ... on Valium. Wondering if perhaps one of those knives was lodged in her head, I looked around to see if I should call for help. But no one else seemed to be paying her the least bit of attention.

Equal parts of alarm and intrigue motivated me to check it out. I didn't want to interrupt her intense focus or frighten her if she was in the middle of some kind of psychotic episode.

Standing quietly on the sidelines, I realised that there seemed to be a pattern to what she was doing. She was fighting off an unseen enemy. Who, apparently, was also operating under the influence of mind-altering substances. The whole dance was carried out in slow motion.

Carefully approaching her, I attempted to break through to her sanity. "Val ... are you ... alright? Do you know where you are? Would you like me to get someone to talk to or ..." I stopped mid-sentence, retracted my hand that had intended comfort, and stood up straight as she burst out laughing.

"Dan, I'm okay." It took her a while to catch her breath, she was laughing so hard. "Quick, get me a chair before I fall over."

I rushed to comply. Sadly, the red wave of humiliation had not receded, and my ears were still burning when I returned.

"Thank you, dear boy. For the chair as well. I haven't laughed so hard in ages." Dabbing gently at her healing face, she captured the few tears that had managed to escape. Then quickly slumped into the proffered chair. "Go get one for yourself and I'll explain."

As I went back to the patio, I thanked the Light that the doors were shut, and no one could have heard what had just happened.

When will I ever feel normal again?

"I was practising an old Chinese art. It was not something developed for the Light. But, centuries ago when it was developed, its creators were incorporating the same principles as ours: focus the mind and train the body, focus the body and train the mind.

"By disciplining both, we allow the life-giving energy of the Light freedom to 'access all areas' of who and what we are, thereby making us stronger in the Light.

"It's also battle training. There are sets we repeat daily so that they become habit and natural movement. In battle, we can trust the programming of our mind, and the trained instinct of our body, energised by the Light, to win. And this brings about maximum carnage, my friend. Maximum. Carnage." Her eyes were lit by a full, face-eating grin.

This was one cold-blooded woman. Single-minded and ... troublesome. Every time I thought I'd managed to put her in a box, I was having to make renovations. Could she not just pick one—or two—character types and give me a break?

Although, coming from a life on the street, and having experienced life in the gangs, this side of her I totally got. But how did she manage that with the vulnerability, and the sharing leadership, and the ... humility thing? It hurt just saying the damn word. I'd been so caught up in my thinking I hadn't realised she'd started speaking again.

"... also train with swords."

"What?"

"Well these things on our backs aren't just there for decoration. Nor are they there just for protection and defence. We have to know how to use them."

I had started to get used to the seriously cool armour they got about in. I mean, they never took it off. Never. They even slept in it. I'd asked Tessa about it, but she said they didn't actually feel it. It was like it wasn't there. Naturally, I asked if I could feel it.

And she was right. I'd been so mesmerised by the way my hand passed through it as I stroked her arm, that I'd missed the fact that Marcus had been standing over me and had to grunt to get my attention. I dropped Tessa's arm like a hot potato and raced off to find some chore to do.

It's a pity really—I'd have loved to have a go at one of the massive swords. I'd always fancied myself as a bit of a ninja. Even though they were more of a European broadsword than an oriental curved blade. Without thinking, my eyes were drawn back to Val's armour and I got lost in the intricacy and detail of her suit. Beautiful. Fascinating.

Val coughed. I froze. Mortified. My hand was centimetres from touching her chest. I could feel the heat of my shame eating me alive. She graciously chose to pretend nothing had happened and moved on. "These"—she indicated the armour and the sword—"are gifts. We don't pick the colour or the detail, the same as we don't pick our Badges.

"Everything we have is a gift—precious things that are given into our care to discover and develop. Just as you have discovered"—she gave me a sly smile—"that the armour, in one sense, isn't there. Yet in battle, against our enemy, it is most effective. Like I said, maximum carnage."

"Why is that … how is that?" I asked her.

"Our enemy is not flesh and blood, but rather things of the 'Other' world, the Unseen. Therefore, it doesn't need to be effective against the Seen world. As I said, it is a gift. A gift given at the time of adoption into the family of the Lord of Light. For those who can see, it's an outward sign of an inward reality. We have picked our side, counted the cost and are prepared to join the battle for the glory of the Light.

"The Light protects us and gifts us with what we need for the fight. Hence the armour." Her face became serious. "Don't ever be mistaken, or lulled into a false sense of laziness. We are at war, and, like I said, it is not just for our mortal lives, but for our eternal souls.

"We are given weapons to train with, to be skilled at, and then to use with precision. As we travel through this world, we will instantly recognise, and be recognised by, our fellow comrades by the armour. We can tell where they are in their journey by its level of clarity and detail."

"Oh." I was gutted. I'd thought I'd been accepted. I'd said I wanted in, I'd made my decision and yet I hadn't received any. Obviously, once again, my face betrayed my feelings.

Val placed her hand on my arm, eyes sparkling. "When was the last time you really looked at yourself, Dan?"

Sitting with her in the garden, bathed in the soft light of the winter afternoon, I looked down and joy exploded like a grenade throughout my body. "Frack me!"

"That, my dear boy, is never going to happen." Her eyebrow raised and her lips twitched with a hint of a smile.

"What? Oh skrat, sorry ... I mean ... grut, oh ... skitch. Uhh ... um ... I mean ..." Swallowing and fighting for focus, I tried to get back to the armour. "When did this happen?"

"We noticed it this morning," she said.

"But Val." I gaped at her. "I'm the same as you. I'm indigo. What does that mean?"

"It means you've been given indigo."

"Will I be like you, Val?" I had to know.

"No. You'll be like you, as you are transformed to be more like the Lord of Light. No one else is like you, nor are you like anybody else. And you're not meant to be. We're unique and we each need to find out who we are. Not strive to 'be like' anyone else. We can be an example and we can learn from each other, but each one of us is a one-off. You may be indigo, but it's a different indigo to mine." She laid a hand on my armoured shoulder.

Yeah, you heard me. Armoured. Shoulder. This was going to take some getting used to. I couldn't wait to check out if I had a sword too. But Val was still speaking. "I look forward to watching your path unfold. And I look forward to journeying with you as long as the Light lets me."

I held out my hand and slowly rotated it, noticing the details in the embers of the afternoon. My eyes travelled slowly over what had been previously inconsequential. I had never really taken much notice or particular care of what I wore or what I looked like. What was the point? If it wasn't directly related to survival, comfort or convenience, I couldn't give a rat's butt.

But this ... this was a thing of wonder, a thing of beauty. A marvel. I was so caught up in checking myself out that I had missed that Val was speaking again.

"... tomorrow morning, first light, you will join us for our morning training. We let you sleep in these last two days, as there's been a lot going on."

"Thanks, Val, that'd be good ... I think."

"It will be easier to check yourself out and get more of the detail when you're disciplined and battle-ready." She obviously knew the kick it was to receive this gear. It was a real high.

"Now, enough of that. I'm seizing up out here. Can you please help me back inside?"

30

MARCUS

I love me wife. I love me life. And I love me coffee.

Thank you.

But I have never been a lover of the morning. For the past twenty-three years, Kait'd been trying to marry me and morning together with less hostility. She still had a way to go.

Once I was up though, I was as happy as a dam at high tide—or would be ... eventually.

Good to see Dan joining us this morning. He'd been busy ticking the boxes. Despite everything that had happened over the last two days. He was still here, still mustard and still working out how to fit his square edges in the curve of this family. Truth be, he was a good kid.

But for now, it was time to start. Walking around the chairs, taking everyone's cups, I pushed the ball to rolling. After taking the dishes to the kitchen, I made me way to the wardrobe and joined the scrummage as we each robed up for the morning's sets. I took an extra handful and passed it to the confused lad. Once we were all ready and armoured in preparation for the inevitable attack of the cold, we moved outside.

The slap of freezing air fought off sleep's last echo. Gasping morning's icy tentacles into me lungs, I buzzed and burned to move. But instead, I pulled the energy in and locked it away. Reaching out, I plucked the calm that swam around me and drank deeply. Well and truly awake, I was now invigorated, alive and ready to go.

When we'd first joined these guys, Val had insisted I lead the morning sets. Me early exposure to this kind of stuff as a kid and me work at the gym was great preparation.

In those early days, Kait and I were at sixes and sevens, trying to find our feet and learn about the Light. Pigs on ice we were. Val and her mum, Joy, threw me a rope by encouraging me to make the most of me knowledge to benefit the whole group. Together, we came up with an extended morning program of sets and stretches. I had never worked with swords before, but Joy was an expert. Val was good with hand-to-hand. And I brought a more disciplined formal routine.

It'd only been six years. Six of the fastest, longest years of me life. Each year, what was became more foreign than what is. Now, both feet were firmly planted in the future, and when the memories took me, I was a tourist. That life was gone. But even though I was no longer that child, those lessons informed the path I trod.

Facing the north, ready to be washed in the rising sun, I stood at relaxed attention. The others found a space behind me. In this time of peace, the first rays climbed over the garden wall to embrace us. We each stood in perfect stillness.

Coming open-handed, we gave everything over to the Light. Approaching empty-handed, we focused on Him alone and gave Him our full attention. There was nothing else. Just Him and me. And so, we began.

31

CONTESSA

S tep.
Breathe.
Move.
Release.

The rhythm of the pattern, the harmony of the group, and the radiance of the Light was a potpourri that soothed my soul. A calming weight that grounded me into the eternity and immensity of the Light.

I could lose myself in the pattern. Release everything into the now.

The feeling.

The movement.

The discipline.

All the thoughts, doubts, accusations and anxieties were unleashed and released.

He is, therefore I am.

Not being a morning person, it took me a while to get used to starting the day this way. It took even longer to see the benefit and appreciate it. And it was only recently that I actually began to enjoy it. But now, it gave me a reason to get out of bed.

Yes, even in the dark. Seriously.

This helped in all kinds of ways. It helped me understand my purpose. In the past year, I had learned that I have a part to play. And to do that well, I needed to be the best I could be.

I still hadn't come close to realising what my best looked like. I was a work in progress. And that was okay, as long as I kept progressing. Abbot was consistent in reminding me that none of us got it right first time. Everyone fell. It was whether you chose to keep on getting up and keep on trying. If you did, that was progress. Well, that's what they all kept telling me.

I chose to believe them.

Kait liked to remind me that each morning was a fresh start. A chance to make over the mistakes from yesterday. A chance to move on. And who wouldn't love that? I, for one, welcomed this gift with open arms. Because every day I made mistakes. A lot of mistakes. But that's completely normal, right? Right.

But now, with a new audience, I was making more mistakes than ever. Which was all kinds of embarrassing. At least when the others watched me, they didn't make it obvious. Dan's stare was like a magnifying glass ... in the sun ... and I was like an ant jumping over hot concrete underneath its focus.

Despite the changes rocking our boat, and the burning at the back of my head, I was starting to see a bit of light with this new set up. There was an extra pair of hands to help with the chores. And an extra body to beat up and spar with in practice. And since I was on edge all the flopping time now, I enjoyed training more than ever.

Dan was a beacon. I could sense exactly where he was.

All. The. Time.

Trouble was, I couldn't relax with him around. Ever. Which is why our morning routine was so important to induce calm. And training was so helpful in releasing tension and aggression. I mean, seriously, who wouldn't embrace the opportunity to go all kinds of hard-core-combat over the person who drove you crazy?

My feelings about him were still tangled. It's hard to explain. I mean, I know we all have walls, but Dan's was a fortress ... with a moat and a drawbridge. And pots of boiling oil. A bit like Val's. He was a loner, a survivor, and a freaking machine. He loved annoying, taunting, and baiting me. Seriously, he'd go out of his way to get a rise out of me. And there were times when he still frightened me a bit.

And yet, at other times, he'd drop the drawbridge and withhold the boiling oil. It was like he considered me an equal. We'd both earned our stripes and come up through the skrat ranks on the streets. These times were rare, mind you. But when he called a truce, I felt ... special. Like I could trust him.

I know, weird. Right?

I planned to find some space and privacy to talk to Kait about it. One thing I was absolutely confident about though: my new comfortable was being thrown to the wind. Perhaps Raph was right. Everything had changed because of Dan.

32

ABBOT

Early afternoon was my favourite time of the day, although my mornings with Sariah in the garden were very special as well. When it came to afternoon lessons I felt I hit my straps, so to speak. It was when I came alive and was able to contribute something of substance. It was the time we spent delving into and discussing the book of Light, *The Way*.

I knew I didn't have much time left before we departed, and I didn't want to waste any opportunity to help Daniel learn and understand the way of the Light.

"Valarie, I believe you made Daniel a promise, or more accurately an offer, to help him understand his dreams. Perhaps now would be a good time to start? That is, if you don't mind, Daniel." Everyone had just returned from a gentle run through the streets. I spoke loud enough to be heard over the ruckus and invited Daniel to join us.

"No. I mean, sure ... that'd be okay." He took the towel he was handed and went via the kitchen for a drink of water. It disappeared in a couple of gulps and the glass was immediately refilled. I guess it wasn't just food, warmth and protection he'd had to go without.

Bringing his glass with him, he joined Valarie and me in the comfort of the sitting room. I hoped the contentment of a sated hunger—and thirst—the security of fellowship, and a flood of endorphins from his exercise might alleviate the stress he would inevitably feel from reliving his nightmares.

He took his seat, rubbed his face with the towel, and looked blankly at us.

I prompted him. "I believe you have a number of dreams, none of which are pleasant. I understand it may not be easy, but are there any you would feel comfortable enough to share?"

Taking another sip, he nodded and began. "I have two kinds of dreams, normal and ... weird ones."

He paused and stared out the window for a while. "My 'weird' dreams are different in the way I experience them. It's hard to explain, but these dreams are really vivid. I can taste and smell. All my senses are active. I'm hyper-alert and when I wake up the memory of them is like they were real. Like I had actually just lived that experience. Sometimes, really simple ones leave me in a physical mess. I have no idea why. Like I said, it's hard to explain, but all the weird ones have the same 'solid' quality about them.

"The first one is not like the other two. It's pretty tame actually. The only reason I think they're related is, like I said, the way I experience it. I've had it a fair few times over the years." He took another mouthful of water before he went on.

"I'm standing on a sand dune overlooking the ocean. The waves are low and it's a dismal, grey winter's day. I can't hear anything but wind racing past my ears. Its salty flavour coats my tongue and stings my eyes. Chilly fingers slap my face and pull my hair and sand flicks up and whips my bare legs. I hug my arms around me for warmth. It's cold but invigorating.

"There is a line of people walking at the water's edge. About seven of them. They're wearing long brown robes with the hoods pulled low over their heads. The first time I had this dream, nothing happened. I stood and watched till they passed, but I woke shaking like a leaf. I don't know why.

"The next time I had this dream it was exactly the same, except the person on the end of the line turned their head and looked at me.

The shivers I felt that time weren't from the cold. Again, I woke sweating and shaking. I have this one every couple of months and it never changed—till my first night here."

He leaned back in his chair after another gulp of water, absently playing with the towel laid across his lap. "This last time, the person looked at me and waved. I smiled and waved back. I had a great sense of familiarity and warmth. A sense of belonging. I woke happy and at peace." He looked straight at me without blinking. I suspected he was looking through me rather than at me. "It's funny. More than anything else that's happened to me over the past three days, this dream confirms I made the right decision." He shook his head, and turned to Valarie. "This is something I brought with me, from my world, and it's like a nod of encouragement. It's really hard to explain, but it's a good thing and I'll go with that for now."

"Are there any other dreams you'd like to share at this point, Daniel?" I asked.

His face paled and his Adam's apple bobbed, "Ahh ... not now. It's not that I don't want to, it's just ..."

His peace evaporated and his calmness dissolved like cool vapour under a desert sun. He wasn't ready. "It's okay Daniel, there's plenty of time. We don't need to rush it. Perhaps you'd like to come to the table and join Tessa for studies?" I stood and held my arm out inviting him to join me. "Whilst I get her started, I would like to introduce you to the book we study. It's an ancient text called *The Way*."

Waves of heightened anxiety radiated from him. I wondered, was he intimidated by reading, study, academics? Or was it Tessa? My Badge only told me which feelings were present, not the fuel that fed them.

I knew he could read, but I didn't know how well. The last thing I wanted to do was shame him, especially in front of the others. So, as tactfully as I could, I broached the subject. "It is good to read the Word to ourselves, but at times it is a wonder to see how much more we pick up by listening, having others read to us."

"Grandpa used to read to me," Daniel offered, "after my mum ... died. He taught me to read really young. We didn't have much, but he did have lots of books." He moved to the table and took the seat I indicated. "He would read them to me until I could read them all for myself. Then, when he was dying, I read them back to him. I tried to take my favourites with me when I had to leave. But I couldn't keep them for long, living on the street."

"To lose one's mother so young is an incomprehensible tragedy. That must have been a confusing and painful time."

His emotions sparked instantly. "I didn't lose her. She was bashed to death in our home."

His anger burned deeply, and rage scorched his spirit. What terrible pain this young man had endured. I gave him time and space to continue if he so desired. But it appeared that he did not.

He pressed his lips together and his nostrils flared with the effort to gain enough air. To his credit, however, he soon had himself back under control. "After living on the streets for a bit, Abraham found me. He took me in and that's where I met Indigo. That's not his real name, but"—he looked to me, feeling the need to explain, perhaps, or to recall—"his skin's so dark, and his hair's almost blue. I called him that to tease him. It just stuck."

He ran his hands over the cover of the book. "Abraham tried to read to the two of us from this book, but we rejected it, and him ... soon after we took to the streets."

He clammed up completely.

So, it was the book that brought back painful memories and opened old wounds. The Light had been after this one for a while.

Help him forgive, help him heal and help me gently lead him further into You through Your Word. Soften his heart and pull him through. Please, in your mercy and faithfulness, hold him tight and don't let him run this time.

I opened the cover. "Have a look, flick through and get a feel for it, and then, if you have any questions feel free to fire away."

I turned away from him and gave my attention to Tessa. By giving him more space, I hoped to reduce his angst and pain. I let him spend some time investigating, and then tried to draw Tessa into the conversation. There is great value and import in being taught by an elder, but there is equal value and wealth to be found in exploring with a peer.

"It's been over eighty years since I first looked at this book, so I forget what that initial experience is like. What were your first thoughts, Tessa?" Her hands twitched, her eyes darted around the room and she chewed her bottom lip. But eventually her gaze came back to me. I smiled and nodded encouraging her to share her valid opinion and soon she was babbling like the merry brook she was.

I left them to discuss it and went to see if Kaitlyn could benefit from some help with the twins. It wouldn't take long for Daniel's stress levels to decrease and he would realise that there was nothing to be concerned about. On the contrary, I hoped that, in time, study would become something he would draw peace and encouragement from.

33

CONTESSA

Abbot was a cunning old fox. It was the first time I'd played the role of teacher and it freaked me out. How did you put what you knew into words that made sense to someone who lived outside of your head?

I hated to admit it, but I envied Dan's boldness. He had good questions that I hadn't thought to ask. Or been brave enough to ask.

I'd been pretty confident in what I knew. But truth was, I was still a newb. We tried talking about what I did know. But kept coming back to a whole lot that I didn't. Plus, we were both struggling with what to do with Raph and Riah's story.

Looking around to see who we could ask, we saw Kait and Abbot's heads bent over the twins in the study area. Val and Marcus were reading in the sitting room.

"Val?" She and Marcus looked up from their own studies as we shuffled our chairs closer to them. Her raised eyebrows and open face invited us to continue. "We were wondering if we could ask you guys something?"

"You just did. Spit it out," Marcus responded in his usual encouraging manner.

"Neither of us seems to be able to get Raph and Riah's story out of our heads," I ventured. They stared at us, blinked and waited.

"What exactly is your question, Tess?" Val took the bait. "It was a horrifying situation, and one of the most satisfying victories I've ever had."

"Kill-hog," Marcus muttered under his breath. Val beamed at him.

"Well ..." I tried to continue but was lost. I looked to Dan.

He just shook his head. "How can a victorious, powerful Light force, who you claim is 'love', allow such a horrendous thing to happen to those innocent kids?" he asked. "Is the Dark more powerful in some areas? What's the go?"

"Before I begin to even try wading into that wasp's nest," Val said, "let me say that I don't think we'll ever truly understand the why of it. Secondly, tell me how what happened to the twins was any different to what happened to you guys. Or Marcus, Kait and Abbot for that matter."

"But they're just kids, Val. Riah was eight years old!" I blurted out. Of course there was a difference.

"Honey, from where we're standing, so are you and Dan." Marcus had entered the debate. "How old were you when you first suffered in Gomorrah, Dan? How old were you when your parents OD'd in the temples, forcing you into the gangs, Tessa?"

"That's kind of irrelevant though, isn't it?" Dan countered. "It doesn't answer the question of why it's allowed to happen."

"Dan, we know that the Light is more powerful," Val said, "and with that power, He created everything and gifted us with free choice. But in order for us to exercise this gift there needs to be something to choose between. So, along with Light, we have Dark. As a consequence, we're all swimming around in this cesspit, being impacted by choices—ours and others'—regardless of the outcome."

"But what is the Light doing about it?" In his anger, Dan stood. "Why doesn't He stop it? Kids shouldn't suffer like that. It's just not right." He was not completely successful in keeping his voice down. We didn't want the twins to know we were arguing over their situation. Like they needed our confusion and anger mixed in with theirs!

"You're absolutely right," Marcus said. "They shouldn't. You shouldn't. No one should. As angry as you are about it, just think how much angrier the Creator is. His beautiful and once-perfect creation destroyed and suffering."

"So, He's powerless to do anything about it, then?" Dan responded in a hoarse whisper.

I was staying out of it. I was too busy taking in what they were saying, and I needed time to process it all.

Please help me make sense of this. I'm not as smart as the others and I'm not as bold as Dan, but I want to understand.

"He has done something about it, and you're part of it," Val said calmly. "So, the question should be, 'What are you doing about it?'"

"What are you talking about? What can I do? I am one person. Are you suggesting I walk out of here and just stop all the suffering in the world?" Dan, red-faced and tense-bodied, continued to stand over Val and Marcus.

"Breathe and focus." Marcus met Dan's anger with a stern challenge, coaxing him to regain a sense of control. It seemed to work. They locked eyes for a moment, then Dan backed down. "You're trying to get your head around a huge issue, and letting your emotions instead of your brain run your mouth is not doing you any good.

"Yes, you are just one person. We all are. And when you put a whole lot of single people together with a common goal and purpose, you have an army. That's what we are, Dan, part of an army. An army that has existed for millennia, including people all around the world. The question we need to ask ourselves each day is, 'What am I doing about it?'" Marcus ended more calmly than he started. Dan slumped into his seat.

From my vantage point, I could see everyone in the room. "We don't seem to be a very scary army," I said. "Obviously, Val, you could scare the pants off anyone. But the twins, Abbot, me ...?"

"But here is the brilliance of the plan, Tessa." Val became focused and steely again. Speaking about fighting altered her. She got all intense and lost her nice bits. Flames shot out of her eyes, and the daggers all over her body sparked in the fire of her Indigo armour.

Thank you that she's on my side.

"You'd think the bigger, stronger warrior would be more effective, but this is not our war. Those of us in this fight are not fighting each other. We represent, or echo, the war of the Others. So, size, age, and the ability of the soldier are all irrelevant. What's important is who your god is. It's also brilliant, tactically. Look at us: broken, old, frail, young, inexperienced. Who would fear us? In our weakened state, they don't see us coming."

Yep, she was definitely on some kind of high just thinking about it.

"But what's that got to do with those kids out there getting hurt?" Dan was like a dog with a bone and I was grateful.

Marcus engaged Dan's rage. "Early on, Dan, before things got so heated on the streets for us, we would go into the city, and, using money from the Soteria Houses and our skills, we did what we could to help those who were in need. Some we brought back for meals and clothed them with what we had, like we did with you.

"We were able to be a part of and witness to some incredible wonders performed by the Light. But after the buzz faded and the signs slowed, the city slunk back into the Dark. Our purpose now is to go in and pull people out of extreme situations. Out of respect and care for Raph and Riah, we don't bring just anyone back now." Marcus's gaze zeroed in on Dan.

"We each have a part to play," Val said, "but none of us has to do it all. We can't. It's pride to think we can. We just need to be obedient soldiers, train hard, stay focused and trust the General who is coordinating the battle. He is doing something, Dan. He is fighting. You are now very much part of that war. Don't forget you have a purpose now. Your life is no longer about you. Remember, choosing to sacrifice despite pain and loss demonstrates love. We have been enlisted to love, and that is the fight. His love saved us, and out of our love for Him, we fight in His war."

34

MARCUS

"Are you scared, Daniel?" I whispered.

It was his second week. I'd been putting them through their paces, pushing boundaries, knowing something big was coming. I had to do all I could to prepare them.

"No, I'm not scared. I could kill her ... or hurt her. No way am I fighting a girl. It's just not right and I won't do it. And you can't make me." He looked to Tessa. His narrowed eyes grew to saucers when her claws grew.

"What do you mean you could kill me? I'm not that useless." Tessa came out with a verbal punch.

I had been surprised and relieved to see that Dan knew which was the pointy end of the sword. He'd sworn he hadn't used one before, but he wasn't alien to its ways.

His street skills were prime. And since hand-to-hand was his daily bread, I'd expected loaves rather than crusts. He didn't disappoint. I was also impressed with his willingness to learn. This one'd go a long way.

In the past, I'd partnered Tessa with the twins for sparring. But this new arrangement would extend her and expose Dan to a different style of fighting. I suspected his aversion to going up against women had something to do with what happened to his mum. But the enemy would know this and use it against him. It was time to turn up the heat at home so they could handle the reality of war.

"I'm not fighting a girl!" He swore.

"Don't call me a girl!"

Not her best comeback. But considering she was mad as a cut snake, her energy was focused on defending her honour, not her wit. In a flash of yellow, Tessa launched, kicking, twisting and striking, attempting to prove her point.

"Let's give it a go and see what happens," I said, but they didn't hear me. They were too busy demonstrating their opinions.

Tessa had him on the back foot. It was all he could do to deflect. But, true to his word, he didn't raise a hand or foot against her. Resolutely, jaw set, he would defend only. The less he tried, the more she raged, her yellow armour blushing red. Her eyes flamed like a wild cat's. I was excited to see that, against Dan at least, Tessa's "thug" was coming into the light.

Whilst she may have been as wild as a bag of cats, I couldn't fight me grin. I'd just been served the cream. This was going to be good. Perfect even.

From then on, I trained them together. Tessa grew in stature, her chin higher knowing she could shock and wrong-foot Dan. She'd always be short on strength, but she compensated with speed, agility, and control.

Stubborn as a mule, in week one of their partnership Dan did not strike back. That was okay. It wasn't wasted. Tessa tried to land hits and Dan practised defending. On the downside, they'd both build up a head of steam in frustration that had to be lanced before they left the paddock. So, I let them release the beast going one-on-one against me as the finale of their work outs.

Sparring was a great way to get to know someone. It was a window and opportunity to learn how they thought and processed things. Tessa and Dan had to learn how to fight against each other as sparring partners so they would learn how to fight alongside each other as allies. It was also a great way to let off steam.

Having a new person in our ranks had thrown Raph, like we expected, and it had also thrown Tessa. But we were most surprised at how Riah had handled the transition. Using our sessions to push everyone harder was a great way to allow them to channel that energy and aggression in a positive way. It kept the aggro on a leash, rather than having them firing it off at one another outside the ring. It was also keeping me on me toes, as I was both pitcher and receiver.

Bearing the brunt of Val's frustration, however, was a harder pill to swallow and recover from. I was as happy as the next person that she was getting her mobility back. But I guess learning how to defend and attack are only two aspects of fighting. You also had to learn how to take a hit, and how to fall, and how to keep on getting up. Val was helping me with this. A lot.

Of course, it wasn't just us who had to adjust to Dan joining us. He had to soften his edges and realign to fit with us. He'd started using me punching bag in the garage more regularly. For him, living in this new environment was creating more tension than could be released through training sessions alone.

Who'd have thought living in close quarters with a bunch of broken individuals would be ideal training for war?

35

ABBOT

Kaitlyn and Marcus had taken the twins and Tessa for a walk in the lull after lunch whilst Daniel had accepted the offer to share more of his dreams with Valarie and me. This one was definitely more intriguing than the last.

"I am galloping across an open grassy plain. I'm on a small horse. Which is completely random, because I have never ridden a horse before. I'm in the midst of a large group and there is a deep and overwhelming sense of 'Oneness'. As we ride, we move together like a school of fish, guiding our horses with our legs, leaving our hands free for fighting.

"We are all equal within the group. This is how we survive. Each one is defined by their special role, each born with a specific gift that determines that role. No one is above the other and no gift is seen as superior to another. Each is valued and critical for the survival and wellbeing of the whole.

"There is a great sense of urgency. We are running out of time. They are coming and we have to be ready. At the border of our land, we stop at the edge of a rugged cliff that drops to another plain below.

"Steam rises off our rides, and a distinct smell of ... animal, I guess you'd call it, I haven't smelled it anywhere else ... fills my head.

The heat of my pony's sweat radiates up through my seat. The animals toss their heads. Impatient snorts are swept away in the wind rushing up the cliff face. We calm and soothe our horses while we wait for the enemy to arrive.

"I, like everyone else, normally fight with a sword, but the sheath on my back is home to a double-headed axe. They all gather around in awe as I reverently remove it from its casing. Despite the dullness of the day, it shines with a light of its own. The blades are honed to a deathly fineness. I know this because of the hours I spend caring for it and tending it. It sings to me as I swing it around my head, reacquainting myself with its perfect balance. It's an extension of me. My senses are on fire with the anticipation of using it. A hunger awakens, for this is my purpose.

"They approach, driving their own beasts madly, whipping and beating them for more speed. Soon they will arrive but will have to climb the bluff to reach us. Then they will have to kill us before accessing our land. We step back and wait. We aren't panicked or worried as we watch them come. They will be spent from the climb. Our horses have recovered quickly for they are fit and battle-ready. As are we.

"Spread out in formation, swords unsheathed, we are calm and patient for it to begin. Battle is common, life is not cheap, but on occasion, blood flows in torrents.

"Our opposition arrive, and my axe sings loudly in my hands as it works overtime. The tribe move to the edges and work from the periphery. Like a magnet, I draw the heat of the battle to myself.

"Experienced in this type of warfare, we all know that the closer they are to me, the harder it is to use the axe. Our short swords are better for close combat, but it doesn't seem to hamper me too much. The battle never lasts long. It never does when my axe is freed. It is so light and easy to manoeuvre, tirelessly separating heads from bodies and cleaving torsos.

"Soon the quiet returns, stilled in grief for our fallen, saddened by the attack, but gratefully accepting our victory as we look over the carnage of the day. The stench of blood, gore and sweat mixes to create the unique scent of battle. The bloodied mud beneath us will soon be carpeted in lush, rich grass as it has been well fed by the spoils of battle. They have all fought to the death, refusing surrender, so we commit their bodies to the fire.

"Then I wake, again shocked and shaken. This one is not as bad as my other one, 'The House,' but it's so strange because I have no knowledge of any of these things. But when I dream them, they are real. I am part of it, living it, knowing it … I have complete awareness."

I could feel Valarie's excitement flowing out of her as readily as the aromas from Raphael's cooking filled our own Soteria House. The story of the dream had awakened her bloodlust and heightened the frustration of her confinement. Being tied down and needing to be helped, constantly exhausted from incessant pain, she yearned to be free. Perhaps, like those in Daniel's dream, to fight and … kill.

It sounded vulgar when put so plainly, but I knew it to be the truth. The people of this city were ignorant of the fortunate fact that Valarie did not hunt humans. For she was lethal.

It could be said that she had a one-track mind, but I knew her and loved her like a daughter. In the big scheme of things, she was calm, wise and patient, but when the battle began, or her blood was stirred, she tended to be a tad … uncouth.

I didn't even have to look at her, but I couldn't resist seeing her so alive and hungry. The fierce smile on her face and the steel sharpening in her eyes. She nodded her agreement of our earlier assessment of Daniel.

I looked back to see that hunger mirrored in him. Oh dear, we may have two of them on our hands. I should warn Kaitlyn and Marcus.

"Did you say you had this dream regularly, Daniel?" I enquired.

"Not every week, but pretty regularly. The fight is different each time, but I use my axe and the outcome is always the same. Why?"

"I don't think it's too hard to see that this dream was preparing you for your future. Not"—he was about to protest—"riding horses, although, one never can tell. It is clear now how you have been able to fit into this life so quickly after spending so many years alone." I could not hide the smile and joy that rose from my heart. "The Light has been preparing you for your part in this family and teaching you about life with Him in a particularly ... graphic and colourful way.

"We had suspected one of your badges was Warfare and, apart from seeing you in battle for myself, I would say this would come very close to confirming it."

36

DANIEL

Abbot was right. I was a fighter. I didn't have anything to be scared of. I could take care of myself. I always had, and I always would. Even in Gomorrah, I got out alive when so many didn't.

The others weren't too far ahead of me on their walk. I could catch up. And even if I couldn't, it didn't matter, 'cause I didn't need them. They were always saying that I wasn't a prisoner here and I was free to come and go as I liked. They'd just asked that I let them know when I was heading out.

Well, I was ready. These walls were closing in and it was time for me to get over myself and get out of here for another breath of city air. I wandered into the courtyard and gave them a heads-up, "I'm just heading out for a bit," as I threaded my way through the half-door and hit the street before anyone could respond.

Flipping a coin in my head, I turned left and started into the rabbit warren at a good pace. I figured if I just kept tracking left then right, left then right, I should be able to reverse the pattern to get back. I nodded to the Warrior who came with me and wondered if he could keep up.

It felt good. I was light and on top of the world, so I upped my pace. It wasn't long till the old thrill was buzzing through me and I was flying the familiar high of being free. Electricity coursed through my veins. I felt stronger and fresher than ever before. I welcomed the pounding of my feet on pavement. In these new shoes they'd given me, the shock was absorbed and the thrum energised me. I was unstoppable. Pushing harder, I broke into a sprint, revelling in the space and solitude. But most of all, I celebrated my own power. On and on I went, left then right, stronger, then left then right, higher.

Finally, exhausted, I had to stop. Impressed my new mate had kept up. More than kept up, he stood calmly by my side as I doubled over, raking in lungfuls of sulphur-tainted air. Ah, the smell of the city. I hadn't realised how much I'd hated it until I'd had a break from it. That was definitely going on the list of things I was not going to miss.

Forcing my heart to slow, I marvelled at the waterfall of sweat that cascaded out of every pore. Never before had I been able to run just for the joy of it. The waste of energy, loss of water, and soaking of my clothes was just too extravagant. But now, not only had the bottomless pit of food and the intense workouts of the past two weeks filled out, strained and hardened my body, they had been accompanied by hot showers, clean clothes, and safe rest. The combination had left me walking on air. I was in control, stronger, fitter and more capable. Lethal.

But now, it was time to walk it out and take myself home. Right then left, right then left, I retraced my path, old mate by my side. It wasn't long before I knew I had made a mistake. It must have been the sprint. I'd missed a turn. There was no need to panic though, the streets were my home, my safety. I was confident I could find my way. I hadn't gone far when voices reached out to me from behind. Smiling I swivelled, expecting to see the others.

"Look, girls, he's happy to see us." A group of women approached.

"The newbie's come out to play." That one licked her grotesquely oversized lips.

I rubbed my eyes, blinked, then gave my head a shake. Either sweat had fogged my vision or I was dehydrated. I couldn't focus. It was impossible. Inconceivable.

Six women approached me. Their bodies sculpted in physically impossible proportions like overworked, underfed mannequins. Surely they weren't real? I must have been having a post-workout hallucination. I looked to my Warrior. He just looked straight ahead. Spinning on the spot, I headed back along the wrong path. I could easily cut across the next parallel street and get back on track.

I turned into the next street and they were there, waiting for me. "Where you going, gorgeous? Don't you wanna play?" That one mutated from obscenely thin to repulsively obese in front of my eyes.

Sick ... I'm going to be sick.

"Did you hear that? He thinks you're disgusting, love." One of the hourglass mannequins pretended to console Body Change mannequin.

"Oh, that's right, he prefers to play with boys." They broke out cackling. All they were missing were pointy hats and warty noses.

I had to get away. I knew these weren't real people. They were the enemy. But I didn't know what to do or how to handle the situation. Again, I looked to my Warrior. He didn't do anything. Didn't move. Didn't speak. Didn't draw his crazy-butt sword. What was the point of a guard if he didn't protect you? Seeking a way out, I turned again. I wouldn't run, that would be futile. Demons could track me anywhere.

I had to remain focused and get myself back to the house. They'd know what to do. Stay calm. Breathe. Walk away. Focus on your escape.

Another street, another confrontation. Every turn I took, they were there waiting for me, cackling and taunting. It was all I could do to stay calm. Well, outwardly calm. On the inside I was a brittle autumn leaf losing more of myself with every step. Sulphur was itching my eyes and irritating my nose. I was cooling off too quickly and my joints protested. My skin and clothing were crusty with dried salt. Everything was piling up, agitating and scratching away at my sanity.

They had me surrounded. My guard was a statue. I was going to have to try to break through by myself. Pretending to be braver than I felt, I approached them. But as I got close, they morphed again. Now they were Commander's men from Gomorrah. One of them played my part, and I was forced to witness a replay of what happened to me in the compound.

Commander walked around his encircled men and stoked them, and his pet, Soldier, into a frenzy. I watched the replica of myself stand bound, half-naked, mute and terrified in the middle of the savage gang. Everything was coming back. Instead of the men, however, now the demonic dolls spurred Soldier on.

I watched frozen in place as it happened all over again. The abuse, the humiliation, and the disabling terror of being recaptured by the gang we'd escaped from. Being bound, stripped to the waist, beaten, and tormented by a psychopath to entertain the men. At the compound in Gomorrah, I'd had to remain silent. Any sign of fear from me would have smashed the scant reserve Soldier had. Even though he'd been kept on a short leash, the Commander wouldn't have cared if he'd let loose. I had released an endless, mindless scream, but only within the confines of my head.

This time, as I was forced to relive the most terrifying event in my life, my resources were dry. This time, I screamed out loud. I gave voice to my terror. I screamed in frustration, in agony, for the humiliation and, most of all, I screamed in anger. I only stopped in order to vomit everything in my gut onto the pavement. They had opened Pandora's box. I knew this would happen. It was the reason I'd never let myself think about it. I knew once I started screaming I would never be able to stop. And I didn't.

I had nothing left in my stomach. So, I retched bile. With every gulp of air, defeat soaked in. With every purge, hope leached away.

The mannequins cackled, their voices echoing around the dark emptiness of my head, "Pathetic."

"Yeah, the little skrat. Thinks he's a warrior. He's a joke." More cackling.

"We've got your number, Little Skrat," a voice purred into my ear, "and I'm gonna frack your brain till your eyes bleed." Soldier's threat, voiced by a demonic doll, and the last of their cackling faded into my all-consuming terror.

My voice was gone. My throat was stripped. But I couldn't stop screaming. Footsteps came thundering down the path. They were coming back with reinforcements, but I was spent. The only thing I had was self-defence. Instinct kicked in and I rolled into a ball and covered my head. Gasping. Straining my ears for their approach.

Rough hands shook me. If the stupid plinters were dumb enough to come that close, they were going to pay. Without conscious thought I allowed my instincts free reign again. Springing into a crouch I came out swinging. The first went down when I buckled her knees. The second received the heel of my hand under the jaw.

But it wasn't enough. There were too many. Body bound, I couldn't get another swing away. My legs were trapped, and I was lifted off the ground. I threw my head back but met thin air. Hell! Fighting for all I was worth was useless. But damned if I was gonna give up.

I was held in a vice, but I felt no pain. The rage was on me and I was consumed by fire. I wasn't strong enough to fight Soldier physically. I had to think my way out. Keeping my eyes shut, I stopped struggling and played possum. Maybe I could trick the kret into loosening his bind.

As I forced myself to relax, to try to think my way out, a voice broke through the fog. Hot breath at a shattering volume. "Dan! Daniel!"

I froze. Gathering my courage, I opened my eyes as Marcus brought me back from Gomorrah.

Realisation washed over me like sunrise and I broke. I was safe. I could stop. My strength evaporated as the remnants of adrenaline dissolved. Marcus caught me as I slumped in his arms, trusting his strength to hold me. Then the tears started.

He embraced me like the father I never had. I soon became aware that Kait was hugging the both of us. They had come for me. My last resolve washed away, and I sobbed freely into their arms.

They were gracious and patient with me, waiting for me to make the first move. Kait seemed edgy, her hands fluttering all over the place. I managed to pull in enough oxygen to relocate my centre and to regain my sanity.

Eventually, I stepped back from them and finished pulling myself together. "Fancy meeting you two in a place like this." My croaky attempt at light-heartedness fell flat amidst all the tears and snot covering my face and Marcus's shirt. I couldn't stop shaking.

"Yeah, we dropped the twins off home and the three of us decided to take a quiet walk to get some peace, but all the screaming put an end to that."

Skrat, Tessa was here somewhere? I didn't want to be seen like this. Not by her. I was grateful to Marcus for giving me the heads up. Kait was having none of it.

"Dan, what happened? Are you okay?" Her fidgety arms turned to steel as she wrapped them around me again and hugged me fiercely. Despite only coming to my chin, she possessed the ability to cradle me. To give myself more time to recover, I let her.

What could I say, how could I explain my extreme stupidity and arrogance? How could I give them the details without telling the truth?

I have been so foolish. I am so not ready for this. Help me. Please.

Sensitive as always, Kait released me, and I did my best to explain. It hurt to talk, but it hurt more to remember. I glared at my Warrior. Stoic, he stared back. "My guard seems to be broken. He didn't help me out. I thought you said we were free from attack, Kait." My shame transformed my confusion into an accusation I hadn't intended.

Her palm cupped my cheek. "Oh, sweetheart. We are free from physical attack. Your Warrior was keeping them from physically hurting you. Without the Light's decree, they would have been all over you. Your Warrior stood by you, a reminder to them to keep their hands off." She ran her hands down my arms and gave me a professional once over. "You're not injured, are you?" Alarm in her voice.

"No." I flicked an apologetic look to my guard, he nodded his head in acceptance. I had so much to learn. Pouring over what had happened, I considered the Freaky Mannequins and their verbal attack. "They knew my weak spots I guess, and they used them. I can't fight women and I'm not ready to face my past."

"They weren't women, Dan. Demons aren't male or female. They're whatever will cause you the greatest damage." Marcus spoke the sobering truth.

"Yeah well, like I said, they knew my weak spots," I said.

"You want to talk about it?" Kait hobbled beside me as we turned. Noticing her wince, I put two and two together. Damn it! They hadn't attacked me, but I sure as hell had laid into Kait.

"Not yet, thanks. But Kait, I am so sorry, are you okay? I never meant to hurt you, I would never hit or ..." I couldn't speak. A lump the size of China was lodged in my throat.

"Dan, it's okay, I'm tougher than that." Again, her palm comforted my cheek. "Next time, I'll be more careful."

Even in this, she was gracious. I knew I had hurt her. I accepted her forgiveness, but her limp was duly noted. I looked to Marcus. "Sorry, and ... thanks." I was surprised he hadn't made some lame comment about his swelling jaw, but I was equally grateful for his silent forgiveness.

Tessa, whiter than her normal shade of pale, crept out from the shadows. Her dark eyes engulfed half her face. Her fingers knotted in the hem of her shirt and she fidgeted from foot to foot.

Marcus threw one arm around my shoulders and the other around his wife's waist as they walked me home. No one asked me any more about it, but the offer was left out there to take up at any point. It was just one more thing to be grateful for—that, and the unexpected comfort given by Tessa's small, clammy hand fluttering into mine. I firmly grasped it and let her cold skin soothe my fire.

37

DANIEL

It had been just over two weeks in the Light and the days fell into a surprisingly easy rhythm. One thing that was troubling me, though, was that I had started having The House dream again. I guess meeting the demonic dolls brought that on.

Thanks girls, or not-girls, as the case may be.

But this time round, things were different. They were better. In the dream, I was still an active participant of some pretty freaky stuff, but I wasn't scared anymore. And a gift I was not going to look in the mouth was that I was able to use my sword and armour to protect myself and others. I started preparing to talk to Abbot and Val about it. But not today.

In the meantime, however, I used my free time to practise my sets in the grey box of a courtyard in front of the house. But I was torn. It was good to be outside, to see the sky. After living on the streets for so long and sleeping almost under the stars, I still needed time outdoors not to feel claustrophobic.

But I still wasn't ready to go back out on the streets by myself. Everyone was pretty cool about it. We would go on short walks so that Val could stretch her legs and start to get her stamina back. They made it look like it was for Val's benefit, but I suspected they were doing it for me as well. It helped.

The other thing that was really troubling me was Tessa. Being outside was a good way to cool my blood and distance myself from her. Out here, in my box, I couldn't see her. And when I lost myself in the meditation, I didn't think about her either. I was finding it harder to honour my pact to give her space. She was like an earworm in my brain, working its way so deep it was making compost, especially since my rescue.

Tessa wasn't needy and desperate like the girls I knew on the street. She didn't throw herself at me or try to con me with sex like the girls from the gangs. She was independent, but wasn't above asking for help. She was focused, graceful and elegant, and also a bit of a klutz. But the most intriguing thing was the joy that blasted from her like heat from a furnace. Maybe it had something to do with her yellow armour? Who knew? But somewhere along the way, she'd transformed into beautiful—I mean, like, full of beauty—and hot, all in one little package. I don't think she had changed, but now that I knew her better, the way I saw her had changed.

When I watched her spar with Marcus, and when I got to spar with her myself, I saw a whole different side of her. Since my attack, I appreciated the wisdom of Marcus's plan and had started to engage her. I knew I had to. It was a weakness. I still wouldn't go hard-core at her. But I could see it was helpful for her as well. She had to learn how to fight off guys so she wasn't so vulnerable. And I needed to face what the Dark threw at me.

Her face, which I once thought of as pretty peculiar, now held me captive. She was creating a lot of energy in me, and I wanted to honour my promise of keeping my hands off her. And, well, I knew if I touched her, I may not be able to stop. So, I did everything I could to avoid her.

Having my guitar and the opportunity to play was a tonic that also soothed my mind and cooled my blood. Music helped everything. And this courtyard had great acoustics. Val was happy for me to spend time out here, but she insisted on the front door being kept open. At first, I thought it was because they wanted to keep an eye on me and what I was doing. But Kait assured me it was so I never felt like I was shut out. I could be separate when I needed it, but always connected.

Riah made it clear though that the door had to stay open for the music. I was learning her sign language, and she made it known that she loved it when I played. If she was inside drawing when I was outside playing, she would open the small front windows and make sure the door was as wide as it could go. My heart broke when I remembered that she used to sing. So, often I would play just for her. I would listen for her coming inside, then I'd stop what I was doing and play. She would respond by popping her head around the corner of the door and gifting me with one of her smiles.

Soon after I claimed the space, she had Marcus bring out some pot plants she had made just for me. Filled with life and colour, this grey space took on a totally different feel. It was still warm and comforting, but more welcoming and, well, just an awesome place to be.

Shortly afterward, she also brought her chalks and started transforming my grey haven into another Eden. Someone must have told her about my old place in the park, because she made it look like we were being embraced and sheltered in the arms of a huge tree. She was good.

Was it a natural talent, was it learned and practised, or was it her Badge?

Not sure, but, fraggling hell, she was amazing. And our afternoon down time settled into a companionable partnership. I would play and she would draw.

I usually lacked the confidence to sing, but when I lost myself in the music it just came out. I would sing the songs Abraham had taught me and the ones I made up. I got so used to Riah being there I soon forgot her presence and I lost myself to the music. I was safe, fed, and warm. I had a purpose and I was at peace, except when I allowed thoughts of Tessa to enter my head. But in my contentment, I couldn't help but sing.

Obviously, sound travelled, and the others soon asked me to play for them as well. They already knew the ones I'd learned from Abraham, and they taught me some new ones. At the close of each day we'd retire to the sitting room, finishing as we'd begun, in communion and reflection on the Light. And I would play.

Val pointed out to me one morning as we did our sets that my armour was getting thicker thanks to all the training. Sometimes I got high on just checking myself out.

Life had fallen into a surprisingly comfortable routine. But if I didn't get out into the real world again soon, I was going to go nuts. I needed to get back to the streets, where life was real and raw. I wanted a breather out in my world, where I was at home and I wasn't the misfit newb.

38

KAITLYN

"They say you are supposed to add the wet to the dry. But I have found that if I add the dry, a bit of time, to the wet, it makes a smoother batch." Raph was giving Dan another cooking lesson.

"What do you want me to do?" Dan towered over his instructor.

We'd all been impressed by the way Dan had eased his way into Raph's trust. Showing real wisdom and insight, he didn't treat Raph like a child. Truth be, in most ways, he wasn't. Providing opportunity for them to see each other's truths had proved successful in raising their mutual regard.

After his initial brain snap, Marcus had come to see Dan in a new light. Now he couldn't stop raving about the lad. And his pride and affection were evidently growing, especially since Dan's attack on the street.

I returned to mending the pile of clothes that I never seemed to conquer. My eyes were drawn to Marcus and Val in the garden going through the motions. It was good to see that, as the days progressed, so did her improvement. It'd been over two weeks. But now she was back to joining us for more vigorous morning sets and helping out with a few things around the house. She had even taken Riah out for a slow jog this morning. I think that may have been a bit ambitious. But like anyone could tell Val anything, especially when she'd been suffering for so long. I found it best to allow her the space to find her own boundaries.

It was interesting to note that the tension of the house decreased in direct proportion to the increase of Val's recovery. A consequence of this, or perhaps a contributing factor, was Dan's diminishing wall. Sariah's badge of Peace had helped. That, and the music she drew out of him. I think all of these things combined were helping him get over his confrontation with the demons. He still wouldn't talk about it and we wouldn't push him. Yet.

"Kait." Tessa came from behind my chair and took Marcus's seat.

I turned to her and smiled.

"Can I ask you something?" Her voice was low, barely covering the laughter and kitchen clatter.

Putting my sewing away, I gave her my full attention.

"I don't know what to do. I mean, I know I don't have to do anything. But I think if I don't figure this out, I'm going to go nuts, I just don't know what to do, and I need your help, I just ..."

I took her hand and stemmed the tide. "Dot points, Tessa." I smiled so she realised I was imitating Val with good grace.

"I like Dan."

"Well, that's a relief."

"No. I mean. I. Like. Dan."

"Is this a problem?" It would help her to put it into words.

"Yes." Her eyes rolled, and she flopped back in Marcus's chair.

"What exactly is this problem?"

"I like him. I don't know if he likes me. He treats me like a friend. You know, a real friend. I think I may even trust him. It's a complete disaster."

"Ahh." I leaned back in my chair.

She chased me, sliding to the edge of her seat. "What do you mean, 'Ahh'? What does that mean?"

"Trust is a scary beast." I cupped her cheek.

"What do I do?" She took my hand and squeezed it in both of hers, her palms hot and damp.

"What is the best possible outcome of this dilemma?"

"We'd be friends. Real friends, like you and Marcus."

"Okay. So, what's the worst possible outcome?"

Her face paled, her eyes grew and glistened, her armour faded. "It'd be like before."

My heart lurched and I pulled her close in an attempt to hug her memories away. I wanted to take all her pain, draw it out and absorb it. I wanted to carry the load for her and give her back her innocence. But I couldn't. I couldn't remove her memories, heal her wounds, or restore her. Only the Light could do that. All I could do was help her build new memories, wrap her hurts in my love, and walk by her as she explored new experiences.

"It won't ever be like before. I promise you."

"How can you do that, Kait?" Her voice lifted and tears fell.

"Because you are different, honey. You're a different person. You are no longer ignorant or innocent. You're a fighter. You are no longer alone. You have family. You're no longer abandoned in the Dark. You've been adopted into the Light."

Colour returned as she sat taller. "So what do I do? About ... you know ..." Her eyes flicked to the kitchen.

"I can't tell you what to do, sweetheart. But I would suggest playing it cool. Wait and see what happens. May I suggest you spend your time building your friendship"—she tilted her head, brow furrowed—"like the friendship you have with Raph and Riah, not like the one I have with Marcus."

I didn't feel the need to emphasise the tactic to go slow as I couldn't see her throwing herself at Dan. She didn't have the confidence. But if I thought she might, or saw evidence that she should, I would definitely caution her. For nothing is more unattractive than a needy, desperate girl turning herself inside out to get a man's attention. Nor did I have any respect for the stupid men who refused to see through the pitiful charade.

"I think he's avoiding me." Tessa pulled me back from unsightly memories.

"Who, sweetheart?"

"Who do you think?"

"Dan?" She was right. He was. But for reasons other than she thought. If he wasn't doing chores, in training, or at meals, he was in his cave, or in Marcus's, harrying the boxing bag. I was confident that it wasn't because he wasn't attracted. On the contrary.

Abbot, never one to gossip, wouldn't spill any beans, but I was aware of him watching the two of them, albeit discreetly, often with a gentle smile. They worked well together in sparring and chores, they complemented each other physically and I suspect mentally. Regardless of what might happen, they were going to be a good team.

"I think he just wants to be ready for when we leave. You know how much the attack on the street threw him." Not exactly a lie. "And, I think he may be feeling the pressure of being cooped up." Also, not a lie. "In fact, Marcus and I are heading out tomorrow for a general reconnaissance—to stock up and do a Soteria House run. We'll invite Dan. You want to come along?"

Tessa shrugged her shoulders and tried for a nonchalant nod. The effect was ruined by her traitorous grin and the spark that lit her eyes.

"We'll make plans after dinner tonight." I picked up my sewing and made myself comfortable. I was equally unsuccessful at hiding my own traitorous grin. Tessa punched my arm. We both laughed out loud.

This time of peace was a blessing, and a haven to rejoice in. But lurking just under the surface was the bitter truth that time was running out.

39

MARCUS

"Time's running out, Dan," I said, "and at the close, you'll need to know the location of the Soteria Houses in case we get separated. You'll also need to know how to get in, so I'd like you up front with me today. Kait and Tessa already know where they are, so, ladies, would you mind travelling in the back?"

Tessa complied and Kait smiled in agreement, knowing I was trying to make up for last time. Dan appeared indifferent as he easily climbed into the cab. It was great to be out and about again. Our strengthened shield held everything at bay, and we could go about without having to worry.

Dan's indifference evaporated, however, like goodwill in a siege when he spotted our guard. Or I should say, how thick it was and how many escorted us. I was so used to it now that I didn't take it for granted per se, but it didn't fly me fancy as it first did. But seeing Dan's response was like seeing it with new eyes.

Going into the city, into their heartland, we were given extra reinforcements. Like Kait said, they would hold whilst the Light's decree was in place, and the guard was a memory prompt. Although, in saying all of that, it didn't mean we weren't the main attraction. They lined the street like an avenue of ugly. Thankfully, since our "time out" had been declared, they could bark as loud as they liked but they were as toothless as gummy bears. We just had to keep our eyes on the Light and pass right through like water sluicing off an oil stain. But they were a constant reminder of what we were having a break from.

Knowing—and not knowing—what was coming put us all on edge. The pressure out here was tangible. People on the street darted about like ants before a storm. A slight smell of sulphur stained everything. Despite our intensified shield, it was as hot as a docker's armpit out here. It was uncomfortable and oppressive. And now it was time to introduce another kind of uncomfortable to Dan's world.

"Before we head into the shops, we'll do a circuit of the Soteria Houses and I'll show you how to get in. If at any point you get separated from the group in the final battle, especially if you have Tessa or either of the twins, keep your head down and make your way to any of these places. Get yourself and the others inside, shut the door and ask the Light to keep them sealed." I risked taking me eyes off the road to take him in. He had to know how serious this was.

Dan nodded his head with resolve in his eyes. This was his area of expertise.

"If it's night, you stay there till morning, then head back to the house. I'm guessing you know how to keep a low profile and not draw attention to yourself?"

I knew he was still shaken by his recent attack, but I also knew he could handle himself in a fight. Again, he nodded.

"It's agreed that if at any stage you are separated from me, Kait or Val, you take lead. Do you understand?"

Again, he affirmed with a nod and a determined look. He accepted this promotion in silence, no questions, and no fake modesty. He knew he was best suited for the job.

"I know you're inexperienced with demons, but you're good in a fight. You're strong, smart and capable, and in the end, a fight's a fight. Your main objective is to protect those in your care, whether it's the twins, Tessa, Abbot or all four. You're the lead. Any questions?"

None.

He was ready. The Light knew what He was doing picking this one.

"So, now that's out of the way, what's going on with you and Tessa?" The cool, hard front crumbled in an instant and he was as nervous as a turkey at Lightmas.

"Wh-what do you mean? I haven't touched her, I swear!"

"I know, lad, don't panic, I'm not here to haul you out. I see you. I see the struggle in you. I see the discipline and the fight you put up not to. So, what's the story?"

A festival of emotion paraded across his face like a Mardi Gras. Poor kid, he went from hardened warrior to nervy adolescent in 0.3 seconds.

"Dan, I like you, trust you, and respect you. We all do. We wouldn't've given you this responsibility if we didn't. Truth be, I want to help you. But I also want to know what's going on, so, in an emergency, I can be aware of all considerations."

That wasn't quite true. It would be helpful to know, but not a necessity. I just thought it might prompt him to spill his guts.

His eyes, saucer-wide, raked the scenery outside. "I don't know what to say," he finally replied.

"Well then, say it like it is, son." It was all I had to offer him at this point.

Tense, awkward silence filled the cab.

"I kind of get the feeling you like her. Yes?" I prompted.

"Skrat yeah! I mean ... yes, I do. That's the problem. I don't know what to do. On the street, girls come and go, we scratch mutual itches. You know what it's like?" He looked to me. A genuine question.

I nodded.

"But that's it. We all kind of live by the same code: use 'em and lose 'em. You can't afford to get close, because ... so many reasons. Mainly 'cause no one can afford trust. It's too pricey."

He was quiet for a moment so I waited, hoping he could get it all off his chest.

"The other reason is, I don't know how to be around a girl the right way, you know … and … all of you guys breathing down my neck and coming over all 'touch her and you're dead' doesn't help."

I had to laugh at that. He was right. Poor kid.

"There's so much to learn. Kait said a girl doesn't want to be with a guy if he can't support her. Well, I got nothing. No job, no skills, no hope of making a living for two. I could barely make a living for one, and that was strongly supplemented by stealing. I don't think that counts, do you?" He eyeballed me. "I've done some seriously bad skrat I'm not proud of, and I've been through … well, let's just say I'm pretty messed up."

The floodgates had opened, and the horse had bolted. He didn't look like stopping.

"With a pride of protective predators to deal with, I've got no idea of what to do or how to go about it. I don't want to hurt her. I've got nothing to offer her and … and I'm not even sure she likes me that way. I don't even know if I like her that deep." Again with the eyeball. This time, pain seeped through. "How the hell do I know if it's more than skin, man. How the hell do I even figure that out? I don't want to hurt her." Eyes cutting the glass of the windscreen. "So, I guess that's what's *not* going on with Tessa and me."

The silence returned, not so painful but still full of frustration. I let him have a break.

As we stopped at traffic lights, the surrounding city buzzed and bustled as it prepared to burn. Heads ducked, bodies closed, faces shut, people weren't interacting, they were retreating. I was torn between gratitude and grief. Forever grateful that we'd been grafted in. Torn for those who'd turned away. But I couldn't help them, they were beyond me. But Dan was well within reach.

I re-entered the fray. "I'll admit, to start with I was wary. I didn't know you or your intentions and I was overprotective. Kait and Val chewed me out over it, even Abbot tried to counsel me. But I saw red and ended up wearing egg and eating me feet, again."

His head whipped round at that.

"Yep, they all told me to back off and let things go. I can assure you that at this point if you guys wanted to explore that question, and were sensible about it, you'd have our blessing."

I let that sink in. The old cab hummed in the silence, gently rocking and rolling as we sailed through the tension.

Then I continued. "Secondly, I totally agree. Trying to understand women is like trying to nail jelly to a tree. I still don't know what to do and how to go about it. The only way I've made it this far is by making mistakes and learning what not to do. Me Kait's awesome and I love her to bits, but after twenty-three years, there's still parts I don't understand. But that's kind of what makes it interesting. Bleeding annoying at times, but I still enjoy the jelly."

He smiled wryly.

"And as far as what's in your past and making a living, it's a bit different now. When you said yes to the Light, you didn't just pick a side to fight on, you said yes to being adopted into His family. You are now an heir of everything that's His. You're a new person with a new identity. All debts are paid. You've been stripped down and rebranded. Along with that, you're now working for Him—you're a soldier of the Light. You will always have exactly what you need when you need it. It may not be what you want, but they can be two totally different things."

I turned right off the main road and drove toward the first Soteria House for the day. "One last bit of advice. The only way you're going to know if she likes you or not is to test the waters." I slowed before I really needed to. But I wanted to make sure we finished this before we arrived.

"After all the skrat Tessa's been through, she's pretty confused about this stuff herself. And you can be sure she isn't about to throw herself at you for fear of more rejection. When you get under the sunshine exterior, her bubble is thin. Take it slow and see where you end up. Although, there are boundaries. Definitely no sex until you're married ... if you get that far. Do you hear me?"

He thought I was joking.

"I mean it, Dan. Sex is an amazing gift. It's incredible fun, but on the deepest level it's the bonding of souls. It is only to be shared with your life partner. I'm serious, Dan." I waited till I held his focus. "do you hear me?"

More sheepish now, he nodded his head. "I hear you … Dad."

"Good." I parked the truck. "Enough of that, except to say, you can come and talk to me about anything at any time. As long as I'm around, I'm here for you … son."

I knew he was having a go, but damn, it felt good to be called Dad. "Do you know this area at all?"

Releasing a pent-up breath and relaxing his shoulders, Dan scoped the perimeter, "Vaguely. I've passed through before. I'm pretty sure I could get to my tree from here."

We climbed out of the truck and I noticed Tessa was looking subdued but happy enough. I led the way to the old wooden building shaped like a box. Worn wooden doors greeted us on the landing at the top of the stairs. I had heard that beautiful gardens used to skirt the outside of these buildings, edged with lush green lawns and large shady trees. Now, dirt and weeds reflected the truth. No one cared or had use for these places, except for us. Dan turned to me. "So what now?"

40

MARCUS

"Tessa has done this before, so we'll get her to show you what to do," I said.

We all shuffled places in the cramped space and Kait backed down the stairs to give Tessa a bit more room. The girl worried the hem of her shirt and chewed away at her bottom lip.

"Relax, Tessa. Low breath, and clear your mind of everything but the Light."

She exhaled and her shoulders relaxed as she stepped forward and took over the job of giving the instructions. "Place your sword into the crevice between the doors. Start high, then slide it down till it reaches the lock. Like this." Her face was a mask of calm. "You don't have to try too hard. It's not you doing the work, but the Light in you. This only works if you are a child of the Light living in the Light."

Her eyes glowed and her armour flashed as she followed the routine. As the sword touched the lock, we all heard the click and slide of the bolt inside being released. Bouncing on her toes, she removed her sword and went to move inside. I stopped her and resealed the doors, waiting to hear the lock resetting itself.

"Your turn, Dan."

We reshuffled so Dan could claim centre stage on the stoop. I stood behind him. "Remember, relax and focus on the Light. It's not your strength, but His." I laid me hand on his shoulder to reinforce the truth. "You're already chosen. If you are actively living in the Light you will be given access into His haven."

I removed me hand. He rolled his shoulders, released a breath, dropped his head and locked onto the Light. Then drawing his sword, he opened the door. The look of pure excitement momentarily wiped all age and stress from his face and once again he was a kid opening presents at Lightmas. Before we went in, I reminded the kids to say a word of thanks for entry into this sanctuary.

I would never get tired of the welcome we received entering a Soteria House. Abbot had told me the name meant "salvation" or "safety". The buildings were a safe haven for any true child who needed it. When you crossed the threshold, peace hit you like a sledgehammer. Even though people hadn't met here for years, the Spirit of the Light still lingered.

The dark wood interior gave a cool and calming embrace. A relief from the sulphuric pressure outside. Filtered light speared through the remnants of the picture windows set at regular intervals high on three of the walls. Beams of colour cut through the shadows, revealing swirling dust motes stirred by our entrance.

The long wooden seats arranged in rows invited visitors to take time to dwell and focus on the symbol of Light hanging on the end wall. This one was bathed in a waterfall of colour from two hidden windows recessed in small alcoves, one on either side. We were home. The same feeling we got from every Soteria House we entered, especially our own.

Dan was stuck in the entrance, speechless at the sight. Kait hustled him and Tessa forward so she could get in and shut the door. She moved around the kids and made her way over, rose up on her toes and gently kissed me. Taking me hand, we watched them, especially Dan, as he experienced this for the first time. It was a great moment to witness. I let them have a moment to soak it all up, before

I had to break the silence. "Dan, come with me and I'll show you how to access the safe box."

I led him down the central aisle to the front of the building. At the left-hand side, in the front corner attached to the wall was a metal box ornately decorated with symbols of the Light. The top was scarred with a narrow slot.

"People have always felt the need to give to the Light. Some treat it like a kind of talisman. Abbot told us that years ago when people met openly in places like this, you didn't actually have to be a child of the Light to get in. Anyone could come in and join in the gathering. It was another thing people thought would help them in End Times. They believed that if they came each week to the meeting and put money in the box, that would be enough."

The look of surprise on their faces affirmed the danger of this useless ritual.

"Yeah, crazy, I know. I guess they thought more of the process than they did of the Light. Sadly, the practices didn't save them. You heard Abbot's story? Just because they did these things didn't mean they were Children of Light. If you're not authentic, you don't get the armour. Then, in a battle, you've got nothing to save you. They didn't understand that you can't buy this armour. But even after the Soteria Houses closed, people still hedged their bets. They still come and feed the boxes."

"But how can they do that if they can't get in?" Dan asked the most logical question.

"There's a slot in the wall on the outside of the building that opens straight into the side of the box," Kait answered. "This way, people can stay in the Dark and not be seen giving to the Light."

"But why do they want to stay in the Dark? What are they scared of?" Tessa asked the oldest question of all.

"Because it's their choice and they are scared of what will happen to them if someone sees them supporting the Light," Kait said. "They would be ridiculed, mocked, they might lose their job, or, as was Abbot's case, their life may be threatened. It costs a lot to live in the

Light, sweetheart. You know that. Most people aren't prepared to pay that much."

"But they think they can buy their way in with money?" Dan screwed up his face.

"People are strange beasts at best, son. But this money was given to the Light, to be used by the Light, to further the work of the Light. And in this place at this time, that's us." It was time to get moving. "Kait would you like the honour today?" She smiled, removed her sword and, whispering a word of thanks, gently slid the tip into the slot.

Once again, there was an audible click and the lock was released. Removing her weapon, Kait opened the lid and peered inside.

"There's a letter." Her voice hitched. Removing it she read aloud:

Help me. I don't know what to do. I know something is happening. I know the Dark is coming. I'm scared and don't know what to do or where to go. Please help me. I work at The Plaza in Renald's—the cosmetic section. Please help me.

~E.

Kait finished reading then looked to me. "Well, I guess we know where we're going later today." This was obviously the "something else" that needed seeing to.

"It could be a trap." I wasn't too sure about this. It was far too easy to just drop a note in the box. We got notes occasionally, but normally they were hate-mail and abusive letters.

"It could be genuine." She smiled as she emptied the other contents.

This would all be gone soon. The box, the building, the whole town. As a rule, we never took all the money in case other Children of Light came by and were in need. The contents were the same as last time, except for the addition of the note. And since this was the end, there was little point leaving any.

"We'll go about this the same way we go about everything else. Eyes open, on guard and prepared," Kait said.

She was right of course. "We'll still follow our plan, and then last of all, we'll swing by this place and check it out."

The kids had been silent through it all. It would be good for them. We were in for the pennies and the pounds, and even though Dan was still wet behind the ears, it would give them both necessary experience. "Take a good look round, guys. You won't see this building again."

"It just so sad." Kait gave voice to the collective mood.

"Yes, but this is just a building. It's special only because of who has lived here. Buildings will come and go, but His presence will never be taken from us," I said.

"I know that, but the history of this place. What it meant to so many people and what took place here. The celebrations, the connections, and the community. But then again, as you say, this is just a building. Out there is a city full of people about to be lost," she said.

What could you say to that? In a cloud of sadness, we filed out and closed the door for the last time. The rest of the morning was tainted with sorrow as travelled to each of the Soteria Houses to check, clear and farewell. We were grieving the loss of these wonderful buildings and what they stood for. To us they represented security. They'd provided a means for us to survive and offered shelter in conflict.

We were also mourning the loss of a city and the thousands who lived here. They'd made their choice. They'd opted to cling to the Dark and live in the shadows, and now they were going to suffer the consequences. 'Twas such a waste. But, if you chose to lie down with the dogs, you'd be getting up with the fleas.

This whole situation highlighted the eternal, unanswerable question, "Why us?" Why were we chosen? Why were we elected from the multitude, to see? Why were we invited to belong? Why had we been offered adoption? There was nothing different about us. I guessed we'd never know. It seemed that the line separating us from all the rest was paper thin and a mile wide. Weaker than vapour, impervious as steel.

Once we'd finished the rounds, we headed in to get supplies. It was disconcerting to be preparing for the end in the midst of societal blindness. Although they may not have known exactly what they were in for, it was becoming as pleasant as prickly heat in the inner suburbs. Individuals rushed about, while groups loitered. Never a good sign. Even though the shield still held, our holiday was well and truly coming to an end.

41

KAITLYN

Nothing concrete was coming to me about meeting with "*E*". I was just picking up sensations of importance mingled with hints of great risk. We proceeded on high alert. The SOS could be genuine, or bait for a trap. Either way, we had to investigate. We could not abandon a Potential.

Please, help us stay vigilant and not drop the ball so close to the end game.

After storing the cold food in the eskies and stowing the rest of the supplies safely in the truck, we flew by the produce store on our way to the Plaza. Renald's was an expensive chain of department stores, usually situated in upmarket shopping malls of the inner suburbs.

I guess one good thing about this one was that the car parks were wider than normal, accommodating the nerves of drivers of very expensive cars. We'd be able to park the truck close by and not have to walk a mile. At this stage of the game, I didn't want to be stranded too far away from transport.

I noticed Dan flinching, his eyes flicking left to right, taking in the vast number of our audience. We'd warned him what to expect. But warning wasn't experiencing. But thankfully, neither was experiencing the same as encountering. There would be plenty of time for that later on.

Coming into the city for the first time with the Sight was always going to be a shock. Thankfully our guard was thick, and we were assured we were safe. Tessa reached up and laid her hand on his shoulder. Once she had his attention, she flipped the front of his helmet down. He breathed deeply as they shared a smile. They were going to be good for each other.

As we walked through The Plaza on our way to Renald's, we let Tessa and Dan take the lead. This way, we could keep them in our sights and within reach. They drew most of the attention from the enemy, who were aggressively straining at the Light's barrier. I knew we were safe, but Marcus and I stayed close to Dan and Tessa. I couldn't bear the thought of either of them falling back into enemy hands.

Thank you for your extended guard at this time. Watch over them and keep them safe ... all of them.

Normally we would check the shop first before meeting up with a Potential. But since the cosmetics section was at the entrance of the ground level, and because we knew we were under extra protection, we headed straight to our meeting. I could see Tessa's attention was torn between staying focused on the mission and trying to ignore the enemy ... and the bags and shoes that spilled out from the cosmetics. I hoped in our new place I could take her shopping without the risk of dying.

We all had our eyes peeled as we worked the area. Dan naively wandered into the lair of the perfumeries—gateway to lingerie. On foreign ground, he soon fell prey to the lure of the advertising, the packaging, and the scent. Oh dear, he was going to be eaten alive.

No sooner had I thought it than it happened. Perfectly sculpted women—silicon wrapped in store uniforms—swarmed to him. Poor thing was like a deer in the headlights not knowing where to look. I quickly glanced at Marcus and noted his and Tessa's expressions.

Each of us watched with what appeared to be different feelings: pity, pride, and fury.

Tessa's face was coloured with rage.

"Sweetheart, I think he's out of his depth and rapidly drowning. He may need saving," I suggested quietly.

"He's doing alright. He'll be just fine," Marcus puffed. "I might go and see what he's up to." Tessa and I rounded on him immediately in utter disbelief. "Or maybe, I'll stand here with you, me beautiful wife."

"Did you see that? That woman dropped that sample on purpose so she could run her hand down his leg, and he could see straight down her top!" Before Tessa could finish her sentence, another of the sirens had completed a full body brush across his back, making sure her chest implants left imprints in his shirt. Tessa was a volcano ready to erupt.

But then Dan turned around. The look on his face was a mosaic of helplessness, frustration, and anger. Oh Lord, it was the Demonic Dolls all over again, but these were human. Teeth clenched, he was desperately looking for an escape. If they'd been men, I suspect he would have enjoyed punching his way out. But he wouldn't raise a hand to a woman, as we well knew.

They had him surrounded. His eyes locked with Tessa's and the message was clear: "get me out of here or it's going to get ugly".

Her yellow armour was tinged with red and green. Her hand wrapped around the hilt of her sword, and she caressed it before passing me her bag. Throwing her shoulders back, chin up and small chest puffed out, she advanced into the throng. As she arrived, so too did her fake, sickly-sweet smile.

She actually had to elbow one of the women out of the way so she could get to Dan. But they had their own way of hitting back. One of the Amazons bent down to her level, got in her face and said something we couldn't hear. Whatever it was hit home. My poor girl deflated instantly.

Dan turned to look at her, calm softening his features. "Contessa, there you are!" He wrapped his arm around her shoulders and, quick as a flash, she rose up to her toes and pulled his head down so she could fully kiss him on the mouth.

There was neither hesitation nor implied innocence. She was staking her claim and countering the attack, girl-style. Her hand dropped to his butt and she giggled. "There you are, I've been looking all over for you. Time to put your toys"—she eyeballed each of the remaining women with a snarl—"away and come home, we have so much to do."

The whole tribe stopped and stared at her. Some I'm sure had not understood her insult, but it created enough of an opening for her to free Dan from their clutches. I heard her mutter something like "bucking riches" on her way back to us. She could have been making a social comment on the ills of rampant consumerism. But I doubted it.

When she returned, she was still fired up, armour ablaze and jaw clenched defiantly. Firing daggers with her eyes, still grasping Dan's hand, she challenged us with a look: "what?"

Marcus's eyes shone with unshed tears, whether from pride or laughter, I couldn't tell. He roughly embraced her and loudly kissed the top of her head. "I love you so much I think I'm going to explode. That was better than a month of Sundays in the middle of May."

That took the wind out of her sails. The shock that had been on Dan's face now rested on hers, and the smile that had been on mine was mirrored in Dan's eyes. I reached over and stroked her cooling face. "Come on, honey, we're here for a purpose. Back to work, people."

This time, staying clear of the Sensual Sirens, the two of them took the other side of the department. Tessa still staking a firm claim on Dan's hand, which he willingly submitted. I also discreetly steered Marcus away from any temptation in that region as our search continued.

"I can see you," a small voice rang from behind the main counter.

We all turned and took in the bashful girl that had spoken. Like the very expensive products she sold, she was immaculate, perfectly presented, and encased for display behind a glass counter. She was beautiful and flawless. Whether that stemmed from the natural gift of youth and genetics, or from the blessing of wealth and a scalpel, was hard to say.

"I know who you are. Did you get my note?"

42

DANIEL

Marcus, Kait and Tessa froze. It mustn't have been a trap. The girl was genuine. How else could she see our armour and know who we were? I stood back with Tessa and let Marcus and Kait take the lead.

"My name is Kait. This is Marcus, Tessa, and Dan. We would like to help you."

"I'm Ebony," she said.

She looked down and did this sideways glance thing when she said her name. I'm sure she flicked a glance to me, but it was so quick, I couldn't be certain. Maybe she was as freaked out at the Dark's goons as I was. And she didn't have a helmet to shut the plinters out.

Thanks for mine and for Tessa giving me the heads up.

Regardless, I was still having trouble reconciling the fact that my nightmares were now walking with me during the day. I shut them out and let Kait's conversation drift over me as I relived the assault of the Perfumery Pirates. With my visor down, I checked them out, from the corner of my eye. Yep, they were definitely human.

I'd thought it was just on the street that girls were like that. It was one of the things that drew me to Tessa. The fact she wasn't after a quick fix, a shallow, self-gratifying high whenever and from whomever. All the girls I had known were for sale. Some sold themselves for the high of drugs, some just sold whatever they had for money and power, and the poor sold themselves for necessities, or the haze that helped you forget.

I'd thought that pretty much summed up life for everyone on the street. But here? These people were rich. They had it all: homes, food, and the luxury of choice. It made me sick. Made me realise how much I didn't fit into "normal", and how grateful I was for my new family.

I took a gamble and released Tessa's hand so I could place my arm around her tiny shoulders. I just wanted to get closer. I was so grateful for her. She seemed to be as different as I was, and that made me appreciate her even more. I got a buzz when she responded by placing her arm around my waist and nestling in.

I went back to considering the slick check-out chick who had written the note. Seemed she wanted in. I didn't blame her. Living in this jungle every day would be enough to drive anyone to their senses. If you looked for the signs, under her make-up you could see she was a "natural" like us. And her clothes weren't as tasteless as those around her.

"I live out of town at my parent's house," she said, naming the most prestigious estate on the eastern side of town.

Figured. She looked like money. But I guess the Light is for everyone, not just the down and outers.

"Ebony, this is not the best place to talk. Are you able to take a break? Can we meet up with you somewhere more discreet?" Kait led the conversation. Being a woman, she was probably best suited to engage the nervous girl. Ebony's darting eyes kept flicking between Marcus and me.

"I can't take a break now. I have just returned from one. That's why I didn't see you when you first came in." Her voice rose as her eyes kept darting around nervously.

"What about after work? We could come back," Kait said.

"Yes, that would suit. Tomorrow. I finish at 4:00. I'll meet you by the main entrance at 4:15. Don't make contact with me in the open. You can follow me to my car, and we'll talk there."

Talk about Twik Princess. But as soon as I thought it, I felt bad. I'd already jumped to the wrong conclusion with one girl. I should wait and see before labelling this one. Although, she was uppity ... and obviously a princess. So, if the shoe fit ...

"Okay." Kait was doing a great job of staying calm. "Then we can arrange to go somewhere quiet to discuss things after that. We'll wait for you at the main entrance at 4:15 tomorrow afternoon."

There wasn't anything else to say and Ebony was growing more edgy the longer we stayed. I don't know who was more relieved when we made our getaway. Marcus's blue armour and Tessa's yellow were both tinged with the same sparks of red. We all turned, giving everyone and everything wide berth, and left the shop.

I'd been looking forward to getting back to the city, my home. But instead, I felt like I'd just waded through an ocean of tar and was in desperate need of something clean and fresh. Back at the truck, no one questioned or even raised eyebrows as Tessa and I climbed in the back together. I kind of hoped Marcus would take the long way home ... slowly.

"Thank the Light there are windows in here. Travelling in the back would be a nightmare without them," I said, making small talk. After the intimacy in the crowd, the privacy was awkward.

"It used to be a horse truck, that's why there are sliding windows and storage boxes along that side. The ramp was converted to a roller door for convenience, and above the cab, behind all the stuff that has already been packed, is a loft bed. It's quite large. Kait and Marcus sometimes spend the night in here."

As soon as the words were out of her mouth, the red rocket launched from her neck and burned to cover her whole face. She ducked under the strap of her bag and placed it on the floor between us, then found a secure place to sit as the rumble of the engine shook everything with the anticipation of moving. Not to be put off, I moved the bag and took its place next to but not touching her. I also prepared for the lurch and sway of the return trip.

"Well, it seems like a really practical kind of truck. I had wondered what the holes in the floor and roof were for."

"That's from the barriers that separated the horses. Did you know that when the truck isn't packed, you can also access a small door from the cab into the back? It's where the grooms could duck back to check on things rather than having to stop the truck all the time. The twins love using it."

"Are you serious? That sounds cool. How big is it?" I was genuinely interested.

She ran her eyes over me and blushed again. Quickly looking away, she answered, "I can fit through it easily, so you probably could too, but it might be a bit of a squeeze."

Looking at everything but me, her eyes finally found something very interesting in the far corner and she decided to lock on to that.

Silence.

"Thanks for helping me out ... back in the shop." I figured it was time to address the elephant in the truck. The space back here was too small to accommodate all three of us.

"That's okay." She graced me with a half-grin, then looked away before continuing. "At first I was really annoyed, but then I realised that you were getting pretty angry. I figured you didn't have any trouble punching those guys for me. But these weren't guys, and ... it was no thrift shop." Finally, she looked my way again and a ghost of a smile hovered over her lips.

"Hang on a minute, why were you annoyed?" I challenged her.

Far out, if this girl got any redder, she'd self-combust. I waited patiently, eager to hear her answer, giving her time to find the words.

"I didn't like the way they were behaving around ... all over ... you. And at first, I thought you were enjoying it, and that annoyed me ... a bit," she said.

"A bit?"

"Okay, it annoyed me a lot. But then, when you turned around and I saw your face, I kind of saw red and got really skitched that they would do that to you. Kait suggested I should help you out. So, I ... ahhh, thought that I would. But then that ... girl ... called me ... well, you know what she called me." Her voice dropped with her head. "I should be used to it. Back in the gang, they all used those names for me. I guess it's just been a while … but it still hurts." She went silent.

I was also remembering the first time I met her and how easily I cut her down with a simple look. I was just as bad as those twiks in the shop and I felt like skrat.

"Why did you call me Contessa?"

"What? Oh, well … the Dark Lord called you that. I know I have heaps to learn, but I've picked up that he knows stuff. He's evil and freaky, but Val said he's really smart. So, I figured it must be your proper name.

"Abraham, Indy's dad, used to say that there was power in names. Anyway, I didn't like the way the Dark Lord used it. It sounded filthy. But it's a special name. It reminds me of royalty. I wanted you to hear your name like it should be said—with respect. And I wanted to remind you that you aren't the sum total of what others see or think. They may've called you that in the past, you may have even believed it, but we've been given a clean slate, remember? But, far out, you've got nerve. That was some comeback."

"Um … sorry about that, I didn't mean to embarrass you, I just thought with those leeches, direct would be … um … best." She stammered to a halt.

I leaned over, gently took her chin in my hand, and turned her reluctant face toward me. I then met her lips in the gentlest, softest kiss I could manage. Inside I wanted a hell of a lot more, but I didn't want to blow this.

"Direct is good. I like direct, Tessa …" She had a look of wonder in her eyes and the red of her cheeks had faded to the most beautiful pink flush. "Thanks. I really appreciated that you did help me, and how you helped me." I then put my arm around her shoulders, and she snuggled in. Resting my head back on some random bag of something, I shut my eyes and just enjoyed the moment.

"That girl …" The sentence died on her lips.

Not moving, I asked, "What girl?"

"The. Girl. The girl we went to find, Ebony."

"Yeah, what about her?"

"She was kind of pretty, don't you think?" She was hesitant, but I wasn't that much of an idiot.

I hadn't moved but watched her out of the corner of my eye. "I guess, if you're into that kind of thing. She was a bit too perfect for my liking. I prefer girls who are real, who can get messy, and who can move like a cat but be a klutz at the same time. I like girls who aren't afraid to try things and get them wrong, and a girl who can laugh at herself. But there is nothing hotter than a girl who can fight like a tiger and dance with a blade. Oh, and I definitely prefer blondes."

We both settled back, and Tessa nestled into the crook of my arm. Perfect. Yeah, I reckoned I could do this. I reached into her bag and pulled out an apple.

"What was that?" She seemed ridiculously upset about something.

It was hard to talk with my mouth full. The juice was running down my chin and the sweetness exploded in my mouth. "Wha-wa-wha?" I mumbled.

"That!" Indicating my apple.

Hello. Welcome back, Twik Princess. I could sense my arch nemesis stirring. Man, this girl could grow prickles at the most inopportune times. "It's an apple."

She hit me with one of those looks. The ones girls get. I don't know where they get them from, but they all have them. Do they go to "look school" or is it chromosomal?

I guess now was not the time to ask.

"I can see it is an apple, Dan. Where did you get it from?" She'd morphed into predator bird.

"Your bag?" I offered.

"What do you mean you got it from my bag? I didn't put any apples in my bag."

"I know. I did."

"What? When?"

"Ahhh ... at the shops." Obviously.

She shot me another look, this one sideways. "When did you go into a food shop?"

"I didn't. There was a fruit barn in the mall outside Renald's and they had displays in the aisle."

"But we didn't stop." I was now getting a full-frontal face frown, with her eyebrows so low they seemed to blend with her eyelashes. The eagle was aiming for a kill.

Can't I just have nice Tessa back? Please?

"I know. We just walked past. I'm not trying to be thick, but I don't understand the problem." I reached across her to her bag and pulled out another one. "I got one for you too." I tried to pass it to her, but it was like the thing was poisoned the way she squeaked and threw her arms up in defence.

"Flopping hell, Dan. What other stolen merchandise did you put in my bag?" Her outrage blossomed like blood splatter after a knife wound. I didn't understand.

"I only took two apples, Tessa. I didn't have time for anything else. Sorry." That last bit was pure acid, but really, she was going way over the top. Seriously, there were hundreds of the things and I only took two. And I got one for her. Granted, it probably wasn't the best idea to put them in her bag, but I didn't have anywhere else to put them. So much for being nice.

"I can't believe you stole those and planted them on me. What if someone had seen you and I got into trouble." Her arms were crossed, and her body was closed. "But not only that, stealing is illegal. Somebody has to make up for that out of their wages." She had started on some holier-than-thou speech, so I shut her down quick before she could build up a head of steam.

"Whoa! Back up there, Tessa. First, I never get caught. You were perfectly safe. And secondly, that's not how it works. In the fruit and veg shops, they throw out buckets of produce every day. Most people won't buy anything that has a mark on it or looks too old. They only put the cheap stuff in the bins out the front to lure people into their shops. The good stuff, the expensive stuff, is inside. The free stuff is in the bins out the back. They're not allowed to give it away to people.

They normally off it to farmers if they can, or it just goes in the skip. So, two apples are no big deal."

"I cannot believe you are trying to justify stealing and planting stolen goods on me." She sat there looking like her overreaction was defensible, happy she'd had the last word.

Check.

"I cannot believe you think this is such a big deal." We'd see about that.

Countercheck.

"It's a crime."

"It's survival."

"You're not dying."

"I was hungry."

"We're having lunch as soon as we get back. You can wait."

"Well maybe you can. I can't. And I didn't know that."

Check and check-fracking-mate!

Equally annoyed, we shuffled apart from each other and sulked in our prospective corners. I couldn't believe her inability to understand. Nor why she had to make such a big deal of it. I made a point of eating both apples, one straight after the other, as loud as I could. They didn't taste as nice this time. But I wasn't going to tell her that.

It was not a peaceful silence that accompanied us home. And once again, Tessa stormed out of the truck as soon as we were let out of the back. Maybe she'd worked out that this was a good way to get out of helping with the groceries. Princess.

43

RAPHAEL

Abbot and Val said it was time to start packing, so while the others were out, I started pulling the kitchen apart and putting it in the boxes that we had been gathering. We only had space for two cartons of my kitchen things. I had to decide what we really needed and what we could do without. Val said in the new place we could replace things that got left behind. But we did not know how long we would be on the road. I was to take essentials only.

I knew we had to leave, but I did not want to. This was the happiest, safest place we had ever been. I knew we would stay with them, and they would keep us together, and we would be safe in a new place, and everything would be okay. But I did not want to leave.

Val explained to us that when the time comes for a city to face judgement, the Light pulls out the faithful and rescues them before everything gets smashed. Everything. I could not even imagine what that was like. I could not even think about it. When I did, my head hurt trying to picture it. Then my heart hurt. Instead of thinking about it, I packed.

Val said that the Light had provided this Soteria House for us. When they had arrived four years ago, there were only four of them.

She said now that we were eight, the Light was going to give us a bigger place with more room for everyone. She reminded me that Marcus said if the yard was big enough in our new place, I might be able to get a goat and learn to make cheese. Abbot said he would help.

Val said that we would find new Children of Light in the new place, that our family would grow, and we could help more people. She said if we tried, we could think of heaps of things that would be great in the new place. But she said it was right to feel sad about leaving our home too.

I knew we were leaving soon. Very soon. So, I packed most of the kitchen stuff and only left out the things we used every meal.

It was hard to leave our garden behind, but I tried to use as much of our produce as I could. I made big quiches and minis, and a huge veggie lasagne that could be cut up and served cold. That way we could have leftovers for lunch tomorrow and on the move if we could keep everything chilled.

I would get as many avocados from the tree as I could, every single day we had left. I wanted Ri to have a huge stack to last as long as possible. I would miss my tree. It had held me, and helped me disappear when I needed to. Soon it would disappear. Tears blurred my vision as I sat in an island of containers and utensils.

Riah and Abbot had been packing the garden tools and the books. The big old computer that everyone called the "dinosaur" would stay, and we would only take Kaitlyn's laptop. They packed all our schoolwork, then Kait and Tessa made a start on the clothes. Tessa packed the laundry. We did not have much stuff, so it did not take too long. Marcus had a big job of sorting the garage. At different times Kait and Dan helped him. But it was hard for him to decide what would stay and what would come with us.

Val said not to stress over deciding what to pack and what to leave. She said things can be replaced, people cannot. The main thing was that we were safe and together.

They were home!

"Hey Raph." Tessie stormed into the room without stopping to give me a hug like she normally did. I guess she really needed to speak to Val and Abbot. She was all red in the face again. She was always red now. Since Dan moved in.

It did not take long for her to have their attention.

"He's a thief!"

44

ABBOT

Waves of hurt, confusion, and anger rolled off Tessa as she burst through the door. She stuttered and spluttered her way around the room, arms punctuating part sentences that began and ended with huffs. The sitting room was scarcely big enough to contain her. She was a raging storm. Impatient for everyone to get there. Her jet-black eyes challenged everyone to hurry up, so she could release her vitriol to the maximum effect.

"Raphael, could you please go outside and help Sariah sort through the last few things in the shed?" I made an attempt to clear the battlefield to reduce the damage.

Raphael was equal parts relieved and annoyed at being asked to leave. He was curious to know what was going on, but he was also nervous of Tessa in this state. He was wary of conflict, and Tessa had never revealed her emotions quite so violently.

When the rest of the council arrived, they took their seats, all completely unaware of what was going on. Except for Daniel, of course, who sat stiffly in his chair, mask on, guard up, and eyes hooded. His clenched white knuckles gripped the arms of his chair, the only outward evidence of his distress.

He didn't know what to expect, but he felt isolated and alone, betrayed and hurt. Kaitlyn felt mildly confused and curious, but Marcus's hackles had risen automatically, triggered by his protective nature. He was not sure who was at fault but was on tenterhooks after the last outing, frightened of what was about to erupt.

Best we begin. "Who is a thief, dear one?" I knew exactly who she was talking about, but thought it best to clear the air first and state the crime so Marcus could retract his claws and engage his brain.

"Dan, of course!"

Of course.

"What did he steal, Tessa?" Valarie gently entered the fray.

"Apples!" she said.

"Apples?" I repeated.

"Yes. Two apples! And he planted them on me."

We all looked at each other in shared confusion. "Dear heart, I just want to get this straight and then we can sort it all out before lunch ..."

"Ha. Well, you'd better make it quick and feed him before he feels the need to go out and steal again." Collapsing in her chair, bringing her legs up, with her arms wrapped about her knees, she glared at Daniel. Both her offence and defence were set.

Daniel looked straight ahead and didn't make a sound. From her chair next to his, Valarie gently placed her hand on Daniel's and took in the both of them with her cool grey eyes, saying nothing.

Marcus let out a lungful of air. "Is that it?"

"What do you mean, 'is that it'?" Tessa screeched. Kaitlyn quickly rose and went to comfort her.

"Well ... I just want to make sure we're all on the same page. That's all," Marcus said. "Dan, did you take some apples?"

"Yes."

At least he didn't lie.

"And did you put them in Tessa's bag?"

"Yes."

"Where'd you take them from?" Marcus continued, not unkindly.

"The fruit barn in the mall outside Renald's," Dan confessed.

"Are you serious? We were all with you, then. I didn't see a thing.

You didn't notice, Tessa?" He looked from Tessa to Kaitlyn. "Did you see him?" Kaitlyn shook her head, bewildered. "Man, you are good! I never saw a thing."

Everyone stared at Marcus, even Daniel. Kaitlyn screwed up her face and shook her head at Marcus. He didn't seem to get the message.

"What? I'm not saying it's okay to steal. We all know that. Well ... except Dan, that is. But seriously, can we not give credit where credit is due? The kid is good at his art."

Feelings of relief and gratitude swam off Daniel to mingle in the pool of emotions pouring off everyone else: confusion, hurt, and pride.

Valarie once again represented the voice of wisdom. "Dan, the reason we don't steal is that, as Children of Light, we trust Him to provide all that we need. We are an example to everyone that His goodness is rich in mercy and there is nothing He can't provide. We are also charged with caring for our neighbours. So, we don't take from them, so as not to increase their burden—which is also the reason we wouldn't put others in the predicament you put Tessa in. It wasn't fair to use her or endanger her like that." She ended the lesson then shifted her gaze. "Tessa, where did we find Dan?"

"In the shops." Thrown by Valarie's question, her anger was momentarily forced off track.

"What was he doing?"

"Stealing," she answered, in a milder tone.

"Why was he stealing?" Through it all, Daniel had not moved. He continued to stare outside. Valarie had not removed her hand from his.

"Because he needed clothes for winter, and he didn't have any money to buy them. He had to save what little he had for food." Tessa finished the declaration in a whisper. But then self-justification overcame humility and she sparked up again in order to save face. "But he doesn't have to do that now! He is with us!"

My poor girl was drowning. "Tessa, you have been with us for over a year and you have had time to adjust from your old culture into the new. Dear heart, you have come so far, and we are all so very proud of you, for the battles you have won fighting your own demons. But like the rest of us, you have a way to go."

Kaitlyn tightened her grip around Tessa's shoulders, and I continued.

"You know that some things change right away, but other things take time. Dan has only been with us for just over two and a half weeks. Look at what he has been through and how much he has changed. Please don't be too hard on him." I smiled at the boy, in an attempt to ease his discomfort. "He did steal two apples, and I guess after today he'll think twice before he does it again." I sent him a wink.

His head and shoulders dropped.

"But Tessa, please look at the big picture. Look at his progress. Look at his heart, dear one. Praise him for how hard he is working and help him to overcome the struggles. Don't throw blocks in his way that hold him down or hinder his growth."

"Right! Time for lunch. I'm starved because I didn't get any apples." Marcus shut the case and we were free to move on.

Kaitlyn rose and held out her hand to a downcast Tessa. "Come and help me unpack and get lunch."

Time was running out. Kaitlyn had informed us that she had received word that we would be leaving in two days' time. And there were some things that just had to be done before we left.

"Daniel, I don't know how much more time we have, but I feel I need to offer you the opportunity to share your last dream with us. The one you call 'The House'? There is no pressure, but I would very much like to help you whilst I can, as none of us know the future ... well, with certain clarity that is." I smiled ruefully in the knowledge that I knew enough.

I didn't want to reveal too much, but I wanted to help him if I could. I also believed it would be helpful to have it out in the open before the final battle. He needed to find peace in this and come to terms with whatever happened in Gomorrah, but we couldn't push him.

Valarie gave Daniel's hand another squeeze and we both looked questioningly at the lad.

"Maybe, after lunch?" I suggested.

He turned to face Valarie, then met my gaze. Dropping his chin, he gave us the briefest sign of acceptance. Valarie then eased her way out of the chair and headed into the garden to get the twins.

"Please don't be angry with Tessa. She is fighting a lot of emotion at the moment and she doesn't know what to do with it. She is still learning, like you are. But whatever you do, do not ever feel like you are alone or that we would ask you to leave. We all stumble and fall—that's the easy part. The hard part is remembering to be gracious with each other in the fallout, as we try to get up again. You are loved, you are one of us, and we are very proud of you. We give thanks to the Light every day for bringing you into our family. Whatever you do, do not forget that."

Again, he acknowledged this—or at least that he had heard what I said—with a nod of his head, then with glistening eyes walked to the garage and shut the door. Soon afterward we could hear the all too familiar sounds of leather pounding leather.

45

DANIEL

"I am standing at the window of an old house, looking over the front yard, which runs unhindered to a quiet dirt road. When I look left or right, no trees or other obstacles interrupt the clear view. There are no cars parked on the street or houses inhabiting any of the lots either side. Apart from the equally ancient house directly opposite, the landscape is barren."

It was after lunch, and the rest of the family were involved with the next stage of packing. Abbot and Val had invited me to join them in the sitting room for another round of "dream delving".

I took a jagged breath and continued, "There is a group of people with me and we all stand frozen, waiting in speechless terror. Waiting for the final light of the day to be extinguished, and along with it, the warmth and security it brings. Paralysed in mind and body, I can smell our collective fear as it thickens in the evening breeze.

"I think the scent of our despair calls them. There is no room for rational thought or reasoning. We have nowhere to go, we have nowhere to hide. We have no way to fight them and no way to protect ourselves. Once again, like every other night, we are to be the offering.

"All eyes are trained on the house opposite and the high, chain wire fence that surrounds it. Why it's there, I have no idea. It doesn't keep them in. Every night they come and, like impotent slabs of meat on a plate, we wait to be taken.

"The hour has come. The nest spews forth its vile occupants. They fly, crawl or amble over and through the fence into our house, through the window where we stand watching. For all of us, hope was a mist that had been burnt away long ago by repetitive slaughter. Most run screaming. Some just open themselves, gibbering and slobbering in gormless surrender. I fight and desperately cling to the remnants of my defiance and resolve, so that they, too, don't abandon me.

"I run. Silent, trying to grab the kids, herd the ones who are still thinking, who haven't given up. I try to hide. I try to save as many as I can. But it doesn't work. It never does. We are always taken. We are always butchered. Sometimes I'm lucky and I go first. Other times they make me watch whilst they tear apart and gorge themselves on the others.

"It's weird, you know. I don't feel pain, but I feel them tugging and pulling at my flesh as they rip at my throat and hook into my stomach. They hold me and make me watch as they eat parts of my body. Laughing and cackling as their long, taloned claws dip into my gut and pull out bits, like I'm a living smorgasbord. I can't feel pain, but I hear the screams and weeping. I hear the laughter and sneers. I hear the shattering of my bones. I hear the ravaging and mauling, the gurgling of air rushing through my ripped windpipe and punctured lungs. Then, eventually, I am allowed to leave. Everything goes black. I wake up. And then, the next night, it happens. All. Over. Again."

The dream had been cast into the waking. In a sense, it made it more real, and palpable. I tried to get my emotions back under control. I reminded myself it was just a dream. It wasn't real. I was awake and I was safe. That scary kret out there, with his freaking, whacked-out, adjustable demonic dolls, couldn't get me. My dream was not real. It was just a dream. Deep breaths. Calm down. Toughen up. If I could just stop sweating and shaking, I'd be okay.

Please make it be okay.

"I can understand why you'd be concerned about going to sleep if that's what was waiting for you," Abbot said. He raised his eyebrows at Val, and she stared back at him. Again with their mind talk, or whatever it was. "You told us you'd had the beach dream again since being here. What about the horse, or this, the house dream? Have you had either of these two dreams again since you've joined us?"

"Yeah." It was hard to explain, hard to find the words. The dreams weren't only the heightened senses I experienced during the actions or events. They involved intense emotion as well. Staying calm and in control when I shared them was difficult to master.

The emotions I felt were also burned into my mind, so when I relived them, awake, I relived everything. The feeling of vulnerability and inadequacy. The feeling of being skrat-scared and totally incapable of doing anything about it. The inevitability of defeat and failure. The paralysing terror of being torn apart and eaten alive. The sickening desperation and extreme mind-frack of being made to watch others—children—being raped and eaten, alive, in front of you.

There were other things that I worked hard to forget, but I couldn't. There were things I would never speak out loud about what happened in The House. Reliving the pony dream was okay, same as the beach one ... but this one was almost beyond me.

"I've been back to The House."

"What was it like this time, Daniel?" I knew Abbot could sense my emotions, but he asked anyway.

"I've had that one a few times since I've been here. The first time it was different. The first time I had a plan. I knew that I had things I could do. We didn't have to just sit and wait for the inevitable slaughter and defeat. We could fight them.

"The first couple of times, I tried to hide from them, outside the house so it looked empty when they arrived. But they found us. The next time I got everyone to run, to get away from the house. We didn't have to stay like dinner on a plate. But they caught us.

"The next time I made weapons and handed them out. Some of us stood up to them and fought them. We didn't have to lie down and take it. We could grow claws of our own. But they beat us. But at least we were doing something about it and didn't just go down like defeated little fra— ... frigates who couldn't do anything about it.

"The last time I had this dream, I realised I didn't have to let them in. I remembered your story, Abbot, and how Val came into your grotto. I had been looking at it the wrong way all along. I had been a victim waiting for punishment or ... disaster to happen. Then even when I tried fighting back, I was still looking at it from the perspective of a victim, letting these creatures into my territory. But I have the authority to keep them out. They didn't have to come into my house, they didn't have to come in and destroy us if I didn't let them. If I didn't let them in, they couldn't get in. Then I realised what the fence was for.

"The last time I had this dream I watched at the window, eager for the sun to go down. Ready for the battle to begin. This time I was terrified and excited at the same time. The sun set, the light lingered. People came away from the window and stood behind me. They were scared, jittery. Nerves were raw, and everyone was on edge. I felt it at my back like a wave pushing me to the edge of the window and holding me there as the twilight made way for the night.

"And then they came.

"But this time I watched as, in slow motion, everything moved silently through the thickest molasses. Momentarily I forgot my purpose, transfixed by their retarded movement. As they neared the fence I snapped back to attention and roared, The tension added with my fear amplified like a cannon. 'No! You will not pass!' The tension added to my fear amplified my voice like a cannon.

"They stopped. They screamed. Back to normal speed. Back to normal volume. The noise was deafening. But they didn't go past the fence. They couldn't go past the fence. They bucked and tore at it, they fought each other and screeched. Intense hatred, all directed at me, but they couldn't get to me. It's hard to put into words just what it was like, but I was shocked ... stunned ... overwhelmed with relief and surging with the satisfaction of victory.

"Finally, I had worked it out. I woke up and have not had that dream again."

"Nor will you," Val stated with confidence. "You have learned your lesson. You don't need to go back. You have been groomed for battle, and life in the Light, so that the transition would be easier for you. Even before we met you, before you were aware of the Light, your life on the street, even your short time with Abraham, and your dreams, have been a training ground, preparing the soil.

"The road that lies in front of you is narrow and complex, but it is straight. Your purpose in the Light is to fight—to fight for the Light in you and around you. To keep yourself pure and protect others. But you are not alone. You know this and it sits well with you. Not only do you enjoy the battle, you have been made for it and this excites you. You have been given your heart's desire."

Turning slightly, she looked at Tessa. "Yes, He grants us our heart's desire because He is the one who sows the desire in the first place."

I didn't know how long Tessa had been standing there and I didn't know how much she'd heard. I couldn't work out what I felt about her at the moment. I was still hurt by her betrayal and extreme over-reaction. I hadn't intended to glare at her, but I guess I was inadvertently advertising the way I felt. I hated being so transparent. They all knew what I was thinking. The lack of privacy, even in my own mind, was seriously doing my head in. I turned, not wanting to give away more than I intended, and decided it was safer to look at no one.

Rather, I focused on my knees and started to, in a pretty controlled way, freak out.

My armour ...

What the hell was happening to my armour?

It was dimming. I looked over to Abbot, who nodded. "Your armour is an outward sign of an inward reality. If your armour is dim, it is merely reflecting the quality of the Light in you. If the Light is strong, so too is your armour. When you allow the Light in you to give way to the Dark, the Dark gets a beachhead into your defences." He spoke calmly, in a voice that only Val and I could hear.

"What do I do?" I was frantic. "How do I get it back?"

"Identify that which is blocking the Light in your life, and remove the block," he said simply.

I looked back and forth between the two and got no more information. Then Val made a point of looking from me to Tessa, and I followed suit. She shuffled her feet and seemed undecided. Red as a beetroot and fidgeting with the tea towel she had twisted into a knot, she timidly made her way over, perched on the edge of her chair and turned her knees toward me. She wouldn't look at me. I didn't have Abbot's Badge, but I could tell she was feeling like skrat.

At this point, so was I. I didn't hate her. I was just pretty cut that she had dobbed on me, and I was angry. And ashamed.

46

CONTESSA

Sodding. Flopping. Poo.

Why was I always the one stuffing up? Why was I always the one feeling like skrat? Why couldn't someone else have to be the one apologising to me for once?

This. Just. Sucked.

I couldn't even look at him.

I know I overreacted. I didn't even know why. Now he hated me and … flop. "Dan … I'm sorry for the way I acted. I'm sorry for …"

What exactly was I sorry for? He was the one who stole stuff. That shocked me more than anything. I could see that was part of the life he'd come from. He'd come so far in other things. I was forgetting he hadn't got it all sorted yet.

I guess I'd been disappointed. Truth was, I'd wanted him to be different to the other guys. To be better than them. I wanted him to be able to carry my trust. I wanted to feel safe around him. I'd wanted an ally. I'd wanted him to be as good as Marcus. I guess I just wanted him to be perfect.

But I wasn't.

So, how the hell could I expect him to be perfect? He was still so new.

After hearing some of that stuff he had been dreaming, and only being able to guess at what happened in Gomorrah. And how he had to deal with all of that, out there. On his own.

Skrat!

How exactly am I supposed to sum all of that up? I have to own this and girl up. He did the wrong thing, but so did I. I'm sorry for so many things. First to You and then to him. I know I'm not accountable for his actions, but I am accountable for mine. Please forgive me. Please help me.

Okay, it was time to be humble. Right? Right.

I looked him in the eye. Reminded myself it wasn't about me, and continued by summarising the key points. "Dan, I stuffed up again and I'm sorry. I hope you can forgive me for overreacting. I'm sorry for being a complete butt-head."

Val held back a laugh, Abbot's eyes sparkled, and Dan looked like I'd just told him the Freaky Mannequins were coming to tea.

"About time you learned to see the heart of the problem, Tessa," Marcus called out from the kitchen. Thankfully, I still had the balled-up tea towel in my hand. I pegged it at him. Also, thankfully, most of the kitchen had been packed up, because my shot went wild and landed where the glasses used to live.

"Don't worry, dear heart, stress has marred your shot." Abbot was his usual wonderful self. "Keep working at it, I have complete faith in you."

I turned back to Dan to hear his verdict.

"It seems weird that I was the one who stole stuff and 'endangered' you, and you're the one apologising. I was pretty skitched. But in truth, I knew stealing was wrong. And so was using you. But it didn't stop me. Mainly because we were out, back in the world I was used to and ... I kind of slipped back into old habits. It was instinct. I was hungry, there was opportunity, I took some food." He dropped his eyes. "I'd wanted to get back out into the streets to feel comfortable once again. To feel at home. But I realise after today it will never feel like home again.

"It wasn't till you went ape about it that I realised that I had screwed up. I thought you all might throw me out and I was furious at you for dobbing and threatening my security. So, if you're going to apologise for being an butt, I'll raise you by apologising for being a buttier butt."

He smiled at me and I almost wept with relief. I will admit, only to myself, that at the mention of butts, I had to acknowledge his did look mighty fine, especially in those jeans I picked for him.

"Great, now that you two butts have managed to sort that out, get them over to the kitchen and help finish the packing. Kait and I have to head out to meet up with Ebony." Marcus was a hard task master, but I was happy for a healthier distraction. Especially when I saw the look on Abbot's face after my trip down imagination lane.

Eeeky beeky.

I jumped up and dived in to helping out with the chores. First, it helped hide the flame igniting my face. But then, as we found purpose, it helped us move on. To find a rhythm again. Everything went pear-shaped, though, when I focused on what we were actually doing. Packing to leave our sanctuary. That's when my heart broke. Again.

This had been the first safe place I'd been given in years. This was my home, and this was my family. I was torn. I wanted to go with them, to stay in their protection, but I didn't want to leave Sodom. Or this house, to be more precise.

I was angry that we were being forced out. I had whinged and cried, "Why can't we stay? Why do things have to change? I don't want to go." But as I watched the twins prepare to leave and saw how they appeared to be at peace about it all, despite their age, their history, and the past they'd been saved from, I was ashamed of my sulkiness. If they could do this without the tantrums, I could hardly break down and cry about it. But I wanted to.

47

———————

MARCUS

Ebony was making herself as popular as a skunk at a garden party with this lark. This was our second attempt to meet up with her. The first, a fisherman's goose hunt. We'd waited over an hour at the entrance, totally exposed, and she was a no-show.

So, Kait and I'd ducked inside to where she worked and were given a bleeding note from her colleague. Apparently, she'd been sick and left early. The note was full of apologies and worded real nice. But me blood was set to boil. She was hiking well beyond the horizons of me grace.

Today was take two. We were to meet same place but, thankfully, an earlier time. It would take a direct order from the Light for me to let anyone out on the streets near dark these days. Things were hotting up and people were shutting down.

It would just be me and Kait this time. We didn't want to risk any more than we had to, since we were heading out tomorrow. Driving through the streets on our second trip in two days was grinding away at me nerves, especially when I thought about our safety ... and fuel consumption.

We weren't the only ones feeling the vibe. Some shops, and every fuel station we passed, had closed early. I'd already filled the jerry cans. But we needed full tanks when we left.

All this running around was just pumping extra pressure into an overly charged cooker. I knew everyone deserved a chance, and the Light would rest on those whom He would. But, bleeding heck, Ebony was not the only one we needed to consider.

"Calm down, Marcus. Think of this as quality time together."

"What are you talking about, woman?"

"You need to calm down and stop brooding. Why not put the energy into finding something positive to think about?"

"Positive? You tell me what there is to be positive about." I regretted the words as soon as they left me mouth. Driving through these hostile streets with me amazing wife, secure in the Light, I had plenty to be positive about. "Sorry, love, you're right. I'm just worried, and you know as well as I do, we don't need these distractions." Again, I'd said the wrong thing. "I know, I know, bringing a soul into the Light is not a distraction. It's what we're about. It might be a nuisance to us ... to me, but it's life-altering to them." The closer we got to the city centre the more closed shops, shut doors, and secured shutters we passed. "I guess I won't feel better till we're all out of here and everyone's safe."

"You know you can't guarantee that, Marcus." Kait's voice barely carried above the growl of the engine.

"Yeah, I know. Well, I'm trying to." I took me eyes off the road to look at her. "Why do you put up with me?"

"Cause you're good looking and a great cook." She returned me look and smiled. I saw the truth in her eyes.

She was right. Spending time with her was a treat. Being in an ark of safety was an added bonus. It had been an eon since it had just been the two of us.

Thank you.

We spent the rest of the trip in relaxed—well, less-stressed—conversation and semi-good humour until we got to the mall.

"There's a space."

"Kait, I can see for meself. And I can pick me own park."

"I know. But wait, that one's closer."

I refused to answer and scouted to find a park as close as possible, other than hers. If it had been a time of peace, I would have picked a park as far away from the entrance as possible. She knew this and, in response, punched me leg and winked with a gorgeous grin, barbed with heat. The right kind of heat. She slid from the cab before I had turned the engine off and met me at me door, hand out, smile sly. Lord, I loved this woman.

We'd decided to go straight to Ebony's department to see if she'd shown up today, before setting up for the wait. I threw me arm around Kait's shoulders as we walked through the mall. I needed to hold her close. To feel her warmth, her strength. I knew we were safe from the Unseen ... for now. But the Others weren't our only worry. The demons had begun enlisting a human army in their fight against us. Groups of people milling, hostile, and on edge were fruit ripe for the picking. And the Others, insidious as cancer, whispered in their ears, enticing them to dance an evil beat.

Our guard had tripled. And as we approached Renald's, I went back on alert. Me hackles were standing at attention. We were in a dead end. Whispering circled us as the shops erratic heartbeat slowed and unified. Like we were behind the eight-ball, and the cue was lining us up for a strike.

"Hi there, I was wondering if Ebony was at work today?" Kait asked the plastic-looking girl behind the counter. Disgust transformed her face as she gave Kait the once-over. The wisps of positivity that had clung to me evaporated like scotch mist.

"What's it to you?" Her words dripped with dismissal.

"We were supposed to meet her today and we just wanted to check if she'd come in."

Miss Plastic's contempt didn't require words.

"Wait, are you Kait?" Another girl leaned over from where she'd finished serving a customer.

"Yes." We ditched plastic-girl number one and engaged the second.

"She rang and left this for you." Kait took the note. "She said she was really sorry to miss you, but said something about having to make her decision and final preparations?" The girl bobbled her head and giggled.

"We understand, thank you." Patience must be one of Kait's Badges.

I attempted to radiate some of her grace as we trekked our way through the fledgling mob the enemy was brewing. I sensed Kait loosen her muscles, we edged away from each other. Close, but room enough to manoeuvre if needed. I doubted the Others would break through our guard, so our swords stayed sheathed.

Fighting demons was one thing, and fighting humans was another. Fighting both together was a twik of epic proportions. And not an ideal date night. Our guard was prime against the demons, they were also effective against the blind and ignorant humans. But at times, a few mortals ignored the barriers erected by our Warriors and leaked through. They needed to be handled with care. They weren't the real enemy, but you could bet your bippy I was not going to sit there and let them walk all over us.

An electric silence surrounded us. Crowds parted and bodies shuffled positions. Narrowed eyes tracked us, shoulders were tapped, and nods pointed us out. Demons wove among the crowds, caressing their pets, purring lies, and provoking anger. Feeling like raw meat, dripping, just out of reach of a pack of dogs, we kept moving.

You've got this, I know. Thank you. You've got us, I trust. Thank you.

An avenue of hostility escorted us back to the truck. I walked Kait to her door, even though she protested, and a guard three-deep surrounded us. She would be safe. Over me dead body if needs be. This I vowed, so this I lived.

Our guard stayed in place as we eased our way back to the house for the last time. As we exited the city and the Unseen climate cooled to steamy, I attempted to nurture an attitude of grace. But each time it broke the surface, me inner junkyard thug ripped it to pieces.

No question, an epic storm was coming, and the Sodomites were puppets of the enemy. Some quiet and sly, others loud and obvious, but all aiming to wreak havoc. Gangs were forming, beating chests and tagging territory. Well, I promise you this, if they came near me territory, I'd beat their chests too. And their heads ... and whip their sorry butts.

48

CONTESSA

Our last evening. Most things were packed, it was just the essentials left now. Tomorrow we would load the truck with the big stuff and the last of the boxes. This was the last evening we'd sit in this room looking into the garden, listening to Dan, with everyone here.

What if something went wrong?

What if someone got hurt?

Oh Lord, I don't think I can take this, I'm going to be sick. I can't sit here with everyone so flopping calm as if everything is okay. I can't breathe, I'm going to scream. I'm going to explode.

I raced from the sitting room in search of the security of my safe place in the laundry. It was too cold to sit outside on the stoop where I normally went. Shutting the door, I dropped to the floor, wrapped my arms around my knees, and wept. Huge. Wracking. Sobs.

Sodom might be a mess, but it was the only home I had known. My parents had made some pretty bad choices, but I had loved them, and they had been laid to rest here. I had been rescued and given security here, in the midst of the increasing chaos. And after tomorrow I wouldn't even have my safe place anymore. Even my laundry and stoop would be gone.

I tried to be quiet, but I couldn't.

I was broken. My heart was in pieces. My mind was shattered.

The door opened. I couldn't even lift my head to see who it was. Snot and tears coated my face like a second skin, but I was too distressed to care. A body heaved down next to me and I took in the comforting scent of Marcus.

My rock.

I could rage against him like the tide. I could fight, struggle and break. And all the while, he would wait to welcome me with open arms, unconditionally.

He didn't say anything. He just took me in, again, and let me cry. Seemed I was doing a lot of that lately. I hated it, it made me cry more.

Marcus left the door ajar, and when my sobs had faded to dense congestion, I heard Dan sharing his gift of music. He had picked up on everyone's mood and was playing a melancholic tune, so beautiful it made me want to cry more. But I couldn't. I had nothing left.

Marcus offered me a towel from a nearby pile to mop up my face. I guess that says a lot about a girl when the men in her life know that a hanky just won't do.

I swabbed the mess and unsuccessfully tried to make myself look presentable. Without a word, Marcus stood up, held out his hand and led me back to the group.

Before we rounded the corner back into view, he pulled me into a bear hug. "Love ya, kiddo. We're gonna be okay. The Light's got us and He ain't letting go." He kissed the top of my head then released me.

We headed back into the sitting room and everyone made a point of not looking at us as we rejoined them. I noticed that Riah was curled up in Abbot's lap and Raph was in her chair, his head on the arm of Abbot's seat. Abbot had a hand on Raph's head whilst his other arm encircled Riah. It was an image that I would never forget.

I would make sure that I didn't.

It was a picture of pure love, overwhelming and indescribable.

I went to Kait and dropped to my knees placing my head in her lap. She stroked my hair, replaying our morning ritual. Truth was, I craved the comfort that comes from routine, the familiar.

She knew that and didn't miss a beat, or a word of the song she was singing, as she acknowledged all my pain. Marcus placed his arm around Kait and his other hand on my shoulder as Dan wrapped us in his music that ministered to and soothed our mourning souls.

I turned to sit on the floor between Marcus and Kait. I needed to be close, to feel their presence. Since Dan's arrival, this had become my favourite time of day, looking into the back garden, listening to him create liquid gold for my soul on his guitar. I knew those hands had been made for music.

In time, Dan finished and I moved to take my seat in the circle as we discussed the strategies for our departure tomorrow. Despite my grief, I was relieved. The not knowing when, had become worse than the uncertainty of what was going to happen.

"Did you know our Dan has names for us all?" Abbot announced out of the blue.

"Really? What are they Dan?" Raph perked up as he dashed across the room to take his own seat next to mine. The rest of us looked to our startled musician, unsure of what to expect.

Dan's fingers halted their quiet meandering, but then the familiar smile crept back into his eyes. "Well, *Abbot*, now that you have spilled the beans, I guess there's no harm." He tentatively looked around at us all, either sizing us up or steeling himself for the revelation he was going to deliver. He looked back to Abbot.

"I think your name means leader of a monastery—"

Marcus coughed.

"—like a priest. Someone they would have called 'Father'. It seems you have either inherited the name that fits you best, or you have grown into the title you were given."

There was a chuckle as Abbot nodded in gratitude at the compliment.

He looked to Sariah with palpable warmth and adoration as he whispered, "Princess." Her smile reflected his warmth. "But I guess there are no surprises there."

Next, he moved his attention to Kait. "Again, no surprises, since you claimed this one yourself, Mamma Bear." Then to Marcus, he nodded his head in respect. "Papa Bear." Kait beamed, but Marcus looked like he didn't quite know what to do with his title. We all laughed. He appeared to accept it with good humour.

Then Dan looked to Val.

Raph couldn't wait. "What do you call Val, Dan?" Bobbing up and down in his chair, he was about to explode with excitement.

"Amazing. Fearsome. Wise. Warrior. Queen." He stated each word as a title. He looked at her with reverence, but then covered it quickly with a grin and continued, "But that's a bit of a mouthful, so I just call her 'Legend', for short." He'd nailed it. We all laughed and cheered with approval.

Except Marcus. "That's way tougher than Papa Bear."

"I don't know. You ever come across an angry bear?" Looking at Kait, Dan continued, "Or a mother bear when her cubs are threatened? I got a glimpse in a shop, once, and the other day on the street." Dan's eyes softened as he took both of them in. Marcus quietly accepted the honour for what it was, and Kait beamed even more and unsuccessfully tried to hide a sniffle.

Building with excitement, Raph pushed on. "What about Tessa?"

Dan looked at me. I believe his pupils dilated. They were darker than their usual faded denim and went a deeper shade of grey. I didn't even think that was possible. Within them was a cauldron of expressions brewing, most of which I couldn't decipher. But truth was, eeeky beeky.

I think I may have melted, just a little.

Okay, a lot.

Yeah well, anyway, this'd be good ... or not ... So, tough guy, what's my name, huh?

"Tessa knows the name I have for her."

I lowered my eyes and tried for the whole knowing, gracious kind of smile. But inside I was like, "What? What do you mean you have a name for me?" Here I was, playing it cool, like Kait said: don't push it, be natural. If it happens, it happens. If it doesn't, it won't. If you force something and it isn't meant to work, it will be really awkward and painful for you, she'd said.

So that's me, playing it all cool and natural. So cool, I was the Ice Queen. But apparently, I was so cold I'd missed it. Whatever "it" was.

"What is it Tessa?" Raph insisted. "Tell us."

Oh. Well. Yeah. About that. "Ahhh ..." I had nothing.

"All in good time, Little Master." Dan saved me.

"Is that my name? 'Little Master'?"

"I've worked with you and been taught by you. I have watched you with your sword and at fighting practice each morning. What else could I call you? You are the master, little man. You are well on your way to being formidable," Dan said.

At this, Raph's chest expanded like a robin, his face just as red, and his eyes sparkled like jewels.

"Well, Grasshopper, that was enlightening. Thank you for sharing with us." Abbot glowed with pride and shifted his eyes to me. I was washed in his affection and love. He knew. He knew it all and still, he loved me unconditionally.

"Good one, Abbot." Marcus laughed with the other "adults" at a joke that the rest of us didn't get. And once again, Abbot had ensured that we were encouraged and uplifted with our victories, rather than sinking into the unknown.

I knew I stood in a place of grace in the Light, and in the lives of each of my family, but I felt compelled to ensure peace between Dan and me.

I didn't know where I stood with him, especially after that whole name thing. But it had given me the courage to find out. For one thing, if it went unresolved any longer, I wouldn't get any sleep tonight and then I'd be exhausted and unfit for whatever lay ahead tomorrow.

49

—————

CONTESSA

Following Kait's advice, I'd invited Dan to join me on the patio after the others had gone to bed. It was freezing. But I had made us each a hot chocolate and we were cocooned in beanies, scarves and our big soft blankets.

The night was beautiful. The air was a high-resolution magnifying glass. If I stretched out my arm, I could've plucked the stars from heaven. The aroma of Riah's garden blended with winter's own distinct scent. Together they smelled of home. Peace. Sanctuary. Heaven. With every creature burrowed away snug from the chill, the night rang with silence. I was sitting in paradise.

With all our extra padding, what would have been "just so" was pretty squishy as Dan squeezed beside me on the two-seater. We had to be careful drinking our chocolate, otherwise we'd be bathing in it. At our backs, insulated behind closed doors, Val, Kait, and Marcus stayed up "reading", whilst Dan and I were outside "talking".

The moment was beautiful, but as I let it drag on it became all kinds of awkward. I had issued the invitation, and the silence intensified as Dan patiently waited for me to speak. The trouble was, I knew what I wanted to say, but didn't know how to say it.

Please, please help me find the words.

"Tomorrow we go into battle, and … we need to make sure there is nothing negative between us," I began.

"Oookaay."

This was not going to be easy.

"Dan, I feel like I need to say some stuff and it's really hard, but it's also really cold out here, and so I'm just going to say it."

"Oookaay."

"Dan … I like you and I feel a connection with you. But, I have been walked over, devoured and spat out by every person I know … apart from those six people inside. And apart from them, there is no one, not one soul, to whom I have given my trust. But, despite trying to keep you at a distance, you've managed to get under my defences and steal my trust regardless. And that scares me." So far, so good. Honest and to the point. I could do this. Deep breath, onward and … onward.

"And I don't know what to do about it. Yes, I find you attractive. I'd have to be a blind, deaf, senseless fool not to."

"Uhh … thanks … I think."

I ignored him and kept on my roll. Truth was, if I stopped now I knew I'd never get going again. "But I know what attraction does to people, how it controls them and how they abuse others because of it. Attraction is dangerous. Trust is dangerous. But put them together and they're all kinds of … scary.

"What happened in the thrift shop really threw me. And then you saved me …" My nerves tripped into anger at the memory of feeling hauled back into my old life. I knew my tone contradicted my words, but, as it all tumbled out, my anger gradually faded, and my nerves returned.

In force.

"Then, witnessing your attack on the street tore me up and I realised how much I really cared about you." Anguish morphed into self-doubt. "And then, watching those piranhas in the shop … and what they said to me … then you said … what you said … and then you kissed me … and then I … blew it with the apples."

I could have stripped off and laid spread-eagled and felt less exposed than I did now.

"I'm really confused ... and lost and ... at sea ... even though I've never been to sea ... maybe that's why I feel so sick ... Anyway, I think it would be really helpful, before we went out tomorrow, if we could set some parameters, or clarify some roles, or figure out some guidelines, or, you know, some kind of ... something ..."

"Ooo—"

"Do not say okay again."

"Umm ... thanks for clearing that up?" He took a huge breath and held it for an eternity. Let it out slowly, then ... nothing.

"Well?"

"Well, what?"

"Have you got nothing to say?"

"I'm not sure what I'm supposed to say. Thanks for sharing ...?" His voice rose as his face scrunched.

"Oh. My. Word. I just humiliated myself by sharing all that stuff and that's all you've got to say?" I sloshed my hot chocolate. It was no longer hot.

"Listen, Tessa. You already know I don't trust easily either. In fact, before I met you guys there was only one person who I trusted. And for all I know, he's dead. So, you already know that I trust you. And that I like you. What more do you want me to say?"

"Dan, I didn't know that you trusted me, and, I only know you like me enough to restrain yourself from killing or maiming me. But apart from that, I got nothing."

"What do you mean? I sleep here every night. Of course I trust you. Like I'd expose myself like that in enemy territory."

I'd not really thought of it like that. But before I could comment, he continued.

"And how could you not know that I think you're amazing, and the only restraint I have to use is keeping my hands off you?"

Brain. freeze.

"What do you mean? Keep your hands off me." Chills froze my heart. Did he want to hurt me too?

I couldn't breathe.

I couldn't move.

Flight or fight?

"Whoa, Tessa. Calm down. I am not going to hurt you. Your trust is safe with me." He leaned back and gave me some space.

I breathed. Centred. And tried really hard to be rational.

"I respect you, and I care for you too. It's obvious. Well, it is for the others." He slumped back against the chair. "Marcus has already spoken to me about it. Do you really think your guard—Other and human—would let me stay if they thought I was intending to hurt you? I've been playing it cool, because I thought that you were either not keen, or not too sure about me." He turned his whole body towards me and trapped me with his very scary eyes.

Heat flooded back to my body and my heart pounded.

In a good way.

Thank you for my family. Thanks for watching out for me.

"Contessa, you are the most kick-butt, hottest girl I have ever met. You are so different from all the others. For the first time, with you, I feel like I have met someone who can stand beside me. I love that you are as graceful as a cat in a fight and like a dancer in life. I totally get that the Light gave you yellow armour. You're total sunshine. But I also really love that you've been through stuff. Not how you were hurt, and you're now scarred. But because you understand what it's like. What it was like for me."

I was breathing easily now and was lost in the wonder of his words. I had no idea where it was all coming from.

"Did you just pinch yourself?" His disbelief came out in a snort.

"I just needed to make sure I wasn't dreaming." What had been pleasant warmth turned to heat. What could a girl say in response to all of that? So, mustering all that grace and sunshine he spoke about, I stared blank-faced back at him and said the only thing I could. "Wow."

"I know stealing is wrong, I also knew it at the time. I just really screwed up. I already knew I wasn't good enough for you, or to be in this family. I still don't know why the Light picked me. I am completely unworthy." His focus shifted to his cup. "And when you called me out, it confirmed my doubts. I don't know what's expected of me. I'm constantly torn between feelings of euphoria and debilitating self-doubt. I'm also really struggling, being this close to so many people. But I can't explain how, over the past few weeks, I've grown really attached to everyone, I mean, like, I really care for you all. But most of all, I've been struggling with not knowing what to do about you."

"What do you want to do about me?" I whispered. I could no longer look him in the face. I so desperately wanted to know. But I wasn't ready to hear the truth.

"Well, I kind of ... was hoping that ... maybe, because I was going to be hanging around with you guys, that ... if it was alright with you, I mean ..." His supple body tensed, his hands were trying to tie a knot in the cup's handle. "Only if you were happy and cool with it, that is, I'd be happy to, ahhh ... but, only if you wanted to ..."

I glared at him and made no attempt to hide my eye roll.

"Well ... may-maybe see where this went? Maybe ...? But only if you were keen."

"Oookaay."

His face paled. But then he realised I was having a go at him. Inside, however, my heart was leaping, and I felt like yelling at the top of my voice, "He likes me!" My emotional high dipped to confusion however, when he nudged me forward, indicating I should stand up. I immediately thought that this, whatever "this" was, obviously wasn't going very far tonight. But I couldn't hide my smile when he rearranged his blanket and pulled me back inside, wrapping his arm around me.

"Tessa, I'm gonna need your help." I turned to look up at him, worried he was about to tell me some ghastly secret. "I don't know what I'm doing with this"—his hand bounced between us—"with us. You're going to have to tell me when I do something wrong." At that point, I do believe our connection deepened.

"Deal. If you promise to do the same for me." I held out my hand to shake on it. "Friends?"

He reciprocated. Then, without letting go or releasing me from his focus, he brought my hand to his lips and, through a smile, softly kissed my knuckles.

"Friends," he whispered. I sank back into his embrace. He leaned his head on top of mine. Like I said earlier, I truly was in Heaven.

We were allowed to sit out there for a bit longer before being roused by knocking behind us. Marcus was standing there pointing at his watch, and then pointing to bed. It was hard to believe that I had forgotten we were going into battle tomorrow. But at least now I knew I would be fighting alongside a friend, my best friend, who cared for me, trusted me and respected me.

Now all we had to do was make it out of there alive.

50

MARCUS

It was a subdued morning, but we needed to be prepared. There was no space or time for moping and self-indulgent feelings. It was when it came to the crunch and punch that we were reminded we were active warriors. All this talk of fighting was not euphemism. It was who we were and what we were called to. It just so happened that this was the pointy end.

We'd had almost three weeks of holiday and now it was game on. We needed to get ready for whatever the day would bring. Instead of allowing imaginations to run away, it was important to keep everyone focused. That meant routine and tasks.

Before we went out, we needed to ensure everything was tight, tucked in, and tapered. We'd each know our role and fully understand Plan A, B, C—and D if necessary. We'd be on high alert, looking for anything out of the ordinary. Hard as it was, it was time to leave, and we were confident the Dark Lord would have us dancing his tormented tune, tying us in knots and tempting us to trip up, every step of the way. We had to be ready for every trick he would pull to stop us. Truth be, he was going to make us earn our ticket out of here. If, in fact, we all made it.

"Dan, one of the most important things we do before a battle is ensure our armour is at full strength." His wide eyes were unblinking as I addressed him. "Mostly, we maintain it every day with discipline and learning. And as you've seen, yours has been getting stronger." I flicked me eyes between him and Tessa. "That meeting you guys had last night will've helped. I've noticed that, Tessa, yours has been thickening up as well, like yours, Little Master." Raph's paled face took on a touch of colour.

"Riah, you are, as always, a mystery to me. Yours is looking as good as ever. Whatever you're doing, keep it up." She beamed at me in response.

Dan looked bewildered as he scanned his own armour. Tessa reached over and tussled Raph's hair. He was completely chuffed that his improvement had been noticed.

"Val, do you want to do this? It's more your area." I made the official handover.

"Thanks, old man." She smiled. Not even trying to hide the fire in her eyes. Val was champing at the bit to get out and do something after being holed up recovering for the past few weeks. Complete movement had pretty much returned and she was back to full tasks and training, as the bruises up and down me body testified.

"Dan, we're about to earn our keep," she started.

Perplexed, he looked at her.

"As Children of Light, we have all we need. We are supplied with shelter, food, clothing and every necessity of life. That's our pay, if you like. Our job, what we do in return, is to fight on behalf of the Light. It's why we train, why we're disciplined. Why we struggle and strive. Why we suffer and hurt. It's why we make sacrifices. Part of what we do is to prepare for the battle. The other part is the battle.

"You've not been with us long, but you're about to see the end game to this place, where all the uglies hit the fan in a very messy way." The eagerness of her voice was intensified by her smile and the glint in her eye. "By this time tomorrow, you'll know what we're all about. That is, if you're still alive. We've kind of grown accustomed to having you around." Her eyes roamed the group. "All of us, not just Tessa." Tessa and Dan both reddened like beacons in response.

"So, do everything you can to stay alive. That goes for everyone. Stay focused. This is likely to get ugly. I don't like the feel of it. I don't like random factors thrown in before a battle, and that is exactly what Ebony is. But despite the peculiarities, she's a Potential. So, as far as we know, we are going into an unknown location, to deal with an unknown Target, in unknown circumstances. So, pretty much business as usual." She stopped and looked around the group. We didn't need a pin to drop to feel the tension.

"We will all have to be on guard and extremely focused. It makes this next part of the day exceedingly important. Do not skimp on your preparation. Dan, the Light knows what's going to happen and the Light is in control. The Light is our protection and strength for the fight." She pinned him like an insect. "Therefore, we do everything we can to make sure there is nothing, on our part, blocking the Light. Kait, Marcus, Abbot, I don't have to point out how vulnerable we are in this one. We are three to five." She didn't have to spell it out. Only three out of the eight of us were battle-ready.

The fight was her strength, her Badge and her passion. But nevertheless we were going to be ridiculously vulnerable in this battle.

Val continued, "Dan, as I explained earlier, our armour is an outward sign of our inward reality. If the Light is strong inside us, our armour is strong around us. If the Dark has a foothold inside, we give him an opening to bring us down in the fight. So, we make sure there is nothing we know of that's giving way to the Darkness in our lives. If there is, we take the time to shut it down before we go out." Even though Kait and Abbot knew the drill, they too were hanging off her every word.

"We do this by coming under the scrutiny of the Light so we can see what needs to change. It's not as easy as it sounds, but we need to be fully armed and protected. So, this is what we will spend a good chunk of our time doing this morning. Be brutal and pare away the canker. It's your only hope.

"When we've finished, we'll come together for a meal of remembrance and thanksgiving, finish packing, and then head out. Dan, would you lead us before we go to our quiet places?"

Wide-eyed and white, Dan moved mechanically to pick up his guitar and returned to his seat in the circle and began to play for us. His fingers plucked and pushed the strings around robotically. But as his reflexes overrode his mind, his fingers and shoulders relaxed into their own comfortable rhythm and became animated with a life of their own. Truth be, the boy was gifted. And we were blessed to have him with us. I'd be sure to tell him before we left.

Once again, I thank you for each member of this family. Each a gift. Again, I vow to look after those you have put in me care.

Eventually, the music worked its magic. The words of the songs hit their target. His spirit lifted, his eyes closed, and his heart soared, taking all of us with him to that place of peace. He sang with passion and led us all into our time of preparation.

51

ABBOT

Everyone was comfortable and relieved that this was Valarie's mission and she was calling the shots.

"Right team, this is it. Time to go." With all the furniture and rugs gone, her voice, ghost-like, echoed around the building. Valarie knew we needed to get everyone moving, otherwise the melancholy would drag us down. It was always sad to leave, but the adventure inevitably lay ahead. One could not meet the future if one anchored oneself in the past, too afraid to move forward.

"Marcus, I would like you up front driving, with Kait and Dan. Raph, Riah, I know it will be squishy, sorry guys, but I'd like you on the bench seat. Kait and Dan, your job is to protect the cab. Tessa, Abbot, and I will cover the back." She'd turned to each, ensuring their focus and understanding.

"Marcus, we don't know what the streets are going to be like. From the feel of things lately, it could all go down very quickly, so take the most direct route to the estate. But stay clear of the city. Might be best if we fuel-up this side of town—we know the layout better." Her eyes flinched as she'd punched her thigh with still tender fists.

"The run-around for Ebony has cost us. I didn't want to have to stop on our way out, but we need the truck filled. Carnage could be widespread, and we may not be able to get fuel for some time. Have you filled the jerry cans?"

Marcus gave her a withering look, but then, realising she was just doing her job, merely nodded his head.

"Abbot, we have secured the seats so you can be comfortable for the ride, in and out. We don't know how long this is going to take." Her scowl was not meant for me, but the concern and care under it was.

"Dear girl, I would like to say that you don't have to worry about me, but we both know just how grateful I am. Thank you."

Her face softened into a smile. I knew she was trying to think of everything and was worried about what she didn't know and what she couldn't foresee.

"Does everyone have water? Are there food bags in the front and back?" She looked at Raphael to check he'd done his job.

All serious, and aware of the tension, he replied, "Yes, Val. Each bag has fruit and carbs, just like you said. There is a four-litre cooler in the front and back and I have checked that there is a personal water bottle for everyone as well. I'll put five in the front and three in the back."

"Good man, thanks mate." She looked around the room and back to us all. "Kait, I hate to nag, but are you picking up anything that could help us here?" Her forehead lifted in question and her eyes pleaded for any extra scrap of information.

"Only what I have given you already. Sorry, Val. I don't know what's going to happen with Ebony, but I know we need to go. All I have is that something necessary and important is going to happen and that we have to leave tonight. I don't have a time, but it won't be late when it all comes down. If we didn't have to meet Ebony, I would be suggesting we just get in that truck and get out of here." She edged closer to Marcus. "You're right—this place is going under tonight and the streets are going to be dangerous." The two women locked eyes.

Kaitlyn knew Valarie well enough to understand her concern for the twins in this battle. For Tessa and Daniel so green, and for me not able to hold my own anymore. That, added to so many other unknowns, was eating her up. I knew she loved the fight. I knew it was what Valarie lived for. She revelled in it, but not when so many were at risk.

"What about you, old man, you sensing anything?"

"What do you mean?" Marcus asked.

"You have a Badge for sensing things, having a feel for a situation, but more so for people. I thought you knew that. I need your input. What's your take on things? More importantly, on Ebony?"

"I don't like it. The situation, that is. And I'm not too sure about Ebony. There's no denying she saw us, so she has to have the sight. Although, we do kind of stand out these days, regardless of whether you can see the armour or not. My immediate take on her is not good, but that could be for a number of reasons." His eyes darted to Kaitlyn then back to Valarie. "Not enough to rule her out. We all come in differently." He stood taller, shoulders back, chin up.

They'd known each other for over six years, but I didn't think he considered his sensing a Badge. I was glad. Valarie gave him a nod, and then moved on.

Her eyes ranged the group, resting on Tessa and Daniel standing close together, hands entwined. "You guys okay? Do you have any questions?" Both shook their heads. We'd been through the logistics a number of times over lunch. They knew what they needed to do.

She moved to Raphael and Sariah, my little ones. They were being so brave. I was desperately sad to leave them ... grieved to leave them all. But I mustn't start letting myself sink into that kind of thinking. It wouldn't help anyone.

"What about you guys?"

Raphael and Sariah, too, were holding hands. The weight of the situation and the fear of the unknown rested heavily on them. Both were pallid and subdued. Raphael looked at Sariah and then back to Valarie. "We are okay, Val, we know what we need to do. You can count on us."

Valarie closed the gap in two large strides then took a knee in front of them. With a hand on Raphael's shoulder, she raised her other hand and gently cupped Sariah's cheek and addressed the girl, "Sweetheart, I need you in the front. If something happens, you'll be able to get out and run. Stick to one of the others and run to a Soteria House. Don't look back or wait around, just run. Do you understand?" Searching both their faces intently for a sign and the truth, Valarie was desperate to know they would be alright.

Sariah gave a faint smile and shakily nodded her head in return, then threw her arms around Valarie. Their bond was deep and mysterious. They shared a quick, fierce embrace, then parted.

I am sure that most of the group missed the look she cast to Kaitlyn and Marcus as she turned around. There was no mistaking the resolve however, or the weight of their combined concern.

"Any last questions?" When no one responded, she continued, "Okay team, let's move out. Kids, toilet first. Don't roll your eyes, Raphael. We don't know when we'll get the chance again. If you want to be a warrior, you need to learn, 'Don't go into battle with a full bladder'."

She then raised her eyebrows at Daniel and Tessa meaningfully. The instruction was for them as well.

Even before we entered the truck, the outside pressure and tension became uncomfortably cloying. The air was spiked with the scent of sulphur. Our time was up. We had to leave. And be quick about it.

Kaitlyn embraced me briefly, looked me in the eye and then kissed my cheek. I could feel her grief and the strain she felt at not showing or sharing the knowledge. Then she was gone, and Marcus and Valarie were helping me into the back and settling me into my chair. Once Tessa and Valarie were settled, Marcus and Daniel closed us in, and we heard them climbing into the front.

At last, we were on our way. Everyone in their places and immersed in their thoughts. The truck came to life and we were off. I didn't know how or when I was going to be taken, but I had been given the blessing of knowing in advance and I wanted to take advantage of that.

I could see Valarie look at me in the afternoon light breaking through the gaps in the furniture tightly packed into where we sat. There wasn't much, but it was enough. "Thank you, dear heart. Thank you for coming for me and sharing with me a life worth living."

"What are you talking about?" she said.

"Like Kaitlyn, you are neither insensitive nor unaware. You know this is it for me and I would like our last moments spent in truth, not pretending we didn't know."

I could hear Tessa inhale behind me as Valarie dropped her head.

"Yes, dear heart, you were right. I am not going to make it through this, and I'm okay with that. I am tired and I know I have become a liability—"

"Never! Never say that. You are not a liability. You are one of our greatest assets. Your mind, your Badges, your understanding, your experience ... your compassion, strength ... everything you have is an asset and a gift."

I held up my hand and called her to silence. "Valarie, we both know the truth. Through the Light, you have given me the best ten years of my long life. The time with your mother was brief but ..."

It was hard to hold back the tears now as I thought of Joy and what she had given me. Valarie and Tessa were patient as they waited for me to compose myself and continue. "The sweetest few years of my eighty-five. Regardless of how we feel and what we think, life will continue to roll over all of us, unstoppable and unchangeable. Fighting it is futile and exhausting. Accepting it allows peace, and enables us to enjoy the thrill of the ride."

We couldn't help but share a smile as memories flooded our minds. I may not have been a warrior like the daughter of my heart, but we both loved the adventure.

"The Light has set the course, and we will follow. I just want you to know how much I appreciate you, cherish, and love you. I admire you and, Valarie, my most treasured gift of a daughter, I acknowledge the sacrifices you make for us. I know them all ... and I thank you."

She was not able to speak, nor could I voice any more. I could feel her grief and an uncomfortable sense of relief—it was out in the open and now we all knew.

Behind me, Tessa quietly cried. Valarie squeezed into the space by my chair, perched on the arm, placed her head on my shoulder and silently wept as she released all her grief. I was the last link to her mother, and I was overwhelmed by the strength of her genuine love and appreciation for me.

I let her be, for now was a time to weep and mourn, a time to grieve and be silent. All too soon it would be a time to kill, a time to fight and a time to lose. Tessa wrapped her arms around me and gently rested her head on the back of my shoulder. And thus, we travelled to battle.

52

KAITLYN

I was in the dicky seat, tightly packed between Marcus and Dan. The twins were still small enough to be comfortable on the narrow bed that ran the width of the cab behind us. They sat with their backs to the side of the cab and their legs straight out, entwining where they met in the middle. We were jammed in, but in a safer position than those in the back. But, in truth, if things turned nasty, no place was really safe.

Lightning flashed over the city and Raph gasped. I turned to lay a hand on his leg hoping to reassure him. The sight of his armour catching the reflection of another bolt of electricity took me back to this morning's check after our thanksgiving meal. We had all gone outside and stood in the light while Val and Abbot checked our armour, till they were satisfied we were all ready. Just like the young ones, Marcus and I needed our checks and balances as well.

With his Badges, Abbot was ideal for this. He had taken Raphael aside and had a quiet word, then invited Dan to join them. When they had finished, Abbot spent time with Raphael and Tessa. The three of them worked through some issues relating back to the time before their rescue. It would take Raphael years to get over his torture, if ever. It was a puzzle to us all how Sariah's armour was so strong. Not being able to hear how she processed it deepened the mystery.

I was so proud of our family. That morning my soul was lifted, standing in the sunlight looking at all the rich beautiful colours of our armour on display. We were all traveling well and essential to each other, a truth that would be tested greatly in the hours to come.

We had witnessed the deteriorating conditions in the city during our fruitless trips to meet with Ebony. The gangs were now well and truly in control. All the outer suburbs matched ours now. All reduced to ghost towns. Most were marred with barricaded shop fronts and vandalised street signs, as useless as the smashed traffic lights. The ferocious storm brewing overhead matched the mood of the street, but its activity was a stark contrast to the barren wilderness that surrounded us. Darkness was closing in.

Squeezed in the middle of the cab I could feel Marcus's tension gently coiling around him like fine insulation. Unlike Dan, whose agitation sparked wildly like a cut snake. He was trying his best to stay calm, but he couldn't hide his nerves. I suspected he was having a flashback to the confrontation on the street, which of course had taken him back to his terror in Gomorrah. The enemy had done well to plant that seed of self-doubt and fear in him for today. He was not at his best.

"Dan." I quietly called him from his thoughts and, laying my hand on his knee, looked him in the eye. "Breathe, honey."

"What the fra— frigate do you mean, breathe? I am sodding breathing. You'd know if I wasn't. I'd be dead. At least then I wouldn't have to take in any more of that feral, disgusting smell."

"Oi." Marcus gave him a side glare.

"It is not that bad," Raph piped up from the back.

"Are you serious?" he shot back. Then, looking at Marcus, then over his shoulder, "Sorry. That came out a bit harsh." Shaking his head, he continued. "This smell is doing my head in." He looked back out the window, and took a slow deep breath. "Sorry, guys, I know I can do this, I just need for it to start. It's the waiting that's killing me. I have no idea what to expect, or if I'll do okay. If I'll be what you all need me to be."

"We have no idea what's in front of us, so I'm not going to make any baseless promises"—I squeezed his knee—"I do know, however, that the best, and safest, place to be through it all, is in the Light. Keep your eyes open. The situation on the streets has become even more savage. And it will get worse as evening draws in." I waited till he looked at me. "Focus on the Light and let your training and instincts take over." I paused then narrowed my eyes. "Don't turn off your brain, just your amazing imagination. Now is not the time to let it run free. Actually, that's the last thing you need right now." I could only do so much to encourage him. In time he would be better equipped to do it himself.

Marcus's face was stern as he studied us, then he brought us back to the present. "The fuel station is up ahead. I don't like it. It feels like an ambush. Dan, can you drive?"

"If I have to, but I haven't really had the need or opportunity to be any good."

"Right. We're more likely to be attacked by humans at this point anyway. When we stop, Dan, you're with me. Kait, take the wheel and do not get out of the cab for any reason. And lock the doors." He flicked his glance to the back seat. "Raphael, Sariah, keep an eye on all windows and mirrors. Only unlock the doors when you see that Dan and I are safe to get back in." His hand flicked to the indicator as he prepared to go in. "Kait, keep the motor running. This is not good, but I can't see it being better anywhere else."

As we drove up to the station, the lights were out and the shop windows were boarded up. The overhead lights were on, but flickering like an epileptic's nightmare. The place was deserted but, thank the Light, the pumps were operational. I agreed with Marcus: this was not looking good, but we needed that fuel.

"Raph, call out to the others in the back and let them know what's going on. Keep them updated on anything you see and tell them to be on high alert." With that, Marcus was out of the truck and Dan followed suit.

I shimmied over to the driver's seat. In the side mirror, I could now see Marcus attaching the pump, but I was so focused watching him and Dan, I missed what was coming at us from the passenger side. My heart leaped into my mouth when fists bashed against the side window. Raphael sat like a block of ice, terrorised, staring at the gruesome face leering straight at him.

"Come out and play, pretty little boy."

"Hey!" I yelled, drawing attention to me whilst scanning the scene through the passenger side window. I had made a rookie mistake by watching the action instead of the periphery. Five were coming at us from the passenger side, and more were coming from the shop. They had waited till we were committed, and now it was too late to get away.

"We've got company!" I yelled into the back and started to wind down the window to tell Marcus and Dan, but all I could see was the abandoned pump left hanging in the side of the truck. I wildly looked around till I saw they were already engaged with the first five. The second five were strolling over from the shop, like they had all the time in the world.

That was one for our team. They underestimated us. I knew Marcus said to stay in the truck, but we hadn't been expecting these kinds of numbers.

"Raph, come and take the wheel! I've got to go and help. Riah, come into the front and man the passenger door, but do not get out!"

If I could just get to the back before they made it over to us, we'd have a better chance. I turned off the engine and slipped out the door, waiting long enough to check that Raph locked it behind me.

Big mistake. My desire to make sure the kids were safe cost me. As I turned to run down the side, I was grabbed from behind and slammed into the side of the truck. Stars filled my vision as my head whipped back, followed by a stabbing wave of nausea.

"Hey sexy lady, time to ..."

Foolish and arrogant, my attacker had pinned my arms against the side of the truck but left my legs free. I was angry that they had attacked my family, scared they were going to hurt my kids, and frustrated that they had delayed our escape. I drove my knee up for all I was worth, only satisfied when it connected with his pelvic bone. Leaving him gasping in a pool of pain, I took off again but was stopped short when a hand grabbed my braid and reefed me backward. The attack was so violent I was pulled completely off my feet.

Thankfully, years of practice and training kicked in. I didn't have time to think—only react. I threw myself into the backwards fall and landed on my arms and lower back. I had to keep my head from smashing onto the concrete or it would have been all over. I was in a world of pain. A good thing. It meant I was conscious. But I was also in a world of trouble.

A foot closed over my throat, restricting my breathing. The burning in my throat was intensified by the fumes rising from the diesel-soaked tarmac. Bile swirled in my stomach. The pain in my head was exacerbated by the flashing overhead lights, and the chaos around me.

Both sides of the truck were being assaulted and the chassis, along with everything inside, was being tossed like a dinghy in wild seas. It was not in danger of being tipped, but I could hear the chickens protesting from their rough ride inside. I could only imagine how Abbot and Tessa were coping. The animals' distress seemed to spur our assailants on. I was fighting to stay focused and to think my way out of the mess. But the assault on my senses was not helping.

"Shut the frack up! Get over there and finish them off." The greasy haired, oily voiced leader brought his baboons under control. "We need to get this done already."

Fear for my family triggered my fight response. I tried to get up.

"Not so quickly." Spittle showered my face. Easing the pressure on my throat. "What's in the back?"

"You don't want to go in there," I rasped. It was the truth, but I also hoped it might entice him all the same.

Please make him take the bait.

Out of the corner of my eye, I could see Marcus and Dan still engaged with about five. The numbers remained the same, but the faces had changed. Three inert bodies lay around them, plus the one I'd dropped. From my previous head count, that was all of them, but I didn't know if they had reinforcements. My main aim now was keeping them all occupied so none were free to focus on the twins.

"Grunt, get the back," he ordered. A minion broke away from the fight to obey.

"You really don't want to do that." My throat burned.

He dragged me to my feet, and with a knife to my throat I was hustled in Grunt's wake. Standing a short way off, providing my captor with a human shield, Grunt was given the nod to go ahead. As soon as the latch was freed, the back flew up. Val's leg shot out. I smashed my soggy skull into the bridge of Oily Knife Guy's nose. He didn't drop like Grunt. But he loosened his hold enough for me to move out of the way for Val to finish him off.

The pain in the back of my head exploded in all directions and my world spun out of control. It was well and truly my third and final strike. Forcing myself to stay on my feet, I bent over and wrapped my arms around my wounded skull. A distant groaning broke through the kaleidoscope of colours. Nausea overwhelmed me. I tried to figure out who was in distress. Was it one of ours? Or theirs?

Breathing in and out slowly through my mouth helped me to maintain consciousness and my lunch. It also stopped the groaning. I guessed it was one of us.

I staggered closer to the back of the truck. "You guys okay ...?" Cut off by another tackle from behind, I was spun into complete disorientation. I fought the fierce hold that trapped me. I knew I was weakened. But I only needed to distract until the others could come and help.

Too close to use my knees, arms pinned by my sides. I threw my head back, ready to crack his skull.

Damn it!

He was faster and manoeuvred me to the side. Held at arm's length. Yelling broke through the fog.

"Whoa, there Kait. It's me!"

"Oh." I crumpled into Marcus's arms, this time happy to be

trapped. Happy for him to take over the job of holding me up. My reasoning swam in a wild sea and I struggled to herd thoughts into some sense of order. Again, I attempted to placate the nausea, dim the pounding, and calm my heart by slow breathing.

But Marcus thrust me to arm's length in order to release some steam. "I told you to stay in the truck! What were you doing? Three times, Kait. Three times you went down. We had this. I told you to stay in the truck." Wild eyes accentuated his barrage. His voice almost broke. "Are you okay?" His anger, fear, and shock were fuelled by adrenaline.

I knew this, but it didn't help. Once more, I tried to form an answer, but I was smothered, wrapped securely within his arms. I gave up. I was annoyed that he judged me to be so inept. And bleeding frustrated that he was right—well, when it came to fighting humans, anyway. However, right then, I just wanted him to shut up and hold me.

Tessa, Val, Marcus and I watched the perimeter, the unconscious, the immobilised, while Dan finished fuelling the truck. As he was wrapping up, Marcus walked me to the cab. It was overkill. But I was used to it. I was going to be fine, the pain would pass, and I would be right as rain in a few moments. But he was having none of it. He watched me like a hawk as I climbed into the cab, before racing to secure the back door.

I used the break to check on the twins. They were shaken but okay. They had returned to their bench seat and we were all ready to go when Dan and Marcus made their way back.

Raphael, my darling boy, reached over and gently laid his hands on my shoulders. I could hear his faint whisper. But more importantly, I could feel the warmth of his hands on my shoulders radiating to my skull. The relief almost undid me. But there was no way I was going to show just how much it had hurt. The screaming in my body faded to a hum, and soon was gone altogether. The herd of elephants dancing beneath the explosion of colours in my head had all gone home. The party over. My stomach had settled and the ringing in my ears had stopped. I could breathe.

Despite my mishaps, this gang seemed small in number and obviously weak in rank. I suspected those who would cause real trouble were closer to the city centre where the more valuable merchandise was housed. The higher the rank, the closer they'd plant themselves for when the trouble and looting began in earnest. We had to move and get to Ebony's asap, then get out of this place before it all fell down.

As he drove, Marcus took my hand and placed it on his thigh, covering it in his. Using the twins' sign language, he pumped it twice, only letting go when he had to change gears, then coming right back to reclaim it. We were going to be okay. Whether we survived was another matter.

53

MARCUS

Human be damned. The enemy or not, I'd have killed the lot of them, especially that kret that pinned her to the ground. Praise the Light, Val got to him first. Otherwise, at some point in the distant future, I would have had the slaughter of that piece of skrat playing on me conscience.

But everyone was safe. Thanks to the Light and the shield who had spread out to defend us against the Others as they flew and raged against us. Time was running out. But at least we were moving again. We just had to get out of here.

Please, help us.

I loved Kait, but I was going to skin her. What was she thinking? Me wife was skilled in hand-to-hand, but that wasn't training, and these guys were playing for keeps. Kait didn't have the thug instinct born from living on the blade-edge of life and death. An edge honed by the inability to trust, ever, sharpened by constant threat, scourged by desperation. Unlike mine, her heart was pure. She too would do anything to protect her family, but she was burdened with compassion, grace and mercy. Even when someone was hurting her, she would still consider them, see them, and bleeding well care for them.

Dan did well. I appreciated his experience, and even though it was a serious interruption to our schedule, it was the perfect opportunity for him to let off some steam. But it was bleeding skratty timing for me. Me mood matched the angry sky. Black, grey and blue clouds were stacking, pressure was building, and lightning was sparking. I had to get me rage back under control. I had to calm down and centre again before we got to Ebony's ... or before the skrat rained in torrents.

If I fed me hate, I'd feed the Dark.

Help me!

As we progressed through the streets, I sank deeper into despair and eventually had to bring the truck to a stop. The tide was rising.

"What's going on?" Val shouted from the back.

"Every street leading to an eastern exit is blocked. We're being channelled into the city centre. To keep going is suicide." I slammed the steering wheel. Kait laid her hand on me thigh. I held it, breathed and tried again, calmer, "We'll have to go back and attempt one of the earlier exits. The further we go, the more substantial the roadblocks are becoming."

"Did you leave the back door unlatched like I asked?" Val was making an effort to calm down as well.

"Yes, Val." I knew she was wading neck deep through responsibility, charged with nerves, cocked and ready to fire. So was I. But truth be, I was surprised the back hadn't ridden up yet. The only reason we secured the door was because, with speed, or bumps, it had a habit of retracting, leaving passengers exposed and objects in danger of falling out. But the unfolding trap had thrown a spanner in the works and slowed our progress.

I had to think. We had to get out of this place. Our guard was still in place, but they were under intense fire from above. A golden arc above us, flashing with the intensity of lightning. The Dark rolled around them, and a battle I couldn't track. I had no eyes for them, but I knew they were busy fighting and holding off the Unseen. Our job was to get through. And all around us, the enemy had set up traps using the very solid and tangible Seen.

Val said, "Right, you pick the spot and we'll help when you get there. Give us warning before you pull up, and get as much information as you can—materials, surroundings, company, anything you can think of. Let's go, Marcus, time is ticking."

"On it." I reversed and made an awkward turn, bumping over kerbs as I headed back the way we had come.

"Kait, you call it for Val and Tessa. Dan, take in as much as you can. As soon as we stop, I want you with me. Kait, you take the wheel."

I had driven back past the more substantial barricades made of trucks and cars, concrete blocks and metal skips, to the ones consisting of piled household goods. It would still impact the truck if we rammed it, but the pieces of furniture would be easier to plough through.

I nodded to Kait and she began, "Suburban street. Tightly packed houses. Barricade is half a block in. Perfect ambush situation. No cover on the sidewalks. They'll come from the houses. No visual hostiles. Couches, cupboards, white goods. Stopping now."

"Dan and Marcus, east side. Tessa and I, west side ..." Val's voice whipped away with the wind as she ran up the side with Tessa. Dan was out before I brought the truck to a standstill. I left it idling and yanked the handbrake on before following suit.

Thankfully it was more bark than bite. But either way it was still a bleeding inconvenience. Within the seconds it took me to join them, the others had made a serious impact. Thankfully, we weren't moving house, just bumping and throwing things aside to clear enough space to get through. In less than a minute, Kait had room to start moving. The truck edged forward, gently sliding any overhanging pieces with the bumper. It was when Kait was halfway through, with the sides blocked, the houses around us erupted.

"Stand back!" Kait revved the truck and pushed through the remaining barrier. She was driving slow enough to not permanently damage the truck, but fast enough to convince any resistance to back away. Once the cab was through, she slowed to a crawl. I managed to catch a glimpse of Dan hoisting Tessa up onto the sideboard outside the passenger door. He followed and clung to the inside handle.

Before they slipped out of sight, I saw Dan shield and secure Tessa's body with his own. They were safe.

Val and I attempted to jump into the cramped space of the back. Abbot sat in his chair, his hands reaching for us, his lips moving silently in petition. There was nothing secure to hold onto. We each clung to a side. As I tried to leg me way in, I caught Kait's eye in the side rear-vision mirror, just before she screamed. A mob swarmed out of the houses.

Help us.

Hands gripped me legs and pulled me free. I saw Val fall. The crowd closed around us and started dragging us away. Over the top of the mob, I watched, both relieved and desperate as the security of the truck crept further away. They were safe. The gang was focused on us. But we had as much hope of wax in hell of getting out of this one. Hands pulled and yanked. Boots landed and rucked. I couldn't find me feet. It was all I could do to protect me head.

An ear-splitting crack stopped time. Everything stilled. I didn't move. I was readying for the second act. But damned if I was going to do it lying down. In the breath they'd given, I found me feet and readied me stand. I caught sight of Val, an arm's length to me right. She'd suffered a similar fate. We edged closer. A calm settled upon me with the gift of an ally. We may be going down, but we were going to take many—a great many—with us.

Path set and, with a nod, agreed, we readied for the attack. But it didn't come ... yet. The crack that had pulled the horde off was a bolt of lightning that had struck an electricity pole on the corner of the street. It had dropped onto the house next to it, wires spitting and crackling. Half of the crowd turned and ran back to the house as sparks turned into flames, fuelled by the wind and the bed of crushed wood the pole nested in.

"Marcus!" I turned in time to catch the hand-held fire extinguisher Abbot had pitched to me. Taking advantage of the distraction, Kait had reversed the truck to within reach. The determined, who'd not been drawn off by the fire, remembered their goal and turned back to us. With the odds now reasonable, I welcomed their attention. Between the two of us, Val and I were able to make short work of those who displayed more determination than sense.

Using the fire extinguisher as a cudgel, I made sure our assailants stayed down. Abbot took the weapon from me as I turned to climb into the back. As we scrambled aboard, he sprayed foam into the dwindling crowd to cover us as Kait drove off.

Val clung on to Abbot's chair and tried to brace him, whilst I did me best to shut the door before he fell out and we lost too much stuff. It seemed only a minute later that we pulled up.

"You guys okay?" Kait yelled from the front. Before I could yell an expletive in response, demanding to know why the hell we had stopped again, the cab door opened and quickly closed again. She was letting Dan and Tessa back in the cab.

"Yeah, we're good," Val answered. I caught her smile in the fading light. She had either known what I was thinking and was laughing at me, or she was high from the fight. Either way, I wasn't very fond of her at the moment. Although I was exceedingly grateful that, one, she was on me side, and two, she was here with me. Apart from Kait, I don't think I appreciated and loved another human being more.

54

DANIEL

Finally, the signs indicated we were heading out of town and into the eastern region. We only needed to cross the river—the line separating the haves from the have-nots. Once across, we were free to hunt down Ebony's address. Kait guided us through the extravagant domain where each property, separated by huge walls, revealed obvious wealth without giving away too many details. No wonder they weren't worried about building roadblocks—they'd built their barricades years ago. Either that, or the help were too busy cleaning the silver.

The closer we got, the harder it was to repress the nerves that had been gnawing away at my sanity all day. My mind had fallen siege to thoughts of imminent death, torture, and failure to protect the kids, Tessa, and Abbot, whilst demons tried to eat me—or whatever it was that demons did. Compounding the nightmare was the fragging sulphur smell seeping into everything, the pores of my skin, my taste-buds … it was even getting under my eyelids.

I struggled to focus, because the heavens were going ape-skrat in a damn good imitation of the swirling, muddy waters of the river in flood. Clouds of sixty-five shades of grey were building up, bunching together and coming closer. The sky was not big enough to hold them. They were bubbling over, tumbling and falling down to earth. I could have reached out and grabbed a handful, if I hadn't been worried about what they were hiding. So, regardless of what Marcus and Val said, my Plan A was to stay close to Val, Marcus, and Kait. And if that didn't work, my Plan B was to stick to Val like glue. After that, I had no Plan C.

As Kait reversed as close as she could to the front door, I felt as ready as I was terrified. I wanted for this thing to be over, but my imagination was running roughshod over all the possibilities. I had absolutely no frashing idea what to expect. I felt like I was heading into The House wide awake, but with no second chance if I got it wrong. There was no time for more training or preparing. We were going in, ready or not. In a way it was a relief, it was just that I felt several years too green.

55

RAPHAEL

We were going to be okay. I knew everything was going to be okay. It was scary, but everyone had taken care of us. No one broke into the cab to hurt us and Riah and I were safe. I just had to remember to do my breathing and focus on the Light. The Light was in control and we were going to be okay. We were in the Light and He would keep us all safe.

In and out, in and out. I could do this. Since the barricade, both Tessa and Dan had managed to put an arm behind the seat. Dan had held my leg in a firm and comforting grip whilst Tessa had held my hand, rubbing her thumb over the back of my fingers. Riah was sending me all her peace through our intertwined legs. I was sending what healing I could into everyone. Riah looked pale, but we were going to be okay.

I just wanted Kait to keep driving. I did not want to stop. I did not care about this silly girl we had to pick up. We had been in this city for years, why did we need to stop for her now? She had had plenty of time. If she missed out, that was her fault. We should not have been stopping. We should have been getting to safety. Everyone was brittle and cranky. I wanted to go home.

The others climbed out of the truck and Riah stepped over the seat, but stopped to look at me as I hesitated. She dared me to join her. She would not let me stay behind. I guess if she could do this, so could I.

Everyone thought I was the stronger one, the one who looked after her. But Ri and I knew the truth. As she held out her hand, we continued to pretend. By the time we got down and walked to meet the group, Marcus, Val, and Abbot were already out and waiting for us at the back of the truck.

Val was a fortress to hide behind, a warrior to lead the way. "Dan, Tess, you take flank. I'll take point, and Kait, Marcus, you bring up the rear." She would make sure we were all going to be okay. We had been told that, whatever happened, they would try to make sure someone would be with us the whole time.

"Marcus, what's your take on the situation?" Val asked.

"Me wires are buzzing, but can't get a feel either way."

"Kait?"

"Nothing new."

It was like everyone was speaking in what Kait called "dot points".

"Abbot?"

"I'm being flooded by you all, I'm afraid. I can't get a read on anything else at the moment. There is a lot going on in this group alone, dear heart." I guess it was too much to think Abbot would ever consider using anything as short as dot points, whether it was urgent or not.

"Anyone else getting a read on anything?" I knew I had nothing to offer so I kept quiet and out of the way. I did not want to interfere.

"Right everyone, remain focused. If you see, hear or smell something, speak up. Don't assume anyone else has picked up on it."

I remembered Dan complaining about the smell and wondered if that was important enough to mention, but since he did not say anything, neither did I.

"Eyes on the Light. Arms ready. Follow my lead. Let's go." She was about to walk off, but she stopped. "What's up, Dan?"

"It's just the sulphur smell. It's doing my head in and it keeps getting stronger. It's making my eyes water."

Val looked around the group to see if anyone else was suffering as much as Dan. She narrowed her eyes and jerked her chin upwards like she did when she was making a point to Marcus and Kait. She seemed to think it was a secret sign. But Ri and I were used to secret signs. We saw Val's all the time, even now. But no one said anything, so maybe it was not important.

Thunder roared and lightning screamed as, for hour-long seconds, the night sky became day and the house lights dimmed throwing everything else into negative. I tightened my grip on Riah's hand and hurried to keep up with Val as she stalked up to the front door and knocked.

56

———

CONTESSA

I had to fight back a hysterical giggle. It was like strolling up to the gates of hell for an all-in brawl and politely asking permission to enter. Although, Val knocking with the side of her closed fist was not particularly polite. She managed to create an echo that mimicked the roar of the surrounding thunder. We waited silently in the shadow of the ridiculously large mansion.

Seriously, talk about going over the top.

The place was like a suburban temple.

Eventually the door was thrown open, and Ebony stood beaming on the other side. Val introduced herself and reacquainted our perfect little host with those of us from the shop. If Ebony thought it odd that she wasn't introduced to Abbot or the twins, she didn't show it. She turned gracefully with an expansive sweep of her perfect arm, and a swish of her perfectly glossy ponytail, and welcomed us into her darkly ornate, perfectly ridiculous home.

Even before we stepped over the threshold, I had to admit, to myself only, that I was pretty impressed by the flash interior. It had been like looking at a tall, beautifully decorated cake. You knew it was going to be good, but when four layers of cake, cream, fruit and fondant were revealed, you forgot just how pretty the outside was.

The whole place was branded with the "oh-yeah-we're-rich" stamp.

I'd never seen anything so posh.

Ever.

We were engulfed by the entrance hall and immediately my eyes were drawn to the high ceiling. Beautifully carved cornices topped dark, glossy panelled walls, which ran into an equally dark polished floor.

Long islands of lush, richly coloured carpet lined the hall. Storm-cloud grey mirrored the brewing cyclone outside. Wild-ocean green. Deep blood-red crimson. Velvety midnight black. Intense luxury invited us deeper inside the house. Chairs, covered in the same blood-red that trailed through the carpets, dotted the hallway.

Sure, it was a long hall, but did they really think people needed to stop and rest on the way? Seriously, who needed all those chairs? And, more importantly, who did all the dusting?

Obviously, it wasn't Ebony, who remained bright and cheerful despite the darkness of her house and the chaos in the city. Was she even aware of the atmosphere outside and the disgusting sulphur smell saturating everything?

She was either really good at hiding it, or just really dumb.

Perfectly perky, but seriously ignorant.

I knew Dan was sensitive to this smell. And if I had noticed it getting stronger, he must be really suffering. I glanced over at him. The whites of his eyes were now red, and tears of irritation were threatening to escape.

Ebony must have been really excited about leaving. In total contrast to her attitude in the shop, she actually bounced as she led us through the mansion. We walked straight down the grand hallway past impressive works of art hung on the walls and displayed behind glass.

The place was an art gallery and a museum all rolled into one.

Did she appreciate it, or take it for granted?

It was something we never took for granted. Having an artist in our family and living within a canvas—on the walls inside and the garden outside—we got a front row seat, watching life being breathed into the inanimate daily.

If I'd had time, I would have loved to have taken Riah for a sticky-beak through the whole place.

Ebony lived in an alien world.

This just wasn't normal ... or natural.

I tried to sneak a peek into some of the rooms as we passed, but all the doors were shut. We'd only been given visual access to the wide hall and the library at the end.

Everything about this place screamed money and class.

Growing up here would have been so easy.

I bet she didn't even know how good she had it.

The library was a perfectly square room. And, except for the large double doors through which we entered, there were no exits. A skylight in the ceiling gave a full-on and impressive view of the angry sky above.

How on earth did they keep that window so clean?

Mid grumble, on behalf of the invisible staff, I noticed an elaborately carved balcony forming a second level around the room. It had no stairs. Forget about how they cleaned the skylight, how on earth did they get up to the balcony?

The far wall housed a fireplace that was set up and ready to be lit. In keeping with the rest of this monstrous house, it was humongous. Big enough to cook a whole cow.

This place was really starting to overwhelm me. I felt like Jack in the giant's castle in a totally different world at the top of the beanstalk.

It was all kinds of creepy ... and weird.

I just wanted this to be over so we could get on the road and get out of here. Val and the others were led to three couches that were the centrepiece of the room. They were set up in a U formation, open to the fireplace. Ebony had taken her place and invited the rest of us to follow suit.

Yeah, right.

There was no way I was going to sit down in this freaky house. Thankfully I was given something useful to do instead.

57

MARCUS

Abbot, Raph, and Riah sank down into the lavish couches and Val perched on the edge. The rest of us stationed ourselves around the outside of the setting. With our guard outside occupied by the storm of the enemy, we were to be on high alert.

Catching Kait, Tessa and Dan's attention, I signalled that we all needed to stay on guard. Ebony was a strange one alright, sharp as a marble. I wasn't happy about this. Something was off, but I just couldn't put me finger on it. She, on the other hand, didn't seem put-off by us. Here, in her own house, she was a totally different kettle of fish. I guess we all remove our masks at home. She was in her own territory, firmly in control of the situation, despite the fact that there were eight of us. So, was she innocent, ignorant, or an incendiary?

Val got straight to business, wanting, like the rest of us, to get out of here. "Ebony, it's a shame we haven't been able to meet with you before this. You need to make a huge decision with hardly any time. We are leaving the city now. We will never come back. If you were to join us, you might never see your family and friends again. Do you understand what we're asking?"

"Yes, you are leaving now and not coming back," she parroted.

"If you join us, Ebony, you will be welcome to stay with us, but we don't know where we're going, how long it will take us, and how we'll live when we get there. It's a big challenge to trust the Light for all that you need, not knowing any details for certain. Are you prepared to live like that?"

"Yes, living in the Light is a challenge. You must trust the Light for all that you need."

"Not only that, Ebony. In the Light we are in constant battle with the Dark and unpopular with people. You will be at war. Do you realise this will be your new way of life?"

"Yes, I will be at war for the rest of my life."

"However, if you stay, you will be abandoned to the Dark in this place. The Light is retreating and Sodom will be destroyed. Do you understand?"

"Yes, Sodom will be destroyed," Ebony repeated.

The girl sat there with her eyes wide open and a plastic smile plastered on her face. I trusted Val to pick up on the weirdness, but she would never leave a Potential behind. I could understand why she was trying to impress upon her how big the decision was. Ebony seemed a picnic short of a thermos if you asked me. Maybe she was a dabbler? But regardless of what was influencing her, she had to make her decision now. Pity the girl seemed to lack the equipment needed to make a decision. Informed or otherwise. But enough was enough, we had to go, we couldn't wait any longer.

Val gave it one last push in an attempt to break through the facade. Duty of care and all, we couldn't in good conscience take someone who was not in their right mind. Regardless, we would be out soon. I continued to study the situation and the room in tandem with Kait, looking for any hidden escapes, traps, signs ... anything. It wasn't good. Only one way in and out—death ground. That second level made us sitting ducks if anyone got up there.

If Val didn't wrap this up right now, I was going to intervene. Something was terribly wrong. I knew Kait could feel it too. She may not have been a pro on the streets, but when it came to Other warfare, she was prime. The knife edge Tessa and Dan were walking along was getting narrower and hotter as well. You could taste the tension. Smell the sulphur. It was getting stronger. Enough. We had to go. Now.

58

DANIEL

The lightning show continued above us and the air crackled with electricity. On another night, it might have been beautiful. But now it was just elevating the tension and magnifying the sulphur smell that pushed and percolated through everything like a giant coffee machine. The hairs on the back of my neck rose, and every nerve throughout my body tightened as the chill in the room increased.

I was sick of the immensity of this place. I'd had enough of the smell, the taste, and the sight of everything. I was completely over trying to figure out the mystery of that bloody balcony. I just wanted to get out of here. No longer able to bear looking at the walls, being blinded by the lightning flashes through the sky dome, I focused on the freaky airhead. What was the chick's problem?

It was then I noticed the square table that sat in the middle of the discussion. Made from the same dark wood that decorated the rest of the house, an intricate pattern was carved deeply into its surface. It was infinitely complex. The more I studied it, the more it drew me in. I just couldn't seem to make sense of it. I examined the carving, and became so intrigued that all my immediate worries started slipping away. It was pulling my mind into it as I tried to make sense of it.

After a crazy few weeks, it was a relief to focus on just the one problem.

"Dan." Tess was in my face, whisper-shouting my name, "Daniel."

Shaking myself, I looked at her. "What ... what's going on?"

"I'd like to ask you the same thing. You were in a trance. Snap out of it, man, we need you to focus. We're getting out of here. She said yes." Her eyes narrowed. "You okay?"

"Yeah. Thanks." I shook my head to clear the fog. "Whatever you do, don't look at that table. It's seriously dodgy." Our hands joined and we made our way to join the others and head out of this freak-fest.

Thank you!

Damn it. I spoke too soon. I didn't know where to look as several things competed for my attention. Ebony stepped onto the square table, looked up to the dome window and started moaning. We turned to look at her dumbfounded, when an ominous thud and click boomed. My stomach dropped. I turned to see that the trap had been set. Like the pull of the dodgy table, the locked doors deleted every thought except one.

We were fraggled.

Years later, or possibly seconds, Tessa was yanking at my arm and making some weird noises of her own. I followed her pointing finger. Ebony's moaning had increased. But more importantly, the girl's body was levitating above the table. Yes. Levitating. As in, no freaking strings attached. "What the fraggingly— frigid— frigates, is going on?"

"Quick, push the couches back against the walls. Clear the centre. We need space." Thank the Light, Val still had her head in the game.

We jumped to obey.

"Get rid of the table. But keep it away from the fireplace. In fact, everyone, keep away from the fireplace. Riah and Abbot, get into that corner." She pointed to the space opposite the fireplace, to the right of the doorway. "Raph, you stand in front of Abbot and Riah and don't let anyone pass."

All three of them raced away. I had just finished helping Marcus slide the mammoth table to the corner opposite to where Abbot and the twins stood. I didn't want that thing anywhere near us. With all the furniture out of the way, the huge room looked even more cavernous.

"Dan, Tessa, stand in front of Raph." Val impaled us with her eyes. "Do not. Let. Anything. Pass. Understand?"

There really wasn't any room for misinterpretation. Fight to the death and give no quarter. The enemy would not pass and leave us standing. We nodded gravely, and then ran to take our stand, guarding Abbot and the twins with our lives. We stood side-by-side, shoulder-to-shoulder, swords drawn, and waited.

Please help me do this right and not stuff up royally.

It was strange. I felt that wave of peace—warm golden oil—pass through my body from my head to my toes. Just like the first time the Light spoke to me, and the time I accepted His invitation. My heartbeat strengthened and slowed, my nerves quietened, and my focus sharpened.

"Everyone, breathe and focus. Do not lose sight of the Light." Val's order shook the light fittings. Her eyes did not leave the suspended body of Ebony, or the ridiculously large skylight.

Nerves tingled all over my body. I was ready for whatever came. Tessa stood bravely at my side and I had an overwhelming sense of rightness. This was what I was made for. This was where I was supposed to be. I was more alive in this moment than any other time in my life. But I wasn't sure for how long this life would last. Would I make it out of this? Who knew? Did I have any regrets? I leaned down and kissed Tessa, and she returned my kiss as intensely as it had been given. No. No regrets.

Ebony was still carrying on, slowly spinning mid-air at the same height as the balcony. Marcus, Kait and Val had taken a stand in a semi-circle, a fair way out from us. No one wanted to be under that window or Ebony when she dropped—which she did.

Unconscious or dead, I couldn't tell, but she lay in a heap in the middle of the floor, unmoving. The quiet was a blessed relief now that her fralicking wailing had stopped. But now, the silence screamed.

"Dan, get her. Put her by the wall." Val's eyes didn't leave the window.

Kait ran with me as I darted out. I grabbed Ebony's wrists and dragged her inert body, dumping her against the wall, away from where our small group had taken refuge.

Settling her in the recovery position, Kait quickly checked her pulse. She was alive. Fine. I really couldn't care either way. All I knew was that I didn't want her jumping up and being a pain in the butt in the middle of something.

She could stay where we could see her, but not near enough to put us in any more danger than she already had. Kait was gentle with the girl. I had to work hard not to kick her as I turned and raced back to my station. Everyone had their swords drawn except Val. I was confident she knew what she was doing, but I would have felt better if she at least looked like she was prepared for a fight.

Then they came.

59

KAITLYN

Val let out a primal roar, welcoming the onslaught, but I did not know where to look. Ghastly forms were dropping through the solid window. Demonic hail of epic proportions. Like a tsunami calmly disintegrating a city, I didn't want to see what was unfolding before me, but I couldn't afford to take my eyes off them.

At their arrival, all of the knives that had been buried in Val's body, causing her so much pain, dropped to the floor. She swooped down in one fluid movement and scooped handfuls of them and threw them at each of the humanoid demons as they dropped into the room.

She moved like graceful lightning. Almost too fast to watch, she spun, threw, leaped, and, with deadly accuracy, took out a demonic form with each knife. Twisted, gnarled bodies were dropping and disintegrating like flies in toxic acid, liquefying into pools of black tar that bubbled and melted the carpet and scorched the wood underneath. With their entrance and their demise came an even more intense sulphuric smell, now mixed with singed carpet. At least now we could confirm the source of the stench.

One landed near where Ebony lay. It leaned over her, drooling.

Cracked, burnt skin covered its lean, naked body. Large talons extended from every bony digit. These matched those thrusting from its primate toes. Each made a perfect secondary weapon.

Then, before my eyes, its features dissolved, with one of Val's blades sticking out of the back of its head. I scoped the room, ready for any of her leftovers I would have to share with Marcus. Val was always greedy when it came to a fight. The rest of our group was huddled in the corner, bulging eyes glued to the hell unravelling around us.

Before I could speak or react, Val yelled, "Focus!" Another form dropped within arm's reach of Dan and Tessa, a knife protruding from the side of its neck before it, too, dissolved into a pool of reeking tar. The couple came to attention, eyes alert, and back in the game. I scanned the room looking for more. Nothing moved.

"Sorry, Val." Dan had let his guard down and it had almost cost him. Val nodded in understanding, but it was unlikely he would get a second chance.

"Bleeding hell, Val. Could you at least save some for Kait and me? You are being a complete kill-hog."

She smirked. "Game on, old man. What's your score?"

"Damn it, that is completely unfair." Marcus tried to hide the fact that he was surreptitiously doing a head count and winced at her total of twenty-five.

"Dinner is going to be on you for a month, old man, if you don't get to work soon," she parried.

"Dinner's always on me, Val."

"That's because you always lose."

He met my eyes, scanned my body to check, once again, that I was okay. I smiled and tried to reassure him that I was fine, I loved him, and I was so extremely proud of him, I had faith in him, and he was my hero. It was a long message, but I'd been sending the same one for twenty-three years, so we'd gotten used to shorthand. He returned the message in kind and, within the next heartbeat, we were back in the game.

60

RAPHAEL

We were okay. It was all okay. I looked behind me first to check on Riah, and then tried to ask a question. It took a few attempts before my voice worked. "Is it over, Kait?"

"No, sweetheart. That was just the first wave. The little ones come to soften us up. The others will be here soon. Stay focused, remember your breathing. You're doing really well, sweetheart."

Val was back in charge. "Riah, Abbot, you going okay?"

Abbot glanced down at Riah and smiled. "Yes, dear heart. We're fine. Valiant effort. You were always a pleasure to watch." I had never seen it before, but I think Val may have just blushed like Tessa.

"Little Master, you alright?" she asked.

I was scared, so very, very scared. I had no idea it would be like this. I had always dreamed of taking my place beside them as a warrior. This one thought had kept me going since our time with the Bad People. It had been the dream that had driven me to stay focused and work hard at my training.

And this was what it was all about. If I could not do this, it was all for nothing. If I could not fight, if I was weak, I had no part in this ... with them.

I may not have been as brave as the rest of them. I may not have been able to do as much, but I would do what I could. I would prove that I was worthy. So, despite wanting to run and hide, I would not. I would do my part and fight.

"Yes, Val." My voice still shook, but she smiled, and I knew it would all be okay.

61

CONTESSA

Val had completed her check and seemed confident that we were all okay and doing the best we could under the circumstances. Then she paused

"'Fraggingly frigid frigates'?" she said, turning to Dan. "What's with that?"

"Well ... I'm trying really hard not to swear, Val. And I was really freaked at what was happening. That's just what came out."

"Proud effort." She smiled at him. "I like it."

Then we all turned at the sound of Ebony stirring.

"Okay, guys, what just happened was nothing. It's about to get really ugly. Please, do what you can to stay focused and disciplined. No one can afford the luxury of a brain break. You lapse, someone dies." She then quickly bent down and stowed the rest of the knives she hadn't used in different holds on her armour. Apparently, everyone else felt the same as me and didn't move to touch any of the ones still swimming in pools of demonic tar.

I noticed some of the Others had totally evaporated, leaving the blades gleaming, reflecting the light coming through the roof and the flashes of lightning still piercing the sky. I called out and kicked one blade over to Val.

The light in the room strengthened and became more pervasive, speeding up the removal of the remaining acidic tar like suds on a frypan evaporating over a hot stove. The rest of Val's knives were left gleaming like stars shining in a charred and damaged sky. Dan and I bolted around collecting the remaining daggers and dropped them at Val's feet before racing back to our posts.

"They're coming, they're coming! I knew they would!" Ebony was jumping up and down and clapping her hands like a child at Lightmas.

"What are you talking about, girl?"

Ebony didn't react to Marcus's hostility. She just kept bouncing on her toes. "The Light is coming." She looked at all of us then spoke to Val. "The Light Man told me how to get you all here and then showed me how to contact him. He said he would come and help us. I did just what he said, and he is coming."

The elation radiating out from her was sickening.

"Who is the Light Man, Ebony?" Kait asked quietly, a mixture of confusion and worry in her voice.

Ebony faced her, equally baffled.

Meanwhile, the light in the room grew brighter.

"He used to come and talk to me, first in my head, and then he would visit me in the night. He is light. He radiated light and he is beautiful ... perfect and so charming and loving ... stunning, and breathtakingly ... beautiful." Her eyes glazed, and I felt like I should offer her a hanky for the drool. "He promised me all kinds of things, told me private things." Her pale skin flushed, and she dropped her gaze.

Perfectly perky *and* seriously ignorant.

Marcus, Kait and Val exchanged worried expressions but didn't have time for anything else. Sharp beams of light burst into the room. Laser-like javelins hurled from the heavens landed in a fence around the five of us in the corner. We were trapped. Each beam then took form. Relief visited briefly as fear increased. Our guard had joined us inside. This was all kinds of bad.

They formed a barrier between us and the others. Their form

more solid, intense, and imposing than I had ever seen it before. They didn't acknowledge us at all. Rather they stood impassive, each with their ridiculously large, intimidating swords drawn, ready to fight.

I felt sick.

Val's eyes widened and she nodded in greeting and respect. Her body relaxed and she smiled at them briefly. "Thank you."

They returned her nod, acknowledging her thanks.

"Don't slacken off just because our guard is here. You are all still on duty. You all still have your orders. Stay safe and stay behind that wall. No. Matter. What. Am I clear?"

I couldn't speak for the others, but I wasn't planning on disobeying Val. So, I tightened my grip on my own sword, dropped my weight and breathed deeply.

Ready.

The rotten sulphur stench returned.

Far. Flaming. Out.

With it came the largest, scariest collection of creatures I had ever seen. The last lot had been humanoid. But this wave was a collection of bodies formed by the unnatural match of humanity and beasts. There was neither rhyme nor reason.

No logic or sense.

All of creation mutated and deformed.

Truth was, we were witnessing chaos incarnate.

I wanted to grab the other three and haul them back behind our defensive wall. But, with no option of flight, we all stood and readied to fight.

Help us all.

A resolute calm infused our lightened fortress. Light married warmth and birthed an almost peaceful cleared air. Despite my fear for my family, I was seriously grateful to be on this side of our guard wall.

Ebony was also realising where she would rather be. She screamed when she was hit by the harsh reality of her situation. The girl became desperate in her attempts to join us. "Let me in! Why won't you let me in?"

The Warriors barred her entrance and crossed their swords.

"Ebonyyy, my dark princesss. Don't be ssscared."

I knew that voice.

Ebony, however, whimpered wide-eyed as she turned to face the one who addressed her. Then instantly upped her efforts to claw her way in behind the Warriors.

"Hush, child." The voice changed.

She stopped and turned. One of the demons had changed form, mimicking a Warrior of the Light. "Come to me my little dark princess, it'll be alright."

Her pale, tear-streaked face relaxed. She took halting steps toward the creature.

"Did I frighten you?" he purred.

"Yes, Lord. Wh-what are these ... these things with you? Why won't they"—pointing her finger at the Warriors surrounding us—"let me in?"

"Because we are enemies and we are sworn to destroy each other. You are with me, so they will not assist you." His silky voice was soothing, like a parent calming a child, but it was at odds with his message. Ebony was being lured closer to him, seduced into a sense of calm. But she still flicked her eyes around the room taking in the Warriors, the demons, my family, and the fake Warrior.

So did I.

"But you're the same as them. Aren't you one of them?"

"Oh, did I forget to tell you? How carelesss of me. No, I am not like them ... at all." The hate and sneer in his voice returned. "Now that you are with me, all the people in thisss room"—he wrapped his impossibly large hand around the back of her head and forced her to survey the scene—"with big nasssty ssswords want to ssslaughter you, too."

She tried to break free, clenching her eyes shut in denial.

My heart broke for her.

She'd believed the lies.

She was trapped.

She was lost.

As the masquerading Warrior released her, she dropped to the floor and desperately clutched his feet and begged, "Please, save me."

"You ssstupid ignorant girl!" He spat the insult at her in disgust. The voice then left the creature and, disembodied, it circulated throughout the room. "You are no longer any ussse to me, I only usssed you to frustrate the Light's purpossse and to bring me the prizze I really wanted. You are nothing ... but a worthless, usssed up piece of ssskrat."

The look of terror on her face lasted only a moment. The creature went back to true form. As it did, it flicked its hand. With incredible unseen force, Ebony's body was flung across the room and smashed into the wall, once again blissfully unconscious.

"Another opportunity to negotiate, my ... dearest Valarrrie. What say you? Are you ready to hand over any of your ... charges? Oh, lovely, look everyone, see how their little claws have grown. Ohhh Sssariahhh ..." The lust and vulgarity in his purring voice were sickening. "There is a part of me that growsss when I ssseee you. Would you like to come and ... play with me?"

It was the trigger that started the war. The Warriors stood unmoving as the rest of the room erupted.

"I'll take that as a no." The voice chuckled and reverberated around the cavernous room, encouraging the fighting below. "Fight well, my beautiesss."

Then it was gone.

The heated battle intensified.

More demons dropped to the floor. Our three moved like lightning. They had to manage the onslaught. The size and strength of the opposition were overwhelming.

I wanted to join them, to help them. But the Warriors of Light stood between us.

I didn't know what to do. My concern for them was causing physical pain. I needed to do something. Anything. I had to help. Bouncing on my toes, hands clenched, white-knuckled around my sword hilt I picked up the soft voice behind me. It brought me back to reality.

"Perhaps, my dear ones, we would be better employed if we petitioned the Light on behalf of our loved ones. Ask that the Light sustain and protect them, guide and strengthen their sword arms and that, whatever happens, the Light will prevail." As always, the calm and wise words of Abbot led the way. But I just couldn't see how that could be enough to save them.

62

DANIEL

We all set to the task of asking the Light to protect our family. I didn't know what to say or how to do it properly. I didn't know if there was some special formula or words I was supposed to say. Our guys were hard at it and they were flagging. For every demon they took out, another was waiting to take its place. It seemed that there was an endless supply of the Dark's minions waiting to meet the Swords of Light.

The three stood back-to-back and moved with each other in a kind of deathly dance. They all knew the steps and timing, the result of years of fighting together, living together, and understanding each other. They all knew instinctively where the other two were and what they would do. Without even thinking, one warrior could lend a hand to the other when needed, and then continue with their own struggle.

As united as they were, they were all still completely unique. Marcus was like a hammer and relied mostly on brute strength, although he did so with finesse and artistry. He didn't just strike and stab, he tended to disembowel and behead, guaranteeing that none of his foes would get up and stab any of them in the back.

Kait was fast and light on her feet and had razor-sharp mental focus. You could see her brain ticking away. Kait seemed to outwit her opponents, staying one step ahead of them till they met the end of her sword. She didn't toy with them. But with her, it was more like a fast and fatal game of chess.

Then there was Legend. She was light on her feet and fast as lightning, cat-like, but lethal and efficient. She didn't waste her moves, nor was she flamboyant with her strokes. Graceful, like a dancer, though she probably would have punched me if I said it out loud. She was strong, artistic, and athletic, and drew your eyes. Once you started watching Val, it was hard to look away. She was art in motion.

All three of them working together was one of the most beautiful things I had ever seen.

Please strengthen them and just give them the energy to keep going. Don't let them get tired. Help them stay focused. Keep their sword arms limber and their armour strong. Keep them alert to their own danger and each other's.

My eyes were constantly drawn to Val. I think I started to understand the sacrifice she spoke of. The whole "knife" thing. Her armour was perfect. Solid. Mesmerising. She was created to fight, and she loved it. Yet she admitted that her flaw was pride and arrogance. That would have left her open to attack and weak in battle. Her brokenness and the humility brought on by her pain and physical inability brought her closer to the Light and made her more fearsome and lethal in battle.

Kait and Marcus also shone with the Light, each making their own sacrifices in order to fight the Dark's hold in them, to get closer to, and release the power of the Light in their own lives. It was beautiful because it was inspiring. In them, I could see a reason to walk the narrow path. Because what I was now seeing, for the three of them, was the daily internal reality for us all. To choose the Light every day, in every way, was the essence of the fight—it was the real battle.

I kept asking the Light to help them, willing them on. I knew ninety percent of fighting was in the mind. I could see them faltering.

I followed Kait's eyes to the balcony running around the upper floor in the room. It was crowded with more demons just waiting their turn. Her shoulders dropped. My hope faded. The battle seemed insurmountable.

How can they win this? How can they possibly keep going against the constant tide that faces them? You have to do something, you have to help them, damn it.

It was in that moment that the purest sound that creation ever put forth was released into the space behind me. I turned to see Sariah, her face lit up like a beacon, arms raised to the sky, eyes closed, her red armour on fire. Her voice simultaneously shattered my heart into a million pieces and lifted it to the heavens. Raph and Abbot wept openly. I could do nothing but stare, open mouthed at the miracle that was Sariah.

63

CONTESSA

I couldn't believe it. All the time I had known her, and I had never even imagined just how amazing my little sister was.

I was completely and utterly astounded.

Turning my attention back to the fight, I was blown away by the result. Truth was, it had changed them.

It had worked.

The circumstances hadn't changed. A relentless tide of demons oozed out of the woodwork. But our three had lifted, their stance had shifted, invigorated once more. I watched them and willed them on.

Out of the corner of my eye, red flame danced to my left. I couldn't hold back my smile as I watched Riah slip her hand into Dan's. Indigo engulfed Red.

Her song continued. Without interrupting her offering, she looked up at him and nodded, eyes wide in invitation.

He was hesitant. I knew he had no idea how amazing his voice was. Just one more thing I liked about him, his genuine humility. Well … in this, at least.

I linked my arm through his sword arm and encouraged him. "Go on."

He relented and joined his voice with hers.

Instantly I was drawn back to our home. I recalled images I'd secretly stolen of him sitting in the courtyard singing for her, as she'd created artistic wonders for him.

It's funny, I had been enraged by the piranhas in the shop when I thought he was enjoying their attention. And I'd felt so unsure of myself in Ebony's perfect shadow. But I had never felt jealous of Riah's connection with Dan.

As their song continued, I was gently transported to our sitting room. We all sat at the end of the day. A mixed scent of herbs and flowers carried on a warm breeze. The setting sun played over the back fence, dancing through the leaves of Raph's avocado tree. Colours merged and took turns claiming our attention as the shadows increased. We each occupied our place in the circle, lost in thought, engulfed by peace, or overcome with gratitude. Once again, I was there, soaking up the love and unconditional acceptance of the Light, assured of my place and purpose in His family.

Please let them feel the same, remember the same, as they fight for us. Remind them of all the amazing things they are fighting for. Remind them of all the victories and blessings Abbot insisted we celebrate.

I didn't want to taint Riah and Dan's perfect harmony, but I couldn't resist the yearning deep within me. So, I joined them.

We all did.

We stood ensconced behind the unmoving wall of Warriors, sending our hope, joy, peace and love to them by combining our voices to celebrate and acknowledge the greatness of the Light.

Movement to the left distracted me.

Ebony was stirring.

She probably knew better than anyone that, with the library door sealed, there was no way out. Drawing her legs up, she wrapped herself in a foetal position. It looked like she was trying to burrow into the carpet. Or perhaps to wake from this nightmare. Her shoulders shook. I imagined I heard her weeping. But it was impossible to hear anything over the nightmare of the battle that raged in front of us.

When would it end?

Please, just make it stop.

Ebony's movement also attracted the attention of a demon from the upper level. It dropped next to her with a lightness that was contrary to its humungous bulk.

As much as I hadn't liked her at first. And blamed her for the nuisance it was to have to stop here on the way out of Sodom. And hated how she had set a trap for us to fall into the hands of the enemy.

The Dark Lord.

I did feel for her.

She'd been sucked in. Her only crime had been gullibility.

I could relate.

Ebony balled herself up even tighter. The thing toyed with her, whispering things we couldn't hear from its bird-like beak. It stroked her with one of its talons.

Frozen, beyond even sobbing, her body lay motionless. It roared with laughter as a pool of liquid darkened the carpet behind her. Then, drawing a knife, it bent down to claim her when an orange flash to my left burst through the wall of Warriors.

In less than a heartbeat, the demon collapsed, impaled by a blazing orange sword of Light.

Abbot bent over the girl and soothed her. He left his sword buried in the side of the beast, then lowered his frail body to the floor and drew her, tears, mucus, urine and all, into his arms and comforted her. Rocking her gently, his lips moved fast next to her ear.

He had no time. Surely, they would notice him.

"Get out of there!" I know I screamed, but I couldn't hear myself over the roars that surrounded us.

Ebony listened intently to Abbot's words. Then she nodded her head, looking up at him through the muck coating her face. She smiled with the Light in her eyes.

"Run." We were a panicked chorus behind our safe wall.

Abbot took Ebony's face in his aged, peaceful hands and gently kissed her forehead as a sword was thrust through the both of them. They collapsed into each other's arms, embracing in death.

No.

Impossible.

I was seeing things.

It didn't matter how much I rubbed my eyes or shook my head. The scene wouldn't change. Abbot and Ebony were joined in death by the blade of the enemy.

Time stopped.

"Abbot!" The crystal voice of Sariah cut through the chaos.

Barging her way through the Warriors, her sword drawn, she gouged the demon that stood over the dead pair. Her blade travelled up through the thick hide covering its ribcage and emerged out the opposite side of its neck.

The red flames that wrapped around her armour raged with her fury.

Grim-faced, she watched as acidic blood pooled under the demon's collapsed body. She smiled when it began disintegrating around her blazing sword.

"Focus!" Val roared at us. The fight around our three warriors had intensified, stopping them getting to Abbot or Sariah.

More demons were dropping into the arena now that Sariah was out in the open and unprotected.

Oh God, no!

64

DANIEL

I didn't need to think or process. I was on the other side of the guardian wall, fighting. Sariah was on my left and I felt Tessa's presence join me on the right. Even though the three of us were still novices, we had something of the mental connection that the others possessed. And once again, in some section of my brain that wasn't needed for the fight, I was aware of how good and right this felt. To be fighting not just alongside Tessa, but with Riah as well.

But where was Raph? Quickly glancing around, I found him standing frozen behind the wall of Warriors, staring at the body of Abbot. I couldn't spare any thought for what he was going through or for my own feelings of loss. I would have to deal with that when the fight was over. For now, we were all fighting for our lives.

The tide was going against us. We were falling back. The Warriors stood impassively behind us, still protecting the frozen form of Raphael. We didn't dare turn and run for the safety they offered. We wouldn't make it. We were inexperienced and the enemy smelled it, it drew them to us like blowflies to rotting meat.

Surely it wouldn't end like this. I was not ready for it to end, damn it. It was The House all over again. It fragging ... fractured ... frapping ... sure as hell, would not end like this.

They shall not pass.

My blood surged. I saw red. All my frustration, anger and grief surfaced in a battle cry, and I forced my way through the crowd that opposed us. Like an arrowhead, I made way and trusted Tessa and Riah to cover the flanks. I was not as strong as Marcus, or as smart as Kait, and I sure as hell was not as graceful or artistic as Val, but the damned *would not pass.*

With that oath, I was back on my pony, my double-headed battleaxe singing with joy at each death stroke. The haze cleared, calm descended, and once again, time slowed. As natural as breathing, I took my sword in both hands, my arms free from any tension, and swung away at the enemy.

Thank you. Thank you for the preparation, thank you for this purpose, and thank you for this life you have called me to.

We made our way through and they fell before me. I had swum through the tide of the enemy and there were no more to face. I turned to help the girls finish off the ones behind me, but there weren't any. I think I may have maimed most of them and the other two finished off any that weren't dead. I was still in my dream, on fire and looking for more hostiles to kill. But there was nothing ... no one.

Damn it. I wasn't ready to stop. I had only just started.

The five stood staring at me. Marcus and Kait openly smiled in appreciation. Val shook her head in dismay. Tessa and Sariah just looked shocked.

"What?" I buzzed and needed someone, something ... anything to fight. No one answered me. So, I picked on Val, I knew she could take it. "What? Why are you shaking your head?"

"So many reasons. That was a dangerous move. You could have left yourself open on the flank or isolated one of the girls."

"I had Tessa and Ri covering the sides. I had to make a move and break through. They were forcing us back. We had to either give in and die or go hard and possibly win. We won. It worked." In your face, Val.

"You're right. It worked ... this time. But my main concern is that you've been bitten." Val gave her head another slow shake and her mouth dropped.

"What! Where?" I was madly looking myself over, taking stock. My muscles ached, but my adrenaline was still pumping so I wasn't feeling it too much yet. But I couldn't feel any wounds.

Am I going to turn into a demon? Are they like werewolves and vampires?

"Don't panic. I meant you've been bitten by the bug. And I think we have confirmation on one of your Badges. For all three of you, actually." She smiled, but her eyes were heavy with grief. "Tell me, do you still smell the sulphur?"

What the hell was she on about? "I can, yeah. Not as strong as it was just before the uglies hit the fan, but it is still around. Why?"

"I think it's another Badge, or a gift. I'm not quite sure yet. But I think your sense of smell can pick out demons. Since the Warriors are still here, I don't think it's over yet." She called us all back to attention: "Stay focused, everyone."

The room did still stink. Now that I was out from behind the wall of Warriors it was once again noticeable. I looked around the room and watched in fascination as the decomposing demonic bodies faded into pools of black acid. As they dissipated, the smell gradually decreased. But, on Val's orders, we were still on alert. We were all raking the walls for any movement. It wasn't time yet to take in the reality of Abbot or worry about Raph. He was a frozen, pale mass of mess.

"Raph, be careful," Val said as he moved in a trance over to the body of Abbot. He knelt down and laid his hands on Abbot's slack, pale face. Raph's body grew strained and his face darkened with effort.

Skrat!

He was trying to revive him, to heal him. The poor kid was deep in shock.

Sariah joined Kait as she walked over to him and gently laid her hand on his shoulder and softly spoke his name. "He's gone, sweetheart. He knew he was going to die today. He went knowing it was his time."

Raph looked at her, then his eyes widened, and fear painted his face. The truth was finally settling on him.

"Look out." This time Marcus yelled the warning.

I turned to see the biggest mother of a demon that had ever cursed the earth, land in the middle of the room. It was bigger than my mind could comprehend. It became a mountain range separating us from each other. I froze.

65

MARCUS

The kret landed behind me Kait, separating her and the twins from the rest of us. Tess and Dan were off to one side, Val and I on the other. We couldn't get to them. I saw red and charged. One thought only: not Kait. You kret, you are not having me Kait.

I didn't care where I hit it. I only wanted to grab its attention. She was stranded, guarding the twins with no support.

Damn that thing back to hell.

I lay prone on the floor and momentarily took in the scene after being swatted like a mosquito. Its immensity was overwhelming—it stood over all of us, its head near the balcony of the upper level. It had no visible weapon. Its size alone was effective enough for both offence and defence. Without shield or armour, a dark green, wrinkled hide its only covering. Maybe we could find an exposed weak spot.

Tiny, pig-like eyes refocused on Kait, leering, as sheets of drool slimed out of a mouth lined with rows of serrated teeth. It squatted down and reached a massive arm towards them. Unfurling its club-like hand to reveal a paw, pierced with sharp, jagged claws.

I charged and re-entered the battle. Dan and Tess attacked the opposite flank, targeting the hip. Their swords were as effective as tie-wire against rawhide. We all knew they couldn't stop the beast, but they were trying bravely to distract it so it wouldn't harm Kait and the twins.

Time sped up. We were losing. Having no effect. Its skin was unaffected by our swords. This was not the time for technique. We were reduced to slashing and swinging like hacks. We had to stop this thing. Sweat mixed with sulphur, washing me eyes in pain. Me muscles fed on lactic acid. Me heart pulsed with fear.

Finally, I made some ground. Me last thrust seemed to do damage and I was rewarded with a bellowing roar. I'd managed to dig away at its hip joint by sheer force of will. Strengthened and numbed by adrenaline, I forced me sword through the joint up to the hilt and disabled the demon. Pinned in the squatting position the monster raged and spat, swinging its mammoth head back and forth.

I hung on with all I had. Acid gushed from its wound and flooded over me hands. The numbness burned away with me flesh. Pain returned and consumed me. The smell weakened me. The pain assaulted me.

Not. My. Kait. You kret of the Dark.

The onslaught was overwhelming. But me rage was greater. I would not let go. Kait would be safe. This I vowed, so this I lived, or died ... as needs may be. As the seconds escaped, realisation dawned on me. I might be able to save Kait and the twins, but this was it for me.

So be it.

Keep them safe, please. I beg of you.

I was a sitting duck. The beast turned, floundered, and with wild swings, it tried to dislodge me. Or more to the point, me sword from its side.

Val flew to join me and did what she could to shield me from its attack. With its attention on us, the others had space to get to safety. Val's sword danced. Her daggers flashed. She leaped and parried, worried and defended. I might be going down this day, but Val would fall first. It was then a confidence gently settled around me shoulders.

Me heart swelled. I wasn't going to die here and now, at the hands of this demon. Because there was no way Val was going to fall.

Strengthen her, please. Help me hold. Save them. I beg of you.

Once again, the room rattled with the beast's bellowing roar. Its claws clenched, raised to the ceiling. Its grotesque head lolling back and forth, spittle flying. And in that snippet of opportunity, rage distracting its focus, Kait thrust her flaming green sword hilt-deep into its eye.

Digging deep, blanking out the pain, I locked down on the grip of me sword. Me balance gave as its violent flailing threw me. I slipped in the growing pool of gore at me feet that was burning the soles of me shoes. But me hands stayed welded to the hilt of me sword. Val stayed to guard me, as I held the beast crippled.

But now Kait was without a weapon. Me roar of rage challenged that of the beast's. I saw Dan grab Tessa and make a run to safety. Good lad.

Each turn of the demon's head revealed a river of ooze working its way further down its wounded face. In confusion and pain, it screamed again, and with greater effort, tried to rise. Kait lay like a shield over the twins. Now unarmed, she had nothing left to protect them apart from her body. The three of them were isolated next to the bodies of Abbot and Ebony.

Not them too. No!

"Run, Kait!" I screamed. "Get out of the way."

Dan raced in, ducking under wild sweeps of the demon's raging arms, and tried to hurry the three of them out of harm's way. He got Kait to her feet, lifted Riah, then, looking like he was about to physically launch her across the room, he turned and noticed Tessa was right on his heels. She took Raph's arm, tugged him to his feet and hauled him, at a run, back to the corner farthest from the monster. Bless Dan. As soon as Tessa and Raph started away, he then forcefully pushed Kait in front of him. Then, keeping Riah bundled in his arms, shielding her with his body, he followed Kait to the relative safety of the far side of the room.

But not fast enough. The monster caught him in his retreat.

Swiping Dan's back with its claws. His flesh ripped open. The force of the blow combined with Dan's momentum launching him across the room. He dropped Riah in safety and rolled onto the floor.

The five of them were out of the way, but where the hell was Val? As soon as they were clear, she had disappeared. With me hands melted to the hilt of me sword, I was stranded. Damn it. Maybe today was the day after all.

Lord, use me and receive me when the time comes.

66

KAITLYN

From our position, I could see everyone except Val. Desperate, I scanned the room until I spotted her in the farthest corner. With all of the danger and concern for this main demon, we had not given heed to any others that may still be around. We could not afford to lower our defences at any point. Dan was down, Marcus was struggling, the kids were in shock and the wall of Warriors was out of reach on the other side of the giant. On the balcony above, there were only a few small demons left. We needed to get Marcus out of there, now.

With her eyes on the giant, Val drew four knives from the sheath on her leg, and before I could blink, she had thrown two, and the third was in the air sailing towards the last minor demon on the balcony. With the fourth knife secured in her teeth, she had already started her run up when her last blade met its mark in the remaining beast. It followed its comrades, collapsing over the edge, dead before it hit the ground.

Just as quickly, she was on to the next challenge. Picking up as much speed as she could in the short distance, pumping her arms, Val launched herself onto the demon's back, using the beast's lowered calf as a vault. Following through, her next step off its protruding backside, she used her hands to grab onto its shoulders. Then, kneeling either side of its neck, she clamped its bulbous head between her thighs. Her left arm wrapped around its forehead while avoiding its ferocious mouth and the toxic tar streaming out of its eye. She pulled back with all her strength. The beast roared in fury and frustration. It screamed in agony and anger. Val took the knife out of her mouth and like a snake, whipped her right arm around and dragged that blade across its throat.

The force of her thrust ripped half of its neck open. Its scream of rage perished with the severing of its vocal cords. The remaining air in its lungs gushed through the wound as waves of black tar gurgled into silence. This was Marcus's cue to let go. He ran straight into my arms. I clung to him, not ready to release him for at least one hundred years.

Despite its disgorged hip, the reflexes of the dead beast thrust itself upwards, jettisoning Val backward into the air. I don't know how she did it, but she managed to connect her feet with the demon's back, then followed through into a flip and landed in a crouch not far from the toppled creature. The rest of us waited, clinging to each other in relief and disbelief. Staying on guard, Val didn't relax till she had searched the scene, checking the balcony, the corners, the furniture and the fireplace, making sure the room was secure. She barely glanced at the giant, confirming it was dead, and then made her way to join us.

Three slow claps bounced off the walls. With the sound echoing around the stilled, tomb-like room it was hard to pinpoint its origin.

"Well done, *my* lady. I did, asss I alwaysss do, enjoy your ssshow. You are ssspectacular and sure to entertain. Are you certain you won't join me? We could rule the world. I will give you whatever it is that you want."

"I am of the Light." Her countenance dropped. She knew what was coming.

"Lassst chanccce, *my* Valarrrie."

"I fight for the Light."

"So be it. For now. We will talk again soon, *dear heart*."

My heart was still too raw from loss for that last barb not to hit home and dig deep. We were going to miss him. So much. I knew we would go on without him. But right now, I had a hard time thinking how.

67

CONTESSA

Like the flip of a switch, he was gone.

My eyes darted everywhere at once. I needed to see everyone immediately to make sure they were all okay.

Marcus was on his knees. His hands unrecognisable from the burns. His face fluctuating between green and white.

Kait knelt beside him with one arm securely wrapped around him, the other snaking out to ensnare anyone who came too close in a one arm embrace.

Sariah looked around the room, sheathed her sword then went to her brother. She stood taller, walked stronger, weary, but older.

Paled, still, speechless, Raphael stood unresponsive.

Dan wavered on his feet. His shirt ripped to ribbons. A sheen growing across his face.

Val stalked.

But we all stilled when, at last, the Warriors of Light moved. They walked to the bodies of Abbot and Ebony and stood around them.

"What are they doing?" Raph broke out of his stupor. "No!" He fumbled to draw his sword from his sheath. Spluttering and tripping over himself, he charged. Still alert, Val caught him from behind and pinned his arms to his side. In the process she received the full force of his anger, grief and distress.

Kait was able to disarm him while Val restrained him.

"Let me go." He turned the full force of his attack to Val. Kicking and punching he screamed, "Traitor! Let me go. They can't have him."

I couldn't hear the words she whispered, but eventually she was able to turn his body and hold him tight as he wept and released some of his distress.

When his sobs calmed, one Warrior bent over and ever so gently picked up the body of Ebony.

Another reverently retrieved the body of Abbot. Val turned Raph. Kneeling, she embraced him from behind. I'm not sure if she was comforting him or restraining him. Maybe it was a bit of both.

I didn't know what was happening. But one thing I did know, we should not interrupt. I doubt we could have anyway.

"Be at peace, my children. You have fought well."

Power and majesty filled the room. The hairs all over my body rose and I fell to my knees. Along with everyone else, I bowed my head. Our Lord was present.

"Abbot has made the ultimate sacrifice for the life of Ebony. He gave her the opportunity to receive the truth you shared with her tonight and the chance to turn from her ways. She made her peace before she died. Abbot offered the greatest of gifts when he laid down his life for her. That sacrifice was made in love and accepted. It has brought great reward."

In the warmth of confidence, I lifted my eyes to see the Warrior holding Ebony joined by two others.

The three escorting her limp body looked to the sky and, like their arrival, shot back into the night.

Five Warriors remained.

Abbot's own guard gently cradled our fallen friend and was flanked by two others on each side.

"A gift for you all."

Abbot's body was infused with the Light of the Warriors until he shone like them. Before our eyes, age dropped from his face. The gaping hole in his chest closed. Slowly, he stirred and awoke as from sleep. He was gently placed on his feet and stood tall, strong and whole. His hair was thick and dark, shoulders broad and strong. Healing and youth poured into him, transforming his body.

The orange blaze of his armour flashed, power pulsing over and through him. I couldn't stop the tears flowing when I saw him standing tall and resplendent in his beautiful, ornate armour. The Badge of a life in the fight well fought.

"Abbot!" Raphael called out to him, but he didn't respond.

Our beloved companion was looking at something else. Like the rising sun, his face lit with recognition and joy.

A man approached, dressed in a robe reaching down to his feet and with a golden sash around his chest. His eyes were like blazing fire.

We watched on in silence. Shocked. Awed.

Piece by piece the figure removed Abbot's armour, handing it to a Warrior who had walked by Abbot's side for as long as I'd known him.

No. Don't take his armour. How will he defend himself? How will he fight?

"Abbot ..." Raph tried again. His cry gave voice to my own grief.

"He can't hear you, sweetheart, he has already gone. We are being allowed to see him as he will now always be. Whole, happy and at peace. There is no war, no battle where he is going. He is safe." In Kait's attempt to comfort Raph, she had soothed the ache of my heart as well.

She looked to me and smiled. Then back to Val and over to Marcus. Even though her words were a balm, I could see she was frustrated that she didn't have enough wings to nurture all her chicks.

As Abbot's honourable discharge came to a close, we were all confronted with our loss. I had no idea how Val felt, having known him the longest of all. Or of how Raph and Riah hurt because of their special bond with him. All I knew was that I was overcome by my own pain.

It was selfish, I know. He'd earned his rest. He was happy and not in pain. But I only had tears for myself as they took each other's hands and all seven of them ascended like arrows into the stormy sky.

And he was gone.

68

RAPHAEL

He was gone. They had taken Abbot away and he was gone. Forever. I could feel the last tiny threads still holding me together start to unravel and ping like popcorn in a hot pan. Everything was not okay. It felt like two of those horrible monsters were ripping me apart, one on each side, pulling and tearing my heart in two. It hurt so much.

But then I heard His voice.

"Valarie, enjoy a season of respite. Your burden will return, but in my time." She bowed her head and gave thanks.

"Raphael." He was speaking to me. I do not know if it was out loud or in my mind. I could not hold my head up, I was so ashamed, hurt and … and … angry.

Why did you let Abbot die? I should have died. I am the useless one.

"Be at peace. What happened, happened for a reason—my reasons."

"Yes, Lord." *I still hate you, I still hurt so much, I am so … so lost.*

"I hear you and I see you, Raphael. But you need to make a choice. Regardless of how you feel, you must decide. Will you stay with me?"

Did I want to stay? Who else would take care of us? I was hopeless and useless. I had nothing. I was nothing. Who would take care of Sariah?

"Yes, I want to stay."

"Even if you don't understand my reasons and don't like the result?" His voice was a blend of chili and sugar, harsh and kind.

"Where else could I go, Lord?"

"Raphael, do you love me?"

Love? Val said it was acknowledging pain and offering sacrifice despite it. All I knew right then was that I was broken in half and filled with pain. I knew the Light had saved me. Even before I knew Him, He loved me. Abbot had explained to us how the Light had suffered and died for me. He knew what pain was, and still He loved me.

"Yes Lord, I love you."

"Stand and unsheathe your sword." There was no questioning this command. Slowly, I slid my sword from its home and obeyed his command.

"Hold it up, hold it tight, and do not let go."

I really wanted to do what He asked, but I struggled. Then, I felt Him helping me. It was like His instructions weren't just an option to consider. He spoke and gave life to the action. All I had to do was follow and not fight. Lightning struck the end of my sword and it caught fire. I could not let go. I could not move. I wanted to drop it and run. But I was stuck to the spot, my hands glued to the hilt.

The heat. The Light. It was too much. But I would not let go. I would stay and be strong. He would not ask me to do this if it could not be done. So, I knew I could do it. I knew He loved me, and I would be alright. I would not let go. I would not cry.

But it was so strong, and it hurt so much. I would not run, but I could not stand. I dropped to my knees, and then it all passed. The pain was gone. "I did it! I did it! I won!"

"I know your heart burns with hatred for those who hurt your sister. I know your brokenness over the loss of Abbot. I know the guilt you feel for your inaction. Raphael, I know everything about you, and I love you. I have a greater purpose for you, but it comes at a great cost. However, I will not force my gift upon you, it is your choice."

He had cut me open and scooped out all the wounds of my heart and held them up for everyone to see. Every failure exposed in front of the others. I was so ashamed. I was so very weak and useless. I deserved punishment and to be left behind. But He said He had a purpose for me. I did not care what it cost. I did not care how much it hurt. I did not want to be left out—to be left behind. So, I nodded in acceptance. The moment I agreed, the top half of my sword dissolved into ash, leaving a jagged broken blade.

"Your badge is Healing. In return for this gift, your sacrifice is to do away with your desire to kill the enemy. You must fight, for you are my child. You may defend, you may protect, but you will never kill. You are not ever to take another's life. You will keep your broken sword as a reminder that you are, and will continue to be, a soldier of the Light. Your palms are permanently scarred from the heat of my Light as a reminder that your hands are an instrument of healing, for this is your purpose. There will still be some wounds you cannot heal, but if you obey my command, you will be far stronger than you were before. Practise your gift, offer your sacrifice, fight well, and through your brokenness, I will be strong."

As I was swimming in His words and straining to understand their meaning, He spoke to the others.

"Contessa, Daniel, be happy.

"Marcus, Kaitlyn, be at peace.

"Valarie, Sariah, be content.

"All of you, be strong and courageous. Peace be with you, my good and faithful children. You are well loved and greatly cherished."

The silence of His departure rang in my ears. The removal of his presence left an immediate hole in my soul. Yet the darkness that came down when He left was not full of evil. It was simply the absence of the day's light. His warmth and peace lingered until I came back to reality.

Val was on her feet. "Riah, quick, help me find the light switches. We need to assess the damage and get out of here. We can't forget this town is going down tonight."

Riah and Val raced away in search of a source of light. I looked around, seeing everything for the first time.

"Raph, we need you, little man. Can you help Marcus and Dan?"

Kaitlyn sounded desperate.

"Why? What is wrong?" Why was everyone so damaged and hurt? I started to move towards Kait's voice in the darkness just as the wall lights sprang to life.

"Thanks, mate. But do you think you could put that down and give us a hand?" Marcus's voice shook, his body trembled, and his skin was coated in sweat. He was on his knees on the soft carpet, holding out his melted arms. Kneeling beside him, her arms supporting her broken husband, Kait's expression pleaded for help.

I raced to help but could not unfurl my fingers from the hilt of my sword, "Kait, I cannot let go."

She breathed deeply. "It's okay, sweetheart, we'll sort it out." Kait stayed kneeling but leaned closer to me to see as I twisted my sword hilt and showed her my hands.

She would make things right. Very gently, she peeled each of my burnt fingers away from what was left of my damaged sword. The design of the hilt had been burnt into my flesh. I could not help but stare—sickened, fascinated, and shocked.

"Does it hurt?" she whispered.

"Yes." I will not cry. I will not cry. I will not ... cry. Kait engulfed me in her arms. I felt like I had just dived into Riah's big safe bean bag. She was going to make it alright.

"Darling boy, the Light said you were more powerful now. How about you try healing your hands?" She said it so softly and kindly. It had not even occurred to me to heal myself. Normally I could not.

Sariah came and took over the embrace as Kait removed my other hand from the handle. The stench of burnt flesh wafted through the air, drifting out from both my hands and Marcus's wounds. Sariah took the remnants of my sword and put it away in the sheath on my back. I looked at my hands. I shut my eyes and focused on the Light.

Thank you for giving me a purpose and a place in your plan. Thank you for giving me this very special Badge that I can use to help people and even myself.

In my mind, I saw my hands whole, and when I opened my eyes —they were.

69

DANIEL

Raph looked up, eyes wide and a smile stretching from ear to ear. He held his hands up to show Kait.

"Well done, Raph. Do you think you could help Marcus and Dan now? They're in a pretty bad way."

He stepped closer and laid his scarred hands on Marcus's shoulders. He then bowed his head and shut his eyes and I'm pretty sure I saw his lips move but I didn't hear any words. I was finding it hard to stay focused, my body was sweating, and I had started trembling uncontrollably. The pain seemed to be passing, but I was struggling to keep my eyes open and my body upright. I was still on my knees, not having the energy or stability to rise.

Tessa shuffled closer, her dark eyes pools of worry. I tried to tell her I'd be okay. I'd just wait for Raph to sort things out with Marcus and then he'd come over. But only half of it came out. I just couldn't be bothered making the effort to finish my sentence. I leaned into Tessa and she struggled to hold me up as we waited our turn.

Marcus had his eyes screwed shut and his tanned face was glistening white. Kait stayed kneeling beside him, her hands fussing. The first aid supplies were in the truck. Gradually, the muscles in

Marcus's face relaxed and he breathed a huge sigh of relief which turned into a sob. The muscles in his face relaxed and his shoulders dropped. The angry weeping wounds had closed over. The skin on his hands was still red, but he was whole. He wrapped Raph in a bear hug and buried his face in the boy's chest, completely losing his composure.

I suspected that the carpet in this house would be a very nice place to pass out. It was lusher than any bed I had ever slept on, so perhaps now would be the perfect opportunity to give it a go. Tessa's voice faded as I dropped face first onto the floor. I then slid into peaceful, painless oblivion.

"Wake up, sleeping beauty, I ain't gonna kiss you, but Tessie might if you're nice to her." I vaguely heard a slap. "What? I'm sure she would, it would probably hurry him up. We have to get moving." Marcus's voice was the first thing that I was aware of as consciousness returned.

It was followed by soft murmurs, then, "Dan, can you hear me?" Tessa's uneasy voice was close to my ear.

"Wha ... ?" I was still trying to pull my thoughts together—where and what the hell was going on?

She gently shook my shoulder. "Dan, are you okay? We need to go." Rapidly coming out of my stupor, I guessed her mouth would be hovering just centimetres in front of mine, so I took Marcus's advice and snuck a quick kiss.

"Dan! You little ..." She feigned surprise but she sat back on her heels, smiling.

"I told you that'd work, although I was thinking the other way around." Marcus was as tactful as ever. "How are you feeling, son?"

My muscles screamed, the burns down my back had dulled to a savage sting, my head throbbed, and I could've killed a pint given half the chance. "Better, thanks." I winked at Tessa, then struggled back to my knees. I let her give me a hand to stand up. "But seriously, what happened?"

"The wound on your back was poisoned and you were pretty sick.

But Raph had the ability to heal you. It really was miraculous. I would never have believed it if I hadn't seen it with me own eyes. You will have some pretty interesting scars, but then, join the club." Marcus held up his swollen, red hands.

Kait smiled and flicked her eyes to Raph. He was standing nearby with Riah at his side. When he realised I was looking at him, he blushed and dropped his eyes. I went to him and dropped back to my knees, so I had to look up at him. "You saved my life. Thank you, Little Master."

"You saved Riah's life when I should have. I failed," he whispered. His glistening eyes threatened to overflow.

"Not from what I heard. I heard that you're not supposed to kill anything, even these uglies. Not only are you not supposed to, you were never meant to. 'All that happened was supposed to happen.' Isn't that what He said?" I asked.

Awareness dawned on his face. "I thought he was talking about Abbot and Ebony."

"Yeah, I'm sure he meant that too. But for now, I'm seriously grateful for your Badge and how you gifted it to me." I took his hands and turned them over to see his palms. Already the red welts had faded into raised white patterns. From the heels of his palms to the tips of his fingers, a perfect imprint of his sword's hilt strapping was tattooed. "Cool."

He returned my smile and stood tall.

"Dan, you picking up any sulphur smell at the moment?" I looked over to Val as she still stood guard over the group.

I stopped and focused. "No. It's gone." Thank the Light, I was completely over the stench.

"Good. If you ever smell it again, anytime, anywhere, you speak up and let us know. Okay?"

"Sure. Am I your bloodhound now, Val?"

"No. You're my demon-hound, boy." She smiled despite her grief and weariness, and the air felt lighter.

I still felt like hell, but we were back on track. "How is everyone else?" I said.

"Just waiting for you, sleeping beauty. Let's go." Val came and patted me on the back. I couldn't help the flinch. My shirt was torn to ribbons, the skin underneath was healed but still tender.

As we walked to the door, I stepped over some of Val's knives. I quietly asked her, "What about these? Do we need to take them with us?"

"The Dark Lord will send his minions to stick me full of holes soon enough. So, for now, just leave them be. The Light said I had a season of respite and I'll take as long as He gives."

The door was now open and there were nightlights on throughout the house. It was strange to be leaving, not knowing where the owners were, or if they were ever going to come back. What would they think about Ebony? Would they even know?

The seven of us left. We were no longer complete. I couldn't help thinking we were now missing orange. How could we be a complete set without orange? Even though I had only known these guys a short time, I was still trying to come to terms with the loss of Abbot.

My hand was in Tessa's as we reached the front doors. My friend.

Now that I had survived, I was looking forward to seeing what this friendship was going to look like. The Light had told us to be happy. It was a command. So far, so good. If I could only keep my arch-nemesis out of the way …

Sulphur still infected the air outside as it blustered over to us from the city. The pressure in the atmosphere was still oppressive. A dry storm was raging, with lightning and thunder released in barrages from heaven. Even without seeing, I knew that demons were rampaging through the streets, wreaking as much havoc as they could in their last hour. What was happening in our doomed city?

We stood on Ebony's front porch and studied the scene. Wild clouds raged in the sky. Spears of Light, different from lightning, broke through and pierced the night, striking buildings with apparent randomness. They were conduits, streaking javelins of Light, spearing one after the other, like some supernatural escalator racing their cargo to the city.

"Warriors! Warriors of Light are descending on the city." I said.

"They will touch down on the sacred ground of the Soteria Houses and fan out from there." Val had been through this before.

"The war's begun. That's our cue to get out of here." Marcus looked at his hands. They were healed but obviously still giving him some pain.

"You gonna be able to drive?" he asked Val, knowing he wasn't up to the task.

"Sorry, old man, I don't know how long my respite will last and I don't want to be a liability driving the truck." I understood now that her moment in the sun would soon end, and once again she would be reduced to pain and weakness. Her sacrifice was truly that—surrendering something of great value for something of even greater worth. I don't think I'd ever fully understand the cost.

"You know I'll do it, Marcus, and I want you and the twins up front where I can keep an eye on all three of you." Kait took control.

"Dan, Tessa, will you guys travel in the back with Val? We don't know when the knives will be back or how bad it will be, but she may need some help."

"I might be an invalid, Kait, but I can speak for myself," Val said.

Kait walked over and kissed her on the cheek. "Yes, dear heart." The use of Abbot's endearment softened Val's hackles and she graciously backed down, acknowledging Kait's need to tend to her chicks—all of them, including her.

Val returned her familial kiss, handing over control of the mission to Kait who ducked up to the cab to start the engine, getting the old thing warmed up. She then raced back trying to hurry everyone up.

Marcus looked to Val. "Thanks, old girl. That was fun. Sticking with you continues to provide good times. But I'm afraid I lost count." He gave her a quick hug, then tried to escape, herding the twins to the front. But they both slipped away from him and managed to give us all a hug before allowing themselves to be ushered away.

Just before Marcus made it safely into the cab, she shot back, "I didn't. 65–47. I win."

"But what about the giant? That's got to count for something?"

"It did. When I killed it. Looking forward to dinner ..."

He'd shut the cab door on her response, so we followed suit, climbing into the back where we were confronted with Abbot's empty chair. Val's efforts to lighten the mood evaporated like good humour in a bar fight. Still, we needed to get going. I turned and shut us in as Kait secured the latch. Silently, we took our seats and waited for Kait to return to the front and get us under way.

The trusty old truck eased down the driveway and we headed out of town, leaving what we knew, and heading into the unknown. It was the second time I had only managed to escape a city by the skin of my teeth under the threat of death. I was thinking of all the things I would be sad to leave. It was a short list. The list of things I was looking forward to, thankfully, was taking longer to compile.

I was pulled out of my pondering by a loud banging coming from the cab.

"Look out the window if you can." It was Raph calling through from the front. We scrambled up over boxes and gained purchase of some part of the windows. Tessa and me on one side, Val on the other. My immediate view was to the back.

"What is that?"

Val shifted to see what I was looking at. "It's the pillar of cloud."

"Should we be concerned?"

"No, it's our rear-guard. No one can see us. It's a gift of the Light covering our escape."

"But won't it be obvious? They might not be able to see us, but the big pillar of cloud travelling down the road might be a bit of a give-away," I said.

"No, they can't see anything on the other side of that. It's like a blanket. Plus, they're all a bit distracted at the moment."

With our rear view hampered I was unable to witness the total annihilation of Sodom. But like Abbot once said, "One could not meet the future if one anchored oneself in the past." The past was locked in, it couldn't be changed, even if we wanted to. I had learned that it was fruitless to waste time looking back. It petrified your soul and stifled your future.

I looked the other way and saw a pillar of Light leading us out of

Sodom. I guess there was no doubt of where Kait was being led, onward in the Light into the unknown. Despite my grief over the loss of Abbot, I was honestly excited to see what came next.

A NOTE TO MY WONDERFUL READERS

Thank you so much for joining me on the first leg of this adventure into the Light. I hope you have enjoyed getting to know the characters as much as I have enjoyed opening the door and watching them come to life. This book and these people have been rolling around in my head for decades, and I can say in all honesty it is a relief to release them and a pleasure to share them with you.

If you have enjoyed this book, please consider leaving a review. It would inspire others to pick it up as well as encourage me to get back to it and write some more. Although, that's not too hard to do.

Donita Bundy

DANGEROUS SALVATION PLAY LIST

Theme Song: Rescue - Lauren Daigle

Daniel's song: Freedom - Zach Williams

Marcus' song: Soul on Fire - Third Day

Family's song: Hold us Together - Matt Maher

Abbot's song: Farther Along - Josh Garrels

Sariah's song: My Beloved - David Crowder

Kaitlyn's song: It is Well - Kristene DiMarco

Valarie's song: Once and For All - Lauren Daigle

Raphael's song: Mountain Song - Little Chief

Abbot's farewell: The Mission - Gabriel's Oboe

Contessa's song: Even Then - Micah Tyler

Dangerous Salvation Playlist

ABOUT THE AUTHOR

Donita Bundy lives in the Somerset Shire (Queensland, not England) with her husband, two boys, her socially inappropriate cat and irrepressible red dog. She loves creating images with words and, when she's not writing, her camera. Eating chocolate, hanging out with the wallabies and walking the aforementioned red dog are a close second.

When she's at work, and not writing novels, Donita is either teaching writing, designing book covers or contributing to the Gracewriters Podcast. To connect, follow her blog, listen to the podcast, check out the gallery or just keep up to date with what's going on, go to her website and sign up to the newsletter.

For more information
donitabundy.com

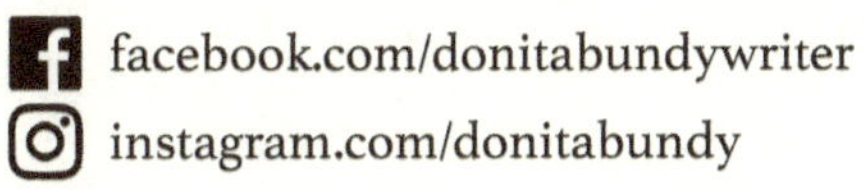

facebook.com/donitabundywriter

instagram.com/donitabundy

ACKNOWLEDGMENTS

I would like to acknowledge my family, who have not only survived but coped surprisingly well with my transition from part-time work, through full-time illness, to a full-time writerly life. It's not been an easy journey for any of us, but their patience and grace has made the production of this book possible.

To Sarah Connors and Ella Green who have shared laughs, tears and coffee. Who have picked up and watched children, kept me grounded and semi-rational, and have stood beside me through bushfires, droughts and famine. For being the other two parts of our three-legged stool: thank you.

To my editor, coach, friend and all-round hand holder, Belinda Pollard, I couldn't have done it without you. Firstly, because I wouldn't know what to do and would still be running in circles chasing my tail. But also for eradicating my plague of commas, cheering from the sidelines, and for the comments in the margins, thank you.

In the early days, when producing this book was just a dream, a steadfast quartet were not only brave enough to read some pretty rough first drafts, they came back for more. For your encouragement and endurance, thank you Ella Green, Lee Cawthray, Ingrid Harris and Stephen Heath.

This book would still be a manuscript hibernating in the bottom drawer if it weren't for the support of the Somerset Shire Council and the Regional Arts Development Fund Committee. I am incredibly grateful for their invitation to be the inaugural Somerset Writer in Residence. Not only did it give me the opportunity to meet some amazing people and form the Somerset Writers Group, it afforded me the funds and time to rewrite (one more time) this story and make a good start on the second in this series of seven.

For my family at our own "Soteria House", for your constant prayers, support and encouragement, thank you.

My earliest memories are of parents who challenged me to push boundaries and reach for the stars whilst keeping my feet firmly planted on the ground and in God. Dad, life would have been very different if you'd been allowed to stay. I miss you still, but thanks for planting the seeds that still bear fruit. Mum, thanks for being my rock, the wall that wouldn't give, and showing me first-hand what it is to be a true child of the Light.

Finally and most importantly, I give thanks to God, who has inspired, carried, prompted and prodded this book over the line. This story, and the library of others associated with it, have been with me most of my life. It is told through the lens of my life experiences, yet it is not my story. It is His. My prayer is that you, my dear reader, will find inspiration, challenge and encouragement to keep journeying the incredible adventure in, and with, the Light.